Praise for
Letters Across the Sea

"Readers weary of European-centric World War II dramas will delight in Genevieve Graham's *Letters Across the Sea*, which centers on the courage and tenacity of Canadian soldiers, veterans, and home-front fighters. . . . A tender, moving tale illuminating a fascinating lesser-known chapter of World War II history!"

Kate Quinn, *New York Times* **bestselling author of**
The Huntress* and *The Alice Network

"I always look forward to diving into a Genevieve Graham novel, because I know I'll be swept away by her meticulous evocation of the past, her memorable and wonderfully observed characters, and her unmatchable flair for shining a light into the neglected corners of our shared past. In *Letters Across the Sea*, she sends us from 1930s Toronto, then under siege by a relentless plague of anti-Semitism, to a different battleground altogether: the last stand of Canadian troops at the Battle of Hong Kong. This is history worth remembering—and fiction that both enlightens and entertains."

Jennifer Robson, **internationally bestselling author of**
The Gown* and *Our Darkest Night

"A beautiful book that tells a little-known chapter of history with incredible humanity. From the neighbourhoods of Toronto to the battlefields of Hong Kong, Genevieve Graham weaves exquisite research, nail-biting tension, and rich characters into a sweeping novel of courage, betrayal, and reconciliation. I loved it!"

Julia Kelly, **internationally bestselling author of** *The Light Over London*
and *The Last Garden in England*

"An epic tale of enduring love, loyalty, and heroism, and a haunting portrayal of one of the most tragic yet overlooked battles of World War II, *Letters Across the Sea* has all the ingredients of a historical fiction masterpiece. Genevieve Graham has delivered once more a powerful, devastating, and ultimately redemptive story that stirs the heart in profound and lasting ways."

Roxanne Veletzos, **internationally bestselling author of**
The Girl They Left Behind

"In *Letters Across the Sea*, Genevieve Graham further cements her status as one of the preeminent writers of Canadian twentieth century historical fiction by illuminating a dark and complex chapter in the nation's past in the decade leading up to World War II. With vivid prose and memorable characters, Graham demonstrates once more her unique ability to inspire, educate, and entertain."

Pam Jenoff, *New York Times* bestselling author of
The Woman with the Blue Star

"A compelling story, meticulously researched and beautifully told—to the point that I was moved to tears on several occasions. Graham is a master storyteller with a gift to touch the heart. I'm so happy to have discovered her work."

Santa Montefiore, bestselling author of *The Temptation of Gracie*

Praise for
Genevieve Graham

"Genevieve Graham captures the reader's attention from the beginning in this exquisite journey to the heart of what makes us human."

Armando Lucas Correa, bestselling author of *The German Girl* and
The Daughter's Tale, on *The Forgotten Home Child*

"[A] page-turner. . . . Graham writes about ordinary people living at important moments in Canadian history, from the displacement of the Acadians to the Yukon Gold Rush to the Second World War. In *The Forgotten Home Child*, she ensures the British Home Children are remembered and honoured."

Winnipeg Free Press

"From icy gales on the Chilkoot Trail to the mud and festering greed in booming Dawson City, *At the Mountain's Edge* gives new life to one of the most fascinating chapters in Canada's history. Fast-paced and full of adventure, this novel is an exciting take on the raw emotions that make us human and the spirit required to endure."

Ellen Keith, bestselling author of *The Dutch Wife*

"Graham has immense talent when it comes to making our nation's history interesting and weaving a riveting story around historical facts."

Niagara Life Magazine

"Graham continues her worthy crusade of recounting pivotal Canadian history in this poignant story [about] the travesties of war both on the battlefield and the home front."

RT Book Reviews, on *Come from Away*

"The talented Genevieve Graham once again calls upon a fascinating true story in Canadian history to remind us that beneath the differences of our birth, and despite the obstacles we face, we're all human underneath. Vividly drawn and heartwarming, *Come from Away* is a beautiful look at the choices we make in the face of both love and war."

Kristin Harmel, international bestselling author of
The Room on Rue Amélie and *The Winemaker's Wife*

"At once dizzyingly romantic and tremendously adventurous, this novel also serves as a poignant reminder of the senseless toll the violence of war can take—and the incredible lengths of heroism humans will go to in order to survive and rescue the ones they love."

Toronto Star, on *Promises to Keep*

"[Graham] has delivered a book that reads like a love letter to a time and place that figures largely in our national identity: Halifax in 1917."

The Globe and Mail, on *Tides of Honour*

ALSO BY GENEVIEVE GRAHAM

The Forgotten Home Child

At the Mountain's Edge

Come from Away

Promises to Keep

Tides of Honour

Somewhere to Dream

Sound of the Heart

Under the Same Sky

Letters Across the Sea

Genevieve Graham

Published by Simon & Schuster

New York   London   Toronto   Sydney   New Delhi

Simon & Schuster Canada
A Division of Simon & Schuster, Inc.
166 King Street East, Suite 300
Toronto, Ontario M5A 1J3

The newspaper article on page 191 is reprinted with the permission of *The Globe and Mail*.
The map of Hong Kong was drawn by Captain C.C.J. Bond and appears in C.P. Stacey's *Official History of the Canadian Army in the Second World War, Volume I.*

This Simon & Schuster Canada edition April 2021

SIMON & SCHUSTER CANADA and colophon are trademarks of Simon & Schuster, Inc.

For information about special discounts for bulk purchases, please contact Simon & Schuster Special Sales at 1-800-268-3216 or CustomerService@simonandschuster.ca.

Manufactured in the United States of America

1   3   5   7   9   10   8   6   4   2

Library and Archives Canada Cataloguing in Publication

Title: Letters across the sea / Genevieve Graham.
Names: Graham, Genevieve, author.
Description: Simon & Schuster Canada edition.
Identifiers: Canadiana (print) 20200293052 | Canadiana (ebook) 20200293079 |
ISBN 9781982156633 (softcover) | ISBN 9781982156640 (ebook)
Classification: LCC PS8613.R3434 L48 2021 | DDC C813/.6—dc23

ISBN 978-1-9821-5663-3
ISBN 978-1-9821-5664-0 (ebook)

To the men and women of this country who offer and often give their lives so that we can keep ours, and in particular to the brave men of Canada's Royal Rifles and Winnipeg Grenadiers, who never should have been sent to Hong Kong. The history books seem to have mostly forgotten them, but I never will.

And to Dwayne, who indulges this passion of mine and brings me wine.

"Although the world is full of suffering, it is also full of the overcoming of it."

—HELEN KELLER

Letters Across
the Sea

If you're reading this letter, that means I'm dead. But I guess you already know that.

I hate to say it, but after you read this, you might be glad that I'm gone, and to my eternal shame, I know I deserve that.

You see, I did something. I made a mistake. I mean, I've made a lot of mistakes, but one in particular has haunted me. At one time I thought I could take this secret to my grave, that no one would ever know. But I've had lots of time to think recently, and I understand now that I can't lie to you any longer.

PART ONE

— *1933* —

one

MOLLY

❧

Just before turning onto our lawn, I stopped, pulled off my shoe, then hopped on one foot, needing to pour out a small handful of pebbles. They'd snuck in through the hole at the toe, and I didn't want to track them inside. I'd gotten used to the routine and barely noticed it anymore. It was so much better than leaky boots in the winter.

As soon as I stepped inside, the smell of corned beef and cabbage coming from the kitchen almost overwhelmed me, wafting like old socks through the house. Mum would be annoyed I hadn't been home to help prepare dinner, but Mr. Palermo had needed me to stay a little later. Fortunately, he'd sent me home with vegetables, though they were a bit droopy. That was one of the benefits of working at a greengrocer. I laid the sad-looking carrots and greens on the counter so I could snap open my purse, then I dropped my weekly earnings into the rusty Folger's coffee can on the counter, which I privately called the Ryan Family's Friday Night Tax Bucket.

At the clanking of the coins, my mother turned from the pot on the stove. The circles under her eyes looked darker than usual, and at the sight of them, I felt a pang of guilt that I hadn't been home sooner. At one time, Mum had taken pride in her appearance. On the mantel were framed photos of her and Dad, taken long before I was born. Above her lacy white collar, her narrow chin was lifted with determination, her dark hair striking, and her expression direct; she'd been in the midst of the suffragette movement, her mind a hundred years away from raising children during a depression. Then there was the photo of her, pregnant with me, holding the little hands of Richie and Jimmy. All alone and raising three babies while Dad was at war. No wonder she looked tired. Now her face was lined, and there were hints of grey at her temples, put there by the efforts of keeping our house of seven running on next to nothing. I missed her smile, and her laughter most of all. The wages my father, brothers, and I brought in each week were so meagre, she'd started taking on mending jobs on top of everything else she was doing. It was too much.

"Thought you'd never get here," she said, brushing straggling wisps from her forehead. "Your father will be home any minute, and the table still needs setting."

"I'll just put these vegetables in the cellar first," I said.

I headed downstairs, into the earthy darkness, and placed the vegetables in the coolest spot of the cellar, away from the canned food. Not for the first time, I wished we had a little white refrigerator like my best friend Hannah had. She and her family, the Dreyfuses, lived just across the street, and I spent a lot of my time over there. Last week, Hannah's mother had poured me a glass of lemonade, and I could still feel that ice-cold drink trickling down my throat. But for my family to save up the five hundred dollars needed for a refrigerator, we'd have to fill at least ten tax buckets, plus we'd still need to eat. Pushing the thought from my mind, I returned to the kitchen where my oldest brother, Richie, was already sitting at the table, flipping through the newspaper with a frown on his face.

I peeked over his shoulder and read a headline about President Roosevelt initiating his New Deal domestic reform program. I wished the president luck on that. Any kind of relief from this Depression was needed in the worst way.

"Good day at work?" I asked.

He shrugged. "You know how it is. Aisles are so empty I could open a bowling alley. Why would anyone come to a hardware store if they can't afford to build anything?"

I felt bad for him, but not surprised. With businesses closing down all over the city, we all wondered how long he'd be able to keep that job.

"You coming to the game tonight?" I asked, hoping to lift his spirits. "It's the season opener."

"Probably not. I've got things to do."

Richie and I had always been close. He was four years older than me, but we'd grown up doing mostly the same things. He was the one who had taught me how to play baseball, with him pitching and me swinging the bat, both of us with our matching red hair and freckles. But once I was old enough to really help Mum around the house, I didn't have as much time to play. I still went to watch games as often as I could, though. Going to baseball games with my friends and family was one of my favourite things to do, and it was also one of the rare free activities in the city. These days, free was important.

Mum gestured for me to set the table, and I got out the old china plates, careful not to chip them more than they already were. Richie lifted his elbows so I could slide his plate beneath the newspaper. I had just placed the last fork on the table when I heard Dad's heavy tread on the doorstep. Richie straightened automatically, and my mother smoothed her hair. That was the effect Sergeant Garret Ryan had on people. As the door opened, my three other brothers trundled down the stairs, somehow sensing he was home.

Dad stepped inside and took off his hat as Mum bustled to greet him.

He was thick in the middle with a shock of bright orange hair and piercing green eyes, and when he wore his police uniform as he did now, he could be pretty imposing. But around Mum, Dad was a pussycat.

He leaned down to give her a peck on the cheek. "Hello, love," he said, then, more gruffly, "Sounds like a herd of elephants in here."

"Quiet, everyone," Mum said, taking his coat and hat. "Your father's had a long day."

I bit my tongue. Hadn't we all? For the past four years I'd worked ten-hour days, six days a week in the back room of Palermo's greengrocer. There, I sorted through crates, picking out the rotten food before stocking the front of the store with the good stuff. Little jobs like that. Most of the time it was quiet around the store. Delivery days like today were hectic, but I liked the busyness. It was rare these days.

The stock market had crashed when I was fourteen. I still remember that day. It was October—a Thursday, I thought. I had been excited, walking home from school, eager to start reading *The Great Gatsby* for a book report, but the streets felt tense, with everyone avoiding each other's eyes. Puzzled, I studied the men standing around the sidewalks, wondering why they weren't working inside. Most of their faces were buried in newspapers. Some turned away when I looked, but not quickly enough for me to miss the fact that they were crying. I'd never seen a man cry before. When Dad got home, he sat us all down at the kitchen table and explained that the whole world had changed, not just our city. His gaze clouded with regret as he told me I would have to drop out of school, and he was going to speak with Mr. Palermo about hiring me. I hadn't understood at first. In that moment, all I could think about was my book report.

I knew the crash was serious, but the reality didn't sink in until the next night. Every Friday, Dad brought Mum a bouquet of flowers. That Friday was the first time I ever remembered him coming home empty-handed. To me, the flowers were before. The empty vase was now.

I wasn't the only girl who had to drop out of school, but my friend Hannah never did. Her father owned a factory in the fashion district on Spadina, so he would manage, she told me. Richie had already graduated. My second oldest brother, Jimmy, didn't go back to school. Only Mark and Liam were young enough that they got to stay. I was ashamed of the envy I felt, watching my best friend and my younger brothers leave for school every morning. Then one day after work, Dad found me out on the front porch and handed me a package.

"Open it," he said.

I carefully removed the brown paper wrapping. "Oh, Dad," I whispered. I skimmed my fingertips over the cover of my very own copy of *The Great Gatsby*. "But we can't afford this."

He reached his arm around me. "I set a little money aside. I want you to know that I'm sorry about the way things have turned out. I know you love school, and as soon as things get better, you'll go back. In the meantime, this is just a little something from me to you."

But I didn't go back to school. And two years later, when Mark turned fourteen, he dropped out too. Now, all of us did our part to contribute to the pot. Richie worked at the hardware store, and Mark incinerated garbage at the Wellington Street Destructor. Liam had a paper route he did before school. Mum had her sewing, and of course, Dad had his job with the police. Only Jimmy was unemployed these days. He'd been working at the Don Valley Brick Works until three months ago, when they'd had to let him go. He'd been looking for work ever since. Still, we were getting by, and we clearly weren't the worst off. Down the street from us, the Melniks had all their furniture taken away.

"Sit down before dinner gets cold," Mum said, carrying the pot over.

Dad took his place at the head of the table, and Mum sat opposite him. Once the rest of us had squeezed in—Mark and Liam at one side and Richie, Jimmy, and me on the other—Dad said grace. My stomach growled as we passed the meat and cabbage around, helping ourselves to the meagre offerings while leaving enough for each other. When we handed the dishes back to Mum, she placed the last two slices of corned beef on Dad's and Richie's plates.

"Thanks, Mum," Richie said.

"Smells good," Dad said kindly.

I looked at my own small plate with its lump of sickly green leaves and a single slice of meat and wished I wasn't so hungry. I slid my fork around the edges, trying to push the food together to make it seem fuller. Then I took a bite of the corned beef and was grateful that I only had one piece. It had the same feel and taste as what I imagined shoe leather would be like.

"How was your day, dear?" Mum asked, her full attention on my father.

"Busy. There was another protest down by City Hall. Dressmakers Union this time. It's always something."

"They're lucky to have jobs," Richie said. "Maybe they should have been working instead of marching around with signs. They'd make more money that way."

Dad nodded as he chewed. "We'd be a lot less busy, that's for sure. Chief Draper is all about keeping 'Toronto the Good' in line."

As I reluctantly took a bite of the overcooked cabbage, I pondered what was actually good about Toronto. All I'd seen lately were hundreds of homeless people lining the streets, endless demonstrations about jobs, homes, rights, and everything else under the sun, and a lot of young, unemployed men joining gangs and starting fights.

My father perked up. "Draper's talking about plans for the Orange Day parade."

Dad was called an Orangeman for more than just the colour of his hair. Ever since I was little, he had lectured us on the importance of our family history and the longstanding feud between Protestants and Catholics. He'd made sure we knew that way back in 1690, William of Orange had saved us from becoming second-class citizens under Catholic rule when he'd defeated King James II at the Battle of the Boyne. William's heirs had ended up forming the Orange Order, a group dedicated to upholding the faith, and my father was a proud member, as were many of Toronto's policemen, government officials, and labourers. Practically anyone could join the Orangemen, as long as they were Protestant.

The Orangemen had been responsible for coining the nickname "Toronto the Good." Over the past hundred years, they had put in place many laws. The purpose of those laws, in my mind, was basically to prevent people from having fun. Like no tobogganing on Sundays. I never understood the reason for that one.

Every July 12, the Glorious Twelfth it was called, the Orange Order held a parade downtown, and my dad and the others always marched in it. I'd grown up loving the pomp and circumstance—who didn't love a parade?—but these days, it seemed a little ridiculous. Not much more than a showy demonstration that the Orangemen were still in power. But I knew better than to mention that to my father.

"The parade always gives people something to look forward to," Mum said, smiling.

Beside me, Jimmy took his last bite. "Is there any more?"

My father narrowed his eyes at Jimmy, looking like an orange cat ready to pounce. "You're lucky to be getting anything at all. I work all day to put food in your mouth, and your mother slaves over the stove. You'll eat what you're given and be thankful for it, or you'll have nothing."

"Sorry I asked," Jimmy said, a familiar note of defiance in his voice.

Jimmy had always been the kid with a cheeky remark, and he was a scrapper. In school, he'd challenged teachers whenever he could, which landed him in trouble, but he was smart, so he still managed to get good grades. Richie, on the other hand, took after our father, a strong, athletic leader who wasn't afraid to get into a fight for a good cause. Dad didn't mind the fighting, but he hated rebellion. He said that as a policeman he dealt with rebels all day long, and he didn't want to come home and have to deal with another one.

The only person in the world who had ever dared speak back to my father was my *seanmháthair*, my grandmother. "Garret, *tóg go réidh é.*" *Be calm*, she would say in Gaelic. It used to soothe him, and me as well. She'd died a year ago, but I still felt an ache in my chest, thinking of her.

"Jimmy's playing ball tonight," I said, trying to ease the mood. "We should all go, like we used to. He's really fast these days. Centre field."

Jimmy flashed me a grateful smile. "Thanks, Molly."

Dad pushed corned beef onto his fork. "People getting fired, losing their livelihoods, us with barely enough to eat, and you want to go to a ball game. When are you kids gonna grow up?"

Jimmy stood, his chair scraping noisily along the floor. "Well, I'm not growing up today. I'm off to play ball. Can't let the team down."

The rest of us braced for Dad's wrath, but it never came. He just sighed and slouched a little lower over his dinner, clearly worn. Jimmy brought his dishes to the counter then slipped out the door.

I glared at my plate, wishing I could have gone with him. I missed the days when we'd all go together, sitting with Hannah's family, having a picnic while we cheered the teams on. Dad had been the most enthusiastic fan of all—especially when his boys were playing—and Mum would laugh at how he whooped and hollered. These days, he didn't laugh as much, and his temper could be quick. But he was a good father. I knew he meant well for us all. It was this Depression. It was hard on everyone.

At last, we finished our meals, and I rose to collect the dishes.

"I can't help you tonight, Molly," Mum said. "I've mending to do before the morning. You'll have to do the washing up on your own."

My heart sank. "Can't one of the boys help? I'm supposed to be meeting Hannah at the game."

"You still friends with Hannah Dreyfus, are you?" Dad asked, his tone shifting from my father to Sergeant Ryan. I recognized the sound of an interrogation. He dabbed his lip with his napkin. "You know, people say it's her kind that are responsible for all this poverty."

I paused, unsure. "Her kind? Are you talking about Jewish people?"

"Them and their communist ideals are causing all these strikes and demonstrations. Now, I have nothing against the Dreyfuses, but times are changing. More folks are blaming Jews these days, and when tempers flare, fights break out. People are getting hurt."

I couldn't bite my tongue this time. "It takes two to fight."

"Not necessarily, in my experience."

"If it's so dangerous, who's going to protect Hannah and her family?" I pressed.

"You let the police worry about that. I just want you to be safe."

I was a little surprised Richie hadn't said anything, but he just grabbed the newspaper and left the table. He and Hannah's brother, Max, used to be as close as Hannah and I were. They'd stuck together like brothers until Max left the city for university.

"Listen to your father," Mum was saying. "Make friends with some of the girls at church. It's safer. Who knows? You might meet a nice boy. You're eighteen, after all." Her lips tightened slightly. "Though you'll never meet anyone with your head always in a book."

My cheeks warmed. The fact that I spent most of my free time reading was somewhat of a sore spot between my mother and me. But books weren't the reason I hardly dated. I just wasn't interested in anyone. Plus, I was needed at home. I didn't have endless time.

I carried the dishes to the sink then rolled up my sleeves. I worked quickly, but I was frustratingly aware that it probably took a whole inning. The second the last plate was back in the cupboard, I tore off my apron and ran for the door, letting it slam behind me. I sprinted past the Dreyfuses' house, knowing Hannah would already be at the game, and jogged along Dundas West, past Mr. Connor's bike shop, the Polish bakery, and the Italian butcher. It was about ten blocks from my home in Kensington to Trinity Bellwoods Park, and my lungs burned the closer I got, but when I heard shouts and cheers coming from the game, happy sounds that filled my heart, I picked up my speed.

I could see the teams now, their ball caps and short pants bright in the last hours of daylight, and I spotted Hannah about halfway up the hill, waving both arms to catch my attention. She was wearing the brown sweater I'd told her was my favourite, with a matching bow tied around her long black hair, and she had a big grin on her face.

Heaving for breath, I dropped beside her and scanned the orange caps of the Native Sons team along the bench, looking for my brother. "How's the game? Has Jimmy been up?"

"Twice. He walked the first time, hit a double last inning. Where have you been?"

"Doing dishes. Don't ask. I'm here now."

She wiggled her eyebrows. "I know something that'll cheer you up."

"Oh?"

She pointed down at the Harbord Playground's second baseman and my breath caught. I would have known that tall, dark figure anywhere.

"Max is back already?" I asked. "When?"

"This morning," she said. "He surprised my mother. I don't think she's fully recovered yet."

A roar rose from the crowd as the batter cracked a line drive, but Max shot out his hand and trapped the ball.

"Three out!" Hannah cried.

I jumped to my feet with her, excited for Max even though I was supposed to be cheering for Jimmy's team.

"Go, Max!" I shouted.

He looked up, and at the sight of his wide smile, I felt a sudden swoop in my chest. How I'd missed him! He'd left for university just before the stock market crashed and everything had changed. Seeing him now, it was like I'd gone back in time to when there were no protests, unemployment lines, or wilted vegetables, to a world that had seemed full of possibilities. I hugged Hannah to me as we cheered, buoyed by the impossible, magical idea that all our lives would turn around for the better, now that he was home. Maybe Max was our lucky charm.

two
MAX

❧

It took a second before Max realized he was staring. Was that really Molly? She sure had grown up over the past four years. If not for the strawberry blond ponytail flapping cheerfully as she waved, and her smile, bright as the sun, he might not have recognized her. He forced his eyes away and took his spot on the bench, finding it a little harder now to concentrate on the game.

After being away for so long, it felt a bit strange to be in Toronto. Like squeezing back into a favourite pair of shoes and discovering they were a little tight, but knowing they'd soon feel like slippers again. Playing baseball at Trinity Bellwoods Park and seeing Hannah and Molly in the crowd made things feel more normal. The only thing that could have made it better was if Richie was there.

Jimmy was, though. He'd come up to Max before the game.

"It's been a while," he'd said.

"It's good to be back," Max replied. "You're with the Native Sons this summer?"

Jimmy nodded and flicked the blue brim of Max's cap. "Not surprised you're with Harbord Playground again."

"Well, they are the only mostly Jewish team around."

"And they have the best players. Tell me, are you out of shape from being stuck in a classroom for so long? Maybe the Sons'll get lucky tonight after all."

Max laughed. Jimmy was a great kid, with more *chutzpah* than anyone he had ever met. On the ballfield, he was always the one to steal a base and get away with it.

"Don't count on it," he said. "Hey, where's Richie?"

Jimmy's grin faded. "He ain't coming. You probably won't see him around much. He's hanging out with a different bunch of guys these days."

Hearing that, Max had felt a little off-balance. He peered over the field, not wanting Jimmy to see how disappointed he was. "That's too bad."

"Yeah." Jimmy slapped Max's arm, then jabbed a thumb toward his team's bench. "I gotta go, but it's good to see you."

For as long as Max could remember, he and Richie had been a team unto themselves, backing each other up on the field. In school, all the kids had wanted to hit like Max and throw like Richie, and the littlest boys had looked up to them as if they were heroes. Even when they were playing on opposite teams, Max and Richie teased each other about having a weak arm or a bum leg to spur the other on. They'd always played their hearts out and walked off the field together like brothers.

Now, in the eighth inning, Max couldn't resist scanning the crowd again, but there was no sign of his friend. There were a lot of other faces he recognized, though. The trampled grass overflowed with people, from the oldest *bubbe* to the tiniest child, all of them talking and laughing, Yiddish, Italian, Ukrainian, and English weaving together like a song from his childhood. He spotted the Beisers in the crowd and remembered his mother's earlier words.

"Mrs. Beiser will be there with her two beautiful daughters," she'd said. "You remember Eva and Frieda? They're always asking about you. Their family is a good one."

"Thanks, Mama," he'd replied dutifully.

The Beiser girls were nice enough, but he wasn't attracted to either, and though he'd never tell his mother, he doubted he could ever marry a woman who couldn't hold up her end of a conversation. For his mother's sake, he smiled at the girls, who were watching him, just as he'd been warned.

As he scanned the faces around him, he felt a ripple of unease in his chest. The various skin tones in the crowd had become more obvious to him lately. Hannah and his mother had tried to keep their letters to him upbeat, but his father had been blunt about the swelling animosity against Jews in the city. Max hadn't been all that surprised by the news. He'd witnessed the growing divide for himself while at university in Hamilton.

"Dreyfus!" the coach called, breaking through his thoughts. "You're up!"

He grabbed a bat and headed toward the plate, a new kind of apprehension buzzing through him. How many of those spectators, how many of his old, *goy* friends still regarded him as their chum? How many now saw him as something . . . less? He screwed his ball cap on more firmly and set his jaw. Time to remind them that he was something *more*.

It was two out, bottom of the eighth, with no one on base. The Sons were ahead 5–4. *Let's tie this thing up*, he told himself.

Standing with his feet apart and knees bent, Max held the bat high and let his body sway slightly, matching the pitcher's rhythm while he waited for the throw. When the pitch came, his focus instantly sharpened, and the ball slammed into the sweet spot, just off the centre point of his bat. The Sons' fielders took off running while the crowd roared, and Max sprinted to first base. He was kicking past second when he spotted Jimmy grabbing the ball and winding up. Just like his older brother,

Jimmy had a great arm, so Max settled in at third. Hopefully the next batter would get him to home.

Jimmy pointed at him. "Almost got you!" And Max laughed out loud.

But it didn't matter, because their next batter struck out and the inning ended. Max grabbed his glove and headed back onto the field.

At the top of the ninth, the Native Sons' first hitter made it to second. After him, Jimmy stepped up to bat. Jimmy wasn't as good at bat as he was in the field, so Max moved in a little.

"Come on, Jimmy!" he heard Molly yell.

A swing and a miss. Jimmy backed up a step and kicked the dirt. He was the only one of the Ryans who didn't have a fiery head of orange hair, but his temper was just as sharp as theirs, especially when it was directed at himself.

"Get in there, Jimmy!" Molly shouted again. "He's got nothing! Eye on the ball!"

A slight, almost imperceptible nod, then Jimmy was back at the plate, setting up his stance. He angled his body toward the pitcher, then *crack!* The ball shot off his bat, and he ran toward first base as it headed up, up, up. It was a good hit, and too far for Max. He held his breath as it descended, watching his teammate, Pavlo Oliynyk, labour across the field with his glove held out.

"Get under it, Pav!" Max shouted.

It should have been an easy catch. From across the field, Max could practically feel the thud of the ball landing in his own glove. If it had been Richie instead of Pavlo, he would've snatched it out of midair and shot it home. But Pavlo was a foot shorter, and so was his reach. The ball plopped down just off his glove, and by the time he picked it up and lobbed it to the infield, Jimmy had run home, and so had the fellow ahead of him. It was now 7–4 for the Native Sons.

Max bit down on his disappointment and acknowledged Jimmy's hit with a nod. It wasn't like they'd lost the entire game. They still had a chance, albeit a slim one.

When it was time for Harbord Playground to hit again, Matteo Rossi was first up. He swung, and the ball plowed through the infield, bouncing between legs and around players. It was a beautifully messy grounder, and it got Rossi to first. Snooky Rubenstein, their shortstop, was up next. He made it to first base, and Rossi moved to second. One batter later, all the bases were loaded, and it was up to Max to bring Harbord to victory.

Adrenaline coursed through him as he strode toward the plate, blocking out the cheers and jeers of the crowd. He settled into his stance, raised the bat, and stared down the pitcher. In his mind, there was only one way this was going to go.

Max belted the first pitch, sending it chest height into left field, slicing through the fielders. He took off, putting everything he had into his legs, relishing the crunch of gravel under his shoes as he sprinted past the bases. Flying toward home, he nearly collided with the three runners in front of him, but they all turned, leaping onto each other in celebration while the rest of their teammates rushed from the bench. The crowds on the sidelines went crazy.

They'd done it. Harbord Playground, 8. Native Sons, 7. It was the best feeling in the world.

Pulling out of the team's embrace, Max spotted Hannah and Molly squeezing between people, on their way to him.

Hannah hugged him tight. "What a game. You were terrific!" she yelled over the noise.

"That was a fantastic hit!" Molly said from behind her.

She was even prettier up close, her green eyes set off by the pale blue of her dress, which he recognized as one of Hannah's hand-me-downs.

"Thanks, Molly. It's good to see you."

"I'm so glad you're back!" she said, reaching for a hug.

He breathed in the fragrant warmth of her hair as she squeezed him. "Me too."

"Okay, okay," Jimmy said, wandering over. "I'll admit that was a good hit."

"Ha! High praise coming from you," Max said. "You weren't so bad yourself."

"I almost had you there."

"Almost," Max teased.

The whole walk home Max felt like he was on top of the world. He loved his studies and had finished at the top of his class, but he'd been so busy he hadn't realized how much he'd missed being home with his friends. He snuck another peek at Molly, walking on Hannah's other side. It didn't seem like that long ago they'd been kids, throwing the baseball around, and she'd been giving him grief for trying to coach her while she was up to bat. Now she was a beautiful young woman. So was Hannah, he realized, looking at his sister with fresh eyes.

Day had given way to dusk, and the lights in the various store windows had been turned off for the night, but some things were still easy to see. When they passed a pawn shop with a big white sign in the window, Max's smile faded, and he stopped walking.

HELP WANTED. NO JEWS.

He'd seen signs like this before. He'd felt outraged whenever he passed them near the university, but seeing them in his own neighbourhood felt like a punch to the chest.

Molly paused beside him. "They're everywhere now. Stores, restaurants, parks, even the beach." She wrinkled her nose. "Oh, and we also have 'Swastika Clubs.'"

Unease spread over him like a cloak. "Swastika Clubs?"

"They claim their only intent is keeping the boardwalk clean of litter," Molly told him as they started walking again. "But they're not talking about picking up trash."

"Yeah, I get it."

"I'm sorry. The signs bother me, and I'm not even . . ."

"Jewish? You can say the word." His response came out harsher than he intended, and she looked straight ahead.

"Of course."

"Sorry, Moll. I shouldn't take it out on you. It just gets tiring, seeing this kind of stuff. It's not as if we did anything to deserve it."

"I know," she said. "It's easy for me to say, but I try to ignore it. Hannah says she won't dignify it with a response."

"That's one way to deal with it." He had a few others in mind.

Up ahead, Hannah and Jimmy were laughing, and Max was sorry he'd missed the joke. He needed to laugh more. Even his mother had said so. He forced himself to put the sign out of his mind and jogged in front of the others, then turned to face them, walking backwards.

"How many times do you think the four of us—plus Richie—have strolled down this sidewalk?" he asked.

"Since we could walk," Molly said, catching up. "Mum said I actually took my first steps on this sidewalk."

Jimmy chuckled. "We all did. She figured if we kept falling on the concrete we'd learn faster."

"Liam still gets bloody knees, and he's twelve," Molly said, then she looked at Max. "Do you remember when he was little and skinned his knee on the school playground and you rescued me?"

"I don't know if I'd say I rescued—"

"You did!"

He remembered it well, and he was pleased to hear she did, too. Years ago, he and Richie had been playing catch on their lunch hour, each trying to throw harder than the other, when one of Richie's pitches had gone uncharacteristically wild. It was headed directly to where Molly was crouched, bandaging Liam's knee, about ten feet out of Max's reach. Max hadn't thought twice, just thrown himself into the path of the ball. He'd never been so relieved to hear the *smack!* in his glove, inches from her face.

"Richie was screaming at me to get out of the way," Molly said, "but by the time I looked up it was too late. That ball was coming so fast I figured that was the end of me."

"Nah. I'd never let anyone hurt you," he said.

She smiled. "That's what you said to me back then, too."

"I remember that," Hannah said. "Richie was yelling at you to *pay attention next time*, and I—"

"You yelled at *him* to pay attention," Jimmy said. "Then the two of you had a huge argument. The whole school was listening in. It was great."

"I won, even though we both got detentions." Hannah lifted her chin. "Oh, look. There's poor old Mr. Rabinowitz."

If Hannah hadn't said so, Max wouldn't have recognized the widower he'd known from the synagogue, with his hunched frame draped in tattered clothes. They nodded at him as they passed, but Molly stopped to say good evening.

"On your way home?" she asked.

"Yes, yes, *sheyne meydel*," he replied, blinking cloudy eyes. "Long day at the factory. I've got to get home for dinner. On Thursdays, Mrs. Rabinowitz makes chicken and potatoes."

"You're a lucky man. Have a lovely evening," she said, and they watched the old man wander on down the block.

"I didn't know you knew him," Hannah said.

"Oh, he and I have the same sort of conversation just about every day outside Palermo's. I don't think he remembers though."

"You know he's a widower?" Max asked. "There's no chicken dinner waiting for him."

"Yes. Mr. Palermo told me. But he still thinks she's cooking for him. He must be so lonely."

That was pure Molly, he thought. Kindness ran all the way through her. "You're still at Palermo's?"

"I'll be sorting fruit and vegetables for the rest of my life."

"It's not for the rest of your life," Hannah assured her.

"Just until you become a world-famous writer," Jimmy said, draping an arm around his sister's shoulder.

Molly flushed, a sweet burst of pink Max remembered well. She and Richie could never hide their emotions behind their pale, freckled skin.

"You're writing?" Max asked. "What about?"

"It's nothing, really. I'm not that good."

"She's being modest," Jimmy said.

"He's right; she's a natural." Hannah beamed with pride.

"You're both biased," Molly said. She turned to Max. "I'm writing my grandmother's stories. Her family couldn't read or write, so she memorized them and told them to me before she died. Like she told me about the *Gorta Mór*, the Great Famine. It's what forced my great-grandparents to leave Ireland for Canada in 1847 with my grandmother and her five siblings. Such an awful story. Lots of them died during the sea voyage to Toronto, then more died of typhus after they arrived. We think *we* have it bad! My grandmother lost two of her sisters." She pressed her lips together. "I'm talking too much."

"No, I think it's fascinating," Max said, thinking about his own great-grandparents. They had immigrated to Canada to escape a different set of problems in Poland. "Really."

"*Seanmháthair* always had great stories," Jimmy said. "I wonder how our family would fare if we took that journey now. If the sea and the typhus didn't get us, I bet we'd have killed each other anyway."

"We wouldn't. Just you and Dad," Molly said, elbowing her brother.

Hannah looked at Max. "I told Molly she should write for a magazine or a newspaper."

Molly rolled her eyes. "Yeah, sure. How many women do you know who are doing that?"

"Actually," Max said, "I was just reading about a woman journalist named Rhea Clyman. She's even Canadian. I'll bring you something of hers," he offered. "She's really impressive."

"You'd be good at writing for a paper," Hannah said. "You'd tell all sides of the story."

"I don't know. Maybe," Molly replied. "Maybe someday I'll go back to school and take writing classes."

But from the soft sigh in her voice, Max could tell she didn't quite believe it.

A memory drifted into his mind of her standing in his family's kitchen years ago. Too small to reach the counter on her own, she'd dragged in a stool and climbed onto it, her short, twin braids falling forward as she watched his mother cook. Her eyes had darted between the pot and his mother as she asked endless questions clarifying what she was cooking, what was in it, why she was making it. That's just how Molly was. All her life, she'd looked for answers.

She might not believe she could do it, but Max did. "The world needs honesty now more than ever," he told her. "Don't count yourself out, Moll. You might be exactly what we need."

three
MOLLY

❧

I ducked under the low rafter just past the door of Palermo's back room, hugging the crate of lettuce to my chest, then I set it on the counter so I could sort through it. The first head I grabbed was still solid and healthy, so I placed it in the "keep" crate, which would go out front when I was done. The second one I touched was slick and soft. I tossed it into the garbage and reached for the next.

I had worked at Palermo's for so long, I could almost pinpoint which item was rotten from ten feet away, just by the smell. Lettuce wasn't the worst-smelling vegetable, but anything spoiled was unpleasant to handle. I was used to the slippery leaves though, and I barely thought about them as I picked through, just like I barely noticed the uneven, wobbly floorboards by the tomato crates. The quirks of Palermo's were just a part of who I had become.

I peeled off the outer leaves of the next head of lettuce, wondering if I could salvage any of it. By the time I was finished, it was about the size of a child's fist, which wasn't enough for anyone. Still, I set it aside.

Tomorrow was Tuesday, delivery day, when fresh stock came in, so today I sifted through the week-old fruits and vegetables. As repulsive as some of the produce could be, this was how I helped people the most. Mr. Palermo always kept a few crates of overripe apples, yellowing broccoli, soft potatoes, and things like that, stacked in the back. The food wasn't rotten, only slightly past the time when most people would have eaten it. But these days, not too many people could still claim to be "most people." The majority were one meal away from the soup kitchen—if they weren't already there.

Palermo's had gone through a lot since my first day four years ago. The store was quieter now, and desperately in need of paint. Warped wooden cartons piled high with fruit and vegetables no longer overflowed onto the sidewalk. Food was too dear to put on display, and too much of a temptation to many. Besides, stock was so low it all fit inside now.

I was grateful for my job. A lot of girls worked at the Eaton's garment factory, and I'd heard rumblings of the strife they put up with—long hours, low pay. It was thankless work. Sure, I had long days, but my job wasn't hard, and that meant my mind was free to wander.

Today my thoughts were on Sunday's sermon. "Thou shalt love the Lord thy God with all thy heart," the minister had read, "and with all thy soul, and with all thy mind. This is the first and great commandment. And the second is like unto it, Thou shalt love thy neighbour as thyself."

I'd heard it a thousand times, but yesterday the words had given me pause. There I sat with my family, in a beautiful church, surrounded by well-meaning, dutiful Protestants, when I spotted Phil Burke a couple pews ahead of me wearing a pressed brown shirt with a swastika pin on his chest. Last week, Hannah and I had seen him and his Swastika Club, wandering in and out of local shops and bullying Jewish customers.

I seemed to witness more prejudice by the day. Protestants against Catholics. Orangemen against immigrants. Employers against employees. Government against the people. Some of the people around me in church who were nodding in agreement with the idea that we should all "love thy neighbour" were the same ones banning Jews from their stores. The hypocrisy sickened me.

I threw a bunch of soft carrots into a crate with more force than necessary at the memory of Max's expression when he'd seen that sign at the pawn shop.

"Molly?" Mr. Palermo's lean, rabbit-like face peeked through the door.

I looked up, a questionable cabbage in one hand. "Yes, Mr. Palermo?"

"Mrs. Collins is asking for a quart of fresh tomatoes." His bushy white moustache twitched. "None of the ones up here seem to suit her."

"Be right there."

I grabbed a quart of the best-looking tomatoes in the room and headed to the front.

Mrs. Collins's face widened with a smile as soon as I entered. She was a tall, blond woman, and today she wore a neat green suit. A matching cloche was pulled stylishly low over one eye. Mrs. Collins was one of the few people I knew who seemed relatively untouched by poverty.

"Molly, dear. So nice to see you. You're looking well."

"Thank you," I said politely. I handed the tomatoes to Mr. Palermo, and he started wrapping them up.

"I was talking to Ian about you last night," Mrs. Collins went on. "You know, he's over at the *Star*. He's hoping to become a junior reporter soon."

"I'm happy to hear he's doing well, especially in times like these."

"Here you go," Mr. Palermo said, holding up the package.

She made no move to take it from him. "I'm sure he would love to see you sometime," she pressed. "Maybe the two of you could have dinner."

I remembered Ian Collins from school. He was three years older than I was and a nice enough boy, handsome in a relaxed sort of way, but I didn't really know him. My mother made a point of saying that was because I had never taken Mrs. Collins up on her suggestion. Besides, she said, what was there to know? He had a good job, and his family was well-off. He was Irish and Protestant. But the truth of the matter was that Ian had never asked me out. I didn't know what I'd say if he did.

"Thank you for thinking of me, Mrs. Collins, but I'm afraid I'm too busy these days."

"Of course," she said through a tight smile. She handed over the cash and gathered her purchases. "Always nice to see you, Molly. Please give my best to your mother."

Once she was out the door, Mr. Palermo returned to his paperwork behind the register. "You can't put her off forever," he muttered.

"Oh yes, I can," I assured him, heading to the back room.

I *was* busy. If I did have spare time, I wouldn't be wasting it on Ian Collins. Or on any boy, to be fair. I'd gone on a date or two, but I was usually so bored by the end of the night I could hardly wait to close the door behind me. Hannah thought I was a riot, turning them down. She loved going out on dates. I knew that most girls my age wanted to settle down and become wives and mothers, but I just wasn't ready for that, as much as it frustrated my mother. It seemed all I'd ever done was take care of my siblings. I wanted to do something else. Something for me.

I hadn't meant to tell Max about my writing, though I supposed that was all right. Growing up, he'd never made fun of me, never made me feel like a little girl like Richie sometimes did, but it had been four years since I had seen him and in that time, he'd gotten a degree. He'd grown up. His face was darker, shaded by the black outline of his beard, and he was leaner, probably from so much studying. But he still had the same smile, and he still hadn't laughed at me. He'd been encouraging about the idea of my writing, and last night he'd even brought over the article by Rhea Clyman, the journalist he'd mentioned before.

Rhea's story tore my heart apart. She'd written about the Holodomor, the ongoing, brutal genocide of Ukrainians by the Soviets. Her article described the deserted villages, the starving people, and the children who she wrote were down on all fours like animals, eating grass because there was nothing else for them.

When I'd finished reading, it was a moment before I could speak. "Imagine, going all the way there by herself," I said to Max. "What a dangerous mission. Especially for a woman."

"This was actually her second time there," he said. "The Soviets expelled her last September."

"For what?"

"She went to investigate reports of political prisoners and exiles being used as slave labour in camps. In her story she called one of the prison towns a 'town of living corpses.' The Soviets were furious."

I couldn't imagine having that kind of courage, to travel all that way then reveal a story like that to the world, putting herself at risk. Then again, that's exactly what I wanted to do with my writing. To make a difference somehow—though I didn't see myself heading to the Soviet Union anytime soon.

"Molly?" Mr. Palermo called again.

"Yes?" I stooped through the doorway, wiping my hands on my apron.

Mrs. Rossi stood at the counter, her boney fingers curled around her handbag, her eyes downcast and sunken beneath her black scarf. Behind her waited her two youngest sons, their clothes hanging off their little frames. Mr. Rossi had been my school principal, but he'd died last year of a heart attack, leaving behind his wife and six children. She took in mending jobs, like my mother did, so she could be with her kids, but it was never enough. Matteo, her oldest, worked two jobs.

"Hello, Mrs. Rossi," I said. "Matteo played well the other night. It was a good game."

"Grazie, Molly," she replied softly.

Mr. Palermo fixed me with a steady look, and I nodded. "I'll be back in jiffy."

I loaded up an empty box with as much salvageable produce as I could find, then I returned to the front and placed the box in Mrs. Rossi's arms.

"Grazie. *Dio ti benedica*," she said, quietly leaving.

Mr. Palermo and I didn't say anything more, and I went back to work. There would be two or three more visits like hers today. We did what we could, but none of them were easy on our hearts. I had planned to bring a crate to the Melniks down the street from us, but just the other day, they'd been put out of their house, and I hadn't seen them since.

The day passed slowly, with far too few customers trickling in. I finished packing boxes for the poorest customers, making up an extra that Mr. Palermo requested, then swept and tidied the back in preparation for tomorrow's deliveries. At the end of the day, I stopped by the counter to say goodnight to Mr. Palermo. He was hunched over the counter, papers all around him.

He held out a hand. "Molly, I need to speak with you."

His gaze went to the ceiling, like it did when he was trying to figure out a problem on the register. When he met my eyes, my heart sank. I knew from his sad expression what he was about to say. I put one hand on the counter to steady myself.

"The store isn't as busy as it used to be," he began, sounding defeated. "I can't afford to stay open every day. I think I'm going to cut down to just three days a week. I'm still figuring it out. I'm sorry, Molly. I have to let you go. I wish I didn't have to."

He went on, and I nodded, but my mind had already rushed home. How was I going to tell my family I was out of a job? I supposed I could take in laundry or babysit, but that wouldn't bring in nearly as much as the store had.

Mr. Palermo's eyes were shining, which brought a lump to my throat.

"It's all right," I said. "I understand. I do. Thank you for letting me work for you for so long. I learned a lot. I enjoyed it here."

Mr. Palermo put his wrinkled old hand on mine. "If business picks up again—"

"Please don't worry about me," I said, pressing a finger against my chin to keep it from wobbling. "I'll find a job somewhere. You take care of yourself." I turned to go.

"Molly, take that last box for your family, would you? Tell your father I'm sorry."

I knew he was watching me as I left, because I felt the weight of his guilt on my back. Only when I was out of sight did I reach up to wipe my tears away.

four

MAX

ෆ

Max wandered into the kitchen and placed a gentle kiss on his mother's cheek, making her smile as she braided the *challah*. Other than his bedroom, where he studied in quiet, the kitchen, with its rich, spicy fragrance, was Max's favourite place in the house. On the table he spotted a plate, artfully covered by a cloth, and he inhaled the sweet aroma of latkes.

Pretending he didn't know, he lifted a corner and peeked underneath. "What's this?"

She looked over her shoulder. "You know what, *bubbala*. It's for you."

"My favourite," he said, sitting at the table and helping himself. He'd missed her cooking so much. "Thank you, Mama."

"More studying today?"

"No, I'm going to the factory this morning. I haven't been yet. I should see if Papa needs help."

"He would like that, but stay a few minutes with your mama. I want to hear you laugh."

"I laugh plenty, Mama." But he knew she had a point.

She placed a cup of tea before him then sat across with her own cup. "You work more than you laugh. You are young only once, my son. I see other boys outside, doing things that boys like to do. You should do those things."

"Yes, Mama, but will those boys become doctors? Will they make their mamas proud?"

"You make me proud already." She eyed the latkes. "Save some for Hannah."

On the table by his father's chair lay a folded issue of *Der Yidisher Zhurnal*, Toronto's Yiddish newspaper. The headline was bold and intriguing. Max slid it closer.

"Maybe you shouldn't read too much of that," she suggested. "Too much hate in this world. There's nothing we can do about it but be sad."

In a way, she was right: there was nothing they could do about what was happening with Germany's new chancellor, Adolf Hitler, and Eastern Europe. But the *Zhurnal* also reported on issues and rising tensions happening in the city. Toronto was like a hot tin roof these days, with people hopping from one cause to another, demanding jobs, homes, and fair treatment, extolling communism, walking lines of tension as strained as a tightrope. Max needed to know every inch of that tightrope so he could navigate it expertly.

He scanned the Yiddish type. "It does no one any good to wear blinders, Mama."

His mother observed him a moment, then she got to her feet again. She never could sit still for too long. "You sound like your papa."

"With most things," he agreed. "Papa wrote to me about the League for the Defence of Jewish Rights."

He'd felt so proud, learning his father had been a part of the league's first meeting that April at Massey Hall. There, various Jewish organizations had come together to address rising anti-Semitism in Canada and beyond, trying to decide what to do about it. Unfortunately, after the first meeting, his father had written to him that the leaders of the movement had argued incessantly, including about who would be on the *shtadlanim*, the committee that would negotiate with the government. *Too many political agendas*, he'd lamented. Max wasn't altogether surprised. In his experience, they could barely get a roomful of men in their synagogue to agree on anything, let alone the whole country. Still, the formation of the league was an important step.

His mother swept in with the teapot, topping up his cup before he was halfway done—her loving way of keeping him with her a little longer.

"Your father talks of little else," she said. "Protests and meetings and boycotts and who knows what. Who wants to hear about that?"

Max wanted to hear about that. His heels tapped under the table, eager to get going.

"It's killing you, sitting here with your mama, isn't it?"

"No. I just—"

She laughed. "It's all right. Go on."

"Thanks." He drained his tea then gave her another peck on the cheek and headed for the door.

Outside, the morning air was warm, but from the weight of it, he could tell the afternoon was going to be steamy. At least for now it was pleasant. As he passed Palermo's, he popped inside to say hello to Molly, but when he asked if she was around, Mr. Palermo shook his head then apologized, saying he was too busy to talk. Since he and Max were the only two in the store, it seemed odd, but a lot of things were odd these days. Max wished him a good day and left, almost bumping into Richie outside the hardware store next door.

"Hey, Richie. I was hoping to run into you sometime."

"Max." Richie gave a sheepish half grin. "I heard you were back."

There were so many things Max wanted to say, but he didn't know where to start. He nodded toward the store. "You on a break?"

"Yep," Richie replied, sliding his hands into his trouser pockets.

Max wasn't used to the strained pauses between them. "I missed you at the game."

"I haven't played in a while. Not much time for it. And the fellas don't play, so, you know."

"The fellas?"

"I don't think you'd know them."

"Oh." The seconds ticked past. "Sorry to hear that. It's not the same without you."

"Yeah, well. Things change," he said. "You weren't here. I did other stuff."

Max felt a familiar pang of guilt at the reminder. During the last year of high school, whenever Richie had come to the Dreyfus house, Max had his head buried in his books. He still felt bad for having to turn his friend away so often.

"I needed to study. I needed to get the marks for the scholarship."

Richie hesitated. "You know you're the guy who could get everything right without even trying, yeah?"

"It's not like that."

Richie had no idea how hard Max studied. Still, Max knew he had it pretty easy in comparison. Unlike the Ryans, his family didn't need him to work, so he'd been able to put everything into winning the scholarship.

"Can I ask a question?"

It struck Max that the old Richie would have just gone ahead and said what was on his mind. "Sure."

"Why did you go to McMaster in Hamilton instead of the University of Toronto?"

Max's mouth went dry, and he struggled to think of a believable excuse. There was no way he was going to tell Richie the real reason.

"There was . . . I wanted to study under a specific professor at Mac."

At the time, the truth had been devastating. Now it was just embarrassing. Deep down, Max understood the University of Toronto's quota for Jewish students wasn't his fault, but he still felt humiliated over their rejection. It also made him angry every time he thought about it. Practically anyone else could march right into the university, but even if he'd gotten full marks on every subject, Max wouldn't have been permitted into the hallowed halls.

Richie nodded slowly. "I see." He looked like he was going to ask something more, and Max braced to tell another lie, then Richie's attention shifted past him. "I gotta get back to work. I'll see you."

Max checked up the street, wondering what had prompted Richie to leave so abruptly, and spotted a group of four boys walking his way. He recognized one of them, Phil Burke, from elementary school, though he'd never known him well. Phil's bleached white polo shirt was buttoned to the top, and a cigarette was propped behind one ear. Max watched him run a hand through his slicked blond hair then lean toward the other boys, saying something Max couldn't hear. All their eyes slid to Max, and anger stirred in his gut. He'd seen this too often at McMaster. As they passed, all four glared as if they each had a personal score to settle with him, but Max stood his ground. Didn't matter how many knuckles Phil cracked, Max refused to be intimidated.

By the time he arrived at his father's warehouse on Spadina Avenue, some of his fury had faded, and he tried to push the rest away. It was midmorning, and there were two delivery trucks parked outside. A small crowd of people moved in and out of the building, their arms full, and Max remembered that Fridays were delivery days, sending stock to stores. As he approached, a tall, bearded man in a white shirt stepped outside, his sleeves rolled up to his elbows.

"Papa!" Max said.

His father turned, arms open. "Max, my boy. You're here to help?"

"Of course. In exchange for lunch?"

"I will gladly buy you lunch if you help with all this."

For the next two hours, Max and the others worked through the rising heat of the day, loading boxes of brand-new dresses, trousers, and coats while his father checked and double-checked inventory lists. When they were finally done, sweat rolled down Max's face, and some of the workers' shirts were drenched through. His father caught his eye and tipped his head toward the deli up the street.

"Let's go see Harry Shopsowitz. He's been asking about you lately."

Max had forgotten how quickly his father walked. He had always taken long strides, his hands folded behind his back as if he was thinking hard. As a boy, Max had taken great pride in being able to match the speed of those steps. Now he was as tall as his father, but he still had to make an effort to keep up.

"It's good to see steady business, considering the times," Max said.

His father shook his head. "Two trucks, and they weren't even full. Before, it was four or five. But I have to remember to be thankful for what we still have. Saul Rubenstein, you remember him? With the leather coats?"

"Of course." Saul had been his father's best friend for years, and Max played on the Harbord team with his son, Snooky.

"He's barely producing a quarter of his old sales. He's afraid he might go bankrupt."

"I'm sorry to hear that."

About a block away from Shopsy's Delicatessen, Max spotted another sign: **JEWS NEED NOT APPLY**. "It's worse than I thought," he muttered.

"What is?"

Max jabbed his thumb at the shop. "That sign back there. In the window."

His father waved a hand. "That's been going on since the beginning of time. Your Zeyde Ira and Bubbe Rachel lived through worse. They were strong people, them. You remember that, Maxim: you come from strong people."

When he was young, Max had found the story of why his grand-parents fled Poland to be thrilling, in a dark, frightening way. On Christ-mas Day 1881, after Christians gathered in the Holy Cross church in Warsaw for mass, a false rumour had spread that there was a fire in the building. Twenty-nine Christians were killed in the subsequent stam-pede. Then the rumours took on a life of their own, and though there was no proof, people claimed the Jews were responsible. For three days after that, any Jewish store, business, or home near the church was targeted for destruction by rioters. When Max's fourteen-year-old grandfather was chased by a man with a hammer, the family decided it was past time to leave.

In Max's young imagination, he had been in Warsaw, fighting back, defending the neighbourhood. His father had put a stop to that way of thinking.

"Do not wish violence upon yourself, Maxim," he'd said. "Our lives on earth are short enough. Your grandparents were wise to come here. They didn't have two pennies to rub together, and they didn't know but one word of English between them, but they were safe here."

Max's grandparents had settled in The Ward, a slum in downtown Toronto that housed hundreds of other immigrants, including Ital-ians and Chinese. Through odd jobs and hard work, Max's grandpar-ents eventually managed to move out and buy a house in Kensington, where Max's father had been born. These days, most of The Ward was gone. The ramshackle homes had been replaced by massive stone buildings.

At Shopsy's Deli, Max and his father took a table near the window, and before they even sat down, other patrons stopped by to greet them. His father had always engaged with the people of their community, and their connections went deeper than simple friendships. Max stood back and watched the conversations, enjoying the custom.

"Ezra, how are you?" they asked.

"You see my son Max is back?"

"Good to see you, Max. You're looking well. So tall! How was school? Are you a doctor yet?"

Max shook their hands and answered politely, explaining that he had another four years to go, and they all nodded.

"Good for you, Max. We're all proud of you."

As more people greeted them, Max was reminded of a special truth. Despite the prejudice and animosity his community experienced, he knew that no matter where he went in life, he would always be a member of this family. His people were like bees, working hard, and always recognizing each other as friends and kin.

When they were finally alone, Max and his father sat, then Max leaned over the table toward him. "Tell me what's happening, Papa. I've been reading the papers, but it's difficult when I'm in school."

"Many interesting things, my son." He smiled up at the young waitress who approached. "You got lox today? And cream cheese?"

"Always," she said.

"Sounds good. Max?"

"I'll have the same. And coffee," Max added. "Okay, Papa. Tell me what you were gonna say."

"Well, your mother probably told you all about it."

"Not all, but I got the feeling that whatever you're doing, she'd rather you stop doing it."

He chuckled. "She's probably right. She usually is."

"What about all the talk of strikes? Do you worry about the labour movement?"

His father shrugged. "Why should I worry? I'm good to my employees. The trouble with socialism in our industry is that there's not much margin. The workers want more money, but I don't have much to give. If they push too hard, they force me out of business, and we all lose. But most of my employees are Jewish. Why would we fight among ourselves when the world is already fighting us?"

"Tell me what's happening with the League for the Defence of Jewish Rights." Max paused, leaning back as the waitress set down his coffee. "Thanks." He turned back to his father. "I've read the headlines and your letters, but I want to hear it from you."

"It's a good organization, I think. Rabbi Sachs is in charge, along with Shmuel Meir Shapiro."

"The editor of *Der Yidisher Zhurnal*."

"Yes. Many, many people came to the April meeting. Some weren't even Jewish. And now, Jews across the country are starting to come together. The irony is that the Nazis want to persecute us, but their hatred is pulling us together. We're getting stronger because of them."

"I'd like to come to a meeting, Papa."

His father reached across the table and patted Max's hand. "Since you were little you wanted to get into the fight. But you, you're going to be a doctor. The first in our family to go to university. You remember telling me that? What were you, twelve?"

"Twelve."

"And you had a plan. Best doctor *and* baseball player in the world, you said. Then you got the scholarship, and your marks—you're top of the class." He shook his head, marvelling. "Oy vey, what a brain you've got. Why would you want to get mixed up in politics? No, you have other things to spend your time on."

Max pulled his hand away. "Papa, I'd like to be involved. This is too important."

His father let out a long sigh. "Okay, okay. I will take you to the meeting tomorrow. Your mama's gonna kill me." He tapped the table with one finger. "You know, your mama's a smart woman. You must find yourself a smart woman, Maxim. One who thinks for herself." He smiled. "Without smart women, we men often do stupid things."

The smoke-filled meeting room on Beverly Street was crowded with men young and old, taking up chairs and leaning against the walls. His father pointed a thick finger toward the other side of the room.

"I'll be over there with Saul," he said. "You stay here."

"Fine with me, Papa. There are too many thick grey beards up there for my taste."

His father chuckled, stroking his own salt-and-pepper chin as he walked away. Max scouted the crowd for familiar faces, then he heard his name, and an arm clamped around his shoulder.

"What, I can't go a month without seeing your sorry face?"

Max grinned at the sight of Arnie Schwartz, his roommate from McMaster. Arnie was a half foot shorter than Max, with thick black eyebrows that arched up in a way that gave the impression he was laughing at everything. He always looked disheveled, but he was smart and he had a wonderfully dry sense of humour.

"I could say the same," Max said. He held out a hand to Arnie's younger brother, Samuel. "It's good to see you, Sam."

Samuel shook his hand. "Welcome to the assembly of the League for the Defence of Jewish Rights, where all the important men in town meet."

"And they let you two in?" Max teased.

"Oh yes," Samuel said, rolling his shoulders back. He was even shorter than Arnie, but his big personality made up for that. "We make all the big decisions. Those old guys up front just take the credit."

"Arnie tells me you're getting married, Sam. *Mazel tov*. When's the big day?"

"Next spring, she says. Lucy is in charge of everything, of course. I hope you'll come."

"If I can," Max said. "So, what else is new? Arnie and I have been living under a rock at school."

Samuel happily filled him in on all the gossip about their old friends. Some were married, a couple had moved out of the city, but most were working in the textile industry on Spadina, alongside Max's father's factory.

"You need to come out from under your rock more often," Samuel advised. "Or you'll never find a wife."

"Don't worry about that, little brother," Arnie said. "What girl is not going to want to marry a tall, dark, handsome doctor?"

From behind Max came a voice he hadn't heard in a while—and one he'd rather hoped not to hear again. Glancing over his shoulder, he spotted tall, spindly Yossel Abelman making his way toward them.

"Here we go," Arnie said under his breath.

Yossel was a few years older than Max, with a scraggly beard and a nose that looked as if it had been broken at least twice. He was a passionate Zionist, and ever since learning that Max wasn't, he delighted in starting arguments with him.

"Yossel. It's been a while."

"Tell me, Max. Have you had your fill of persecution yet?" Yossel asked right away, settling into a seat across from Max. "Shall I tell you again about our homeland? It would have no Irish, no Italians, no Catholics, no *goyim* at all. It would be a place of peace and strength. We are always running. There, we would never run from oppression again."

Max straightened, aware of curious faces leaning in to hear what he would say. "I didn't know you'd been running, Yossel. No wonder you're so thin. Tell me, are we Jews to hide away for the rest of our existence? Run away, as you say, with our tails between our legs? I say no. We travelled thousands of miles to get here because we want more out of life."

Yossel let out a sharp laugh. "More of what? More torment?"

"More than just ourselves," Max replied. "You Zionists want to shut yourselves off from everybody else. If it were up to you, you would be an armadillo, curled into a ball to keep all your soft bits safe. You'd only talk with like-minded people, excluding yourselves from the rest of the world—"

"And that is somehow worse than being in another man's world but living in fear and humiliation the entire time?"

Max had no plan to live in either fear or humiliation. Since being home, he had tried to ignore the signs populating the city and the glares from people like Phil Burke, knowing that if he let those things get to him, they won. He wasn't afraid of them, just annoyed. In this world there would always be bad people, but good people existed too, like Molly, Jimmy, and Richie. Max chose to believe his friends were part of the quiet majority.

"Come on now. We all know we need a homeland," Yossel was saying. "Even you, Maxim. A home is where one feels safe to be himself. He can believe what he believes and worship how he wants to worship, and he has no fear of being persecuted. There is no home here for us."

Max didn't agree, but he and Yossel would never see eye to eye, so Max decided to lighten the conversation.

"I don't know," Max said, folding his arms. "You *kvetch* all the time, Yossel. I want this. I want that. If you get your own homeland, you'll never have anything to complain about. What will you do with yourself then?"

"Yossel will always find something to complain about," Arnie said, and the young men around them laughed.

Yossel leaned toward Max and gestured for him to come closer. "Maxim, my friend," he said, lowering his voice. "I admire you. You are a *mensch* who knows what he wants. If they let you, I am certain you will be a great doctor someday."

"If they let me?"

"*If* they let you. I understand the quota for medical school at the University of Toronto is even lower this year. Isn't that where you plan to go?"

Max hesitated a beat. "That is where I *will* go."

"Sure, sure." Yossel moved back again and waved his hand in front of his face, like he was batting away a fly. "But you know, we all like you, Maxim Dreyfus. So don't worry. When you have to start sewing seams in the factories with the rest of us, we will still welcome you."

"The only seams Max will be sewing is in surgery," Arnie countered.

More laughter, but Max didn't join in this time. Yossel's words had struck a little too close to home.

"You still boxing, Max?" Samuel asked.

"A little," he replied, glad to change the subject.

"Good. We'll need you ready to go when the Swastika Club comes out."

"I heard there are over four hundred of them," Max said. "Are you expecting me to fight them all?"

Samuel puffed out his chest. "There are only about forty, and they're never all together. I'll take a couple off your hands if it helps."

"You gonna be like Baer, Max?" Yossel teased. "Be a hero and take on the Swazzies?"

They all knew he was referring to Max Baer, the American boxer who had just defeated Max Schmeling. Schmeling was a German heavy-weight, a former champion, and Hitler's prize fighter. Baer only had one Jewish grandparent, and yet he had proudly worn the Star of David on his trunks. Arnie and Max had listened to the fight on the radio when they were at school, cheering Baer on as he took Schmeling down.

Arnie shook his head. "It's better that Max keeps those surgeon hands safe."

"You're right. Don't worry about the Swastika Club, Max," Samuel replied. "We have our own Uptown Gang."

"Order!" a voice called from across the room. "This meeting will come to order!"

"I'd like to meet that gang. They sound fun," Arnie whispered, making Max smile.

Rabbi Sachs stood at the front of the room, not far from Max's father, waiting for quiet. He was a bald, serious-looking man, and one of the few in the committee without a beard.

"This is an unofficial meeting to address the increase in the city's anti-Semite activities and discuss how to counter them in a peaceful manner." Rabbi Sachs adjusted his round, gold-framed glasses and slowly scanned the room. "Among other things, we will be addressing the Swastika Club and their symbol, which they insist has nothing to do with Hitler."

Derisive chuckles rippled around the room.

"Today, Shmuel Meir Shapiro and I will collect ideas from you that we will put forward for the committee to consider."

Max craned his neck to get a better view of the editor of *Der Yidisher Zhurnal*. Shapiro was a stocky man with a neatly trimmed salt-and-pepper beard and a no-nonsense expression. He sat behind Rabbi Sachs, writing notes, then lifted his head and briefly studied the faces in the crowd, as if memorizing them.

"Our Women's Committee has been working hard on the efforts to put sanctions on German-manufactured goods, and many local businesses have complied," Rabbi Sachs continued. "All Jewish businesses have, of course. It's the others who aren't convinced."

"The *goyim* don't believe what is happening in Germany will affect them," someone said, drawing a few eyes.

Rabbi Sachs nodded. "Then we must show them it will."

"Jews must boycott those businesses," Yossel suggested. "We don't need them."

"But we do," Shapiro countered, tucking his pencil behind one ear. "Which of us is selling fruits and vegetables? Do we own hardware stores? I know of very few Jewish businesses handling those things."

"How do we make it clear that the rising threat from Germany will affect them?" Rabbi Sachs asked.

"We should put a full-page advertisement in the *Telegram*." Yossel's tone suggested he was surprised no one had already thought of this. "We can tell people what is happening, and we can remind them that we are not the enemy."

Beside Max, Samuel whispered, "Correct me if I'm wrong, but I don't think the people who read the *Telegram* will believe that."

Max nodded. Of all the papers, the conservative readers of the

Evening Telegram were among the least likely to side with the Jewish community. Yossel should know that, he thought.

More suggestions were thrown out, ranging from printing educational booklets to picketing outside noncompliant stores. Shapiro alternately wrote things down or shook his head while Rabbi Sachs encouraged more input, but none of the ideas seemed exactly right to Max. As the night wore on, the room got louder, with each man trying to outthink his neighbour. That's when Max remembered something Molly had said when he'd asked about her parents after the last baseball game.

"My dad's excited about the upcoming Glorious Twelfth," she'd said, rolling her eyes dramatically. "The big Orangemen parade—it's the only thing that seems to bring a smile to his face lately."

"A rally," Max declared, cutting through the din. "We should hold a rally."

Shapiro stood. "A protest? A parade? What do you envision?"

Nearby, Max's father nodded at Max with encouragement.

"Why not both?" Max said, a swell of purpose rising in him. "We could start on the street, maybe meet outside the Minsk synagogue, and march down the main streets until . . ." He thought it through. "Queen's Park. The legislature can't ignore us if we're there. If there are enough of us, that is."

Shapiro was nodding slowly. "A lot of arrangements would have to be made to get something like that going. Permits, police. But yes. You have something. The committee will discuss this."

"If I might make one more suggestion," Max added, fighting a little guilt. He hoped Molly would forgive him—and that her father never found out whose idea this was. "If there's enough time to arrange it, I suggest the rally be held July eleventh."

"Why's that?" Shapiro asked.

"Because July eleventh is one day before the Orangemen's parade. If nothing else, it will give everyone lots to talk about."

Shapiro raised his face to the ceiling and let out a laugh that came straight from his belly, and the rest of the room joined in. "What's your name?" he asked, taking up his pencil. "I want to make sure I have it spelled right."

"This is Max Dreyfus!" Arnie yelled, grinning. "D-R-E-Y-F-U-S."

Beside them, Yossel refused to meet Max's eyes, but Max beamed. He was part of this now, for better or worse, and he was filled with resolve. He could hardly wait to see what happened next.

five
MOLLY

꘎

I stood back from the mirror, checking to see how I looked, but my view was distorted by a diagonal crack cutting through the glass. Keeping that in mind, I examined my reflection sideways, trying to decide if wearing curlers had been worth the sleepless night I'd had. Normally I wouldn't have bothered, but today I was paying special attention to my appearance.

"Today I get a new job," I informed my warped reflection as I gently brushed the curls out. From between my lips, I took a bobby pin and pinned a lock of hair, then added another one to keep it in place. I leaned in a little, noting the definition of the bones in my face. We were all getting thinner these days.

At least I didn't have to worry about what to wear. Hannah had seen to that. When I'd listed my limited options, she'd frowned at me.

"No, no. Those won't work," she said, kind but firm. "I'm sorry, but that pink cardigan reeks of mothballs. You need to air it out before you wear it again. My father always says in order to be successful, you need to look like you already are. Lucky for you, I have the perfect dress. I wore it the other night when I went out with Abe, and he couldn't take his eyes off me."

Her infectious attitude lifted my mood as it always did. "You could have worn a paper bag and he would have acted the same way."

Hannah's eyes twinkled. "I know. I was almost afraid he was going to propose over dinner."

That led us deep into a conversation about whether Abe was the right kind of boy for her—we agreed that he wasn't—and whether she thought she was ready to become a homemaker—she said she definitely was.

"What else am I going to do with myself?" she asked.

"And what about children?"

"Lots," she said, looking pleased. "All I want is a home of my own and a family to take care of."

I envied how sure Hannah was about her future. All I knew was that I wasn't ready for the exact thing she wanted.

Before I left, she ran inside then returned with a smart navy dress draped over her arm and an almost new pair of Oxfords in her other hand, which I promised to keep clean and unmarked. Even with my cracked mirror, I could see the dress was perfect, though a little loose. Cut in the latest fashion, the waistline hung around mine, and the short sleeves ballooned out slightly. The shoes were a vast improvement over my own.

The trouble was, no matter how well I dressed and how hard I tried to convince myself, I knew my chances of finding a job were bleak.

Three weeks ago, when I'd started searching, I had scoured newspapers for ads, but found nothing that applied. A lot of the jobs were for men, but far too many families were like mine, in dire need of more than one income. Not yet discouraged, I'd set out door-to-door, looking for hiring signs in the shops lining the streets, but within the first block it had become apparent that I couldn't depend on those. They hung in a couple of windows, but not many. Most signs simply said, **OUT OF BUSINESS**. Others said, **JEWS NEED NOT APPLY**, but I dismissed those shops, holding on to hope that something better would be up ahead. So far it hadn't appeared.

As I turned to leave my room, I stopped by the tattered armchair that had once belonged to my *seanmháthair*. For years, it had sat by the window in the living room, but after she passed, my father had brought it up to my room.

"You remind me of her," he'd said after her funeral. As much as I was hurting, I'll never forget the depth of pain I saw in his eyes that night. "You're just as strong as she was. I hope you'll use her chair and keep telling stories."

Now, I rested my hand on the worn upholstery and closed my eyes, summoning her dear old face. "Send me some magic, *Seanmháthair*," I whispered, then I headed downstairs.

"You look nice," Mum said, glancing up from her mending.

"Hannah lent me the dress and shoes," I confessed.

She nodded, and I could tell she wanted to say something. Maybe comment about my Jewish friends, like Dad had.

"Good luck" was all she said. I took that as a good omen.

Something in the air felt different today, or at least that's what I told myself. I stepped outside and smiled at the sight of Max walking by. His gaze swept up from my shiny Oxfords, over Hannah's svelte navy dress and my fancy hair, then stopped at my face. Admiration shone in his eyes, and an unexpected wave of pleasure rolled through my chest. I'd never felt that way around him before, but I liked it.

"Where are you off to?"

I slowed, nearing him. "Job hunting still. I'm not having much luck."

"I would hire you in a second," he said. "You look fantastic."

My cheeks flushed, but only partially at the compliment. The other part was embarrassment. He had inadvertently reminded me of what Dad said after I'd told the family I was unemployed.

"It's all right," I had assured them. "I can work for Mr. Dreyfus. Hannah said so. It's not as bad as the other factories. He's good to his workers, and—"

"No," Dad said flatly.

"No?"

"It's too dangerous. With everything going on right now, Jewish businesses aren't safe." He scowled at the table. "I'll ask around. See who's hiring."

"You'll find something else," Richie offered helpfully.

"Yeah?" Dad jabbed a thumb in Jimmy's direction. "This one's been looking for a job for three months now, and he ain't brought home a penny."

Beside me, Jimmy seethed, but for once he didn't say anything in response. I took a breath for courage then threw out the next pitch.

"I would be all right working there, Dad."

"I said no. It isn't safe."

It annoyed me that he was treating me like a child. "I'm eighteen. I know what I'm doing. And Mr. Dreyfus would—"

"I said no!" he shouted, his face tomato red. "You will not work for a Jewish business. That's the end of it."

Later, Hannah asked if I wanted to speak with her father about a job, and I'd burned with shame over the fact that her religion was the reason I couldn't say yes. So, for the first time in our friendship, I had lied to her. I said my parents didn't want me working in a factory because they thought it was unsafe. Under her scrutiny, I had to turn away. Then she swiftly changed direction, asking me what I was planning to wear on my job hunt. It was like she'd swept the whole question under the rug, and I was so grateful.

Standing in front of Max now, I wondered if Hannah had told him.

"Don't worry, Molly. You'll find something," he said cheerfully, easing my fears. I didn't see any questions in his expression. "Which way you headed? Can I walk with you?"

"Dundas, Bathurst, up to Bloor Street . . . Who knows after that."

"I'm headed the other way. Gonna go see my father." He gave me a wink. "Good luck today. I know you'll win 'em over."

But Max was wrong. Today was no different from any other. I lost track of how many people shook their heads and sent me away. By the afternoon, my feet were sore, and I was overheated from walking the hot sidewalks. Then, just when I couldn't face another rejection, I found myself standing in front of the Smith Brothers' Bookstore on Brunswick, and I felt a flicker of hope. The store had a small white awning over its window, and its name was written in gold script on the glass. There were no **HELP WANTED** or **NOW HIRING** signs, so I knew before I stepped inside that there was little chance of finding a job there. But it was a *bookstore*. Maybe this was the magic I'd asked my grandmother to send. She'd known my love of reading better than anyone.

I patted my drooping curls into place, checked that I was still put together all right, then walked inside. The store was a long, lone room divided into rows and aisles by crowded wooden shelves, and the planks beneath my shoes were lightened by well-worn paths weaving between shelves of Fiction and Nonfiction, Children's Books, and Biographies. The air smelled like paper, and I felt almost dizzy with the desire to riffle through every page in the place.

An older, cordial-looking gentleman stood at the counter, clad in a white shirt and short brown tie, his brown trousers hooked to suspenders. He was about fifty, I estimated, with thinning hair and round spectacles.

"Good morning, miss." His voice was low and rumbly. "Can I help you find something?"

I pushed my earlier rejections aside and bestowed upon him my most winning smile. "As a matter of fact, I'm hoping I can help you. My name is Molly Ryan, and I cannot imagine anything more wonderful than working here. Are you Mr. Smith?"

"Yes, I am." His mouth twisted to the side, and it struck me that he seemed familiar. "I'm sorry, but we're not hiring at the moment."

But from the appearance of the store, they needed help. The shelves were dusty and the floor needed mopping. Even from a distance I could see a lot of the books weren't shelved in the right places.

I stepped toward him with conviction. "I'm a good worker. I can clean and do other things you don't want to do."

He peered at me over the rim of his spectacles. "What experience do you have?"

I told him about my work at Palermo's. "Mr. Palermo would be happy to provide a positive reference on my character and work ethic."

"And your parents? Who are they?"

"My father is Sergeant Garret Ryan, with the police force."

His eyes widened slightly, and I remembered where I'd seen him before: at the Glorious Twelfth march last year. Mr. Smith was an Orangeman.

"I know your father well." He cleared his throat, considering. "As I said, I'm not currently hiring, but as a courtesy to him, I am willing to give you a chance. I'll pay fifteen cents an hour for the first week, during which I will monitor you. Then I'll decide whether to let you go or keep you on for one dollar and seventy-five cents per day."

I had never been more grateful for William of Orange. Fifteen cents an hour wasn't great, but a dollar seventy-five a day was a fortune compared to Palermo's. Plus I'd be working with books. I felt giddy with joy.

"You have a deal, Mr. Smith."

I was still grinning when the little bell over the door jingled and a young man entered the shop. He slipped off his fedora then ran his fingers through a mass of black hair, fluffing it a little before replacing the hat.

"Good afternoon," I said eagerly, keen to try out my new job.

"Good afternoon," he replied. "I'm looking for a book recently translated into English. I'm hoping you might have it, but it's a little obscure. *The Radetzky March.*"

"Oh! I've heard of that book," I said excitedly. Max had mentioned it to me in passing. "By Joseph Roth, right?"

I turned to Mr. Smith, but he was frowning. "We don't have it. Never have, never will."

The man's jaw flexed. "I see."

I didn't. I glanced between the two, confused.

"We don't serve your kind in here," Mr. Smith said, his voice sharp.

I stood frozen in place, unable to speak. The young man's keen eyes shone with the same hurt I'd seen on Max's face that night we'd walked home from the baseball game. After a moment, he quietly left the store, and Mr. Smith latched the door with great deliberation. Then he strode behind the counter and pulled out a blank piece of paper. He wrote something on it, then shoved it in my face.

"Your first task is to put this in the window," he said. "Now."

I dropped my eyes to the sign. **NO JEWS ALLOWED.** All my joy drained to my toes. "I don't understand," I said slowly. "Why can't he shop here?"

Mr. Smith's face was blotchy with indignation. "I don't want their filthy money. This is a clean, reputable store where people can feel comfortable and safe when they're shopping. I won't have Jews tracking their stink into my shop. They can stick to their own bookstores. Maybe those places carry those communist rags, but I won't. Now put the sign in the window."

The paper shook in my hands. I was desperate. The box of old vegetables Mr. Palermo had given my family was long gone. Last week we hadn't had enough money to buy meat. This job could save us.

But as I stood there, I heard my grandmother's weary voice telling me about the Great Famine.

"It nearly killed them all," she'd said. "My mother told me people ate whatever they could find to survive. The story goes that a selfish woman in the next village stole her wee niece's crust of bread. The child died from need of it, and the very next day, the woman's sister died of grief. The woman herself lived forty years on, and never a day passed without regret at what she'd done." She'd touched my hand. "Remember that, my girl. *Is fearr bolg folamh ná croí briste.*" Better an empty belly than a broken heart.

And when I thought of my heart, I saw Max and Hannah.

"Miss Ryan?"

A terrible swelling jammed in my throat as I placed the sign on the counter rather than in the window because *oh*, I wanted this job. But it was as if he'd handed me a bouquet of flowers with a razor hidden within the blooms. Knowing what I had to do broke my heart into a million pieces, but not doing it would have been so much worse.

I looked him in the eye. "I won't put such a hateful thing in the window, Mr. Smith. I can't. Of all the places, a bookstore is where people can escape the ugliness of the world. It's not a political place or a religious place or anything like that. It's a personal place." I gestured around the room. "I don't understand how you can find room for hate in all this beauty."

"You are wrong, young lady." His expression was granite. "A bookstore is a place of business. It is commerce. I own this store, and I have certain standards I must uphold in order to keep it inviting for my regular customers. If I allow someone like *him* in here, there is damage done to the store—"

"What damage? He just wants to buy a book! He'll just buy it somewhere else. Don't you want the money?"

"It's the store's reputation. It's *my* reputation."

I could tell there was no point in arguing. There was only one more thing I needed to say, if I could get it past the knot in my throat.

"Thank you for the opportunity, Mr. Smith, but I cannot work here after all."

That took him aback. "What are you saying? You'd choose *them* over this job?"

"I need a job more than you know," I said quietly, "but what you did to that man is wrong. The thing is, Mr. Smith, given a choice between the two, I'd choose common decency."

I felt an aching sense of loss as I stepped outside, then I was engulfed by a crowd of tired, grey-faced labourers holding placards and sounding off about working conditions. I couldn't even do that, I realized, since I'd just given up a job. And yet, a small part of me stood a little taller. I would go hungry because of my decision, but I would never regret what I'd done.

six

MAX

❧

Max flipped the page of his textbook and wiped sweat off his brow with the back of his hand. It was only noon, but the temperature in his bedroom was already unbearable. He'd been reading about a fascinating new electro-mechanical invention, built just a year before by an American physiologist named Albert Hyman. Powered by a hand-cranked motor, the machine could generate electrical impulses to help a struggling heart pump blood at regular intervals. Hyman called his invention an "artificial pacemaker." It was all very compelling, and Max wanted to dig deeper into the research, but the heat was making it difficult to concentrate.

Hannah knocked on his door. "Ready for the beach?"

"I thought you'd never ask," he replied, closing the book and grabbing his swimsuit. "Just let me change."

"We'll be waiting," she said over her shoulder.

Max snapped the straps of his swimsuit over his shoulders, then pulled another shirt on top and reached for a towel. When he stepped outside, Molly was already on the front porch, talking with his mother and sister. She was wearing a bright red dress, and her pale, freckled skin was protected from the sun by a large, practical hat. Heat shimmered in the air around her.

"You have no idea how much I've been looking forward to this," she was saying. "Church went on forever."

"It's a perfect day for the beach," his mother agreed, handing a basket of food to Hannah. She smiled at the trio as they headed out. "Have fun!"

Hannah led the way along the sidewalk, puffing a breath up into her face. "Come on. Let's walk faster. Maybe we can create our own breeze."

Across the street, Max spotted Richie heading the other direction. "Hey!" he called. "You coming to the beach?"

Richie's gaze passed over the three of them. "Nah. I'm meeting some guys."

He continued on without so much as a wave, and Max felt a pang of regret.

"Never mind him," Molly said. "He's like that lately. We'll have more fun without him." She looked up at a house as they passed. "I feel so sorry for people stuck at home. It's too hot to be inside."

"Ah, but this is Sunday, the Lord's Day, remember?" he teased. "They *can't* come outside. I'm telling you, every Sunday they should call this city 'Toronto the Boring.'"

Way before he was born, before even the Great War, the government had created the "Lord's Day Act," which prohibited stores and movie theatres and just about anywhere someone might want to go for entertainment from opening on Sundays. Even swing sets in playgrounds were padlocked.

"Max," Hannah said, a note of warning in her voice, but Molly laughed.

"But isn't it just like Shabbat for you?"

"She's got you there," Hannah said.

"Sort of," he admitted. Every Friday at sunset, the Dreyfus family lit the Shabbat candles, and the next twenty-four hours were filled with blessings, food, and family. He found the tradition to be calming, the connection to God and their ancestral lessons reassuring. "But why does Eaton's cover their windows every Saturday night? What's that for?"

Molly raised her pale eyebrows. "Why, that's obvious, Max. You don't want to be tempted to window shop on a Sunday. The devil is out there, just looking for window shoppers."

"Ah, that's completely understandable."

"I'm glad you see my point." She grinned. "I've missed your humour."

"I haven't," Hannah said, rolling her eyes.

"Well, you won't be missing my brilliant humour this fall," Max said, proud as could be. "I just got my acceptance from U of T. I'll be going to medical school right here in Toronto."

Molly stopped. "What? Really?"

Hannah nodded. "He got the letter Friday."

With a squeal, Molly threw her arms around his neck. Her hat toppled off, landing on the ground behind her, but she didn't seem to notice.

"Congratulations, Doctor Dreyfus," she said, an inch from his ear. The tickle of her breath on his neck raised goose bumps along his arms. "I am so proud of you." After she released him, she turned to Hannah. "You knew about it and didn't tell me?"

"I made her promise," Max said, picking up her hat and handing it to her. "I wanted to surprise you myself."

"Everyone's glad he'll be home." Hannah elbowed Max. "Mama told Mrs. Beiser and the other ladies at the synagogue yesterday. Now all they can talk about is wedding bells for their daughters. The competition is heating up, I hear."

Max checked Molly's reaction, but she was looking ahead, toward the streetcar stop. "You and Hannah," she said. "You'll both be married off soon, and I—"

"And you'll still be turning down dates," Hannah finished for her. "Honestly, Molly. It's time to think about the future."

"Not today," Molly said in a singsong as they boarded the streetcar. "Today I'm thinking about the beach."

An hour or so later, they got off as close as they could to the beach, and Hannah led the way toward a spot on the grass, just beyond the boardwalk. The beach was as crowded as Max had ever seen it, with umbrellas propped up side by side to shelter everyone from the sun. Even those who didn't plan to go in the water had stripped to their swimsuits, hoping to cool down.

Everything was perfect until he heard a woman in the distance shout, "Get outta here, you filthy Jews! We're trying to keep this place clean!"

Max bit down on his anger, not wanting to start something today, but Molly spun around, her hot Irish temper on full display. "Hey! You can't—"

Hannah grabbed her arm. "Never mind them, Molly. Come on. Let's just enjoy the day."

"Never mind them?" Molly sputtered. "How do you put up with that?"

Max was surprised by the force of her fury. Molly allowed herself to be pulled along, but she kept glancing back over her shoulder at the woman, who had disappeared into a crowd of people greeting each other with a bold "Heil Hitler," their arms extended.

"No one's doing anything to stop them!" she cried. "What right do they have to say things like that?"

"They have no right," Max replied evenly, "and they have every right. It's hateful, but it's free speech. It's up to us how we respond."

"But you didn't respond at all," she said, glaring accusingly up at him. "It isn't as if it will go away if you ignore it. What about that sign we just passed? Didn't you notice it?"

Of course he'd noticed it. **NO DOGS OR JEWS ALLOWED** was

kind of hard to miss. But he was puzzled by Molly's reaction. Hadn't she suggested he ignore that sign in the store window? Now she was practically shaking with anger. He was about to ask what had changed, when Arnie came loping toward them.

"I heard this was where the action was today," Arnie said, hands sunk deep in his trouser pockets, "and where all the beautiful girls were heading, so here I am. Why the glum faces?"

"We were discussing that sign back there," Max told him.

Arnie tapped his temple, half hidden under his careless mop of hair. "Ah yes. I memorized it as I came in. Very important."

"Does it actually mean anything?" Molly asked. "Are you really not allowed to be here?"

"It means nothing," Max said. "There are no laws about where we can or can't go. This isn't Germany yet."

"But the things those people were saying," she insisted. "Do they have any idea how hateful they're being? Don't they read the papers?"

"Well, it depends on which one they're reading," Arnie said. He handed Max a piece of yellow paper. "For you."

Max recognized it as the flyer for the rally the league had been organizing and tucked it into his shirt. He'd read it later. "Thanks."

"Let's not talk about this," Hannah begged. "Please, Molly? I don't want to talk about politics."

"All right. But I still think—"

"Not another word," Hannah said, taking her arm and dragging her ahead. "This day is about fun. Let's find a good spot to sunbathe."

"Well, if it isn't Max Dreyfus and Arnie Schwartz." Max's old school friend David Bohmer approached from their right with his hand outstretched, though his attention was on the girls.

Max shook his hand. "David. How are you?"

"Still in the shoe business?" Arnie asked.

David was tall and lanky, not yet having grown into his muscles. Max thought he probably never would, judging from his father's slight build, but he was a good-looking, genuine young man with a glint in his eyes. Max had always liked him.

"Sure, sure," David said. "Business is good. As good as can be expected, anyway. Hey, is that your sister over there? She gets more beautiful every time I see her."

Max lifted an eyebrow. "You're no good for Hannah. She's a smart girl. No time for a *meshuggener*."

"Ah, you don't know." David winked. "Some girls like the crazy ones. Who's the *shiksa*?"

"You remember Molly Ryan," Arnie said. "She was in school with us."

"Don't tell me that's Molly."

The girls had spread out a blanket and were peeling off their summer dresses, leaving them in a pile and revealing their bathing suits beneath. As Molly leaned down to slip off her shoes, Max followed the long, smooth line of her legs in a sort of daze. When had she gone from being the adorable little girl next door to being a woman he'd admire in a magazine?

"Wow. She looks incredible," David said, reading Max's mind.

"Put your eyes back in your head," Max told him, his grin a little forced as he swallowed a strange new sense of possessiveness. *She's here with me.* He handed David the basket. "Here. You carry this."

They headed toward the girls, and David plopped down by Hannah, proudly declaring that he'd brought lunch.

"In our basket." Hannah laughed.

"Sure, sure. But it's here, ain't it?"

Arnie and Max joined the others and tossed their shirts onto the pile. The sun beamed down from a cloudless sky, and Max revelled in the simple heat baking his skin. Over by the girls, David was busy praising the virtues of lace-up, mid-heel Oxford shoes.

"I'm telling you. Come to the store. I have the softest leather in stock. I can make you a pair of shoes you'll never want to take off."

Hannah smiled politely, but Max could tell she didn't realize David was doing his best to flirt with her. David hadn't bloomed like the girls had, so she saw him as an old schoolmate, nothing more. That's when Max noticed Molly discreetly nudge his sister then tilt her head slowly toward David. Hannah's eyes widened and she shook her head ever so slightly, but Molly was nodding. Max watched their silent communication with fascination.

"What about you, Molly?" David asked, interrupting without knowing. "Such beautiful feet as yours deserve the best."

"They might deserve it, but my pocketbook can't afford it," she told him, still grinning at Hannah. "Thank you anyway."

"I'm sure we could make a deal."

"No thanks. Eaton's doesn't exactly pay the kind of wages it would take to buy a brand-new pair of shoes, no matter what kind of deal you offered."

Max knew she was working at Eaton's. When Hannah had told the family over dinner, his father had frowned and declared that Eaton's was a sweatshop compared to his own factory.

His mother had nodded. "That girl has been crossing the street to our house since she was born. We can't let her rot in that place. She's *mishpocha*." Family.

"She can work for me," Max's father agreed.

He was always doing that, offering jobs to people who were down on their luck. Max wasn't sure how long he could continue to do so, considering business these days. Then Hannah told them Molly couldn't take the job. She said that Mr. Ryan was concerned about Molly's safety.

"Safety?" his father echoed. "My factory is safer than Eaton's."

"I guess that's up to her family to decide," Hannah replied.

Max had been disappointed for Molly's sake, knowing his father would have treated her well. She would have been much happier. He hated to think of her working in a place like that.

Molly glanced up as if sensing his gaze, and for a moment, he couldn't look away. The sunlight caught her eyes, the shine of green and hazel made almost transparent by the light. His skin tingled with her attention, as if she had touched him.

"Max," David said, breaking his trance. "I hear you're gonna be in Toronto this fall."

Max nodded and tried to listen, but his attention was still on Molly, who was talking to Hannah again, her slender fingers twisting her ponytail into a loose, shining coil at the back of her neck. The sharp, inquisitive girl he had always known had matured into a fascinating woman who shared his exasperation with the state of the world. But what held his thoughts were the differences the two of them faced within it.

seven

MOLLY

❧

Max was watching me with that earnest expression of his, and I smiled back, slightly embarrassed. I hoped he hadn't overheard our conversation. David and Hannah had been talking about *Brave New World*, and I'd felt oddly out of touch. Usually Hannah and I had lively discussions about books, but lately I'd been reading more newspapers. It had started because I'd been scanning the pages for a job, but the headlines had caught my eye. There was a lot, I'd realized, that I didn't know about the world.

"So what *are* you reading?" Hannah asked. I could tell she was disappointed I hadn't read *Brave New World* yet.

"Well, did you know that one in five Canadians is dependent on relief? In the Prairies, farmers are at over sixty per cent. On top of the Depression, they've gone through years of drought, and the dry heat brought in a plague of grasshoppers, then hailstorms . . . Saskatchewan's income has fallen by ninety per cent in two years."

She looked at me like I had two heads. "That was not what I was expecting."

I tilted my head toward Max, then whispered, "Do you think Max is going to marry one of the Beiser girls?"

"What?"

I grinned. "You said you didn't want to talk about politics."

She lay flat on her back and draped her arm over her eyes, against the sun. "Honestly, Molly, sometimes I don't even know you."

"Of course you do," I replied.

Thinking about newspapers reminded me of Arnie's earlier comment, about how people's understanding depended on which paper they read. Dad always had a *Telegram* lying around to use as a fire starter, but one day I'd been on the sidewalk and spotted a copy of the *Toronto Daily Star* sticking out of the garbage, so I grabbed it, thinking they might post some other jobs. Right away I'd noticed the different tones of the papers. The *Star* wrote a lot more about what was happening in Germany and the Soviet Union than the *Telegram* ever did. Richie argued with me that the *Telegram* did, once in a while.

"Most of those basically deny anything is happening over there," I said.

"Then maybe they're not happening," Richie replied.

"But the *Star* reports them," I insisted. I'd pulled out an article from June 3 by a reporter named Pierre van Paassen that said over 120,000 people had been imprisoned by Nazis in Germany. "The *Telegram* never even mentioned it," I said. "Listen to this: *'What is happening at the present moment in Germany? The burning of books, the incarceration of liberals and pacifists, socialists—'*"

"Yeah, but the *Star* was banned from Germany for spreading misinformation," he said. "So keep that in mind."

"I don't know, Richie." My finger slid down the page. "*'Only men who are afraid of the truth try to ban it. Only men who are afraid of reality try to shut their eyes to it . . . They call revolutionary a regime that burns the masterpieces of modern literature and the latest depositions of science, while leaving the people, by way of philosophical nutriment, the incoherent drivel of Adolf Hitler and Rosenberg's political discussions, whose reading reminds one of a debate in a lunatic asylum.'"*

"Sounds more like an opinion than reporting," he said with a shrug. "Don't buy into it."

But the *Star* had opened my eyes, and Arnie's comment piqued my interest.

"Speaking of reading," I said, looking over at the others. "Arnie, when you were talking about newspapers, did you mean how the *Telegram* and the *Star* report things so differently?"

Arnie perked up. "Partly. Ever heard of *Der Yidisher Zhurnal*? It's Toronto's daily Yiddish newspaper."

"Why would she have heard of that?" Max asked wryly.

"Good point. Molly, allow me to introduce you to a paper you haven't yet read."

"And probably never will," Hannah said. "Honestly, do we always have to talk about serious stuff?"

"It's important," I said.

Hannah set her hat on her face. "I've heard this a thousand times. I'm going to take a nap."

David smiled at Hannah. "Sounds like someone needs a lemonade."

She peeked up at him. "Actually, yes. Thank you."

David jumped up and headed over to the lemonade stand, while I scowled down at Hannah, slightly annoyed. These days, she never seemed to want to talk about what was going on.

Arnie rubbed his hands together. "All right, Molly. What do you know about Hitler?"

"He's the chancellor of Germany, he hates Jewish people, and he has a ridiculous moustache."

"All moustaches are ridiculous," Hannah muttered from under her hat.

"That's more or less the basic story," Arnie said to me, "but there's a lot more you don't know."

"It's not your fault," Max assured me. "You've only read what the papers report on."

I looked back at Arnie. "Okay, so tell me."

"Neither the *Star* nor the *Telegram* ever talked about German politics until Hitler was pronounced chancellor this past January. They never even mentioned his name. But by that point, the *Zhurnal* had already run multiple stories on him and the Nazi Party. Have you heard of Joseph Goebbels?"

I shook my head.

"He's Hitler's minister of propaganda. The *Zhurnal* ran a piece about Goebbels's plan this spring, which was called—and I quote—'*How Nazis Will Exterminate the Jews of Greater Germany.*'"

I shivered despite the heat. "Exterminate?"

"Interesting, isn't it? How nothing was written about that in either the *Telegram* or the *Star.*"

"I remember seeing something in the *Star* just this month," I said, thinking of Pierre van Paassen's article. "About 120,000 people in German prisons."

"Yeah," Max said. "They constructed what they call a 'concentration camp' for political prisoners back in March."

"The *Star* only recently started reporting on some of the big headlines that the *Zhurnal* covers." Arnie counted on his fingers. "Like the maltreatment of Jews, the mass exodus of scientists and academics, the confiscation of Jewish money, the removal of Jewish doctors, lawyers, teacher, actors . . ." He looked at Max. "Oh, and the fact that Jewish people are no longer allowed to matriculate as medical students."

Max's mouth twisted, his eyes on the ground.

Arnie continued. "Last April, they ran the story about the German Student Union's '*campaign against the un-German spirit*' on the front page. In May, the union burned all the Jewish-authored books. They called them un-German and said, '*The Jew can only think Jewishly. If he writes German, he lies.*'"

My mind flashed back to Mr. Smith refusing to carry *The Radetzky March*, and I shifted uncomfortably on the blanket. I still hadn't told anyone about that day at his store.

"So the *Star* has stepped up," I said. "But if the *Telegram* mentions any of those things, they say they're not true, or at least that they're not as serious as is being claimed in other places. Or that Jewish people are just causing trouble, which gives idiots like Phil Burke and the Swastika Club the ammunition they need." Max and Arnie were both nodding, so I continued. "I understand journalists interpreting subjects with a bias. That's only natural, because everyone sees things through their own eyes. But this sounds more like censorship."

"And that comes down to the editor," Arnie agreed. "If the *Telegram* is determined to ignore what's happening, they'll put their best misinformation journalist on it."

I paused. "There are so many stories out there, how do we know what's really going on?"

Arnie grinned. "Have one of us read you the *Zhurnal*."

He couldn't fool me. "It's not that easy, Arnie. The *Zhurnal* can say whatever it wants, too."

"Arnie!" David called from twenty feet away. "Come help me carry these!"

Arnie got to his feet. "I'll be back," he promised.

"I'm coming too," Hannah said, jumping up. "Anything to get away from this conversation."

After Arnie left, Max pointed at my forehead. "You're doing that wrinkly thinking thing."

"Am I?" Self-conscious, I put two fingers on the spot above the bridge of my nose and smoothed out the crease. "I guess I'm still confused. Why would a newspaper hide these stories?"

"I imagine that sometimes—"

"And if we accept that the other papers are hiding things, how can we know for certain the *Zhurnal* isn't as well?"

"Well, if you—"

"I could read a dozen newspapers reporting on the same thing differently. How do I know which is the truth?"

I stopped, realizing he was staring at me, a bemused sort of smile on his face.

"What?"

He lifted one shoulder. "I'm just listening."

"And? What do you think? How do you know the truth, Max?"

"I suppose you can't ever know for sure. Not really, unless you're actually there. Like everything else, the more you read and educate yourself, the better."

There was a hole in that argument, too. "But based on this discussion, the more you read, the less you actually know for sure, isn't that right?"

He chuckled. "I do love the way you think, Molly Ryan. I meant it when I said you'd make a great journalist. You ask the right questions, and you go after answers like a terrier."

I looked at the grass and started picking at it. "I don't know, Max. That dream seems very far away these days."

"Life's hard right now for everyone. Things'll improve."

"I used to tell myself that," I said, "but every day it's the same, and it's not getting any better. Trust me on that."

Sympathy shone in his eyes. "So . . . you're working at Eaton's. Want to talk about it?"

I hesitated, still feeling guilty—and disappointed—that I wasn't working for Mr. Dreyfus instead. Until now, I hadn't talked with anyone about Eaton's—no one else had asked.

"I should be grateful I have a job, I guess. They say one in three people is out of work right now. But Eaton's is the one place on earth I never wanted to work."

"How is it?"

I rubbed the tips of my fingers against the callus on my thumb, a habit I'd started doing every time I thought of work. "As bad as everyone says. Hundreds of women crowded into a room with rows and rows of sewing machines. It's always noisy—not from talking, because we can't talk—from the machines. And it's hot. I don't mean hot like today. I mean it's like they squeeze all of the day's heat into one stuffy room and never open any doors." I inhaled, relishing the bouquet of grass, sun, and water. "I can't tell you how sweet the air smells right now."

"I'm sorry, Moll."

"It's like a dungeon. And the work never stops. The boss . . ." I shuddered. "He times us with a stopwatch. We have to sew a certain number of garments or we're not paid. The first week I was there I was short by one jacket, and I went home with nothing after a full day of work. I show up, cut, and sew until my blisters grow blisters."

"At least you're bringing home some money."

"A little. But pay for women has been cut up to fifty per cent in those places. It used to be $12.50 a week, but I'm lucky to make eight dollars now. I feel like I'm going backwards. I feel like—"

I stopped, at a loss. It was too painful to describe it. Too degrading.

"You can tell me," he said.

I looked into the soft, sturdy landing of his deep brown eyes, and knew he was right. If anyone would understand, it was him.

"I feel like the bits and pieces of thread I have to sweep up at the end of the day. I feel like . . . debris."

But the warmth that softened his expression assured me that I was more than that, and my stomach suddenly felt as if it could float from all the butterflies in there.

We both looked up when Hannah's shadow passed over us, and an unfamiliar sense of shame sank in my stomach. I was uneasy, and yet I wasn't sure why. It's not as if I'd done anything wrong.

She handed me a cup of lemonade, her gaze direct. "Are you two gonna sit here with serious faces all day?"

I faltered and took a sip, afraid of what she might be thinking. We'd known each other for so long we could practically read each other's minds. But she didn't say anything more, and I exhaled as she went to grab our towels.

"You know," Max started up, drawing me in again. "I was thinking that you—"

Hannah dumped a towel over Max's head. "Come on, big brother. Let's go swimming."

The rest of the afternoon sped by, laughter and conversation blending as we rotated between swimming and sunbathing. The sun felt exquisite on my skin, but I had to wrap a towel around my pale shoulders so they wouldn't burn. When our stomachs began to grumble, we ate the *rugelach* Mrs. Dreyfus had baked for us, then Max splurged on ice cream. He knew I couldn't afford to buy a cone, but he also knew I wouldn't say no if he offered me one. For a little while, I forgot about the humiliation of my job and the hopelessness of the city, and I had a wonderful time.

When the sun started to set, we gathered our things and headed back to the streetcar stop. Hannah, I could tell, wasn't feeling well. The sun had worn her down. David stepped in at the first opportunity, gallantly lending her his arm and offering to walk her home, even though we were already going the same way. I thought the effort was adorable, and from the look Hannah gave him, she did too.

The sidewalk was less crowded now, the pace sluggish but easy. The worst heat of the day had dissipated along with the sun, and the breeze tickling my slightly sunburnt skin felt like a caress. Tomorrow, perched on my hard wooden chair and hunched for hours over my sewing table, I would cling to the memory of this day while I waited for the clock to count down to closing time.

Arnie turned off at an earlier street, and as we waved goodbye, I suddenly remembered something. My hand went to my head.

"I forgot my hat."

Hannah groaned.

"I'll go with you," Max said, already turning.

"Are you sure? I'm so sorry."

"It's fine, Moll. It's a nice night."

David and Hannah headed on toward home, and under the gathering dusk, Max and I walked in silence. After a few minutes, he said, "I've been thinking about what you said. About feeling like debris. I know it's tough, but when things get hard for me, like when it feels like I'll never get through all the studying, I remind myself that this isn't what it will always be like. This is just a step in the road, and we have to keep moving forward. Someday this Depression will be over. Things will go back to normal, and everyone will be working regular jobs again."

I thought of Palermo's, then let that memory slip away. What if I followed his advice, but instead of just accepting a regular job, I went back to school? Maybe I could finish my high school degree, then try for journalism school. He was right, of course. This was just a low point. I had to keep reaching for more.

"When that happens, a girl as smart and beautiful as you will be able to do whatever she wants."

I felt my cheeks warm and was thankful for the camouflage of my sunburn. "Beautiful? Oh, stop."

"What? You don't believe me? Why, you could be a movie star, Molly Ryan." The corner of his mouth curled. "And I'll tell you what else. I'd pay to go watch you every single day."

"You're funny."

"If only I was kidding."

I looked at him but didn't respond. I wasn't sure how to. Something had changed between us. I heard it in the softening of his voice, and I felt it in my pulse. Like an electric current humming through the air, drawing me to him. It felt so real I could almost see it, and it unnerved me.

"Here," he said, pulling out the yellow paper Arnie had given him. "I meant to show you this earlier. It's for a rally coming up on Tuesday. The first of its kind in Toronto."

I skimmed the flyer under a streetlamp, stopping when I ran into Yiddish symbols I didn't understand. "A rally? About what?"

"Hitler, Germany, what's happening here . . . My father and I are involved with the League for the Defence of Jewish Rights, and they organized it, but other groups have jumped on board. A lot of labour unions are showing up, protesting the same working conditions you described at Eaton's."

I thought of Richie's comments about protests being a waste of time. I had my own doubts about whether they accomplished anything. "One of the ladies at work told me about a protest two years ago, with about five hundred dressmakers. She said it was awful, and it failed. All they wanted was a fifteen per cent pay increase, but the whole city ganged up against them."

"This one'll be different," he said. "So many people will be there, it'll be impossible to ignore. Even the factory owners are preparing. Everyone's closing down at three o'clock. That's how big this thing is."

"They're closing at three? Even Eaton's?"

He nodded.

I held up the flyer, curiosity taking over. "All this Yiddish . . . Would I be . . ." I left the obvious question hanging.

"Don't worry about that," he said as we walked along. "There will be a huge mix of people there."

Thinking of the crowds reminded me of Dad. "The police will tear the protest down, you know. They always do. My father said it's basically their job to drag speakers off podiums and arrest them."

"Not this time. The whole thing is entirely legal. Mayor Stewart cleared it. Chief Draper is even going to be there."

"Draper? The upholder of the enduring obstinacy of the Protestant Brotherhood of the Orange Order?"

Max laughed. "That's a mouthful. Better not say it too loud, Moll."

I made a show of scanning the empty streets. "I think I'm pretty safe, don't you?"

"Well, no matter what the Orange Order thinks, Draper's orders are to keep the peace."

I looked at the flyer again, and something about the date caught my eye. "Kind of ironic that this rally is the day before the Orange Day parade, isn't it? Tuesday we listen to revolutionary speeches, then Wednesday we'll hear the Orangemen do the opposite. They'll have a few choice words to say about communism and the unions if Tuesday's march is as big as you say it's gonna be."

"I'll admit, the date was kind of planned that way on purpose."

"Oh?"

"It was my suggestion," he said, a hint of pride in his voice.

"Troublemaker."

"You bet. So? You gonna come with me?"

His crooked grin was irresistible, as was the idea of being at his side at something like this. "You want me to?"

"I do."

"Then I will. How will I find you?"

"I'll meet you outside Eaton's, and we can walk together."

The upcoming week suddenly looked much less bleak now that I had Tuesday to look forward to. "I'm excited. I'll—"

"Well, well, well. What do we have here?" Phil Burke suddenly appeared. Behind him, half a dozen boys spread out like a pack, swastika badges on their chicken-hearted chests. A shiver of fear ran through me—not for myself, but for Max, who angled himself in front. If this led to a fair fight, I knew he could handle himself. But between the gang and me, he was badly outnumbered. I looked around for any passersby to maybe come to our aid, but the streets were empty and dark.

Phil took a step toward Max. "Get away from Molly, Jewboy."

Max didn't budge.

"Get lost, Phil," I snapped.

Phil ignored me. "I saw you and your kind down at the beach," he went on, crossing his arms. "Jews ain't allowed there."

"Says who?" Max asked.

"Everyone. We're keeping our beaches *clean*. You didn't see the signs?"

"So you saw us down there," I said, "but you waited until Max was alone before you went after him. Such courage."

"Then again, maybe you missed the meaning of the sign. It's written in English, not Jewish." Phil finally met my eyes. "What do you say, Richie? This dirty Jew's messing with your little sister. You gonna let that happen?"

Richie? The group separated down the middle, and I stared in shock at my brother. A shiny nickel badge was pinned on his shirtfront, embossed with a bright red swastika.

"Richie," I gasped. "What are you doing with these idiots?"

He avoided my eyes. "Leave him alone, Phil. They're just friends."

"Makes no difference," Phil said, his teeth bared. "A Jew is a Jew. He don't get a free pass just because he's someone you grew up with. He needs to learn a lesson like they all do."

I heard the distinct *pop!* of someone's knuckles, then Phil wheeled on Max, leading with his fist. The sucker punch crashed into Max's jaw and sent him backwards against me, but I held onto him, keeping him upright. It took only a second for him to recover, then he stormed back at Phil, hands up like a boxer. But the other boys joined in as I'd feared, and Max disappeared beneath their fists. Only Richie stood apart.

"Stop them!" I shouted in his face. "Make them stop! He's your friend! He's *our* friend!"

But Richie didn't move. His face was as red as mine, from shame or anger, I didn't know, but I could tell he was biting back words. Any other time he'd have yelled at me, but he knew very well he couldn't deny what I'd said. Only when I turned to pull one of the boys off Max did he reach out his hand and grab me.

"Stop it, Molly. You'll just get hurt."

"Then you need to do something!" I yelled, trying to wriggle out of his grasp.

From behind me, I heard a shout, and I knew the voice right away. I had never in my life been so relieved to see my father in his uniform.

"What's going on here?" he demanded as he approached. "Richie? Molly? What's all this?"

I stretched my arm out toward the boys, who had all backed away. A couple of them had bloodied faces, and I was glad of it. "They—"

"It's nothing, Dad," Richie said. "We were just leaving."

"Are you now?" His attention passed between the gang, Richie and me, and finally landed on Max, who was getting to his feet, touching his bleeding lip with his tongue.

"We were at the beach with Hannah and some friends," I said. "I forgot my hat, and Max offered to go back with me to get it."

Dad was still focused on Max. "You should go home."

Max straightened. "I will, sir. We just have to get her hat first."

"Don't blame him," I said, stepping forward. "These bullies came after Max just because he's Jewish." I glared at Richie. "He has a right to go where he wants without getting pushed around, just like anybody else."

My father's fury turned on me, and I trembled under the solid weight of his authority, just as I had as a little girl.

"I won't have you talking back, Molly Ryan. I've told you how I feel about you being with— It isn't safe." His voice was tight with control, but his eyes flickered toward Max. "And I was right. Look what happened. Just go home. Now." He glared at Richie. "You go with her." Then he studied the rest of the boys, memorizing each face. "I don't want trouble on my streets, boys. Keep it to the beaches, or you'll answer to me."

Phil Burke lifted his chin, as if he'd just been given marching orders. "Yes, sir."

My jaw dropped. *Keep it to the beaches?* How about *Disband at once and stop beating people up*? I looked from my father to Richie, alarmed to see such a striking resemblance between them in that moment. I started to say something, but Max touched my arm.

"Let's go, Moll," he said.

I scowled at Richie. "I'm going with Max. Don't bother coming."

So many emotions swirled through me as we walked away, but I resisted the urge to hang on to Max's arm for support. The worst was a terrible sadness. My big brother was a Swazzie. Not only that; my father had looked neither surprised nor angry about it.

eight
MAX

❦

The crowds were already bunching up when Max reached Eaton's, just after three o'clock on Tuesday. He peered over heads, fighting nerves as he sought out Molly among the women leaving the factory. He hadn't seen her since Sunday night when he'd walked her home. Did she regret standing up to her father and brother? Would she still want to go with him today?

Then she stepped outside and scanned the faces around her, the sunlight catching the copper shine of her hair. She smiled when she spotted him, and they worked their way through the crowd toward each other.

"You came," she said. "I wasn't sure—"

"Me too," he said, even happier than he'd expected. "Besides, I had to bring you something." From behind his back he drew her sunhat from the other day.

"Oh, Max. Thank you. How did you get it?"

"I went back in the morning."

She put it on, squinting up at him from under the brim. "How's your lip?"

"It's nothing," he assured her.

She staggered toward him when someone shoved through the crowd, and he caught her in his arms. She smelled sweet and a little dusty from work.

"You okay?" he asked, suddenly shy.

She nodded. "Let's go."

With one hand on the small of her back, he guided her through the crowd to Queen Street, and they joined the mass of people moving westward. They would march to Spadina, then north to Dundas, east to University in a sort of three-sided square, then finally arrive at Queen's Park, where everyone would congregate.

Molly's smile was a mile wide, and her eyes darted everywhere, at the signs and banners and faces. He couldn't blame her. He'd never seen anything like it in his life. Among the sea of signs, a group of young people waved a long, vivid banner of red and gold with the words "Young Communist League" painted across its length. Just like on the flyer, most of the slogans were written in English as often as Yiddish, and they represented every group imaginable: Headgear Workers, Fur Workers, Bakers, Single Men's Unemployed Association, and more.

"I can't believe this all started with your father's group," Molly said. "He must be so proud."

"There ended up being about fifty different Jewish organizations involved. Most won't be happy to see so many other groups here. They'll see them as hijacking the cause."

"Yeah, but having so many people makes it too big to ignore. I had no idea some of these groups even existed. I mean, there's the Finnish Anti-Fascist Group. I didn't even know we had Finnish people here."

Max hadn't either. "Not many in Kensington, that's for sure."

"I see the I.L.G.W.U.," Molly said excitedly, spotting a series of white placards. In their middle, a green circle made up of the words

"International Ladies' Garment Workers' Union" was pierced by the likeness of a sewing needle. "Look at that sign from the Furriers' Union."

"'*Hitler Is a Skunk, and the Furriers Will Cut Him to Pieces*,'" he read. "Top marks for originality. See that one over there?" He pointed to a sign with the words "Bill 98," crossed out by a big, black X. "That's about Section 98 from Canada's Criminal Code. It's been around since just after the Great War, basically to stop communism and any other group with plans to affect change through force. If charged, a person could go to jail for up to twenty years. That's why the Young Communist League wants it repealed."

"Twenty years? I'm no fan of violence, but that seems pretty extreme." She frowned. "Speaking of which, I don't see any police. That doesn't make sense with a march this big."

"Chief Draper's supposed to be here. Did your dad say anything about it?"

"I haven't spoken with him since Sunday night. And I didn't tell him I was coming today." She shrugged. "I suppose it doesn't matter. Everyone's behaving."

When the parade reached University Avenue, they followed the streetcar tracks north until the pink-purple stones of the Ontario Legislative Building rose before them. Veins of protestors streamed into Queen's Park from all directions, jabbing the air with signs and banners, coming together in a pulsing heart of protest.

"Come this way," he said, tugging her toward where he'd arranged to meet up with his family.

"Max, Molly, over here!" Hannah called when she saw them. His parents stood just behind her, in the shade of a tree, and Max spotted David standing with them. Good for him, he thought.

"I see you got your hat," Hannah said to Molly as they drew closer.

"Actually, your brother got my hat," Molly replied.

Hannah raised an eyebrow at him. "You're a hero."

He chuckled. "Kind of an exaggeration."

"Well," she said into his ear once Molly was out of earshot, "I'm pretty sure that's how Molly saw it. Watch your step with her, brother-of-mine."

He stopped. "What are you talking about?"

"I'm just warning you. Back away if you know what's good for you both. Can you imagine what our parents would do if— I don't even want to think about that."

Confused, he watched her walk toward David, wondering why she'd said that. Max was enjoying his conversations with Molly, but he hadn't done anything to suggest that they were more than friends, had he? Still, Hannah had noticed their closeness, and a sense of foreboding settled like an anchor in his chest. Growing up in the patchwork neighbourhood of Kensington, the lines between communities had blurred, but only so far. He knew that. And Molly did too. She could never date a Jew.

"Maxim, my boy." His father held his arms out toward the crowd. "Look at this. You did this."

"Hardly," he said, forcing a smile. "I made a suggestion. Everyone else did the work."

"I'm just glad everything has remained peaceful," his mother said.

"Hey, David," Max said, giving him a meaningful look. "Didn't expect to see you over this way. Where's your family?"

"Somewhere other than here," David replied with a playful grin.

"I didn't think you'd be here," he heard Molly say to Hannah. "You don't like political stuff."

Hannah elbowed Max. "He made us come."

"I didn't *make* you, but I'm glad you came. I think it's important that you be here to witness all this. You can't always be an ostrich."

"Nothing wrong with ostriches," Hannah said, but she was smiling, her eyes twinkling in the sunlight. He could tell she was enjoying herself, and he had a feeling David had something to do with that. She lifted her hand to her brow, shielding her vision. "Hey, isn't that Jimmy?"

He squinted through the crowd and spotted Molly's brother standing near the flagpole, chatting with a few ball players Max recognized.

"I thought he'd be at work," Molly said. "I guess they got out like I did."

"Jimmy got a job? That's great news," Hannah said.

"Yes. Finally. He's doing something at the Heintzman factory, but I'm not sure what. He doesn't talk about it."

"Heintzman?" Max repeated. He turned to his father. "Didn't they just lay off—"

"Jacob Weiss and Aryeh Dvorkin, yes. They were told the company couldn't afford so many workers in this economy. I didn't know they were hiring."

A bit of the colour seeped out of Molly's face, but Mrs. Dreyfus squeezed her arm. "We're happy for Jimmy. He's needed work for a while. It's just difficult. Aryeh's mother doesn't know what they're going to do."

Max knew both boys. Their families had come here from Germany only five years before, and these days, new immigrants who couldn't make their way in Canada were being sent back to their home country. A shiver ran down Max's spine at the thought of going to Germany at a time like this.

"Tell her the boys must come and see me," his father said. "No one is going back to Germany."

Max sighed. "You cannot hire everyone, Papa."

"I can hire some."

Max felt guilt coming off Molly in waves. "It's not your fault. Don't let it bother you."

"He's right," Hannah said, but Molly didn't look convinced.

A loudspeaker squawked, making everyone jump, then Hannah nudged Molly. "Hey, you'll probably want to stand with Jimmy for this instead of with us. Papa wants me to listen to the Yiddish speaker with him and Mama, so—"

"There's a Yiddish speaker?" Molly asked.

"There are so many people here that there will be several speakers," his father replied. "They'll address the crowd in different sections of the park so we all will be able to hear their messages. Some will speak in Yiddish, others in English."

Max wasn't sure what to do. The plan had been to stay with Molly, but Hannah's unexpected warning had burrowed in his brain.

"I think Jimmy wandered off," Molly said, scanning the area near the flagpole where a different group had now gathered. "Maybe I'll come with you, and you can translate."

His father looked at Molly kindly. "But that won't do. You need to understand the words. Max, you go with Molly. Take care of her."

"Of course," he said.

The family headed away, but not before Hannah shot him a look, which he answered with one of his own. Then Molly turned to Max. "I'm sorry. Which speaker did you want to listen to?"

"I'm with you, Moll. Come on. I know where we should go for the best view."

He guided her through the crowd toward the base of the Sir John A. Macdonald statue, and she stepped onto the base for added height.

"Can you see well enough?"

She stood on her tiptoes. "I can see some of it."

He nodded toward the statue. "Let's go a bit higher."

Without hesitation, she stepped closer to him, and he wrapped his hands around her waist then hoisted her onto the statue so she stood beside Macdonald's cool metal feet.

"Much better!" she beamed. "I can see everything from here. You coming?"

He braced his hands on the platform beside her and launched himself up. From their perch, they took in the throngs of people, the waving signs and banners, and the various stages set up around the park. A contagious energy filled the air. He could tell from intermittent cheers rising like waves around them that the speeches were underway elsewhere, but theirs hadn't started yet.

"Best seat in the house," he said.

Molly's gaze had dropped to a couple of women that he recognized from earlier, outside Eaton's, and he noticed her unconsciously rubbing the tips of her fingers with her thumb.

"You okay?"

She nodded, sheepish. "Seeing all these causes being protested in one big, united front . . . It feels amazing. Our backgrounds, races, and religions are different, but we're all coming together. I feel like we might actually be able to change some things."

Max took her hand in his and touched the calluses, put there by hours and hours of drudging work.

"You've worked hard your whole life, Molly, just like so many here. Today is for all of us. That includes you."

He wasn't sure if it was what he'd said or if it was simply the emotion of the day, but suddenly she was looking at him, holding him with those green eyes, and he couldn't turn away.

"Thank you for bringing me, Max," she said.

"The factory would have let you go anyway."

"It wouldn't mean as much without you." She hesitated, and he could swear he felt a shift between them. "Everything means more when you're with me."

He suddenly felt the need to say something. Something he shouldn't say.

"Molly, I—" he began.

"Ladies and Gentlemen, your attention, please!"

A voice called from the direction of the legislative building, and Max caught the rest of his words before they got him in trouble.

"Welcome, welcome, everyone! Thank you for coming out today and showing solidarity with so many causes. We are stronger together, and in this city, as we face rising prejudice and violence, we need each other more than ever."

Max listened hard, ingesting every syllable, letting them feed his mind and soul. Beside him, Molly was transfixed.

"We stand with our brethren in Germany who are being subjected to the Hitler regime's hateful persecution of the Jews," the man continued. "The Nazis plan to rid the world of the working class and of anyone who dares sympathize with them. They burn books and ban public gatherings. They deny citizens their right to free speech. We cannot allow their ignorance to poison this city. And we cannot assume that today's event will guarantee change. We must be militant in our struggle to stand up for people, no matter who or where they are, and fight for their human rights."

Molly shivered involuntarily, and it seemed the most natural thing in the world for him to wrap his arm around her shoulders and pull her close. She leaned into his chest, and he held her for the remainder of the speeches, amazed at the way she could make him feel both strong and yet helpless at the same time.

It seemed to Max that everyone who had stayed home the day before came out to celebrate the next day, lining up along the sidewalks and waving Union Jack flags as the Orange Day parade passed by.

"You know, we could get away with just about anything today," Arnie said. He and Max had grabbed a table by the front window of Shopsy's Deli before the other regulars came in, and now they were watching the procession. "We could rob a bank."

Max gave him a sideways glance.

"What? All I'm saying is, the police are all busy, marching in their little parade."

"I wouldn't call it a 'little' parade," Max said, picking up his pastrami on rye. "Three hours long this year, they say."

"Good. We'll have lots of time to rob that bank."

Molly's father would be in the parade today, Max thought as he observed the crowd. She'd told him that she had no plans to attend, though she hadn't told her dad of her decision. "He won't even notice," she'd said.

Max passed a copy of the *Telegram* to Arnie. "Have you seen this?"

"Not yet. I heard they estimated yesterday's crowd at anywhere from twelve thousand to twenty-five thousand."

"Yeah. But read this letter to the editor."

Arnie brushed some crumbs from his wrinkled jacket, then cleared his throat. "*If the Jews of Germany encouraged disloyal parades of the kind witnessed here on Tuesday,*" he read out loud, "*is it any wonder that Hitler planted his iron heel on their necks? You can't expect but a grunt from a pig, but we will not see our war memorials desecrated.*" He threw the paper down. "Utter rubbish. I expect nothing less from the *Telegram.*"

Max tapped the corner of his mouth, staring at Arnie.

"What?"

"Mustard."

Arnie wiped it off with his thumb, unconcerned.

"Considering how many thousands of angry, frustrated people were there," Max said, "I'd say it was an extremely calm rally. And I didn't see any 'desecration.'" Though he had wondered if the offended letter-writer had been talking about Sir John A. Macdonald's monument, where he and Molly had spent the duration.

Arnie let out an exasperated sigh and pointed at the door. Max looked up to see Yossel stride into the deli, along with a few others from the synagogue. Predictably, Yossel came right over and claimed the seat across from Max, a smug smile on his face.

"If I didn't know better, I'd think you were following me," Max said.

Yossel kept his eye on Max as he lit his cigarette. "I saw you at the rally yesterday."

He took a bite of his sandwich. "So you *are* following me."

"Who was the pretty girl?"

The pastrami went dry in Max's mouth.

Yossel blew out a ring of smoke. "She looked like a *shiksa.*"

"Not that it's any business of yours, but that was Molly Ryan. A good friend of mine."

"It looked like you two were close," he replied.

Had Yossel seen Max put his arm around her? Had he noticed that Max spent almost as much time watching Molly as he did the speeches? Across the table, Arnie was watching, waiting on Max's response.

"Sure we are." Max set down his sandwich. "We grew up together. Molly's Hannah's best friend. She's like another sister to me."

He found the words surprisingly difficult to get out, but it was important to reassure everyone around him that he had no romantic inclinations toward Molly. The trouble was, he couldn't reassure himself. When he looked at Molly now, he saw so much more than just an old friend.

"Lucky you, to have such a friend as that," Yossel replied. "She's gorgeous."

"And smart." Max raised his eyebrows. "Are you lonely, Yossel? No friends of your own? I can see how that might happen. You have a habit of rubbing people the wrong way."

Arnie barked out a laugh, but Yossel didn't smile. "Maybe she can be my friend, too."

Max tried not to react, but Yossel was annoying him more than usual today. "You really ought to try and make your own friends," he suggested. He got to his feet, set some money on the table for the food. "I have to go. You coming, Arnie? We still have time to rob that bank if you want."

Half a block away from the deli, Arnie raised his voice over the clamour of bagpipes. "So you were with Molly at the rally?" he asked. "That's why I didn't see you with your family."

"Is there something wrong with that?"

Arnie hesitated. "Listen, you know I love Molly. She's a great gal."

Heat rose up Max's neck. "She is."

"I saw how you looked at her at the beach, Max. Listen, I know it's none of my business, but you already got punched once for being around her. Maybe you ought to back off, my friend. One wrong move and you could find yourself in a world of trouble."

Max's instinct was to deny his attraction to her, but Arnie would see right through his lie. And Arnie was right. It was time for Max to wake up. First Hannah, then Yossel, and now Arnie. Besides, Molly hadn't said or done anything to encourage him. He was going down a path he had no right to walk. It was time to change direction before he got lost.

nine
MOLLY

❦

'd decided on the blue dress for tonight's ball game. When I'd worn it to the season opener, Max's team had won. I liked to think it had brought them luck, and tonight they'd need whatever luck they could get: it was game three between Harbord and St. Peter's. Both teams had won a game so far and tonight was the elimination round.

Nerves rushed through me as I dressed, my fingers fumbling over the buttons. Despite getting out early from work, I was still running late. Jimmy's game was happening first, and I'd promised him I'd do my best to make it for the end of his game, but it wasn't looking good. At least I'd get there for Max's. I reached for my hairbrush—and heard the sound of fabric tearing.

"Darn!" I glared at the small rip in the bodice seam, wondering if I had time to sew it up. Or I could change into something different, which I really didn't want to do. I examined the material, my seamstress eyes assessing the damage. Not even an inch long, not an important seam. No one would notice, I decided. And I would be mindful.

Tonight was the end of the season, the end of summer. It usually felt like a dismal time, but it didn't seem as bad this year, because I had decided to go back to school. Max was right—things wouldn't always be like this. So I had signed up for night school. I would finally get my high school diploma. Classes would start in just over two weeks. Going to school while working was going to be exhausting, but if I could finish high school, I could apply to journalism school, and my life could move forward from there. Maybe someday I could even write for a living. When I was around Max, the world seemed full of possibilities.

I watched my smile fade in the mirror, thinking about the rally. That entire day had been magical, and when he'd put his arm around me, I'd known he was as happy as I was. But that happiness had been an illusion. We both knew things could never work out between us that way. If Hannah found out, she'd be livid. And our parents? It was foolish to even imagine it. Except, no matter how I tried to ignore my feelings, I felt like a ten-cent piece being drawn inexorably to a magnet. Max had withdrawn since the rally. He was the smart one. On the other hand, here I was, having told myself so many times to put those thoughts out of my mind, wearing a dress that I hoped he liked, and rushing to cheer him on at his game.

When I got downstairs, Dad was sitting at the dinner table. Things had been awkward between us ever since the other night, and we hadn't spoken much. Meanwhile, Richie and I avoided each other whenever we could.

Dad set last night's *Telegram* partially down then slid a package toward me. "I got something for you."

"For me?" I said, touching the brown paper. He nodded, and I tore it open to find a new copy of Agatha Christie's *The Thirteen Problems*. I clutched it to my chest, taken aback. "Dad, thank you. You didn't have to, but I'm so glad you did."

"I wanted to. As a treat, since you're going back to school and all. I'm proud of you for doing it. I hope you haven't read that one yet."

"I haven't."

He observed me over his black-rimmed reading glasses. "I bought it from a friend of mine," he said. His voice took on a different tone. "Smith's his name. Owns a bookstore. Know the man?"

My gut clenched. "You know I do."

"Imagine my surprise when I'm paying for that book and he tells me that you were asking about a job there. He said he was gonna bend the rules, seeing as you're my only daughter. He was gonna give you a job. I was glad to hear it, thinking that it seemed like a perfect job for you, since you're always reading. But he says you quit." He arched a thick, orange eyebrow. "Tell my why. Why would you quit a perfectly good job when other folks are lined up to get one?"

"It doesn't matter, Dad. I got another job. I'm bringing home money."

His jaw tightened. "He says you lost your mind when a Jew came into the store, and he wouldn't sell him a book."

I set my book down and met his steely blue eyes. "I wouldn't say it was me who lost their mind."

"Molly, your foolish decision means you're bringing home less money, which means your family is eating less. You've got to understand priorities. You can't let your friends determine what you do for a living."

"What? No! I chose that job myself."

"You chose to work in the factory?" he asked flatly.

I looked away.

He sighed. Suddenly he looked older and more tired than I'd seen him before. "I've told you before. There's too much trouble around Jewish people these days. What happened with Max, that kind of thing is going on more and more. Be smart about who you're with. Stay safe. And stay away from Christie Pits tonight."

I crossed my arms. "No one's gonna stay away from there tonight, Dad. It's Harbord Playground against St. Peter's in the quarterfinals. Jimmy's playing with the Native Sons right now, as a matter of fact. It's the end of the season run."

He scowled. "It's more than that, and you know it. When the Swastikas started waving that emblem of theirs around on Monday, they guaranteed a big crowd tonight, and for all the wrong reasons. I hear there might be trouble." I could hear real concern in his voice. "So I'm asking you to stay home. It's bad enough you went to the rally. That was like painting a target on your back."

He hadn't mentioned the rally to me. "The rally was peaceful. Besides, I can take care of myself." I paused. "Is that why you're home early? You're working at Christie Pits?"

He shook his head. "There's a bunch of unemployment bums rallying at Allan Gardens. A couple of units'll be at Christie Pits, but we'll have most of them at the Gardens."

I thought of Mr. and Mrs. Dreyfus, Hannah, and Max, just across the street, getting ready for the game. They wouldn't stay away because of threats; they would face them. We all knew there was a possibility that things might go wrong tonight. We'd been there on Monday when someone had waved a swastika that they'd sewn into their coat. After the game, the hateful symbol had been painted on top of the clubhouse roof, too. What Dad didn't understand was that, no matter their religion, the Dreyfuses were my second family. If something bad did happen, I wanted to help them.

"I'm going," I said, turning away. "Thank you for the book, Dad. I'll take it upstairs later."

I was reaching for the door when I heard him speak again.

"There will come a time when it's us versus them, Molly. You'll not be able to walk away from that."

Us versus them. Did he really feel that way? My mind was still turning over those words as I crossed the street and fell into step beside Hannah. I tried to put on a smile for the Dreyfuses, but it must have failed, because Hannah bumped my elbow. She could always read me.

"What's wrong?"

"My father warned me not to go tonight. People are saying there's going to be trouble."

"I'm not worried." Max sounded more than confident. He sounded eager. "If they wanna fight, we'll be ready."

Mrs. Dreyfus frowned. "You don't mean to fight, do you?"

"Times have changed," Mr. Dreyfus told her. "Max is only saying that if they start a fight, we will be prepared. You remember what they said at the rally? We cannot sit by and let ignorance take over this city. A man does what he has to do."

She looked away. "Violence is never a good thing."

"Neither is having your head beaten in," Max said.

"What is it with boys?" Hannah asked. "It's like they can't wait to hit something."

I winked. "They want to impress us."

She gave me a sideways look. "And are you impressed with anyone in particular?"

All I could think of was Max, walking behind us, keeping his distance. "I have no time for romance. I'm focusing on going back to school and getting a career."

When we reached the edge of Christie Pits, Max jogged toward the Harbord Playground's bench on the northwest diamond. Jimmy was already across the park, managing centre field for the Sons. I squinted toward the scoreboard. It was the bottom of the ninth—I'd missed his game, but I was glad to see the Sons were up 5–4. Jimmy'd be happy with the win.

We headed up the hill to a quieter area, away from the main crowd but still with a good view, then Hannah and I looked back down. There had to be a thousand people behind the Harbord Playground's bench on the first baseline. On the other side, by the third baseline, there were at least as many St. Peter's fans. I noticed a couple of newspapermen standing near the benches with their notepads, and I wondered what they would write about the game. Was there anyone here from *Der Yidisher Zhurnal* to report on the Jewish players?

Mr. and Mrs. Dreyfus laid out their blanket, while Hannah and I watched the players warm up. Balls shot from glove to glove, landing in well-seasoned leather pockets with satisfying smacks, and Max picked them out of the air like apples on a tree. His movements were so natural, controlled yet fluid. It almost looked like a dance.

"Jeez," someone said nearby. "Dreyfus has an arm like a cannon. If he can hit like he throws, we can't lose."

Hannah and I grinned at each other. What the man didn't realize was that Max hit *better* than he threw.

"I'll see you after the game," Mr. Dreyfus said to his wife, leaning in to kiss her cheek.

"Say hello to Saul for me," she said.

"Remember what I said, yes?"

"Yes. We will go home if things get out of hand."

He nodded, then smiled at us. "Enjoy your evening, girls."

"Saul Rubenstein is having money trouble," Hannah explained to me. "He needs to talk with Papa."

Jimmy's game ended across the park, and what looked like a thousand more spectators trickled toward our diamond to enjoy a doubleheader. I tried to spot Jimmy among the crowd, but couldn't. I imagined he'd sit with his teammates.

Warm-up over, the Harbord Playground players took to their bench while St. Peter's headed onto the field. Snooky was first up to bat, and he drove a grounder into a lousy spot, but St. Peter's fielders weren't organized. They tripped over their own feet, and the ball bobbled loose.

"Go! Go! Go!" Hannah and I screamed, jumping up.

Snooky stopped at second. Pavlo was up next, slugging the ball beyond all the fielders.

I was already losing my voice. "Home run! Go Pavlo!"

Harbord was up two almost right away, but St. Peter's came back swinging and tied it up. The fans taunted each other predictably and yelled at the players, but as the game went on, I felt the tone shift. The jibes and hollers became uglier, made up mostly of sharp barbs about

Jews. Beside me, Hannah and her mother were visibly tense, as was I. I could tell Max and the other Jewish players were doing their best to ignore the noise, but a couple of them were pacing quietly behind the bench like frustrated tigers.

When it was finally time for Max to stride to the plate, I noticed the St. Peter's fielders back up, and that made me smile. They knew to give him room.

"Come on," Hannah muttered. "Right field. That guy always drops the ball."

"Come on, Max," I echoed.

Max's line drive rocketed past St. Peter's, between right and centre field, exactly where Hannah had willed it to go, and the ball gave a giant bounce, sending the fielders running. Max made it to third base easily, but by then the fielders had sent the ball home, so he stayed there. His shoulders rose and fell with his breaths as he adjusted his cap. I couldn't take my eyes off him.

Then a shout rose up, and I looked away.

"Heil Hitler!"

About thirty boys near the front had leapt to their feet, their right arms held straight out. I recognized the Willowvale Swastikas from Monday night, and I watched in dread as hundreds of Harbord fans rushed toward the agitators. Mrs. Dreyfus gathered Hannah and me to her like a mother bird, while below us, the game ceased. From the way he leaned, I could tell Max longed to be on that hill, putting a stop to the Nazi shouts with his fists, but he and the others stayed where they were, their eyes on the fight. After a couple of minutes, the hostilities began to ease, though the combatants, bruised and bleeding, had to be dragged apart by the opposing sides.

And then, a few feet behind the Swazzies, I spotted a familiar red head. Richie. My heart sank to see where he'd chosen to sit. I should have been surprised, but I wasn't. I looked away, determined to ignore him as the game resumed, but I kept looking over, angrier every time. I could feel the tension among the crowd building, like a barn packed with dry straw. It seemed only a matter of time before someone dropped a match. And Richie would be right in the middle of it. Had Max seen him there?

In the third inning, the same group yelled "Heil Hitler!" again. Then someone shouted, "Kill the Jews!"

My pulse stilled with the very real tone of the threat, and my gaze flew to Max, standing like a target in the field. The Harbord fans shouted back, words I couldn't discern through all the chaos, and I was glad to see a couple of policemen finally arrive and rush in to speak with the offenders. After the shouting abated, the game began once more, but my stomach still rolled. I'd come to see baseball, not blood. Dad was right. If it weren't for the Dreyfuses, I would have left already.

The score stayed even at 5–5 as the innings flew by. Max was all over the place, catching impossible throws, hitting pitches that shot like bullets. Then St. Peter's caught a pop fly, and they were suddenly up 6–5.

Hannah had grown quiet beside me, so I nudged her. "You all right?"

"Yeah. It's just . . ." She scanned the crowd around us. "I wonder where Papa went."

"The game's almost over. He'll be back soon."

"Unless our boys can tie it up," she said with false cheer. "Then it's another inning."

"I'm sure he's okay," I said, putting an arm around her.

The chances of Harbord Playground winning were bleak at this point, but I told myself there was always hope. Then, right before Max was due to step up again, Pavlo hit a fly ball. There were already two out, and I gripped Hannah's hand, praying the St. Peter's fielder would miss it, but we all heard the ball land in his mitt, ending the game 6–5 for St. Peter's. Their fans roared in celebration as the winners sprinted to the middle of the field for a celebratory hug. On the other side of the diamond, the Harbord team milled around their bench, slapping each other's backs and shoulders, commiserating.

"Oh well. It was a good season," Hannah said, getting up to fold the blanket.

The sun had mostly set, and the breeze had picked up, raising goose bumps along my arms and reminding me that summer was almost over. As much as I'd miss the games, I was quietly relieved. Lately, the season had seemed less about sport and more about spite.

Just then, Mrs. Dreyfus let out a cry of alarm, and we turned to see. Across the field, on a small hill called the Camel's Hump, a large white sheet had been unfurled. In its centre had been painted a massive black swastika, its four crooked legs splayed with hate. From the corner of my eye, I saw Max and the others grab their bats and charge toward the banner, then the whole field seemed to move in a giant, converging wave as hundreds of spectators joined the stampede. I couldn't look away, as horrifying as it was. Shouts of "The swastika! The swastika!" swept over the crowd, and when the players swung their bats, the agitators blocked them with broom handles, bricks, lumber, and iron pipes—weapons they had obviously brought on purpose. In only seconds, Christie Pits had become a battle zone.

"Where are the police?" Hannah cried. She and her mother were holding each other, panic in their faces. "Where's Papa?"

Among the thousands of people down there, I couldn't see more than five or six uniforms, and they were clearly overwhelmed.

"We have to leave," Mrs. Dreyfus said, her voice trembling.

"No, Mama! We need to stay and find Papa. He and Max need to come home with us."

And Jimmy and Richie, I thought, desperately scanning the field.

Mrs. Dreyfus held a hand toward the field. "What could we possibly do to help them, Hannah? We have to go now. Your papa told us to go." She was close to tears.

Hannah and I exchanged a glance, but we both knew she was right. We had to leave, if only to protect her mother. Our challenge would be crossing the field, since the fighting had boxed us in. We packed the blanket into the basket, then Mrs. Dreyfus held it against her like a shield, and we hooked our arms through hers. My pulse drummed a warning in my ears as we descended the hill, but we had no choice except to merge into the unpredictable rhythm of the fight. I angled out in front and the three of us wound between strangers in a chain, bumping and tripping as we went. When a man stumbled against me, I shoved him away, trying to clear a path before us, but there were too many struggling bodies, not enough space, and the awful shouts and cries were deafening. Hannah yelped then ducked when a bat swung near her head, and I gripped Mrs. Dreyfus more tightly.

"Come on!" I yelled. "We have to go faster!"

They nodded, their expressions set, and we pushed through.

All of a sudden, something sharp and hard cracked against the side of my head, and I cried out in pain.

"Molly!" Mrs. Dreyfus held me up. "Are you okay?"

I nodded, spotting a piece of brick on the ground by my feet. There was no way to see who had thrown it, so I clenched my jaw against the throbbing in my temple and moved forward.

"David!" Hannah yelled.

To our right, David had been thrown to the ground, but he jumped back up to face his attacker. Blood streamed from his nose, but there was fire in his eyes. He looked far from defeated.

"Come on, Hannah," Mrs. Dreyfus said, tugging her forward. "He can take care of himself."

We were almost through to the other side when I spotted a dump truck pulling up alongside the park. Out of it leapt a couple dozen men, armed with pipes and broom handles and—my heart stopped—a pickaxe. I thought of Max, Jimmy, Mr. Dreyfus, Richie, and our friends, somewhere in the path of that, and I had to restrain myself from running after the man. I watched in horror as the fighting overflowed onto the street, and more trucks arrived, bringing more men and weapons. When we were finally out of the fray, I turned back to an inconceivable sight. Everywhere I looked, I saw furious, bloodied faces, torn clothes, and tears.

Because of what? Religion? Race? A fascist leader a world away? But I knew the truth was much simpler than that. Ignorance had been the match to light the straw.

That's when I remembered the two reporters I'd seen at the start of the game. They were somewhere in the middle of all this, and if they were any good, they were writing it all down. I knew what Rhea Clyman would do. And I suddenly knew what I had to do.

"You should go," I told Hannah. "I have to stay."

"What? Why? You can't do anything here."

"I need to see what's happening. I need to write down the truth."

Her eyes widened. "No. Not tonight, Molly. Come on. It's dangerous."

"Don't worry. No one is coming after me."

She touched my cheek, and her trembling fingertips came away wet with blood. "No?"

I winced. "They weren't aiming for me."

"We can't stop you," Mrs. Dreyfus said, then she kissed my brow. "Please stay out of the worst of it. Come home in one piece." She looked desperately across the field. "If you find them—"

"I'll bring them home."

I watched them leave, then I turned back. It was easier to bully my way through the fighting now that I wasn't tethered to anyone, but I stayed on the outskirts, swerving to avoid men pushing past. Behind the clubhouse, I paused to catch my breath, then I peered around the corner at the brawl. I could watch from here, I realized, and stay out of the worst of it.

The more I saw, the more I wished I had my pen and paper, but I was determined to set it all down in my mind so I could record it later. By now, the police had arrived, and I counted a couple dozen at least, but I didn't see my father. Those on motorcycles went to work breaking up scuffles on the streets, while mounted policemen and officers on foot rushed into the crowd, but I couldn't see how the police could possibly quell the riot.

A hand clamped onto my arm from behind, and I whirled around, heart racing. Phil Burke stood before me, practically glowing with victory despite a bloody lip and a swollen eye.

"Look who's here!" he said. He checked around us. "Where's your Jewboy?"

I yanked on my arm, but he held tight. "Leave me alone, Phil."

"It's okay, Molly," he said, drawing in close and shooting fear through my veins. "I know it's all an act." He gave me a wink. "You're a good little Orange girl at heart, just rebelling is all."

I was shaking so hard my teeth were chattering, but I ground them together to hide it. "Go away."

"Come on, Molly. Play nice."

He reached out, fast as a snake, and grabbed me around the waist, ripping the seam of my bodice where it was already torn. With one jerk, my body was pressed against his, and he walked us both forward until my back slammed against the clubhouse wall.

"Get off me!" I jammed my hands against his chest, but his grip tightened even more, his hips pushed against mine. "Leave me alone!" I screamed, but my panic was swallowed up by the noise of the fighting.

He was so close I could feel his breath on my lips. "I don't think so," he said.

Suddenly Max was there, his fist a loaded weapon. Phil dropped like a stone, and I fell forward into Max's arms. I buried my face in the crook of his neck, inhaling the sweaty, dependable smell of him. I never wanted to let go.

After a moment, he took a step back, noticing the torn bodice of my dress. "He didn't . . . ?"

I shook my head.

"But you're hurt." He touched my cheek softly.

"So are you." Blood trickled from a cut above one of his eyebrows, and there was another smear beneath his nose.

"It's nothing. What are you doing down here, Moll? You should be at the top of the hill, safe. Or at home. Where are Hannah and Mama?"

"They went home, but I couldn't leave."

He frowned tightly at Phil, motionless in the dirt. "You're in danger here."

"So are you," I said again.

"But this is my fight, Moll, not yours."

I closed the gap between us and placed my hand in his, adrenaline making me brave. I couldn't hear the crowd over the thundering of my heartbeat. "This is my fight too, Max. It's us versus them, and I'm with you. I've always been with you."

He glanced down at our hands, then back up at me. He shook his head. "Molly, I've thought about this—about you—every day . . . but you know we can't. I'm sorry. I've been trying to stay away to make it easier on both of us."

He was right. But when I looked into his eyes, all the reasons why faded into the background.

"But we can," I said, knowing I was wrong.

Something melted in his expression, and I reached for him. My fingers wove through the damp hair at the back of his neck as his arms went around me, then he leaned down and I closed my eyes. When I felt the whisper of his lips on mine, the world and everything in it was suddenly gone, a million miles away.

"Molly," he whispered, his long, dark lashes soft on his cheeks.

"What in God's name—"

Max was ripped from my arms, and I saw him hit the ground hard.

"Get the hell away from my daughter," my father roared, swinging his baton.

I grabbed his arm. "Dad! Stop!"

He threw off my grip, focused solely on Max. Dad's face was beet red and slick with sweat, and his lip was drawn back in a horrible snarl. I'd never seen him so angry.

"I came to make sure my daughter was safe," he shouted. "But it turns out you're more of a threat than the rest of them, taking advantage of her like that." He took in my ruined dress then raised his baton. "You've some nerve."

Max crouched before him, his arms over his head like a helmet. "No, sir. I'd never—"

"Don't you dare speak!" Dad shouted. The baton came down on Max's arms, and he cried out in pain.

"Stop!" I screamed, throwing myself on top of Max.

I closed my eyes and braced for the blow, but it never came. When I looked up, my father no longer stood there. Instead, he was on his back, unmoving, his policeman's cap two feet away, his face slack. The fighting continued around the field, but those closest to us had withdrawn at the sight of a fallen policeman. Phil had scuttled away like the cockroach he was.

"Dad?" I whispered, a shiver of panic racing through me. I crawled toward him and touched his face, but he didn't react. "Dad? Wake up."

Max rose stiffly, holding his arms where he'd been hit. He pressed his fingers against Dad's neck, feeling for a pulse. "He's alive. Just unconscious."

Fresh tears of regret rolled down my face. Dad had asked me not to come, and I hadn't listened. He shouldn't have gone after Max, but he was just trying to protect me. It was all my fault. I should never have acted on my feelings. I leaned down so he could hear me over the noise.

"Dad? Can you hear me?"

"Molly!" Jimmy cried, dropping beside me. I was so relieved to see him. "Is he okay?"

Mr. Dreyfus suddenly appeared from around the clubhouse, out of breath. His expression was dark with fury and concern until he saw Dad on the ground. "Is he all right?"

"I think he was hit," I told them both.

Mr. Dreyfus pulled Max to him, carefully touching the cuts and bruises on his face. "I saw him hitting you. I came as fast as I could."

Jimmy picked up a brick lying near Dad's head and studied every face around us, his glare ferocious. "Who threw this? Did anyone see?"

No one said anything.

Then Dad groaned and opened his eyes.

"Dad," I cried with relief. "You're awake."

"Molly," he said, then his brow furrowed as he remembered. His eyes narrowed at Max, and he struggled to sit up. "You bastard," he said.

"No, Dad! Max didn't do anything. He rescued me." Anger crept back into my voice. "He saved me, and you hit him."

Mr. Dreyfus spat to the side with disgust. "You crossed a line, Garret." His eyes passed over me then locked onto his son. "Come on, Max."

"Papa, I'm all right. I need to—"

"What you need is to come home with me right now. We're done here." He glared down at my father. "Too bad that brick didn't kill you."

My jaw dropped, stunned by Mr. Dreyfus's venom. Yes, my dad had done wrong, but so had Max and I. I looked at Max, then at my father, and I held my breath, afraid I might be sick.

"We're leaving now, Max," his father said.

Max's eyes were on me as he leaned on his father's shoulder, then he limped away, sticking to the outer ring of the fighting. When they reached the end of the park, Max paused and turned back. Even from there I felt his lips on mine, and it felt like goodbye.

Dear Molly,

I didn't know if I should write this letter, but I didn't know what else to do. If I could have seen you one more time before I left, I could have said everything in person, but we both know that wasn't possible.

I guess by now, Hannah's told you that the University of Toronto changed their mind and rejected me. Before you object to their asinine decision, you should know this has nothing to do with my marks. I never told you before, but the reason I left Toronto in the first place was because of the quota U of T had on the number of Jews allowed there. It appears they lowered their quota even more this year, and as a result, I was cut. So my plans all changed at the last minute. Instead, I'm at Queen's, in Kingston, for the next four years. It's not bad, but it's not home.

So much happened after Christie Pits. So much anger and injury. I think about your dad a lot and pray for his recovery. I know your family is struggling even more now, and I am so very sorry for that. I feel responsible. But when I remember that moment between us, I cannot regret a single thing—other than the outcome.

What I need to know, Moll, is do you still believe in us versus them? Are you still with me?

If the answer is yes, please write back. Either way, I want you to know that I have always loved you, Molly Ryan, as a friend, now as something more. I miss you very much, and I hope with all my heart that I will hear from you soon.

Yours,
Max

PART TWO

— *1939* —

ten

MOLLY

❧

Left widowed with three young sons," I muttered to myself as I typed, but my voice was buried beneath the hubbub of the *Star* newsroom. I pulled the paper from my typewriter, then checked it over again out of habit.

```
DIES IN A JAIL CELL
NORTH BAY, SEPTEMBER 10, 1939. — A
CORONER'S JURY FOUND THAT HOWARD J.
MORTIMER, 39, OF NORTH BAY, ONTARIO,
DIED IN HIS JAIL CELL OF A BRAIN
HEMORRHAGE. HE HAD BEEN ARRESTED FOR
BEATING HIS WIFE, WHO CLAIMED HE HAD
JUST COME HOME AFTER A DRUNKEN QUARREL
WITH ANOTHER MAN. MRS. MORTIMER HAS BEEN
LEFT WIDOWED WITH THREE YOUNG SONS.
```

"Poor old Howard," I sighed. "You should have just gone straight to bed. At least you won't have to go to war."

The rest of the newsroom clattered with two dozen or so men, blustering around between typewriters and telephones, all of them evidently on an important assignment of some kind. I put the page in my outgoing tray and reached for the next brilliant, one-paragraph work of journalistic integrity on my desk. *Truth and Accuracy, Fairness, Impartiality, and Humanity*, I thought with a sigh. The ethics of journalism, as I'd learned at school. It was just too bad *Something Interesting* wasn't included on the list.

I was distracted by the activity around me. As of last Sunday, Canada was at war. For an entire week, the country had held its breath, waiting for Prime Minister Mackenzie King to announce that we would join Britain against Hitler's Nazi Germany. The prime minister had seemed determined to do it in his own time, making it clear to Britain that we were an independent country now. Today's announcement had thrown the newsroom into an excited chaos cloaked in sobriety—it would have been unseemly for the reporters to admit that they were practically salivating at the stories they needed to write.

I scanned the next article before me: an all-British military band playing an all-British programme at Christie Pits on Sunday. The name of the park brought me back six years, but I shoved it aside, as I always did, and told myself to focus on my work. If I added the names of the band's pieces on the programme, I might be able to stretch it to three paragraphs, I mused. Then again, no one was going to flip all the way to page thirty-two to read it, so I supposed it didn't really matter. I rolled another piece of paper into my old Underwood, slapped the bar down, and got to work.

"You planning to go to that?"

I jumped. Over my shoulder stood Ian Collins, hands sunk deep in his brown tweed trousers. "You scared me," I said.

"Sorry," he said, flashing an innocent smile. "I didn't realize you were so mesmerized by the notices." He peered past me, his blue eyes fixed on the note about the band. "Looks very entertaining."

The first day I'd arrived at the *Star*, I'd been nervous about actually being inside a news office, and eager to make a good impression. I'd also been terrified that Ian Collins, now a senior reporter, would spot me, so I'd hidden behind my typewriter. After so many years of dodging his mother's pointed suggestions that we go out, now I would see him every day. I'd rehearsed various apologies, preparing for the moment we finally spoke, but it turned out there'd been no need. Ian had been friendly from the start and put me at ease, commiserating with me about his mother's persistence. He'd shown me the ins and outs of the office and introduced me to my new coworkers.

Now he came around to the front of my desk and leaned against the corner. He was undeniably handsome, with his sandy blond hair and relaxed but muscular build, and his smile could charm cheese from a mouse. I was flattered by his attentions, but then again, I reminded myself I was the only woman in the place, other than a few secretaries.

"Don't make fun," I said. "Listen, if you'd like to hand me something a little more interesting, I'd be happy to work on that instead."

"I couldn't help it," he teased. "You looked so serious over here."

"What are you working on?" I asked, trying to keep my envy from showing.

"Just a little opinion piece on making the war official."

"Just a little opinion piece," I echoed wryly. "I'm typing up theatre listings next."

He raised his eyebrows. "Have you figured out what you want to see? I was thinking of going to the *Wizard of Oz* tonight. Care to join me? As colleagues, of course," he added.

I hesitated. While I may have misjudged Ian all those years ago, based solely on his mother's tenacity, I still wasn't ready to start dating. My parents needed me, now more than ever. And besides, I wanted more than this tiny desk where I typed out community notices. As attractive and nice as Ian was, he was a senior reporter. If I dated him, I had a feeling I'd never be taken seriously in the office.

"I can't," I said quickly. "We're having a big family dinner tonight. It's going to be a full house."

Disappointment flickered across his face, but he nodded, standing again. "Maybe another time." He pointed at the short stack of papers I'd typed up. "Want me to take those over to Mr. Hindmarsh?"

I shook my head. "I need to walk around. I've been sitting in this chair all morning. But thanks."

I watched him move away, stopping at a couple of desks to chat with fellow reporters, and I felt a pang of regret. What was I so worried about? It was only a date, after all.

I spent another half hour typing up the theatre listings, then I got up and stretched, dropping off my work in the editor's tray. As I left Mr. Hindmarsh's empty office, Roger Waters, one of the junior reporters, put a hand on my arm.

"Sweetheart, get me a coffee? Two sugars."

I pulled my arm away. "I'm not a secretary, Roger."

Across the newsroom, Ian looked up. My cheeks warmed with embarrassment.

Roger frowned. "You don't have to be so testy. I just wanted a coffee."

"Yeah, well, you can get your own."

Averting my eyes from everyone in the room, I marched back to my little desk in the back corner. After years of night school and journalism classes, I fumed, this was where I'd ended up, being asked to get coffee and typing the most insignificant things. Practically the whole world had gone to war, and I was collecting recipes for a new feature Mr. Hindmarsh felt would "really give wives a lift." It wasn't as if I'd expected them to send me overseas, like a couple of the other reporters, but I thought I'd at least get something interesting to do. My thoughts went to Rhea Clyman, as they often did these days, and I wondered what she was up to. Probably interviewing starving prisoners in Poland or something.

Thinking of Rhea brought me back to the hot summer days six years ago when Max and I had talked about what was wrong with the world and our city, and then the riot that had changed our lives.

After the fight, Dad had fallen terribly ill. In the first week of his bedrest, Mrs. Dreyfus had brought food to our house, along with well wishes for him, but despite our need, Mum wouldn't accept the food. She said awful things to her, including barbs about Max "taking advantage" of me.

I'd tried to explain to my parents what had actually happened that night. They'd refused to listen when I said Phil Burke had attacked me, then Max had saved me. Since Phil had already run off by the time Dad had come upon us, he only knew what he'd seen: the unimaginable crime of his daughter kissing a Jew.

The final straw had been my mother accusing Mr. Dreyfus of throwing the fateful brick that had struck Dad. Max's mother had left our house without a word, and I'd cried as I watched through the window, seeing the grief on her face. Since that day, neither she nor Mr. Dreyfus acknowledged any of us, even if we saw them across the street. A wall had come down between our families.

I hadn't imagined it might extend to me as well, though. I'd gone to Hannah's house a few days later, since I hadn't seen her or Max since the riot, and I needed to talk to them both.

"Mum's just upset. It'll pass," I said when Hannah answered the door. Her face was tight with anger. "I'm sorry for what she said."

She folded her arms. "This has nothing to do with our mothers. This has to do with you. And Max."

He'd told her about the kiss, I realized. "Hannah, it just happened."

"It shouldn't have. You both know better. Look what happened. This is all your fault."

It was like she'd slapped me. I looked down at my scuffed shoes, the Oxfords she had loaned me then never asked me to return. Ever since the kiss, I'd felt sick with guilt over what had come out of it, but that hadn't stopped me from thinking about it. I needed to talk to Max. I needed to know what he was thinking.

"Can I talk to him?"

She laughed, but it was a hard, bitter sound. "I see why you're really here."

"No, Hannah, it's not like—"

"He's not here. He's gone to school, but not in Toronto. Somewhere else."

My jaw dropped. "What? Why? Where is he?"

Her face softened slightly. She shook her head. "I'm sorry, Molly, but it's better if you don't know. You two need time apart."

Oh, I wanted to be angry. I wanted to shout at her, to tell her she had no right to decide what was best for Max and me, but I couldn't. She was right. I'd been wrong.

"I understand," I said, blinking hard. "And I'm sorry, Hannah. I'm sorry about everything. Please don't hate me."

Her eyes glistened as well. "I could never hate you. But I think maybe you and I need some time apart, too."

That short walk home was the loneliest of my life. I hid in my room and sobbed myself to sleep. When I left for work the next morning, I ached to see her. But I buried myself in a numbing routine of home, work, night school, and home again, and I got used to being alone. Over time I realized that Hannah and I had been growing apart for a while, and the pain faded.

Not long after, Hannah married David Bohmer, and I was happy for her. I still remembered that day by the beach when he'd tried so hard to gain her attention. Now she had all the shoes she'd ever want, as well as two beautiful children, but my heart hurt with the knowledge that I'd only met her little girl and boy on a handful of occasions. Time had changed everything.

I tried to put Max out of my mind, but he stuck stubbornly to my thoughts. I wrote him letters but never mailed them. I imagined him at school and wondered if he ever thought of me. If he did, did he miss me?

Did he regret what we'd done? He'd told me we shouldn't cross that line, but I'd foolishly leapt across. And I didn't think I would ever forget the way that moment had felt. How we'd been suspended above everything else, sharing a perfect kiss.

But then it was over, and my world fell apart.

The one good thing that had come out of the riot was that, after I had calmed down enough, I'd written an article about what had happened. I talked about the ugliness of the mob, about how bullies had infected others through intimidation, sweeping innocent people into a frenzy of over ten thousand brawlers, pounding on each other for four terrible hours. When the fighting was over, I asked, how many of those men were proud of themselves and of what they'd done? How many went home that night, feeling confident that they had been in the right, and that the stranger they'd slugged with a brick had deserved it? I tried to remind readers that none of us was perfect. Without mentioning Dad, I brought up the concept of "us versus them," and made it clear that I didn't believe that to be true. Instead, I wrote, the goodness within us was only as good as how we treated our fellow humans.

I made it into a letter to the editor, and with a trembling hand, I delivered it to the *Star* the next morning. My heart sang to see it printed the day after that. My first piece of writing in print. When I applied for a job at the *Star* six years later, I presented my best stories and put that letter on the top of the pile as a reminder. That day, the legendary Mr. Henry Comfort Hindmarsh, managing editor of the *Toronto Daily Star*, hired me as a junior reporter.

The big clock on the newsroom wall ticked to five o'clock. Outside, the rain was coming down in sheets, so I gathered my coat and handbag, then reached under the desk for my umbrella. As I passed by Ian's desk, he raised a hand.

"Have a good night with your family," he said, warm as always, and I thought again about maybe saying yes to him next time.

The rain pounded my umbrella as I rushed toward the streetcar, dodging puddles and wishing I'd had the forethought to bring galoshes as well. Inside, the streetcar aisle was slick, so I clung to seat backs until I found an empty one. I settled in and gazed out the streaming window, my thoughts still on the riot so long ago. That night had marked a change for the city. Things were still tumultuous, noisy with continuing protests and prejudice, but there had been no more major uprisings after that one. I liked to think that maybe a few people had read my letter and taken it to heart.

Then just this past August, seven hundred or so local German Canadians had gathered near Maple Street, showing their support of the Nazis. The following Monday, when their leader, Martin Kaiser, returned to his job as a foreman at a factory on Geary Avenue, his coworkers had a few things to say to him, then a fight broke out. As soon as I heard about the brawl, I'd braced at my desk, hoping Ian would take me with him to the scene, but that wasn't up to him. Instead, I was tasked with writing about a church bazaar. Ian and another reporter got back to the office hours later, and he told me the factory floor had been covered with bloody towels.

The streetcar stopped at Spadina, and I got off to wait for the one headed north. By the time it arrived, my shoes were soaked through, and my teeth were chattering from the cold. As we rattled past Mr. Dreyfus's factory, I found myself thinking about Max again. Once, he'd been the sun and the moon to me, but we'd been so young. Now, when I looked back, I regretted my actions that day. As much as I wanted him, I hadn't given any thought to how it might affect others, and my selfishness had caused so much needless pain. I hadn't spoken to Max in years, and I'd only seen him a handful of times through my window. Other than to visit, he'd never returned after his four years at medical school, so I assumed he was working somewhere else. Maybe, like Richie, he was married. I hoped he was happy. I really did.

That fall, Richie had joined the police force, and I thought his decision had a lot to do with what had happened to Dad. During the first few weeks after the riot, I'd occasionally come home from work and seen the two of them in Dad's bedroom, talking quietly between themselves. Then Richie had applied and was accepted into the police force, and Dad seemed to like the fact that there was still a Ryan in uniform. A few months later, Richie married a quiet, pretty barmaid named Barbara, and I'd become an aunt two years ago to sweet little Evelyn. Barbara was pregnant with their second baby now, and she'd positively glowed the last time they'd come over for dinner. Her hands rested on her belly, and I'd felt an unexpected twinge of envy.

Tonight, when I stepped out of the rain and into the house, I could smell ham in the oven. Mum was leaning over a pot, the steam rising into her face. I noticed her apron was covering a neat new dress, which made me smile. She deserved that.

"Hi, Mum," I said, dropping my week's pay into the Friday Night Tax Bucket.

Only my youngest brother Liam and I were still living at home these days, and the Depression was easing a little, so things had improved around the house. But without Dad working, there was still pressure to contribute. Fortunately, my eight dollars a week at Eaton's had grown to almost thirty at the *Star*. I'd even been able to set some of it aside for myself, for the future.

Over the past year or so, life in Toronto had slowly improved. More jobs had opened up, and the need didn't seem as dire. People started shopping again, though they were still prudent in their purchases.

My brothers were all working and doing well. Mark had lucked into a job driving streetcars, and that's where he'd met his wife, Helen. Love at first sight, he'd said. She couldn't find the right coins, but he'd taken one look at her and let her ride for free. Helen had a curly brown bob and a lovely smile, and she clearly adored my brother.

At my voice, Mum looked up from the stove. She seemed better these days, though she was understandably drained from tending Dad. "How was your day?"

I shrugged out of my dripping coat and hung it by the door. I didn't want to tell her how discouraged I was at my job, not after everything I'd done to get into this field of work.

"Busy. So much going on now that Canada's fighting."

She turned back to the pot, shaking her head as she stirred. "I had hoped it would never come to that. Didn't we learn anything from the last war? Oh, the stories your father told me. Not that he talked much about it." She sighed, sounding resigned. "Molly, dear, if you're not too tired, would you please set the table? The boys should be here any minute."

From the cabinet I took out the set of plates I'd bought for her last birthday, then pulled out a few of the older, chipped ones. Our evenings were quiet affairs with just Liam, our parents, and me, and he was gone most nights, either at work or out with his girlfriend, Louise. So it was usually just me, alone with my parents. I didn't mind. Mum had stopped encouraging me to date long before, grateful for my help with Dad. Then again, she had been quietly pleased to hear I was now working with Ian.

Tonight it would be all seven of us in one house again, plus four more. The normally sober quiet would be smothered beneath love and laughter, I hoped.

As I finished setting the table, Liam wandered into the kitchen. At eighteen, he had grown taller than all of us. His shoulders had thickened from working with Jimmy at the Inglis factory, which had recently turned their appliance assembly line over to the manufacturing of Bren machine guns in preparation for war.

Liam sniffed the air appreciatively. "Your pea soup is the best, Mum. Louise is gonna love it."

She wiggled her eyebrows. "It's a family recipe, dear. Louise can have the recipe if she's a family member, you know."

He laughed. "I will keep that in mind."

"Would you bring the high chair from the basement for little Evelyn, please?" she asked.

He nodded then headed downstairs just as the front door swung open, bringing the rush of the rainstorm inside.

"We're here!" Mark announced, ushering Helen in front of him. Jimmy was on his heels, and the three of them stood in the doorway, thumping rainwater off their boots. Mark had put on some weight, I noticed as he took off his coat. It looked good on him.

"Come on in," Jimmy said, holding the door open for Louise, who was just behind him. "Hey, Liam!" he called. "Come and be a gentleman, would you?"

Liam rushed up from the basement with the high chair, then reached to take Louise's coat and umbrella. It warmed my heart to see the love in his eyes.

He planted a kiss on her cheek. "Hi there," he said. "You look beautiful."

Louise blushed, then turned to my mother. "It smells wonderful in here, Mrs. Ryan. Is that pea soup? Oh, I'd love the recipe."

Mum and I glanced from her to Liam, hiding our smiles. "You'll have to ask Liam," she said, and Liam turned beet red.

"Where's Richie?" I asked, scanning my brothers' faces.

Mum shrugged. "Any time now. Mark, would you go get your father?"

"Oh, I'll get him," I said quickly, moving toward the stairs.

Upstairs, I paused at the doorway of my parents' room, watching Dad. He was sitting at the window in *Seanmháthair*'s chair, reading. I'd brought the chair from my room to his six years ago, knowing he'd need it more than I. Dad was a smaller man now, shrunken into himself. Far from the imposing policeman he had once been.

It had all started on the night of the riot. After he'd been struck by the brick, Dad had seemed a little dazed and needed help getting to his feet, but we didn't suspect anything serious, and I was caught up in a cloud of righteous anger of his treatment of Max. When we'd gotten home, he'd said goodnight and I had walked past without acknowledging his presence. I still clearly remember Mum's cry of anguish the next morning. We'd all run into their room to find Dad lying perfectly still in his bed, his eyes wide with terror. When we asked what was wrong, he couldn't answer. Richie raced for the doctor, who told us Dad had suffered a massive brain bleed that caused a stroke, and that we shouldn't expect much improvement. He'd said we were lucky Dad hadn't died right there. Nothing in our lives had been the same since.

When anyone asked, which they rarely did anymore, Mum and I liked to say he was improving. The truth was that not much had changed in the past six years. He could talk, but only slowly and in short sentences. His mind seemed fine most of the time, but his memory slipped sometimes, which meant he missed out on some of our conversations. He'd reluctantly accepted using the cane when he was well enough to stand, and I doubted he'd ever walk without it. But it was the pain beneath his weaknesses that had stolen most of his strength. The knowledge that he couldn't support his family, that he'd never be the man he was before. That lived in the emptiness of his eyes.

I knocked gently on the doorframe, and he looked up. He gave me his approximation of a smile, affecting only half his face, and my heart melted as it always did. I'd never forget what had put him in this position, and I'd never forgive myself.

"Everyone here?" he asked in his wavering voice.

"Almost," I said, settling on the bed near him. "Still waiting on Richie."

"Smells good."

I nodded, then my eyes went to his hands, folded over some paper. I recognized the handwriting as mine. "Are those my stories?"

They shook in his grip. "Mum found them."

He was reading about the Great Famine, the story told to me by his mother. My mind recalled the people in the story, the families torn by tragedy then shaped into survivors. I wished I could have written a happier ending for him to enjoy.

"Those are from so long ago. They're probably really bad."

"They're beautiful."

My throat squeezed at the sight of tears in his eyes. He was much more emotional these days, and I still hadn't gotten used to that.

"It's like your *seanmháthair* is right here." He patted his chest, over his heart.

"I miss her," I said. I wondered what my dear grandmother would say if she were here now. Seeing her son like this, the rest of us spread out in different directions, a war on the horizon. "I still do."

"She would be proud of you." He paused. "I am."

"Oh, Dad."

I wrapped my arms around him and pressed my cheek to his, and his one good arm went around me. What a fool I'd been all those years ago. If I could have gone back in time, I would have held him tight instead of chastising him for going after Max. And while I was there, I would have taken back that impulsive kiss with Max.

"Ready to get up?" I said into his ear, and he nodded.

I straightened gently and helped him to his feet, then I handed him his cane. He caught his balance, then we made the slow walk downstairs. By the time we arrived, the family had crowded into the living room and kitchen. It was so good to see the house full again. Dad was welcomed with hugs and smiles, and I stood back and watched, loving my family so much it hurt. We were different from how we'd been, but we'd pulled through the Depression, my brothers and I were happily employed, and the family was growing. Like in my grandmother's stories, we'd survived.

Five minutes later, the door opened again, and in walked Richie's wife, Barbara, her face red, her eyes puffy, and her arms tight around a bewildered little Evelyn. Richie was right behind her, still in his policeman's uniform. He looked stiff, uncomfortable. I raised an eyebrow at Jimmy, but he only shrugged.

"What's going on?" Dad asked, breaking the silence.

Richie took off his hat then stepped farther inside the kitchen. "I've enlisted," he said.

eleven
MAX

❧

1940

Max shrugged his pack over his shoulder and stepped out of the train onto the frozen tarmac of the Newfoundland Airport. Arnie, David, and he had made quite a journey to get here, sailing to Botwood, Newfoundland, on the *Duchess of Richmond*, shuddering with cold as they were taken to land by tender, then chugging the rest of the way on a narrow gauge railway. Now he walked toward the army barracks with the rest of the Royal Rifles, and Max wasn't sure it had been worth the effort. The airport at Gander, Newfoundland, which was connected to the army's base, was a long, flat stretch of nothing very interesting, set in the middle of a wilderness.

"Sure is cold," David said, falling into step beside him. David was as tall as Max now, and he'd left his father's frail physique behind. "That wind is sharp."

Arnie nodded on Max's other side, his boots squeaking on the snow. "This place is big. Biggest airport in the world, you know."

"Somehow I thought that would make it more exciting," David muttered.

When they'd been told the Royal Rifles were being shipped to the Atlantic coast for duty, Max had been keen to set out. He wanted to get into the fight, and this was the first step.

But once they were on their way to Newfoundland, their sergeant, Sergeant Cox, a slight man in his thirties with short brown hair and a thin moustache, informed them that duty in their case referred to garrison duty. They would not be going overseas after all. They were here to guard this airport.

Construction was going on at what seemed like a frenzied pace, with new hangars and living quarters going up, and another runway being put down. Max imagined the workers were in a rush to finish before the winter storms came, and he shuddered at the thought. It was already freezing, and it was only November.

Crossing the tarmac toward the flat, one-storey barracks, they passed hangars for the Canadian, British, and American air forces, and Max noted the military instalments set up around almost every runway: the pill boxes armed with machine guns, and the uniformed, fully armed Canadian soldiers marching nearby. A fleet of B-18s, what they called the Digbys, were parked along one runway, and barbed wire was set up all around the compound to prevent any airborne invaders from accessing the base.

Max, Arnie, and David had originally joined Toronto's Royal Regiment, but the Royal Rifles out of Québec and New Brunswick had needed a couple of medics, so Max and Arnie had been transferred. Max wasn't sure why David had been assigned there as well, but he was glad to have them both with him. Unlike David and Arnie, Max hadn't had to leave anyone behind. All the married men had been allowed one night at home before setting out for Newfoundland, and when David and Arnie had met Max at the station the next day, their shoulders were sloped with guilt.

"Clara will be all right," Max assured Arnie. "And Hannah's just stubborn. Give them time, and they'll call you heroes."

Hannah was good at guilt. Max had felt the weight of it as they'd shipped out. Especially since he hadn't been the most attentive son or brother over the past seven years. During that time, he'd made the trip to Toronto for only a handful of occasions: Hannah and David's wedding in 1934, the birth of their daughter, Dinah, who had won over his heart a year later, then their son Jacob's bris last year. Other than that, Max had stayed in Kingston, working in the emergency ward at the hospital. His life was no longer in Toronto, no matter how much he loved the people in it.

Then, at the end of July, he'd taken the train home. His parents were overjoyed to see him, their arms wide open for hugs. That made him feel even worse about the news he was about to share with them.

The next night, when Hannah and David arrived for a family supper along with their children, he almost felt like a stranger around them. He'd embraced his sister, very aware of her belly, round with baby number three, shaken David's hand, then hugged Dinah and Jacob, exclaiming about how much they'd grown.

All day, he'd smelled his mother's cooking and tried to stay out of her way so she could get it all done. His patience was rewarded at last with a beautiful meal of brisket with baba ghanoush on the side. She'd even prepared Max's favourite dessert of *rugelach*. As the plates were emptied, the conversations filled, and there was laughter around the table as there should always be. But Max could hardly eat because of the pulsing guilt in his heart. He waited until after the meal to share his news.

"I came home because I'm enlisting," he finally said.

It was like he'd dropped a blanket on a fire, the way the conversation died.

His mother had gone very pale. "No, Max," she whispered.

"What's in list?" little Dinah asked, looking at him then at Hannah, whose face was frozen in shock. One-year-old Jacob began to cry, and Hannah turned to free her son from the high chair.

Max was relieved when his father nodded, stoic as ever, and murmured, "Yes."

His father had been unwilling to talk about his own war experience, twenty or so years before. All he'd said was that war was the worst thing that mankind could do to one another. It was a disgusting, horrendous act of brutality that forced men to go against their own morality. And it was a man's duty to serve.

Over the past seven years, his father had changed. He had redoubled his work within the Jewish community, devoting himself to any and all relief efforts. He'd been on the front line a year ago, petitioning for the rights of the over nine hundred Jewish passengers on board the MS *St. Louis* to come ashore in Canada. Max had never forgotten the letter his father had sent to him, quoting the immigration official who had been asked how many Jews would be considered for entry into Canada in the future: *His answer was that "none is too many," Max. Tell me, how can a man think that way?*

But Max knew it was more than the war that was driving his father. After the riot, Mrs. Ryan's accusation about throwing the brick, and the lingering suspicions had hardened him, made him bitter. He spoke less, but Max could tell he was always listening.

"You don't have to go," Hannah said, her mouth set in a thin line as she bounced Jacob on her hip. Beside her, David studied the tablecloth.

"Yes, I do," Max said.

He'd been prepared for her to push back. Hannah had never been one to discuss politics, let alone war. She'd built a perfect life with her own little family, and from the shuttered look in her eyes, Max could tell she refused to contemplate much more than that. To Hannah, Max should be building a family of his own by now, and working hard in his chosen profession to support them.

She bounced Jacob faster. "Why would you throw your life away like that? You're a doctor, Max. You've worked hard all your life to achieve your dream, and now you can take care of people like you always wanted. That doesn't mean you're supposed to cross the ocean and become a shield to protect them from bullets and bombs. What a waste!"

He fought the urge to snap back. "It's not a waste," he said calmly. "I'll be a medic. I'll be of use. I'll save lives."

"Let other men do that," she said.

"Uncle Max, what's in list?" Dinah repeated, getting out of her chair and climbing into his lap. Her eyes were wide, just like her mother's, squeezing Max's heart. He pulled his niece close, then looked at Hannah over her little shoulder.

"It's my responsibility," he said. "I'm not leaving that up to anyone else."

"Why? You think you're the only one who can save the world? Come on, Max! You don't need to do this!"

"As a Canadian, it's my duty to volunteer." He paused. "As a Jew, I have a personal score to settle. You know it's true, Hannah."

Lips pressed together, she passed the baby to David and stormed out of the house, letting the front door slam behind her. Max looked at David, who offered a helpless shrug. Sometimes Max felt a little sorry for his friend. Hannah had always been a lot to handle, and David would do anything in the world for her.

His mother waved her hand. "Go, Max. Talk to her."

Hannah was sitting on the porch, the wetness on her cheeks shining in the moonlight. The last time he'd seen her cry, he realized with surprise, was after the riot, when he'd told her about Molly. Those had been angry tears too. It had taken Dinah's birth for things to thaw between them, and here he was, hurting her all over again.

"I'm sorry," he said, lowering himself beside her.

She sniffed. "I know. It's just . . ." She wiped her face with her palm. "I know I pushed you away all those years ago, but things were getting better, weren't they? Now you're here, and I . . . I don't want to lose you. Never ever again, Max. I don't want you to go."

He wrapped an arm around her. "I have no choice. I promise I'll write to you."

"That isn't enough. Promise me you'll be careful." Her hands went to her stomach. "This little one needs to meet her uncle."

He gave her a gentle smile. "Okay, but only because you asked nicely."

The next day he'd gone down to Fort York Armoury at the Canadian National Exhibition grounds where the army was posted, and he signed up without hesitation. He passed the medical examination with flying colours, became one of the medics for the Royal Regiment of Canada, and moved into the temporary barracks in the agriculture building. Every stall had been cleaned out and converted into sleeping quarters for two men, but the residual stink of horses filled Max's nostrils from six a.m. reveille to 10:15 lights out. Then Arnie and Samuel Schwartz joined the regiment. Two weeks later, David did as well.

"I don't think she'll ever forgive me," he confided to Max on the first night.

"You can't blame her," Max said, torn between surprise and quiet admiration that David had dared stand up to her. "That baby's coming in two months. You could have waited."

"Could I?" His sharp reaction took Max aback. "Do you think you're the only one with a score to settle? The Nazis are bombing London. What's to keep them from coming here and going after my family?"

Max hung his head. "She'll forgive you."

"I sure hope so," David had replied. "I can't imagine my life if she doesn't."

That's when Arnie popped his head in. "You and me, David. Clara might have loved the uniform, but she hates everything about where I'm taking it." He pulled out his wallet, grabbing for bits of paper as they tumbled out. "Hey, wanna see the cutest kid ever? I mean, look at this little guy. Five years old already. So smart. Spitting image of his father, poor kid."

David's smile returned, and he reached for his own photos. "Oh yeah?"

Now the three of them were in Gander, Newfoundland, where none of them had ever imagined being.

Max held open the door to the barracks. "Home sweet home," he said.

They stepped inside the newly constructed building and followed Sergeant Cox into the sleeping quarters, where two columns of single bunks extended the full length of the room. They claimed one each, side by side, and Max was just setting down his pack when someone said his name.

He turned, then stopped short. "Richie?"

Richie's cheeks bloomed that familiar red, and a tentative smile played at the corner of his mouth. "I thought it was you. What are you doing here?"

"My battalion just rolled in," Max replied, astonished. "You?"

"We've been here a couple of months."

For a moment they stared at each other, neither one speaking. It had been years since they'd last seen each other, and Max could practically feel the history crackling between them, the fibres of their childhood friendship burned into something hard. It was like a physical barrier, looming even higher with the spectres of their fathers on their backs. Max could now clearly see Mr. Ryan when he looked at Richie.

"How's your dad?" he asked carefully.

Richie fiddled with the strap on his pack. "Same as ever. Crippled for life."

Max didn't know if he should feel shame or not when that subject arose. Certainly he felt partly to blame for Mr. Ryan's stroke, but in the chaos of the riot, they'd never been able to prove who had thrown the brick that struck him down. Mrs. Ryan had accused Max's father, and despite his father's furious denials, her accusation had never faded away. Sometimes even Max had doubts. All he remembered was his father rushing to his rescue, livid at Mr. Ryan. The truth was that anyone could have thrown that brick. Even his father.

"I'm sorry to hear that," Max said.

Richie's eyes slid sideways. "It's not your fault," he said, frowning slightly to himself, then he cleared his throat and looked back at Max. "I got duty in a bit. I'd better go."

Max watched him leave, then he turned to lift his pack onto his bed.

"You okay?" Arnie asked from the bunk across the aisle.

He nodded, but didn't speak. He couldn't tell Arnie that seeing Richie had brought back all the memories of that summer. Even after all this time, the pain felt fresh. He could still see that look on Molly's face behind the clubhouse, the one that assured him *I'm with you.* Despite everything that had happened between their families, he had never really stopped wanting to believe she still might be. He'd written to her after the riot, hoping he was right, but after a month of waiting for her to reply, he'd reluctantly made a decision. There were only two things he'd ever wanted in his life: Molly and medicine. When she hadn't written back, he'd buried his feelings, determined that from that point on, it would only be medicine.

But seeing Richie changed all that. The old hurts and the anger from that summer were coming to the surface again, reminding him of the swastika pin on Richie's shirt, and the sharp crack of Mr. Ryan's baton.

The days and weeks and months of waiting for a letter from Molly that had never come. He clenched his jaw against the memories, swallowing the pain. It was bad enough that they were stuck way out here in Gander. Now that Richie was here, he'd have a daily reminder of the biggest mistake of his life.

twelve
MOLLY

꠸꠸

1941

I hugged my handbag to my chest as I strode through the windstorm, muttering to myself about November being the worst of all the months. I closed my eyes against a blast of wind just in time to splash into an icy puddle, which soaked immediately through one shoe. I hissed with exasperation. I'd feel that misery all day long.

"Good morning!" I heard from across the street, and I smiled despite myself.

Mr. Rabinowitz stood at his usual spot on the sidewalk outside Palermo's, his back to the wind.

"Mr. Rabinowitz," I said, hopping across the street. "You should go inside, out of the wind. Mr. Palermo wouldn't mind, I'm sure."

I thought he was looking more fragile than ever, and stooped with arthritis. When he smiled at me, ignoring my suggestion, his eyes were milky. "What a day this is!" he said in his creaky voice. "Reminds me of Poland."

The poor man. I wondered where he slept at night. I knew Wellington House took in homeless men, but I'd read somewhere that the shelters were terrible places to sleep, crawling with vermin and criminals. Maybe he just huddled in a corner or alley, thinking he was at home with his long-departed wife. Maybe it was a blessing not to remember some things.

I reached into my bag and fished out the lunch I'd packed, then offered it to him. It wasn't much, just crackers and a bit of cheese.

He pushed it away. "That's very kind, but it's your meal."

"Oh no," I lied. "My lunch is at the office." I told myself that when I got hungry later, I'd remember the gratitude in his eyes.

The fingers that accepted the food poked through holes in his gloves, and the tips were slightly blue. His coat was old and threadbare, and from its fit I could tell he was now a much smaller man than he used to be. His boots were worn and wet.

"Aren't you cold, Mr. Rabinowitz?"

He waved a hand. "This coat's been with me forever. It'll do. These days they don't make nothing that ain't schlock. Mrs. Rabinowitz will patch this up. Thirty-seven years she's been patching me up." He chuckled, then shivered despite himself.

No one was going to patch up his old coat. I thought of the noisy, whirring sewing machines at Eaton's, remembering the thick grey wool I'd made into so many coats, and I wondered how much they cost.

I was reluctant to leave him there, alone in the bitter cold, but I didn't have a choice. "I'm sorry, Mr. Rabinowitz, but I have to go to work," I said. "I don't want to be late."

"Ah yes, don't let me keep you," he replied. "I should be getting back to the factory myself."

When I arrived at work, the newsroom was darkened by the storm outside, adding to the doom and gloom forever being typed up in the office. Mr. Rabinowitz drifted to the back of my mind as I pulled out the latest news from the war, which brought my daily fears for my brothers back to the forefront. One by one, they'd all gone to fight. Eighteen-year-old Liam had been the last to go, in 1940.

Jimmy had joined the Royal Canadian Air Force, and his brief letters home were messily scrawled stories of danger that kept me from sleeping. In the summer of 1940, he and the rest of the Number 1 Fighter Squadron had flown their one-man Hurricanes during the Battle of Britain, and he'd written with a sort of crazy glee about their first engagement of enemy planes in August.

> *Those bombers couldn't keep up with us. What a thrill to finally get into the fight! We shot down three, and four others took some heavy fire.*

There was a big ink blot, then he continued on.

> *We did lose one of ours, though, and that was a sobering fact to remember as we all touched down at the base.*

The next letter sounded less like a celebration, and it had chilled me to the bone.

> *We weren't so lucky today. The Messerschmitts came out of the sun—you remember what that's like? When you're out in the field and someone pops a fly ball right into the sun? There's no way to see it, then all of a sudden it's in your face. Well, we fought well, but we lost three more planes.*

I kept track of the numbers he sent me. Later, I'd see them printed in our paper.

"Your brother's a hero," Ian reminded me one morning in October as I sat at my desk, staring at nothing. "Thirty-one enemy aircraft destroyed, and another forty or so more damaged. He and his squadron are saving a lot of lives, Molly. Try to think of it that way."

"I'm trying," I'd replied, "but then I think of the sixteen downed Hurricanes, and those Canadian boys who will never see their families again. And I think it could be Jimmy next time. And I can't imagine a world without Jimmy in it."

Liam was just as bad at stopping my heart. Maybe worse. He was with the Royal Canadian Navy, sailing on a corvette through the deep waters of the St. Lawrence, trying to stay above the surface while wolf packs of U-boats hunted from the deep. At least he tried to inject a little humour when he could.

> *I was awful glad to hear from you that Louise is all right,* he'd written privately to me. *It doesn't matter how many times I write, she still seems worried. Please tell her I love her—even though I have probably told her fifty times recently. I keep promising I'll be back so I can marry her, whether she likes it or not!*
>
> *Hey, I wanted to tell you about our cuisine out here, Molly. You know how tired we were of corned beef and cabbage? Well, guess what we eat practically every day out here? Corned beef and <u>powdered potatoes</u>! What I would do for some of Mum's overcooked cabbage right about now.*

I didn't bother writing back to tell him I missed corned beef too. Our weekly individual rations were very restrictive, including no more than a cup of sugar per week and four ounces of butter. Meat was so hard to find, they'd come up with cans of a new, seasoned ham called Spam, and I was not a fan. Vegetables were hard to find these days too, considering everyone's victory gardens were all done for the season. Good thing Mum and I had canned like fiends.

Mark and the Royal Regiment were, so far, as safe as could be in

Iceland, where they were protecting that unappreciative country from Russians. He'd made it clear in his letters that he was not pleased about the assignment.

> *Iceland is dull and most of the locals don't want us here. I*
> *told Helen there's no need to worry about the girls out here.*
> *If any of them say so much as hello to us, they're reported*
> *to the police! We're bored out of our minds. But they say if*
> *Hitler wins Iceland, we lose the North Atlantic, so I guess*
> *this is where they want us.*

Then, just yesterday, we'd gotten a letter from Richie, saying he was in Hong Kong. That had been a big surprise to us all. He'd known they were sailing somewhere, but no one had let the cat out of the bag about exactly where until the second day of the voyage. He wrote that Britain was vaguely concerned that the Japanese might come after Hong Kong, one of their colonies, but the Brits were too busy fighting Germany to do anything about it. Their solution was to send troops from Canada and British India to make a show of force. I'd been worried about him being so far away, but Ian assured me that he was likely the safest out of all my brothers, with the possible exception of Mark. He handed me an article about Hong Kong, and I was relieved to read that no one was overly concerned about any kind of military action happening there. From what I read, even if they did decide to invade, the Japanese were not great fighters, and there weren't many of them anyway. Most were caught up in a war with China that had been raging for four years already. It was understood the Canadian and Indian forces would easily fight them off.

A steaming cup appeared magically on my desk. "Thought you could use a drink," Ian said. "Sorry it's not something with a little more zip to it."

I peered into the cup, impressed. "Is that tea?"

"I have a secret stash. Don't tell anyone."

I closed my eyes and took a fragrant sip, then smiled up at him. "I won't tell a soul."

Since my brothers had enlisted, Ian's friendship had been a real comfort. I knew he was interested in me romantically, but despite my attraction to him, I was maintaining a safe distance. I didn't want to rush into anything. Once in a while he took me to dinner, but he seemed to understand that my heart wasn't in it and was satisfied with my company. He never pressed for anything beyond friendship.

Our mothers, though, saw our relationship through much more optimistic lenses. I warned Mum not to start making wedding plans anytime soon, because my job was the most important thing. She pretended to agree.

Ian leaned over my shoulder. "What are you working on?"

In the last year, I'd begun reporting on some actual stories, but it was still mostly local news. And while Mr. Hindmarsh, in his usual, emotionless voice, said he liked my work, they never added up to more than three paragraphs, and were never printed before page thirty.

I rolled my eyes. "An argument at a church bazaar that led to fisticuffs, if you can believe it. Honestly, Ian. Is that really news?"

He grimaced. "You know what I think, Molly. You got to stand up for yourself in here. Write something that matters to you."

I nodded, drumming my fingers on the desk. Every page in the paper was full of stories from the war, but every day I was reminded that the city's own problems hadn't gone away. I saw people lined up for hours for rations, and the homeless population kept growing. I pictured Mr. Rabinowitz, hunched in the icy wind, and an idea began to materialize. The more I thought about what I could write, the more I felt the almost forgotten thrill of a story rising within me.

Everyone had a story. What was his?

"Free for dinner tonight?" Ian asked.

"Not this time, I'm afraid. There's something I need to do." I gulped down the tea and grabbed a pad and pencil, nearly forgetting my coat in my rush.

The corner of his mouth curled. "Atta girl. I can't wait to read it."

I hustled outside, questions popping into my mind. Why had Mr. Rabinowitz left Poland, and when? What had life been like for him when he'd arrived here? How had he met his wife? I'd only seen her once or twice when I was little, but I vaguely recalled her thick grey curls and wide smile. I tried to remember what Mr. Palermo had said about why she'd died. Was it cancer? Suddenly, I wanted so many answers, and I couldn't get there fast enough.

The wind had died down, and the day was warmer by the time I spotted Mr. Rabinowitz huddled on his regular bench outside Palermo's. Before he could spot me, I ducked into the shop.

"Molly!" Mr. Palermo looked up from the counter, and I noticed his moustache was almost pure white now. "How are you? Your father says you're working at the *Star*? Congratulations."

I smiled. I'd always liked him. "I am, thanks in part to your lovely letter of reference. How are you doing?"

He gestured at the store behind him, slightly fuller than it had been on my last day of work, despite today being late fall. "Things are slowly recovering, I dare say. It's a shame that it takes a war to make things better, though."

He asked about my father, then about my brothers, and we commiserated over the state of the world, then I paid Mr. Palermo for the best of his slightly soft apples.

"For a friend," I told him as I headed back outside.

Mr. Rabinowitz beamed at me before he even saw the apple. Then he looked surprised. "What's this? Oh, what a treat. Thank you." He took a bite, making a satisfied kind of humming noise while he chewed.

"Mr. Rabinowitz, I'm wondering if I can ask you a favour."

"Ask away," he said, taking another bite.

I fought the urge to pluck a tiny bit of apple from his beard. "I don't know if I told you before, but I write for the *Star*."

"Eh?"

"The newspaper. The *Star*."

"Ah yes? Good for you."

"I'm interested in speaking with people in the neighbourhood. Doing interviews. And I am wondering if I could ask you a few questions."

"Oh, ho! You'll make me famous, will you?" He chuckled. "Nothing interesting about me, but I'll answer what I can."

"Let's start with where you were born," I said, pulling out my notepad.

"Bobrowniki, Poland, in 1875," he said. My mind clicked through the numbers, astonished. Mr. Rabinowitz was only sixty-six, but he looked so much older. "My papa had a farm," he said. "I looked after the chickens. It was my job to watch out for those chicks. So sweet, those little yellow things, and their mothers all talking *kuk kuk kuk*."

As I asked more about his childhood, I realized that his memories from long ago were fresh in his mind.

"Did you fight in the Great War?" I asked eventually.

He waved a hand, dismissing the question. "Meh. I don't talk about that."

"I'm curious, though. Can you tell me a little?"

A slight frown. "I was in the cavalry during Szarża pod Rokitną. June of 1915."

My pencil paused. "What's that?"

"They called it the Charge of Rokitna. I lost seventeen friends that day, but I managed to save my friend Piotr. I pulled him out of the way when he was shot." He laughed bitterly. "They gave me a medal for it, but it seemed pointless when so many others had died."

I felt a hitch in my chest, imagining this poor, broken man, young and terrified, desperately trying to save his friend. A hero. Now forgotten on the streets. "Where's the medal? Do you still have it?"

He shrugged. "I threw it away. Should I be proud that I killed other men? I didn't want anything that reminded me of that time."

I changed tacks. "What about your wife? When did you meet her?"

He smiled, a far-off look in his eye. "Ava and I met at our friend's wedding, just after the war. She was a wonderful dancer. I could have danced with her all night," he said. "We got married, then we came to Canada in 1919."

He went on to tell me about their first house and the babies, his face lighting up in wonder at the "six beautiful blessings" that filled its two bedrooms. But that's when his memory started to fail him. He knew the children's names and could tell me the details of each one's birth. He knew stories from their childhood, but his expression grew vague when I asked where they were now. Still, I jotted down everything he said, thinking all the time about how I might weave his words into a story.

That night I started to write, and the story swept through me, filling me with a sense of exhilaration I hadn't felt in months. I kept going long after Mum and Dad had turned in for the night, and the next morning, I was at work an hour early to type it all up. When I'd finished, I scanned the pages for errors, then approached Ian's desk. He was talking with someone on the phone, but his eyes flickered up at me.

One minute, he mouthed, smiling.

After a moment, he hung up and gave me his undivided attention.

"I wonder if you have time to read something for me," I said.

"For you? Always time." He eyed my pages. "What is it?"

"A little something I wrote," I said, placing them on his desk. "I did what you suggested. I wrote something that mattered to me."

I checked over my shoulder as I walked away and saw he was already deep in concentration, reading my words. Minutes later, he stood before me.

"I love it," he said. "In depth, but with such an emotional hook. You should bring this to Mr. Hindmarsh."

My heart swelled with pride. "Really?"

"Absolutely. Want me to come with you? As a supportive colleague, I mean."

"Do you think that would help?"

"Can't hurt, can it?" He handed me back the pages then tilted his head toward the office. "Ready?"

Mr. Hindmarsh's silvery head was bent over his desk, studying an article, but his small, heavy-lidded eyes showed interest when he looked up and saw Ian behind me.

I cleared my throat. "Mr. Hindmarsh, I wrote something that I'd like you to read, if you have the time."

He adjusted his black-rimmed glasses on his nose. "I'm very busy, Miss Ryan."

"You should take a look," Ian said smoothly. "Perfect for what you were talking about at the last editorial meeting. Local interest, poverty, veterans . . . She nailed it."

Mr. Hindmarsh lifted one eyebrow and looked from Ian to me. "Is that right, Mr. Collins?"

The revered managing editor of the *Star* held out his hand, and I gave him my precious story. "Thank you, Mr. Hindmarsh."

I turned to go, but Ian reached for my arm. He gave me a reassuring wink, so I waited beside him, watching Mr. Hindmarsh read.

The editor turned over the first page and set it facedown on his desk. From his deadpan expression, it was impossible to tell what he was thinking. He turned over the second page, and when he was finished, he set all three pages to the side and looked up at me with narrowed eyes.

"I'm very impressed, Miss Ryan," he said. "Have you been keeping all that talent to yourself because you secretly love writing recipes and church notices? Or has Mr. Collins been keeping you too busy with other things?"

I felt heat roar into my face. "No, sir. I would love to write different stories."

"You can do more like this?"

"Yes, sir. I can write anything."

"Excellent to hear, Miss Ryan." He looked at Ian. "Well, Mr. Collins?"

"I'd love to read more by her," he said.

"As would I. Right. This will run tomorrow, if that's all right with you," he said, then he tapped a finger on his desk. "I'm interested in the immigration angle, and how you've brought history right into the present. Could you work on another piece similar to this? 'Where Toronto's From' or something like that."

"I would be happy to." I beamed, despite the fact that I had no idea what I would write.

Back in the newsroom, I floated to my desk with happiness. Ian offered to take me out for a celebratory lunch, but once again I apologized, telling him I had some personal errands to run. Grabbing my handbag, I trotted outside and made a beeline to City Hall, where I asked for recent immigration records and the clerk put my request in a queue. I dashed to the bank to withdraw some money, then I stopped in at Eaton's to spend it. On my way back to the office, I retrieved the records the clerk had collected for me, then I carried them back to the office along with a large, brown paper package, which I tucked under my desk. All afternoon, I kept peeking at the package, humming with excitement as I researched the latest government statistics on immigration. Finally, five o'clock rolled around, and I practically sprinted toward Palermo's, where I knew Mr. Rabinowitz would be.

"What's this?" he asked when I handed him the package.

"Open it," I said, struggling to contain my excitement.

He carefully opened the paper, not wanting to tear it even a little, and deep wrinkles cut into his forehead as he concentrated. I took the wrapping from him as he uncovered the bundle of dark material. Confused, he held it up, watching it unfold then take its shape as a thick, black wool overcoat.

"Very nice," he said, smiling. "A gift for your father?"

I shook my head. "It's for you, Mr. Rabinowitz."

He stared, uncomprehending, then quickly folded up the coat and held it out toward me. "No, no. This is too much."

I put my hands on his. "I hope you will accept it in the spirit it's given. It's actually a thank-you gift. My editor loved your story."

He frowned, confused.

"Yesterday, do you remember that we spoke about your life in Poland?" I pulled out a copy of the story. "My editor wants it to run in tomorrow's paper. I hope you don't mind."

He took the paper, and I held the coat as he read. "Why, I never saw nothing like this in my life," he said softly.

"Is it all right?"

He didn't say anything more as he read, and I bit my lip to calm my nerves.

When he looked up, the faded white of his eyes shone, but his expression was clearer than I'd ever seen.

"I remember now," he said, the words slow and gentle. "Ava. My dear Ava. She was so beautiful, so kind. I loved her very much. The cancer took her from me." A tear rolled down his cheek. "In this terrible world of war and poverty, it's easy to end up alone. You have to remember the good things in life, dear. When you find someone you love and they love you in return, that's a miracle."

Memories stirred within me, and I felt again the wonder of being in Max's arms. Of his lips finding mine. I'd tried so hard to forget, knowing it never should have happened, but now the longing in Mr. Rabinowitz's expression made me want to bring that memory back. To keep it close for the times I felt lost.

He looked at the paper again, shaking his head slightly. "But this story, it's our story. Ava's and mine. I forgot so much. I thought it was all gone." His cold fingers touched my cheek. "Thank you, Molly. For asking me about my life, and for writing it down. It hurts some, remembering she's gone, but it's good to have this."

I blinked back my own tears, then held out the coat. "Will you put it on? Just to see if it fits?"

He examined it closely, his thumbs rubbing the sturdy seams, and I knew he could feel the good quality of the heavy wool. He slipped off his old, ragged coat, and I helped him into the new one. All at once he looked taller. Stronger.

"I don't know how this is a thank-you gift," he said, his voice gravelly with emotion. "You've given me two wonderful gifts today, *sheyne meydel*. I may forget a lot of things, but I promise I will never forget this kindness."

The next day, I flipped through the paper and stopped at page ten, seeing my name printed right above my story about Mr. Rabinowitz, and pride spread through me in a glow. I'd done it; I'd finally broken through. I had earned my place and changed my life again. But even more than that, today I had been given the greatest gift. I would never forget the smile Mr. Rabinowitz had given me in that moment, shining with gratitude. After all the years of wanting to make a difference through my writing, I finally had.

thirteen
MAX

❧

Max dropped his arm over his eyes, shielding them from the dim light within the Sham Shui Po barracks, but that didn't stop his temples from throbbing. Most of the men of D Company, his company within C Force, had left the barracks for the day, leaving only the hush of a few men sleeping or writing letters. Max had overdone it yesterday with that bottle of Johnnie Walker scotch, but he hadn't been able to resist it for only $1.85. Arnie and David had sat across the table from him, downing ten-cent bottles of beer all afternoon, nodding while Max loudly aired out his complaints.

"It's been nearly a year and a half since we signed up," he'd ranted. The scotch had loosened his voice, but he didn't care. He'd been frustrated and quiet about it for months. "Now here we are in Hong Kong, of all places. This wasn't what we signed up for! Eh, Arnie?"

Arnie had wholeheartedly agreed, though he'd happily left the vocalizing to Max.

Today, Arnie and David were out on the streets of Kowloon, enjoying themselves in the sun while Max groaned in his coconut husk mattress. Lesson learned. He'd stick to beer from now on.

Nobody could have predicted the Royal Rifles would end up in Hong Kong. After spending nine chilly months in Gander building runways and hangars, exercising, and fighting boredom, their regiment had taken a train all the way across the country to Vancouver, picking up more men along the way. Max had won the coin toss with Arnie over the window seat, and he'd spent the trip spellbound, staring out at mountains and frothy rivers, blinking as they dove into pitch-black tunnels, then again as they emerged into blinding sunlight. That journey alone had made enlisting worthwhile, he'd thought at the time.

Once in Vancouver, they'd been joined by the Winnipeg Grenadiers. The Grenadiers, like the Royal Rifles, had only ever served on garrison duty, but they'd done it in Jamaica and Bermuda while Max and the others had shivered in Newfoundland. Together they formed C Force. Halfway through October, Sergeant Cox told them they'd be shipping out, but it wasn't until the day after Max, Arnie, David, Richie, and the almost two thousand other men in C Force boarded the *Awatea* and set out that they were told their destination was Hong Kong. They were stunned by the news. Max didn't think he'd even thought about Hong Kong in his entire life. If he had, the place had seemed make-believe. An exotic gem from storybooks, certainly not someplace he'd eventually defend.

"Seems weird to be going to Hong Kong instead of Europe, doesn't it?" Arnie asked one day, standing at the *Awatea*'s rail.

"I guess I don't mind," David replied, the wind riffling through his dark hair. "At least the Pacific will be warmer than the Atlantic. And Hannah will be glad to hear I'm far away from any fighting."

Max sighed. "We might as well be on the North Pole. Garrison duty is all we ever seem to do."

"Oh cheer up, Max." Arnie grinned. "It's a great adventure, you know?

I mean, I know we want to get Hitler, but I gotta say, I'd never be able to travel to Hong Kong if not for the war. I'm kind of looking forward it."

Max's gaze passed over the horizon, at the straight black line of water meeting the greyness of the sky. From the corner of his eye he spotted Richie a little way down the deck, and he looked away. Things between them were like the sea right now: calm, despite a lot of murky currents moving beneath. There were too many unanswered questions, too much unfinished business. Ever since Gander, they'd mostly kept their distance from each other, though when they were put on a rotation together, Richie was cordial. When one of his buddies complained that there wouldn't be a war if it wasn't for Jews, Richie told him to shut up.

"It's not their fault. Hitler's a madman," he'd said, then he'd turned to Max with an apologetic nod.

The gesture had caught Max off guard, and it gave him hope that there might be a chink in the wall between them. At least a possibility to sort things out.

The *Awatea's* first port of call was Honolulu for restocking food and fuel. The harbour was a marvellous site, with the magnificent American fleet of battleships all lined up, floating peacefully at the docks. It seemed ironic to Max that practically the whole world was at war except them. If the U.S. would only join the fight, Max thought, Hitler wouldn't know what hit him.

After a second stop, this time in Manila, C Force arrived on November 16 in Kowloon, Hong Kong's steamy port. They walked down the gangplank in their khaki shorts and short-sleeved shirts to the welcoming strains of a British Army band. Their assignment was to bolster the small, fourteen-thousand-man British garrison against any possible invasion by the Japanese, but they soon discovered that their day-to-day duties consisted mostly of killing time.

"I don't even have to shave my own face!" Arnie had laughed, strolling out of the barracks and into the sunshine after their first night, happily slapping his cheeks. Every member of C Force had been assigned a

Chinese servant, who was paid twenty-five cents a day to shave the soldiers' faces, do their laundry, and generally treat the Canadians like kings.

"Yeah, but you did meet up with that tarantula last night," David teased. "Oh, the way you shrieked! I could have sworn it was your sister."

"I didn't see you rushing in there to grab that thing," Arnie replied.

The Sham Shui Po barracks had been built a decade before as a British Army facility, and its clean, white exterior, surrounded by well-tended parks and gardens actually did feel somewhat like a castle. For the most part, they'd been impressed.

"You'd think they'd have toilets in the barracks though," David grumbled. "Those buckets are disgusting."

After months of grunt work in Gander, the big, beautiful city of Hong Kong was a welcome break. Toilets aside, to Max and the others, who still remembered the shortages and sacrifices of the Depression, it seemed like a place out of the movies. The air was balmy and warm—nothing like the cold weather everyone at home was experiencing—and when they weren't wandering through the city, they got to let out tension in other ways. Max and some of the others took the time to play a little baseball, a few of them having packed a mitt just in case.

At night they were hardly able to see the stars for all the lights of the city. For less than a dollar each, Max, Arnie, David, and the others could eat a feast of rice with tender, savoury toppings of chicken, duck, or fish. Anything to do with shellfish, no matter how delicious it looked, was reluctantly avoided. They might be living in a whole different world over here, but they still had to stick to kosher meals.

The first few nights, they took in all the sights. They danced with beautiful Chinese women at the Dreamland Dance Hall, drank at various taverns, or went roller-skating at the Roller Dome, which was Max's favourite. It wasn't so much the skating that he enjoyed, but watching Arnie battle to stay upright. Max couldn't remember ever laughing so hard as he and David did on those nights. Arnie laughed as well. He was a good sport.

Sheltered within the wild city of Hong Kong, the war seemed very far away. But after a week, the dazzle of the city began to wear off, and Max noticed cracks in the veneer. While popular American music rolled out of the many taverns, Hong Kong's streets overflowed with people in desperate need. Thousands of Chinese refugees flooded in by the day, and Max was haunted by the pleading sounds of orphans crying, "No Mammy, no Daddy, no money! Please, mister!" He did what he could, dropping a few coins into the children's outstretched hands, but it was never enough.

His feelings of helplessness only got worse when he thought about why they were here. Not only were they not in Europe, fighting Nazis, C Force was assigned to garrison duty for a fort that would, according to the experts, never be attacked. According to the Brits, even if the Japanese *did* attack, they only had about five thousand troops gathered across the Chinese border. Those forces, they were told, were weak and had very little artillery support. Their troops were ill-equipped and not used to night fighting—in fact, they avoided it—their aircrafts were basically obsolete, and Japanese pilots were mediocre. There was nothing for Max and the others to worry about, since the Brits stationed outside of Kowloon would make short work of any attempted invasions.

The Allied forces were so confident in the lack of threat that when C Force first arrived in Hong Kong, they discovered all their military vehicles had been diverted to Manila, on orders from the U.S. government. They didn't even have a jeep. As for training, all they had done since they'd arrived were two forty-eight-hour manning exercises of designated areas on Hong Kong island, where they set up barbed wire and familiarized themselves with the area as best they could. Max and Arnie had a refresher in their medic training, which they'd first learned back at Fort York in Toronto. But there was little else.

Right now, Max wished that medic training had included a little more attention paid to hangovers. The headache wasn't going away.

He uncovered his eyes, nudged awake by a velvet touch. "Hey there, Gander," he mumbled.

Gander was a beautiful, purebred Newfoundland dog, practically the size of a pony. He had been given to the Royal Rifles as a mascot during their stay there, and they'd brought him to Hong Kong with them. Now he stood by Max's bunk, pressing his soft muzzle against his hand. Gander could strut at the front of the parade with the dignity of a general and resolutely defend his unit against any curious strays, but he also knew just when to ask a lonely, homesick young man for a scratch.

"You can read my mind, can't you?"

Gander thumped his tail against the cot.

"Mail call!"

With a groan, Max sat up and watched the young corporal sort through the envelopes in his hand. Gander wandered off, distracted by the smell of food coming in from outside.

"Dreyfus!" The corporal shuffled through more mail. "Ryan!"

Down the row, Max saw Richie's hand reach out from an upper bunk, then the corporal made his way toward Max. After handing him an envelope he moved on, calling, "Stevens! Schwartz!"

Smiling, Max slid his finger through the envelope in his hand. It was from Hannah—he recognized her handwriting—and was sure to contain sweet stories about his niece and nephews that reminded him how much he was missing of their lives. He'd vowed to himself that when he got home he'd spend more time with them. Be a proper uncle.

He pulled out her letter, and with it, a newspaper page, which he set aside.

Dear Max,

First of all, I would like to announce that the Dreyfus family genes are running strong in my little family! I wrote to David to warn him: Mama gave Dinah a baseball and a tiny glove a week ago, and you should have seen that little girl's determination. She reminded me so much of you, scowling at herself every time she couldn't catch what I tossed. But then she figured out how to watch the ball, not the thrower, and now she is constantly chasing me around, wanting to play. Well, once Jacob saw that, he wanted to join in, and Mama went right out and bought my three-year-old a ball and glove. The glove is so big on him it keeps flopping his hand over, but I do my best to not laugh. Right now I am holding a napping Aaron on my lap while I watch Dinah and Jacob through the window. She kind of lobs it, he waves his glove around, then she runs to grab the ball before he can. Did we start that way, I wonder?

Max, I've included something extra in this letter. I wasn't sure if I should, but I really wanted you to see. I know you'll be surprised. You and I haven't talked about Molly in a long time—

Max stared at the paper. "Surprised? That's putting it mildly," he said quietly. For a long time, any talk of Molly and the Ryans had been basically prohibited in his family. What had changed?

—and I'm sad to say that she and I rarely see each other these days. I'm so busy with the children, and well, you know. It's hard to fix some things, isn't it? Anyway, she's working for the Star. *I bet you'll be proud to hear that. Enclosed is one of her latest stories. It's actually from a few weeks ago—do you remember Mr. Rabinowitz? It's about him!*

I'd love to write more, but little Aaron is awake and crying now—this boy is always hungry. Dinah says hello to her big, brave uncle (she is such a good girl, thank goodness), so hello from her and everyone here. We miss you so much. Stay safe, brother dear. And promise you'll keep my husband safe. I'm counting on you.

Love,
Hannah

Max's fingers trembled a little as he unfolded the sheet of newspaper, and his heart gave a little thump when he saw the name Molly Ryan, in small letters beneath the headline. *IRA RABINOWITZ: A PORTRAIT OF TORONTO'S LIVING HISTORY.* He ran his fingers over the ink, feeling a rush of affection for her despite all the years between them. The only other time he'd read something of hers was a letter to the editor that she'd written years ago, after the riot.

His eyes fell to the story that followed, and his mind recalled Mr. Rabinowitz as he'd last seen him, seven or eight years ago. Molly's story brought the old man to life. Max hadn't known about his early life in Poland and had never thought about him fighting in a war, let alone earning a medal for valour. Nor had he known about Mr. Rabinowitz's six children, who had married and moved away, spreading across Canada. All he'd ever really seen was a broken man with sad, rheumy eyes. At the bottom of the article, Hannah had paper clipped an addendum, and emotion swelled in his chest when he read that Mr. Rabinowitz's grown children had contacted the *Star* three weeks after Molly's article had run. They had been searching for their father for years.

"Oh, Molly," he said softly.

He dropped his head into his hand and rubbed his face, hearing her voice in her words, then he skimmed his finger over the letters, marveling at what she had done. Somehow, despite everything stacked against her, she'd found a way to achieve her dream.

God, he missed her.

"She's pretty good, isn't she?"

Startled, Max glanced up to see Richie in front of him, peering down at the letter.

"Yeah," he said, quickly folding it up and tucking it away. He and Richie had never spoken about Molly. "She really is."

"She worked hard for it," Richie said. "She went to night school while she was still at Eaton's. I remember how tired she was back then, but she'd been determined. You know how she was. Once she had something on her mind."

Max nodded. He remembered everything about her.

"After journalism school, she kept saying she wanted to work for the *Star*, but I never figured she'd really do it." A gentle smile curled his mouth. "But she did."

It was then that Max felt the wall between them begin to crumble, and with it his reservations. He set Hannah's letter and the envelope aside, then nodded toward the paper in Richie's hand. "What's that?"

Richie took a seat on the bunk across from him and held up his letter. "It's from my wife, Barbara. I don't think you ever met her. You got a girl back home?"

Max shook his head.

From his envelope, Richie pulled out a photograph, then passed it over. "That's Barbara with our daughter, Evelyn. She's three now. And that's the new one, Joan. I've actually never met her, which is kind of hard to fathom. Anyway, Barbara says she's a real talker." He chuckled. "You know what I mean. She's too little to say anything, but she's always saying something."

Max felt a twinge of envy, seeing Richie's happiness. They were both twenty-nine years old, and Richie had created his own little family. Max had never married, much to his mother's dismay. After Molly, no one had been able to hold his interest. Seeing Richie's little girls and the pride in their father's eyes pushed a knot of regret into Max's throat.

"They're beautiful," he said, passing the photo back. "I can't tell from the photo. Did they inherit your red hair?"

Richie flushed slightly, taking another peek at the photo before replacing it in the envelope. "They did, poor kids."

"They must miss you very much."

"I guess. I sure miss them. When I got letters in Newfoundland, it didn't seem so far. Here, well, it's a world away. If I didn't have the photographs from Barbara, I'm afraid I'd forget their little faces." He frowned at Max. "Sometimes these letters are hard to read. I mean, Barbara tells me all the little stories, but I hate that I'm not there to see for myself. Will my kids even remember me?"

"They'll remember you. You'll be back before they're grown."

"I hope so."

"I know what you mean, though," Max said, thinking of home. "If I'm not going to be useful in this war, then I want to be with my family."

Richie nodded. "I mean, it's okay here, right? We're all making friends, doing what we're told to do. We're safe. Nobody's shooting us or anything. But when I see Barbara's writing, or Molly's or Mum's, I just . . . I miss the old life. Remember how easy it was when we were kids?"

Max bristled. "It wasn't always easy."

Richie shifted, his expression tight with regret. "I know. But you and I, we were best friends, weren't we? I mean, before we blew it. We were like brothers. Once."

Max's heart clenched. Richie was right. That's why his betrayal with Phil and the others had hurt so deeply. "Once," he echoed quietly.

Richie continued on, saying more than Max had ever heard. "Nobody ever stood up for me like you did. You always did the right thing. You're the reason I became a cop, you know. I wanted to do the right thing too. Especially after what I did to you. I messed up," Richie admitted in a rush. "I never should have . . . well, there are a lot of things I shouldn't have done. I never should have sided against you, not at the beach that day, not at Christie Pits. Back then, I thought I was tough, you know? One of the boys, going around, scaring people. But I know better now. And when I look at you, I can see how much you hate me. Honestly? I can't stand that. I don't want us to be on opposite sides anymore."

Regret tumbled through Max's chest. "I never really hated you. I was angry. And I was hurt. I mean, I understood why we'd drifted apart, but—"

"Well, you're a better man than I." Richie's gaze dropped to the floor. "That night at the ball game, I was scrapping halfway up the hill when

I saw Phil go after Molly. I wanted to get down there to help, but the bastard I was fighting wouldn't leave off. When I looked again, I saw you deck him, then I saw her with you."

Max closed his eyes. Even after all these years, all the promises he had made to himself that he'd forget her, he could still feel Molly's lips on his.

"I gotta tell you," Richie said, staring at his hands, clenched on his lap. "If I'd been there, I would have gone after you. You know I would have. Then I saw Dad start beating you, and he looked like he'd never stop. And there was Molly, throwing herself on you like a shield." He stilled, then he looked up, his eyes bright with emotion. "It was like somebody turned on the lights for me, and I could see clearly what was happening. Seeing Dad like that, I realized I'd been an ass all along. You and Molly were both adults. It was between the two of you. But I'd started looking at you the way other people did. I had no right. I was your friend. I owed you better than that, and I want you to know that I really am sorry."

Max's chest tightened. After all this time, all the years of feeling betrayed by his best friend, he'd almost given up on ever hearing those words.

"Why now?" he had to know. "Why did you wait so long?"

"I don't know. I guess I was afraid at first. But I've had a lot of spare time since then to think about you, about my family, about this war, about a lot of things. And I've realized that I can't put off fixing what I broke. What if we go to war and something happens?"

"Nothing's gonna happen."

He flashed a reluctant smile. "Yeah, well, in case it does, just know I'm sorry."

"I don't know what to say," Max admitted. "I never expected this."

"Are we good, you and me?"

Max nodded, feeling lighter than he had in a long time. Even his hangover was gone. "Season opener," he said, holding out his hand. "Fresh start."

Richie took it, and the relief that spread over his face felt the same as what filled Max's heart.

Richie started to get up, then he stopped. "There's one more thing I gotta get off my chest, though."

"What is it?" Max asked.

He cleared his throat. "Leaving Molly like that with no goodbye, no message or anything. You should have written to her. It's a small man who would break a girl's heart like that."

Heat rushed into Max's face. "What are you talking about? The minute I got to Kingston I sent her a letter and asked her to write back. She never did. It's not me that ended it."

Richie rubbed his brow. "That doesn't make sense. She was devastated after you left."

"I wrote."

"Well, I know for a fact that she never got a letter from you."

Max felt dizzy with realization. "That means she thought that I . . ."

He knew how much he'd hurt, thinking she didn't want to be with him, but unlike her, Max had escaped Toronto. She'd been there all this time, seeing his house every day, living in the middle of all the memories. *God, Molly. I'm so sorry.* He never should have given up so fast. He should have written again.

"How is she?" he asked Richie.

"She's happy, I think. She loves her job." He paused. "She's dating someone, Barbara told me."

So she hadn't married. Molly had always insisted on putting her career first. Now that she was doing so well, was he too late to give it another shot?

Once Richie had walked away, Max reached for his stationery, took a deep breath, then started to write.

Dear Molly,

I never thought I'd write to you again, but here I am. I hope it's okay, after all this time . . .

fourteen
MOLLY

❧

"Did you eat?" Mum called as I came inside, shutting the first December storm behind me.

Even before I stepped into the living room, I knew she and Dad were in there. I could hear the clicking of Mum's knitting needles and the flapping of Dad's paper. The warm breath of the woodfire touched my cheeks, welcoming me into our quiet home of three.

"I did, thanks," slipping off my gloves and hat. I shook the hat over the doormat, sprinkling it with the melted remnants of a miserable freezing rain, then unbuttoned my coat. "I'm sorry I didn't call. I was working late on a new story."

I was surprised to see an envelope lying on the counter, addressed to me from Hong Kong. Even more surprising was that it wasn't Richie's handwriting. I carried it into the living room and slumped onto the chair, where I readily peeled my feet out of my shoes and sighed with relief. It had been a long day of researching, writing, and rewriting my third piece in the Toronto series Mr. Hindmarsh wanted, and I'd been ready for home hours before. Ian had brought me a sandwich from the deli across the street, then we'd spoken awhile. It was nice. Ian knew how to get me out of my head when I needed to take a break.

"Knitting?" Mum hinted, lifting her needles.

"I will. I just need a few minutes to relax first," I said. Wool socks, hats, and mitts were in perpetual demand overseas these days. I'd lost track of just how many men I could have dressed with all my knitting. Were any of my brothers warming their toes in my socks?

"Those Germans just can't get a foothold in Russia, can they?" Dad asked from behind his paper.

Now that I was at the *Star*, he had started reading it more than the *Telegram*, and he loved to start up conversations with me about the latest news. It kept me on my toes. The *Star* was a busy place, and I didn't always know the headlines. Fortunately, I did tonight.

"Well, it's minus thirty or so up there," I said. "I'm surprised they're even bothering. It's not nearly that here, but I'm still shivering and I've been home for two or three minutes."

"Your father served in Russia," Mum said, her eyes on her needles.

"Russia?" I knew Dad had served in the Great War, but he'd never spoken about where he'd been deployed. Not even when Richie signed up. "Why didn't you ever say anything, Dad?"

"You never asked." He lowered the paper to his lap. "Nobody talks about that part of it anyway."

"Why not? I want to know about it," I said, tucking my feet under me.

"Because it happened after the rest of the world had already declared peace. I was a gunner with the Sixty-Seventh Battery. We were sent to protect Allied assets in Russia from the incoming Germans, but things got complicated."

He looked like he might stop there, so I prodded a little. "How?"

"We were working with what they called the White Russians, but those folks were also fighting with the Red Army. We got caught in the middle, you could say. It's not a good story."

Mum was watching him with a soft expression in her eyes. "It's okay, Garret. She can handle it."

He considered what she'd said, then nodded. "All right. It was November, and colder than you could believe. Lots of snow, and our big guns were stuck in it. When the Red Army troops came up on us, they came from the rear, and we couldn't get the artillery turned." He shook his head, remembering. "The rest of the men spread out, covering us with their rifles while we wrestled those things. They managed to hold the Reds off until the Brits arrived with reinforcements." He frowned at his paper, remembering. "We lost two men. A couple of days later, the Reds killed two more of our guys on reconnaissance patrol. When we found them, they'd been hacked apart by axes."

I wasn't sure what to say. "Oh, Dad. I'm so sorry. That must have been awful."

"And damn cold," he muttered, his nostrils flared. "I wouldn't wish that patrol on anyone." After a pause, he shook the paper and held it up like a shield. "Think the Americans are ever gonna get into this thing?" he asked, steering the conversation to less painful ground.

I was grateful he'd finally shared a piece of his past with me. "Well, there's no rush, Dad. I mean, our own men haven't even seen any action yet."

"And thank the Lord for that," Mum said. She turned to me. "I notice you've been spending quite a bit of time with the Collins boy these days, Molly."

I smiled, imagining Ian's reaction. "He's what, twenty-nine? I don't think I'd call him a boy, Mum."

"Why's he not fighting?" Dad wanted to know.

"He has a substantial heart murmur, according to the doctor."

Dad's eyes narrowed, assessing the idea.

"But you like him, don't you, Molly?" Mum pressed.

I knew what she was asking, obviously. And I knew Ian was thinking along the same lines as she was, but I still wasn't ready to commit to anything beyond dating.

"I'm having fun with him, Mum. That's all for now. He's a smart, funny man, and we enjoy each other's company."

"Good," she said. "But don't wait too long."

Dad was still stewing about Ian's heart defect. "Don't rush into it, either."

Outside, a wintery blast rattled the window, and I turned to my letter, sliding my finger under the flap of the envelope.

> *Dear Molly,*
>
> *I never thought I'd write to you again, but here I am. I hope it's okay, after all this time.*

I caught my breath, and my eyes dropped to the signature: three little letters that set my world alight.

"Molly? Are you all right?" Mum asked, dropping her knitting to her lap.

"I'm . . . I got a letter from Max," I said, barely aware my parents were still in the room. My lips felt numb with adrenaline. I brought the paper closer, squinting at it in the dim light of the lamp beside me.

> *What a day I had. First, Hannah sent the article you wrote for the* Star *about Mr. Rabinowitz. My God, Molly. I had no idea you were working there. Congratulations! Your writing is beautiful. Your portrait of Mr. Rabinowitz really made me think.*

He'd read my article! My heart flipped at the thought. I read those lines again, thinking of Hannah this time, and I felt a stab of regret, realizing how long it had been since she and I had last spoken. I didn't realize she knew I was at the *Star*. I'd heard from someone that she'd had another baby, but her home with David wasn't in the old neighbourhood, and their new place was out of the way.

Just after I finished reading it, I had a real heart-to-heart
with Richie. It was actually the best conversation we've had
in years. He said—

Max and Richie were in the same *battalion*? When I looked up, my
parents were watching me intently.

"Did you know Max and Richie were in C Force together?" I
asked.

Mum leaned forward, worry in her eyes. "He wrote about Richie? Is
Richie all right? Did something happen?"

"No, no. Richie's fine. In fact, he and Max seem to be patching things
up." I followed his messy writing. "He says . . . he says . . ." I stopped, my
blood running cold at his words.

I touched my finger to his signature again, then lowered the letter.

"What is it?" Mum asked.

"Max says he wrote to me a long time ago," I said slowly. In my mind
I finished the sentence: to see if we could make things work. "But I never
got anything from him. I can't understand it."

My parents looked sideways at each other.

"What?" I asked, my skin prickling with uncertainty.

"Molly dear," Mum said carefully. "Your father and I felt, well, things
being what they were, and Max being what he was, we thought it would
be better—"

I stared, my mouth hanging open as her words started tripping out,
faster and faster.

"What did you do?" I whispered, sick to my stomach.

"It was for your own good," she said.

Dad cleared his throat. "We thought it was better this way. Now,
it might not have been the right thing to do, looking back, but at the
time—"

"What did you do?" I demanded again.

"We burned his first letter."

"You *burned* it?"

"But we didn't read it," Mum said, as if that made everything all right. "We never did. We just thought if you didn't know it had come, you wouldn't think about him so much. You could move on."

"Things were heated back then," Dad explained. "With everything that had happened between the two of you—"

"Then his father with the brick, and your father getting so ill," Mama added, putting her hand on his.

I could hardly breathe. Bracing myself against the arms of my chair, I got to my feet, feeling off-balance.

"The brick?" I glared at Dad. "Let's finally be honest about this. Nobody knows who threw the stupid brick. Even if it *was* Mr. Dreyfus, can you blame him? You attacked Max. You were in a rage. You even scared me. If Mr. Dreyfus did throw it, he did it to protect his son. Wouldn't you have done the same thing to protect Richie, or any of us?"

They were watching me with a sort of horror, like children who'd been caught out on something. I wanted to feel bad for them, but all I felt was rage. How *could* they?

I took a shaky breath. "Dad, I'm sorry you were hurt that night. I'm sorry any of it happened. For so long I blamed myself. I kept thinking that if you hadn't felt you needed to rescue me, if I'd listened and never gone to that game, none of this would have happened."

I wished I had a thousand more things to say, to get my anguish out in the open and let my parents experience every tormented heartbeat I felt whenever I'd thought of Max over the last eight years. I shook his letter in the air.

"But now this. For years, he thought that I— Oh, God. Do you know what you did to him? To me? You broke our hearts." Bile burned in my throat as I tried to understand. How could they have done this, then kept it from me for so many years? "You, with your 'knowing better'! I don't care 'what' he was. He was Max."

"Molly," Dad said quietly. "It could never have worked out, and you know it. He's Jewish. You're not. It isn't allowed on either side."

"No, Dad. You don't understand. You never did. It was never about sides." I hugged Max's letter to my chest and looked into their eyes. "It was never about a Jew and a Protestant. It was about Max and me."

fifteen
MAX

❧

"Max! Get over here! You gotta hear this!" Arnie shouted, a note of panic in his voice.

Max was just walking into the barracks when he heard Arnie shouting at him. He, David, and others were gathered around the radio by their bunks, and Max heard the announcer's voice chopping urgently through the static.

"What's going on?" Max asked, ducking through the bunks toward them.

David waved him over. "Japan just attacked Pearl Harbour. They're blowing up all those beautiful battleships we saw. They bombed Honolulu, too."

"What are the Japanese doing in America?" Max asked, stunned.

"Shhh! It's still going on," David said, leaning in to the radio.

"Hello NBC. Hello NBC. This is KGU in Honolulu, Hawaii. I am speaking from the roof of the Advertiser Publishing

Company building. We have witnessed this morning the distant view of a brief, full battle of Pearl Harbour and the severe bombing of Pearl Harbour by enemy planes, undoubtedly Japanese."

"Listen to that," Arnie said, his face pale. "It sounds like total ruin."

Word of the attack spread through the barracks, and the crowd jostled behind Max, trying to hear. He and the others stayed by the radio all morning, listening to updates.

"The city of Honolulu has also been attacked and considerable damage done. This battle has been going on for nearly three hours."

"Why would they do that?" Arnie asked. "America wasn't even in the war."

"It was only a matter of time," Richie said, his hands tucked tight under his armpits.

Max nodded, thinking it through. "They would have probably joined the war soon, and the only way anyone could get ahead of them would be with a surprise attack. They're in it now. They have no choice."

"But what does this mean to us?" Richie asked.

"Means the Japs are busy over there," someone replied. "Means we're safe."

But over the next few hours, the radio crackled with updates, and Max felt tension snapping through the room like a live wire. Japan had gone on to attack the Philippines, then they'd invaded Malaysia. Six hours after Pearl Harbour, the Japanese bombed Hong Kong's airfield, which was being defended by the British forces.

"They've destroyed five RAF planes," one of the men reported, returning to the barracks with updates.

"The Brits will fight them off," Richie said. "Right? They told us it would never come to anything."

Max wished he could reassure him. "I don't know."

"Don't say that," Richie said, holding his gaze. "You never say that."

Arnie let out a slow breath. "I used to think my brother was the one in a scary position, whenever he heads to Europe. Now I wish I was Samuel. This place is in trouble."

Max was positive he wasn't the only one who didn't sleep that night. Try as he might to calm his mind, he could sense the danger drawing closer by the hour. The next day, word got out that the Japanese were in sight of the main British defences and had set up artillery. Max went to Sergeant Cox and asked what was going to happen, but the sergeant said the Canadians hadn't been issued any orders. While the Brits battled the invaders, Max and the rest of C Force paced the barracks, and thousands of Chinese refugees loaded what they had onto wagons. When he asked one of them where they'd go, they waved their busy hands and vaguely said north, then west, toward the New Territories. They'd fled the Japanese before. They'd witnessed what the enemy was capable of doing, and they weren't sticking around to see it again.

On December 10, three days after the Japanese sank most of the American battleships, they torpedoed the British Royal Navy's HMS *Prince of Wales* and HMS *Repulse* in the South China Sea.

"We have to get moving," Max muttered, bracing himself against Arnie's bunk. He felt like a trapped animal. "We have to either fight or retreat. They've sunk all the ships. No one's coming to help us."

But the sense of urgency Max and most of the others felt appeared to be lost on the men in charge. Sergeant Cox maintained a stony expression, though Max could tell from the way his eyes constantly scanned the area around him that he was as confused as the rest of them. Everyone kept repeating what they'd been told, that the Brits would beat the Japs back, and they'd never make it to Kowloon. All they could do was sit tight and hope the people in charge were right.

"Richie," Max said, watching his friend pace. Richie's hands opened and closed, opened and closed, and Max recognized the need to use them. "Let's toss a ball."

Without a word, Richie ducked under his cot and pulled out his glove, and they headed behind the barracks.

"We haven't done this in a while," Max said, pitching.

The ball slapped into Richie's glove. "Feels good," he said.

After they'd thrown the ball back and forth a few times, Richie spoke up. "You remember that incredible game against the Sons? When we were sixteen? You were the best."

"*We* were," Max said. "The two of us. Those were the days, weren't they?"

Richie didn't speak for a couple of pitches, then he paused, holding the ball. "I think we're in trouble here, Max. This feels like the night of the riot, you know? When everybody knew it was gonna be a brawl to remember, but none of the cops showed up. That's how I feel right now. Like, why isn't anybody doing anything?"

Max punched his glove, nodding. He knew the feeling exactly. "We're supposed to pretend it isn't happening."

Richie's eyes went to the sky. "What's that?"

Max turned, startled by the sight of airplanes coasting in on the horizon, traveling swiftly in a wide V. "Think they're ours, coming from Singapore?"

"Sure hope so."

Something dropped from one of the approaching planes, and Max frowned, squinting to see. Then he made out more of the small dark objects tumbling from the sky, and he saw smoke plume up. From somewhere inside the barracks, Gander began to bark hysterically. All at once Max understood, and he and Richie exchanged a look of horror.

"Get inside!" Max shouted.

The first explosion hit the street a block away, and they ran for all they were worth. The *rat-tat-tat!* of machine-gun fire came from the planes closing in behind them, drawing ever closer. At the entrance to the barracks, they threw themselves inside just as the bullets strafed the walls of the building.

"Under the bunks!" Sergeant Cox ordered, and Max and Richie dove under the iron beds as the others had, flinching when something crashed outside. Max turned his head to look at Richie beneath the next bunk, and saw his eyes were closed, his lips moving in prayer.

Half an hour later, when the bombing had ended, they peeled themselves off the floor, stiff from tension and fear.

"That's it," Cox said. "We're out of here tonight."

They got the evacuation orders at last, and C Force set out under cover of darkness. Relieved to finally be in motion, Max slung his pack and rifle over his back and set out into the night, quietly marching behind the others as they evacuated the mainland. They boarded the ferry to cross the narrow Lye Mun Passage to Hong Kong Island, and Max looked back in shocked silence as they set off. Behind them, nothing could be seen of the British-Indian company of courageous Rajput soldiers, left to guard the hill called Devil's Peak, the Brits' final hope of holding the mainland. Ahead of them loomed the forbidding island of Hong Kong, made almost entirely of steep, granite mountains. He could see no escape either way.

Arnie's eyes were wide with panic. "What are we supposed to do once we land there? We have no big guns, no ammo." He patted his belt, touching a grenade buckled there. "I don't even know how to use one of these."

At Hong Kong Island, C Force was split into two groups. The Winnipeg Grenadiers were sent west, while the Royal Rifles covered the east side of the island. As soon as they were organized, Max and the rest of D Company positioned themselves along the water's edge and waited. For five days, they watched explosions rock the mainland. On the fifth day, it fell under Japanese control. Max didn't need Cox to tell him the

Japanese's next target was Hong Kong Island. The enemy was on its way.

As night deepened, Max, Arnie, and David shivered in the muggy night, partly hidden in a ditch. Cox and some of the other senior soldiers were holed up behind them, inside a cement bunker that had been built decades before for the last war. There were tunnels, too, but most were too old and cracked to offer any sort of passage. Max knew, because they had explored them during an earlier exercise on the island. About ten feet away, Max made out Richie's profile, then his pale red hair, just as grey as everyone else's in the moonlight. Richie gave him a nod of encouragement, and Max did his best to appear just as confident, but nothing could reassure him about tonight. He slid his eyes away from his old friend and studied the dark water stretching before them, indistinguishable from the sky.

Waiting, he thought. Waiting was the worst part.

But he had a feeling that was almost over.

David slid closer. "With all this going on, did you guys remember it's Chanukah? Hannah and the kids will be gathered around your mama's table, eating latkes and playing dreidel."

"Pretty dark out here," Arnie said quietly. "Sure could use a menorah right about now."

Max closed his eyes, picturing his family around the candles. He could almost hear the warm voices of years past, filled with laughter and love. *If I don't come home*, he thought, *know that I love you all.*

David patted Max's back. "Don't worry. It won't happen tonight. One of the Brits told me the Japanese never attack at night. He said they have real bad night vision and they get seasick in the dark. Something to do with the shape of their eyes."

Max shot him a look. "That's bologna. Arnie and I studied ophthalmology in our classes," he said quietly. "Everybody's eyes work the same."

David's expression fell.

Max slowed his breathing and focused on the air around him,

searching for a sign the enemy was near. A sound. A flicker of metal. A whisper bouncing off the surface of the water. His senses were so heightened his body was alight with nerves, and he had to force himself to stay calm. *Breathe in, breathe out.* It was getting harder by the second. He could sense the enemy coming. He could feel their approach in his bones.

"Ever have that nightmare where you're onstage and everyone's watching, but you have no idea what you're supposed to do?" Arnie muttered. "That's where I am right now."

Hours passed, and dawn peered over the horizon in a glimmer of orange. Max's eyes were gritty from lack of sleep. He sniffed the air and his stomach rolled with near panic.

"They're almost here."

The whites of David's eyes glowed in the morning darkness. "How do you know?"

He couldn't place exactly how, but he was certain. "You remember playing ball, Arnie?" Down the way, he saw the flash of Richie's smile. He was listening. Max had a feeling Richie sensed exactly what was vibrating through Max's veins right now. "You know when you're in the field and you don't know if a runner's gonna go or stick between bases, but you only have a second to decide? You gotta kind of open your mind, listen with all your senses. That's what this feels like."

He took a long, slow breath, and a tingle raced over his body. He sank a little lower into the ditch.

"They're here."

Suddenly there was a deafening *boom!* and a geyser of water shot into the air as shelling started up from the mainland. The next moment the ground shook beneath Max with the impact of an explosion, and they ducked under a shower of rocks, dirt, and shattered trees. All at once, orange bullet trails streaked through the air, and Max peeked briefly over the edge of the ditch. That's when he caught a glimpse of men in boats.

Max fired straight ahead. "Aim for wherever those shots are coming from, Arnie!"

"I can't see anything!" Arnie cried.

Max grabbed the cold barrel of Arnie's rifle and pointed it. "Just shoot that way!" he yelled. "Watch for flashes of gunfire. Maybe we'll hit someone."

All at once Max could see the enemy, moving smoothly and confidently through the dark, climbing from their boats and closing the distance between them like fog on a warm winter night. Max fired back, visibility better now that the enemy was close enough to see, but it was obvious right away that he and the others were vastly outnumbered. Max felt something hard being shoved into his hand, and he looked down.

"Throw it," Arnie said, gesturing at the grenade. "I don't know how."

"Me neither," Max said.

"Maybe not, but you can throw like nobody else."

Max knew the mechanics, but they'd never been trained on how to use a grenade. Praying he had it right, Max yanked out the pin, launched it, then crouched beside Arnie. The waiting seemed to go on far too long, then there was an explosion that shook the earth. When Max peeked out, he saw nothing but smoke.

"Retreat!" Sergeant Cox yelled. "Retreat! Head to the rendezvous in the mountains."

In the days leading up to this, they'd committed the rendezvous location to heart, and Max knew it was a mile on, in a small cleft between two mountains. He braced then leapt out of the ditch, ducking and swerving in a zigzag pattern, firing backwards as he went, with bullets slicing *zip! zip! zip!* through the grass all around. David and Arnie ran beside him; he could hear their panicked breathing. As they raced past the concrete bunker, he heard one of the senior officers inside shouting into the telephone.

"We need artillery now, dammit! They're here on the island! The Japs are here! We need assistance!" A pause. Then, "No, sir, I ain't dreaming, for Christ's sake. Don't tell me they aren't here. They're shooting down my men while I stand here arguing with you. Get troops down here right away!"

Max kept running, David at his right, and through the darkness he spotted familiar uniforms ahead. He lost sight of them through the trees, then found them again and shifted direction to meet up with the others. *Maybe I'll make it after all*, he thought.

White pain suddenly shot through his thigh, driving him to the ground. His cheek pressed against the sticky wet mud, and through the searing pain, his mind returned to medical school: *Had the bullet gone through? Was it still in there? How close to the femoral artery was it? Could he stop the bleeding?*

David dove flat beside him, took a look at Max's leg, then glanced nervously around. They were in the open, right where they shouldn't be, and Japanese bullets were tearing through the space, grazing leaves and pinging off rocks. David lunged for Max, grabbing him under his arms and dragging him behind a boulder. Temporarily hidden, they made themselves as small as they could and watched the enemy hustle past.

"You're the medic," David panted once they were alone. "What do I do?"

Max peered at his leg in the shadow of the jungle. From what he could see, it was bleeding freely, but it looked like the bullet had only winged him. As long as he didn't bleed to death or develop an infection, it wasn't going to kill him.

He reached for the first aid pack. "You need to make a tourniquet," he said.

David followed his instructions, drawing a strap tight while Max gritted his teeth against the pain. When that was done, Max looked around, shocked by what he saw. He wasn't the only one who had been hit. All around him, the wounded writhed on the ground, tangled among many who lay perfectly still. As their medic, Max knew he had to help them, but he was injured as well, and the enemy still lurked. A bullet chipped into the rocks nearby, and David dropped lower beside him.

Max made a decision. "Go, David. I'm okay."

"Leave you? How can I do that?"

"It's all right." He looked out at the wounded. "I have to try to help the others."

"I can stay."

"For what? You know how to do what I have to do?"

David said nothing.

"Go on. I'll see you at the rendezvous." When David stayed in place, obviously torn, Max shoved him. "Go! Get outta here! I need you to stay alive or else Hannah will kill me. And then where will we be? Go on."

David scowled, reluctant. "You be careful, Max."

"You too. Get going."

David took off, and Max shimmied on his forearms toward the closest body, but he didn't recognize what was left of the man. When the gunfire paused, he struggled to his feet, breath hissing through his teeth at the pain in his thigh. He checked unsuccessfully for a pulse on another man then moved on again, knowing time was running out. He couldn't stay out here alone for long; he had to get to the rendezvous. The pain from his leg suddenly knifed through the rest of him, and he stumbled onto one knee. *Come on*, he told himself. *It's just a cut. You'll get worse if you stay here.*

"Max."

Richie lay thirty feet away, flat on his back.

Max didn't hesitate. Steeling himself, he rushed to Richie, flinching and dodging as bullets rained around him. *Hang on, Richie.* His friend's face was smeared black and bloody, and his green eyes were dim with pain. Gasping at the burn in his own leg, Max dropped to the ground and took in Richie's wounds, swallowing back his grief. Richie's arm was mangled and pulsing blood, he had a long, deep gash under one eye, and his trousers were slick with blood. Max knew immediately that there was little he could do for him. Not here, anyway.

But Richie's red-rimmed eyes stared up at him, so old and so very young all over again, and so full of trust.

Max lowered his face to his friend's. "I can't lie. It's bad."

"I know."

"I'll do what I can," he promised.

The arm was Richie's worst injury by far, and it was really bad. A grenade had done this. Bone, muscle, tissue, all of it mashed together from halfway down his upper arm to what was left of his fingers. Max scrambled to stop the bleeding, furtively watching for enemy soldiers as he worked, rocked by explosions and hunted by random machine-gun fire. He had to get Richie out of here. Normally the army would have set up a field station to take in the wounded, but there had been no chance to do that. That's when Max remembered the old cement tunnel near the bunker. It wasn't guaranteed safe, but it could at least provide some kind of shelter.

"Richie," he said, but Richie's eyes were closed, his jaw slack.

Max jammed his fingers against his friend's neck, searching for a pulse, then relaxed slightly. It was there, just weak. He'd lost consciousness, which was a blessing. When there was a lull in the gunfire, Max grabbed Richie's good arm, hauling his dead weight backward, the way he'd come. The movement jarred Richie awake, and he screamed, reaching for his wounded arm, but Max couldn't stop.

"Hang on, Richie. Don't touch your arm. Just gotta get you under cover." Shooting started up again, and Max dropped onto his stomach beside Richie. "We're almost there."

Richie howled, every tendon in his neck strained. "It's too much!"

Max grabbed for his pack, searched through it, then closed his hand around one of the five tubes of morphine tartrate. Richie never felt the needle go in, but Max saw its effect almost immediately.

When the gunfire moved off, Max resumed his mission, and when he finally reached the tunnel, he discovered he wasn't the first one there. Someone had thought of its protective walls already, and half a dozen men clustered inside, most of them badly wounded. Others stood guard.

The man who seemed to be in charge directed Max to a spot near the back, eyeing Richie as he went. "We'll stay here as long as we can, then we'll take him to St. Stephen's."

Max reluctantly lowered Richie to the ground. St. Stephen's College hospital was in Stanley, at the very south end of the island, and Max had serious doubts that Richie could wait that long before having something done. He was pale as ice, his breathing catching as he laboured through the pain.

Max hesitated, feeling sick. He knew what he had to do to save Richie, or at least to try. He'd done it once before at the hospital in Kingston. But he could never have imagined doing it in this humid, filthy environment with enemy soldiers firing on them. And never, ever to a friend.

"I can't save your arm," he told him. "There's not much left of it. It's gotta come off."

Tears squeezed from the corners of Richie's eyes. "Just don't leave me, Max. Don't leave me here to die."

"I'm right here, Richie. I won't leave you."

Max didn't have a lot of time, and he didn't have the right instruments. He pulled out what he had, then shoved a folded leather strap into Richie's mouth.

"Bite down hard," he said.

Richie passed out almost immediately, and Max was glad of it. As he worked, cutting the remaining tissue, severing the bone, he tried not to remember running the bases with his old friend, chasing each other through the neighbourhood, wrestling just for the fun of it. He needed to focus, to remember his training, not his past. When the worst of the rough surgery was done, he bound the wound as tightly as he could, then tossed the ruined limb deeper into the tunnel before moving on to Richie's leg. The bleeding there had stopped for now, and Max saw it was a superficial gunshot wound, not too different from his own. He taped it up then moved to the deep shrapnel cut on Richie's cheek. As he did that, Richie's eyes opened, tired beyond words.

"Is it done?"

"I did the best I could."

Richie blinked up at him. "I know, Max. You always have." His voice was low, slurred by the morphine and the pain. "I'm sorry. For everything."

"It's okay. It's okay," Max managed, his voice cracking as he pressed his forehead to Richie's, praying to God they would both survive. "We're okay now, you and me. And we'll be home soon. You'll see Barbara and your girls, and we'll have lots of stories to tell them."

Richie hesitated, then he blinked, sending tears down both sides of his face. "Reach into my jacket pocket," he said hoarsely, tilting his head toward it. "Take out the envelope."

Max dug inside, trying not to jar Richie too much, then he pulled out an envelope that had obviously been folded and unfolded many times.

"It's for my family." Richie swallowed. "I need you to send it for me."

His heart twisted, and he had to force words through his throat. "You can send it yourself."

"I know I can count on you, Max. Please."

Max tucked it into his own pocket, by his heart, praying Richie was right.

A couple of soldiers squatted beside them then carefully lifted Richie onto a stretcher.

Max held his friend's tortured gaze. "You'll be okay, Richie. I'll see you at St. Stephen's, all right?"

"We got him," one of the men said. "Get back out there and do what you have to do, soldier. We'll get him and the others out if we can."

Max watched them carry Richie away, his chest constricting with loss. He didn't want to leave, but he had to get moving. He peered through the hanging smoke, listening for threats and searching for an opening. The enemy seemed to have cleared out, in pursuit of Max's friends, giving him an opportunity. When he was sure it was safe, he darted out then stopped short, disoriented. It all looked the same: the jungle, the darkness, the smoke, and the bodies scattered everywhere, their blood smeared black in the early, dappled sunlight. He didn't know which way to go. Then he heard a burst of bullets, and he turned toward the sound, running as fast as he could. Along the way, he recognized landmarks and picked up his pace, closing in on the rendezvous location. Finally, he stumbled into the clearing, and Arnie and David rushed to him, their faces smeared with dirt and sweat.

"What took you so long?" Arnie asked.

He told them about Richie, and their faces fell. They might not have been close, but they'd grown up with Richie. He was one of them, and now he was on the way to the hospital in grave condition. He might not survive. Suddenly everything was too real.

"We're going into the Wong Nai Chung Gap," David told Max as they prepared to start moving again. "Up in the hills. The plan is to stay as high as we can and fire down on the Japs."

Arnie frowned at his leg. "You okay on that?"

"Just a scratch," Max replied. "Let's go."

————

The Japanese offensive was relentless, the shelling worse every hour. For days, they forced the Royal Rifles inexorably south, climbing the tangled, scrub-covered mountains after them, plunging into the rocky ravines, always in pursuit. Laden with weapons, ammunition, and what wounded they could carry, Max and the others fought back. He adjusted to the constant agony ripping through his leg, reminding himself he had no choice; he must run or be killed. And every day, every night, and every mile, he thought of Richie, remembering the trust in his old friend's eyes. Had he made it to the hospital? Was he still alive?

Max's confidence fell every time they lost another man. In brief intervals between the noise of battle, he heard the agonized screams of wounded soldiers cut suddenly short.

Bayonets, he thought, horror vibrating through him.

He saw the fear and hopelessness building in his friends every time they were forced to leave their dead and wounded behind, including

Gander. Their ferociously loyal dog had rushed in and retrieved a grenade that rolled into a group of injured soldiers. He'd run off, putting as much space between them and him, sacrificing himself to save those seven men. Loyal to the end.

One night, Arnie, David, and he crowded into a shallow trench high on a hill, savouring a few minutes' rest while Max was the lookout.

"God, I'm hungry," David said.

They'd run out of food on the second day of their retreat and had to forage. Worse, the Japanese had taken control of the water supply. David reached to the side and yanked a leaf out of a bush, grimacing as he chewed.

While the others rested, Max swept his binoculars slowly across the hill below. From the corner of his eye, he thought he saw movement, but he was so tired he wasn't sure if his mind was playing tricks. He swung the binoculars back, squinting hard, then spotted men slithering out from the trees, seventy yards below them on the slope.

"We've got company," he whispered.

David and Arnie immediately dropped into position, lying on their fronts, and Max joined them, still scouting between the shrubs.

"I count five. They haven't seen us."

Moving slowly to stay invisible, the three friends trained their rifles on their quarry. Max quietly slid a shell into the chamber and took his safety off.

"This has to be quick," he murmured. "Make sure you have them lined up before you fire. We don't want to attract attention. Ready?"

On his signal, the three of them fired as one. Max heard Arnie swear as he missed his first shot, but they had the jump on the Japanese; two of them fell right away. The other three had dropped and were firing back. The boys reloaded and fired, and Max brought down his second mark, but this time David missed, and Arnie shouted, "Jammed! I'm jammed!"

Two Japanese soldiers were left, and they were running, closing in on the boys' position fast. Max's mind slipped into focus, factoring in the enemy's direction and speed, and his gun became an extension of himself.

Reload, fire! When the first man fell, Max adjusted, zeroing in on the remaining soldier. *Reload, fire!*

Then there was nothing left but the echo of gunshots and the hanging smoke.

"We got 'em," David whispered, patting Max on the back.

Max could only nod as adrenaline pounded through him.

David grinned, his teeth white in his filthy face. "You haven't lost it, Max. You got four out of five. Those boys just experienced the firepower of Harbord Playground's finest."

"Ha," Max said, wishing he could laugh. "Just don't ask me to run bases. My leg's killing me."

David's smile faded when they saw Arnie crouched in the brush, curled into himself.

"I can't do this anymore," he gasped. "We're going to die in these mountains."

Max knelt beside him, one arm around Arnie's shoulder. "Hey, it's okay. Just breathe. We're going to make it out. We'll be back home before you know it."

Arnie's panting slowed as his panic began to ease, but a new sense of fear burned in Max's chest. He knew Arnie's terror. He'd seen it in David's eyes as well, and he felt it twisting in his own soul. They were falling apart a little at a time.

What if this was it, he wondered, a shuddering cold jarring through him. What if none of them were getting out of here alive?

―――――

By Christmas morning, the remaining ragtag members of C Force had retreated from the mountains, worn threadbare after two weeks of fighting. Their destination was Stanley Fort, at the south end of the island, where they collapsed with exhaustion, lying flat on their backs on the cement floor of the fort.

"Think we'll ever get home?" David croaked.

Max rolled his head to look at his brother-in-law's profile. Like the rest of them, David was streaked with dirt; some was clumped into his beard. No one had shaved in a week. Hell, no one had taken off their boots.

He started to answer, but David was already asleep.

An hour later, Sergeant Cox emerged from a meeting with the other remaining senior officers, and Max noted the tight set of his jaw. He was not happy about what he was about to tell the men of D Company.

"At one p.m., we will retake Stanley Village," he said, pointing to a building on his map, set behind the village graveyard.

"In broad daylight, sir?" Max asked, his voice hoarse.

Cox reluctantly met their bloodshot eyes. His tongue went to the crack in his lip, which opened up every time he spoke. Max knew that from his own.

"Here's the choice, fellas. We attack or wait here like lame ducks." He lifted his chin. "Except it's no choice at all, is it? We're Canadians. We don't give up."

No one answered, so Cox dropped his shoulders slightly, and Max saw what this was doing to him. Their sergeant looked almost transparent with wear.

"I've never lied to any of you, so I'm not gonna start now," Cox said, his voice more subdued. "The truth is, they don't expect many of us to survive this day."

Arnie lay on the floor nearby, listening. At that, he rolled onto one elbow. "Sir, that's goddamn pleasant news on Christmas morning."

Max smiled while the entire unit applauded. Leave it to Arnie to hang on to his sense of humour to the last. But inside, dread rolled through Max at the cold, hard facts of Cox's news.

David wasn't laughing. "Whoever makes it out of this has to tell the wives," he said after Cox had moved on. He was blinking hard. "I'm not sure which would be worse."

I'll keep him safe, Max had promised Hannah long ago in a letter. He'd never broken a promise to her before. Was there anything he could do to keep this one?

We'll get out of this, Max tried to say, but the words stuck in his throat, burning there.

The next hour or so was spent in near silence. No one complained, and no one begged to be excused from the battle. They were all in this together, and Max felt their resolve just as he felt his own. He cleaned his weapons, stocked up on grenades, then, resigned to his fate, finally fell asleep.

When the time came, D Company quietly followed Cox, staying low and ducking into a ditch across the road from the village cemetery. But the Japanese spotted them within seconds, and the machine guns started up, drowning out the thundering of Max's heart.

"We have to go in fast and hard, and making lots of noise. They won't expect that," Sergeant Cox yelled from the end of the line.

Max scanned the graveyard, noting the Japanese soldiers positioned all over it, surrounded by superior weapons and what looked like limitless ammunition. Beyond them stood the target, a series of what appeared to be empty houses. Max couldn't conceive of any scenario in which the Canadians could reach those houses, but Cox was right. What choice did they have? Behind him, David and Arnie were checking and rechecking their clips. They'd have only five shots before they'd have to stop and reload. No one could afford a jam like Arnie had suffered the other day. That done, they looked to him, and a terrible sadness stretched between the three friends. What would be left of them when this was all over?

"Fix bayonets," Cox called.

Then all at once they were charging, screaming like banshees, firing their precious ammunition. When they got closer, the bayonets came into play, then Max used his fists, roaring with fury with every punch. They heard a shout, then, incredibly, the Japanese started to fall back and flee toward the row of houses.

"Go after them!" Cox shouted.

And then Max was running with the rest of them despite the constant stab of pain in his leg, tossing grenades into the houses, feeling the whoosh of heat burn his skin as they exploded. He reached down to grab a tommy gun someone had dropped, and his whole body shook as he shot the walls of the houses apart.

"We're doing it!" David yelled as they sprinted toward the next group of houses. "We've got them on the run!"

A madness seized Max, and he whooped with laughter, running for all he was worth. If this was it, if this was to be Max's final battle, then he was taking as many enemy soldiers with him as he could. With David and Arnie at his side, he turned a corner and came upon an unprepared Japanese platoon, and the three of them instinctively mowed the enemy down.

Just ahead, the targeted houses looked wide open, and Max careened through the door of the nearest one, hunting for the Japanese. Through the smoke, he spotted enemy soldiers scrambling out of a back window. He gave chase, lifting his gun once more, then he froze when he spotted movement to his left.

"Grenade!" he screamed, wheeling back toward the entrance, shoving Arnie out ahead of him. The three of them tumbled out the door, deafened by the explosion.

"Grenade!" he heard foggily from nearby.

Still stunned, they watched men pour out of the next house just before it exploded, then fell to the ground with the impact. They staggered back to their feet, but the Japanese were there, shooting every one of them down. The enemy had regrouped, and they were like hornets, furious at the invasion.

"Retreat!" Max heard. "Retreat!"

"Come on!" he yelled, grabbing Arnie and David and dragging them behind him. "We're getting out of here now!"

Max's leg held him back just enough that his friends ran past him, but he followed as fast as he could. He could feel the bullets whizzing past, so close, so very close, and David turned to pull him along.

"Hurry up, Max! Let's go!"

The next moment passed in a blur that burned into every one of Max's senses. David was facing him, reaching for him, when suddenly his eyes flew open in an almost comical expression of disbelief.

Then he dropped like a stone.

Max fell beside him, screaming David's name, pumping his chest and pleading for him to *Breathe! Breathe!* despite the savage hole shot right between his eyes. Seconds later Arnie knelt beside him, shaking David's body while bullets thudded into the earth all around them.

"We gotta go! We gotta go!" Arnie sobbed beside him. "Come on, Max!"

But Max stared at David's body, unable to move. He couldn't leave him there. How could he do that? With all his strength, he threw David over his shoulder and started to run, feeling the dear weight of his brother-in-law jarring against him every step of the way. Arnie ran ahead of them, yelling encouragement. Then suddenly Max jerked, his leg giving way when a bullet struck him, and both he and David tumbled across the field, his gun rolling off on its own.

Arnie looked back, panicked, but Max shook his head. "Run, Arnie! Keep running!"

David's body lay a few feet ahead. Max couldn't stop now. If he left David behind, he might as well die. Digging his fingertips into the dirt, he dragged his body toward David's. Then he froze, stopped by the black leather boot appearing in his vision. He looked up, straight into the barrel of a Japanese gun.

"Kōfuku!" the soldier screamed. He looked so young, Max thought. Barely old enough to be shaving. "Kōfuku!"

Through his shock, Max saw David's still form just ahead. All he could think was, *I'm so sorry, Hannah. I'm so sorry, Hannah.*

A slow, smug smile spread expectantly across the face of the soldier, and Max dropped his face to the dirt, his empty hands held to the sides in surrender. There was no use in pleading. There was no escape.

He felt the hot metal barrel of the gun shove against the back of his head, then he closed his eyes, waiting. The rifle's bolt opened then shut with a final click.

Then Max said goodbye.

1,689 OF DEFENDERS CAPTURED BY JAPS AS GARRISON FELL

Ralston Presents Figures in Commons Based Upon Reports from Nipponese Government; Original Contingent Totalled 1,985 All Ranks

By WILLIAM MARCHINGTON (Staff Writer, The Globe and Mail.) Ottawa, Feb. 25, 1942. – Only 296 Canadians from the contingent that, with the British, made such a gallant fight to save Hong Kong must be considered dead and missing, according to a brief statement given to the House today by Defense Minister J. L. Ralston.

At the end of the question hour, Colonel Ralston rose to announce that, according to a message received directly from the Canadian Minister at Buenos Aires, Hon. W. F. A. Turgeon, and which had been relayed to him from the Argentine Legation at Tokyo, the Japanese Government said a total of 1,689 Canadians had been made prisoners.

No names of those taken prisoner or of the casualties were yet available.

PART THREE

— *1942* —

sixteen

MOLLY

❧

Richard Caolan Ryan," I said firmly into the phone. "Yes, I'll hold."

Across the newsroom, Ian looked up. I glanced away, offering a tight smile.

After what felt like forever, the woman returned to the line. "Thank you for holding," she said, her voice dry of emotion. How many of these types of phone calls was she receiving every day? "Now, what was the name?"

I closed my eyes, trying to contain my frustration. For two months, ever since Ian had wordlessly handed me *The Globe and Mail* article about the Battle of Hong Kong, I had been calling the Red Cross and government offices, always asking the same questions, always receiving the same answers.

"Corporal Richard Caolan Ryan. C Force, D Company," I said. "He was in the Battle of Hong Kong. Can you tell me if he's a prisoner of war, please?"

I heard her shuffling papers in the background.

"Hmm," she said. "I'm sorry. I don't see his name here."

"What about Maxim Dreyfus? Arnold Schwartz? They were both medics with D Company. Or David Bohmer? They were all there."

"I'm sorry, miss. If they're on the Red Cross list, their families will be notified," she said. "This is all the information I have."

But no one I knew had been notified by either the Red Cross or the government. It had been over two months since the battle, and we existed day to day in the dark, not knowing how we should be grieving.

"I understand. Thank you." I hung up and dropped my head, digging my fingernails into my skull while I held in a scream. How could no one have any answers? They couldn't have simply disappeared, could they?

Ian appeared at my desk and placed a cup of tea in front of me. "Just because their names aren't on the list, that doesn't mean they're gone," he said gently. "Keep in mind that Emperor Hirohito started this war without agreeing to the Geneva Convention, which makes it difficult for the Red Cross to access their POW camps, let alone get proper lists of prisoners."

He was such a good friend. So patient. Before all this had happened, we'd gotten much closer, even going to dinner and the movies a couple of times. We'd had a lot of fun together. But he looked sad these days, his normal energy sapped by the distance I'd placed between us. Everything in my world had changed since Christmas. I had retreated from everyone, including him.

"I know," I said, rubbing my eyes. I glanced blearily up at the clock on the wall, noticing it was almost five o'clock. I'd gotten practically nothing done all day. At my right stood a stack of paper I had barely touched.

"Have you eaten anything today?" he asked, eyeing the unopened bagged lunch at my left.

"I guess I forgot," I said lamely. "Thanks for the tea." I gulped it down then gathered my things. "I need to stop and get some rations, then go through more of these POW lists from the Red Cross."

I stepped outside, bundled against the raw March cold, and started walking, my mind returning to Christmas as it so often did.

Every day for two weeks, Mum, Dad, and I had shivered beside the stove in the living room, three blankets piled over us as Mum and I knit socks for soldiers and listened to the radio, with its ongoing reports of what the press were calling the Battle of Hong Kong. The cold stiffened our fingers, but it was the awful waiting that made our stitches uneven. We sat in stony silence as the announcer shouted into his microphone about dive-bombing Japanese planes and relentless shelling, reminding us repeatedly that our men were vastly outnumbered. He rattled off the word *casualties* over and over, but no one said how many there were. No one said anything about our boys.

Finally, on the afternoon of Christmas Day, the British surrendered to the Japanese.

Dad had huffed with disgust. "They had to. The Canadians never would have surrendered."

Despite my relief that there would be no more fighting, I still felt sick. We had no idea what had really happened out there. Where was Richie? Where were Max, Arnie, David, and the others? Had they survived? And what did surrender entail? Nobody seemed to know anything about that. It wasn't until February that we finally learned the majority of C Force had been taken as prisoners of war. The rest were either dead or presumed dead.

Recently, telegrams had begun to trickle into homes, notifying families about the fate of their sons. Every time the mail came, my heart stopped in my throat. We still hadn't heard a peep about Richie.

Fortunately, we did hear from my other brothers fairly often. Their letters were comforting to receive, though we knew little about where they were coming from, since they weren't allowed to write specifics. We did know Mark and the Royal Regiment had moved from Iceland to somewhere in England, but that they still hadn't seen action. Mark was the calmest of all my brothers, but as the war worsened, even his frustration became obvious.

Seems an awful waste not to put us to use somewhere . . .

Jimmy wrote sporadically, and I was glad to read that he seemed to be enjoying his winter overseas.

> *Weather's so bad all the flights are grounded, and the squadron's been out clearing runways. I never thought I'd be happy to see snow, but it reminds me of home.*

> *Still no news of Richie?*

Liam's letters from the St. Lawrence frightened me most of all. He was still sailing across the freezing Atlantic, shielding merchant ships and chasing down U-boats.

> *Our last sail to England, we were loaded up with depth charges and we had to store them on the forward decks. That meant the enemy planes could easily have spotted them if they came low enough. I tell you, one shot from them and . . . Oh, boy. That was the worst week of my life, I can easily say. By the time we arrived, I could practically recite the Lord's Prayer backwards.*

I pushed the thoughts of black water and frozen decks aside as I headed up the street toward my house. I had just passed the Dreyfus house when I heard their door creak open.

"Molly?"

I turned, and my heart went to my throat seeing Mrs. Dreyfus's obvious grief. "Is it Max?" I cried, racing toward her.

She stood back and motioned for me to come inside, where the house was warm but still. I caught my breath, seeing Hannah sitting in the corner of the living room, her face a small, white oval in the darkness. She clutched a telegram in her hands.

I rushed to her side. "Oh, Hannah! What's happened?"

"David," she whispered. "Christmas Day. I thought . . . I thought maybe he—"

I threw my arms around her, wishing there was something I could do, something I could say, but all I could do was hold her tight, weeping with her while she clung to me. My mind returned to the day at the beach when a smiling, eager David had offered Hannah his arm to walk her home, and my heart broke. My dear, beautiful friend was a widow at twenty-seven. Her three young children had lost their father. Nothing would ever be the same.

"He's gone, Molly," she cried, her shoulders heaving with grief. "How can he be gone?"

I barely felt the cold when I finally left her house. In a fog, I walked through the door of my own, my head pounding, all my limbs weighted by cement. I took off my coat and boots and started toward the stairs, needing to be alone.

But then I heard a strangled sound coming from the living room, and I stopped on the stairs. Dread pooled in my stomach as I peeked into the room.

"Mum?"

She was wrapped in Dad's arms, and both of them were weeping. He held out a trembling hand, his fingers practically crushing a small telegram. I willed myself to reach for that piece of paper, and fresh tears sprang to my eyes as I skimmed the lines.

> WE REGRET TO INFORM THAT YOUR SON, CORPORAL RICHARD CAOLAN RYAN, DIED OF WOUNDS ON THE 25TH OF DECEMBER 1941 AT ST. STEPHEN'S HOSPITAL, ON HONG KONG ISLAND.

seventeen

MOLLY

❧

Richie was gone. David was gone. No one had heard anything about Max. I tried to convince myself he was safe someplace, just stuck in a POW camp. For me, it was easier to think of him living behind bars than to imagine a world where he no longer existed. But I had no proof.

For weeks afterward, I tried to visit Hannah every day, to sit with her for a few hours at least. Sometimes I stayed overnight. Being together helped us both.

"Thank you, Molly," she said quietly when I arrived one day in May. She hurried over to relieve me of my bag of rationed groceries. I'd picked them up for her on my way over from the Red Cross, where I'd been volunteering on Saturdays to help assemble parcels for the POWs. "I just put the kids down for a nap, so I have a quiet hour to spend with you."

I filled her kettle. With only two ounces of tea rationed per person in a week, we'd gotten used to just drinking hot water, sometimes with a little dried fruit thrown in for taste.

"I thought Clara was coming over," I said as Hannah unpacked the food, waiting for the water to boil.

Clara's husband, Arnie, had been on the list of POWs that had finally come back from the Red Cross, and I'd wanted to talk with her. Ever since Christmas, I had researched all I could about the camps, including the ones in Canada.

Hannah bit her lip and folded the empty grocery bag. "She's not coming," she said, looking at me through eyes that had aged years in a few months. "She got another telegram yesterday. Arnie got sick, apparently. He died."

I felt a stab of pain for Clara. Arnie and I hadn't been overly close, but he still made up part of my memories of that wonderful summer of 1933, teaching me about newspapers, teasing David about all his talk of shoes, and I knew he and Max had been close.

"What did he die of?" I asked.

"They called it an 'unspecified illness.'" She busied herself, pouring the water and bringing cups to the kitchen table.

"Do you think Max was with him?" The words were out before I could stop them.

Hannah shook her head but didn't say anything. We rarely spoke of Max anymore. We knew nothing of where or how he was, but I got the impression that Hannah and her parents didn't hold out much hope.

"How's Ian?" she asked.

I shrugged. "He's fine, I guess. I haven't had much time for him lately. You know, with work, and Dad, and volunteering."

"And me."

"You're one of my top priorities," I assured her with a smile. "You and Dinah, Jacob, and Aaron."

"But you and Ian got along great, didn't you? I remember being so shocked when you actually started dating. In the old days, you couldn't even stomach a second date with other boys."

"He's a good man," I said, sipping the hot water, sweetened with a bit of apple peel. She would have made the rest of the fruit into something mushy for little Aaron, I imagined. "Very thoughtful."

"What's he like?" Hannah asked, sitting back. "Is he smart?"

"He is," I told her. "And funny. Everyone likes him."

"Including you?"

"Yes," I admitted coyly. "Even me."

She paused. "You can't wait forever, you know," she said gently.

"What are you talking about?"

Her shoulders slumped a little. "Max. You can't wait for him, Molly. He's gone."

I braced out of habit, prepared to argue. Anything to help me believe.

"You know," she said slowly, "I was so mad at you back then."

Heat rose up my neck, reminded of that night. After the one blunt conversation Hannah and I'd had in her doorway, we had never spoken of it again. I'd thought we'd left it behind. I'd hoped we had. But deep down I knew that moment would haunt us until we exposed it.

"I thought I hated you," she went on, and a fresh wave of pain rippled through me. "I wanted to. The idea that you might truly love my brother in that way had never occurred to me until that night. The way we were raised, it didn't seem possible. Sure, I knew you had a crush on him. We all knew you did, I think. But looking back, I guess anyone could see it was more than that. The way he looked at you, the way you were always asking about him . . . Molly, it took me a long time, but I understand now. You really did love Max. I guess you can't choose who you love, can you?"

I looked away, suffocating on memories and regret. "It doesn't matter anymore. I moved on."

"But it does matter." Her dark gaze was intent. "I need to apologize."

"What for?"

Hannah reached across and closed her warm fingers over mine. "I love you so much. You're my sister."

"And you're mine," I said, glad to finally close the chasm between us. I'd missed her so much.

She nodded. "When Max told me he'd kissed you, I was upset, but I guess I also wanted to protect you both, so I pushed you apart from each other, and away from me. You could never really be together that way, and you'd both be hurt so badly when you finally faced that truth. But I had no right to judge you, or to try and manage your life. And I'm sorry."

"Oh, Hannah," I said, pulling her into a hug. "It's all right. I've always known it was done out of love."

She drew back, sniffling. "But you have to stop waiting for him."

I opened my mouth to speak, but she continued.

"I know you are, Molly, whether you admit it or not." She took a deep breath, settling herself. "When David was killed, I lost my husband, the father of my children, and the love of my life. I feel like I lost half of myself. But the time we did have was wonderful."

My heart twisted with grief for her.

"I know you want to believe Max will be back. God, Molly, I miss him every single day. I hate not knowing what happened to him. I mean, like your family, we don't even have a body to bury." She sniffed again. "But he's not coming back. You need to move on with your life."

"Why are you saying this?" I whispered.

"Because I want you to be happy. I don't want you to miss out on what David and I had."

I sat back, needing to breathe. To understand. She wanted the best for me, but I still wasn't sure what to do. We didn't know about Max. Not for sure. What if he was still out there somewhere?

But I knew what she was saying. How long was I willing to wait? Especially since I knew Max and I never could be together that way even if he returned one day. Was I wasting my life waiting for the impossible? Was I holding on too tight? Could I allow myself to let go? To accept he was gone? Was I strong enough to do that?

The next morning when I arrived at work, Ian was typing at his desk, a pencil behind one ear. He smiled uncertainly as I came through the door, and I despised myself in that moment. When all the terrible news had started up in December, I had retreated from our friendship without an explanation. I'd let any feelings between us run cold. He hadn't deserved that.

I headed toward him, intent on apologizing, but he spoke first.

"I've done some investigating for you," he said.

I grimaced. "I know. I've fallen behind in my work. Thank you for picking up after me."

"No, not that. That stuff's up to you," he said wryly.

I walked behind him, peering over his shoulder at his typewriter. "What's this?"

He pulled the paper out and presented it to me. "I know how hard you've been researching Hong Kong. I wanted to take something off your plate, so I started looking into this."

"The St. Stephen's Massacre," I read out loud, my blood running cold. Richie had died at St. Stephen's. I'd never forget that. It was the one aspect I'd never worked on, because I didn't know if I could bear the truth.

He studied me, concern etched in his face. "It's really gritty stuff. When you're ready, I can tell you about it."

"Gritty?"

"Not gonna lie, Molly. It was awful. The Japs achieved a new level of savagery that day."

My stomach rolled with dread. Funny how I was always determined to expose the truth in my articles, and yet I shied away from this. I needed to face what had happened. It wouldn't be fair to Richie if I didn't.

"What do you think about going for a walk?" I asked. I didn't want to be in this noisy, impersonal room for a discussion like this. I needed air. And I wanted to be alone with Ian. "It's a beautiful day."

His eyes widened with anticipation, and I knew Hannah was right. This was what I needed to do. I needed to push myself. I needed to move on.

"I'm ready when you are," he said.

I could tell from the moment we left the building he was bursting at the seams to start talking. He was an enthusiastic man to begin with, and he'd always been attentive to me, but it had been a while since we'd last had a good talk. Now that he was back at my side, I realized I'd missed his company more than I'd been willing to admit.

"How are you feeling?" he eventually asked.

"I'm getting better," I told him. "I had a good talk with my friend Hannah. She had a lot of wise words for me, and I'm taking them to heart."

"I'm glad. You deserve to be happy."

"I do." I glanced up at him. "And so do you."

He watched me a minute, assessing. "Are you saying that if I made dinner and invited you over, you might come?"

"I might," I said, smiling.

That familiar twinkle sparked in his eyes again, and I was so glad to see it. "All right. I'll make something edible from my ration tickets. Maybe spaghetti."

"I like spaghetti," I said, then I tilted my head toward the park on our right. "Feel like telling me about St. Stephen's now?"

He inhaled through his nose. "You sure?"

"As sure as I'll ever be."

We made our way toward an empty park bench, and I prepared myself as well as I could. He had brought notes, but he kept them rolled inside his coat pocket. He had all the information in his head.

"At the same time that D Company faced their last stand, fighting at Stanley Village, there was an attack on the St. Stephen's College hospital, at the south end of the island."

I nodded. That much I knew.

Ian reached into his shirt pocket and took out his cigarettes. He offered one to me even though he knew I never accepted, then he lit his, blowing a stream of smoke away from me.

"There were about a hundred Canadians and Brits at the hospital, including doctors and nurses. Other than the medical people, the rest were wounded men."

So Richie had been one of the wounded, I realized. When had he been hurt? Where? Would I ever know?

Ian squinted, drawing on his cigarette again. "About two hundred Japanese attacked the hospital Christmas Day, claiming they thought it was a fort, despite the hospital flag flying outside."

"The patients were unguarded?"

"They were in a hospital. No one's supposed to attack a hospital. And all our fighting men were busy elsewhere."

"Go on," I said after a moment.

He regarded me carefully then set both his feet flat on the ground, as if he was bracing himself. "The two doctors in charge of the hospital barred the entrance, but the Japanese killed them both."

My mouth went dry. I swallowed, reminded myself that this was war. Hadn't Dad described something similar?

"It only gets worse from there, Molly. It was a massacre."

I took a breath then nodded, steeling myself. I had to know. I couldn't ignore the facts. My brother deserved that.

"The Japs stormed into the hospital and bayoneted about sixty of the ninety-three wounded men to death." Ash dropped from Ian's forgotten cigarette. "They— They cut them to pieces as they lay in their beds. They showed no mercy."

"Oh, God. Richie," I gasped.

He'd probably felt safe there, under the care of the doctors. People were supposed to feel safe in hospitals, weren't they? I clenched my hands together, squeezing until my nails cut into my palms, imagining the panic he must have felt, the screams that had cut through the day and night.

Ian handed me a handkerchief, and I wiped at my eyes.

"There were also seven Allied nurses and a bunch of Chinese nurses, no one seems to know how many. The Chinese nurses were taken away and never seen again. The Canadian and British nurses were attacked and . . ." Ian turned his face away. "They were raped all night. Five of them survived."

Bile seared my throat, and I covered my mouth with a trembling hand. When at last I found my voice, it was barely a whisper. "How could they do that?"

"You know how," he reminded me gently. "You've been studying their POW camps. These guys don't follow any rules. They believe if a man surrenders, they have forfeited their soul, and they're less than human. That they actually deserve to be treated that way. But here's the kicker: the Canadians never surrendered. The Brits did, hours *before* that attack. But the men of C Force never did." He stubbed out his cigarette in the grass, grinding it in with his shoe. "In the morning, they made the survivors carry all the bodies, mattresses, and whatever else they could find, then burn them all. Once that was done, they started marching them to North Point Camp."

"The POW camp."

"And nobody knows much more than that."

I sighed. "Because the Japanese won't allow the Red Cross in." I stared at Ian's handkerchief, crushed in my hands. "But by that point, Richie was already . . ."

Ian lifted my chin with one finger, and I saw the sympathy in his shining blue eyes. Then I saw the love behind it, and I let myself go. I reached for him, and he wrapped his arms around me, holding me tight while I wept into his warm, welcoming chest.

When my sobs slowed, we drew apart, and I caught the pleasant tang of his aftershave as his cheek brushed against mine. I looked into his eyes, feeling truly comforted for the first time in so long, then I tilted my face toward his, finally ready for more.

He paused, inches away. "Are you sure this is what you want, Molly?"

"I am," I said. "I just needed time. There was so much going on, with the war, my brothers, and everything else. I needed to sort through everything."

"But even before then," he said, searching my face. "I don't know. We were having fun, but you never seemed to want anything more than friendship. I knew you wanted to focus on your career, but I thought it was more than that. And I would never push you if you didn't want to go there."

"Establishing my career was part of it." I paused, leaving words unsaid. "My life has changed, Ian, and I'm moving on. I'm ready to walk down that path with you."

The corners of his lips curled in a sweet smile. "I've been hoping that someday I might hear those words." It surprised me to see just how vulnerable he was, and I was ashamed that I'd taken him for granted. "I've been crazy about you since the moment you first walked into that newsroom."

I felt his breath on my face, then his lips on mine, his kiss warm and gentle.

"I can't tell you how long I've wanted to do that," he said.

My hands went to the lapels of his tan-coloured coat, and I drew him back toward me. "Then do it again, please."

eighteen
MOLLY

❧

It was impossible not to smile at Ian, bouncing in time to "A String of Pearls" while his fingers tapped the steering wheel. Outside the car window, the golden leaves of October and the dry, harvested fields flew by, warming themselves under a cloudless sky. It was a beautiful day for a two-hour drive, and for a little while, the war and all my troubles seemed very far away.

"Ever been to Bowmanville?" he asked, sticking a cigarette in the corner of his mouth and working his lighter with his thumb.

"I haven't. I've actually never been outside the city at all."

"Really?" He grinned, then leaned into the little flame. "That's where I was born."

"I thought you were born in Toronto, like me. It must have been so nice growing up out here, in all this space."

"We moved to Toronto when I was just the cutest little tyke you've ever seen. I think I was seven. From what I remember, Bowmanville's a nice little town." He rolled down his window and hung his elbow over the edge, and the wind played with his hair. "Too little for Mom, though. She hounded my father to get her to Toronto or else. That's how I heard it, anyway."

He glanced in the rearview mirror at our staff photographer, Freddy Morris, sitting in the back seat. Freddy hadn't spoken a word the whole way. In fact, I had never heard him say a word at the office, either.

"How about you, Mo?" Ian asked. "You ever been out this way?"

"Nope," Mo grunted, and that was it for the rest of the drive.

Mr. Hindmarsh had sent the three of us on assignment, saying there was a situation at a POW camp in Bowmanville that needed covering. He'd handed Ian the folder, but Ian had nodded toward me, suggesting I take the lead. Just last month I had been promoted to senior reporter, and Ian knew there was no one in the office who'd done as much research on POW camps as I had. This would be the first one I'd ever seen outside of photographs.

I'd been looking forward to today for a couple of reasons. First, the POW camp. After everything I'd read, I wanted to see the real thing. Second, I needed to get out of the house, if only for a while.

Last month, my baby brother Liam had come home, wounded inside and out from fighting at Dieppe. His face, once so handsome and eager, was masked by horrible pink scars from a fire, and the agony of what had happened still burned in his expression. Because of nerve damage, he could no longer use his right hand, and he was blind in that eye. He wouldn't meet anyone's gaze and had steadfastly refused to see Louise, no matter how many times she called or left a note. He preferred to sit alone in his room, but when he came out to the living room, he wanted to be in darkness, the orange glow of his cigarette the only light in the room. He was constantly tapping one foot, like he was waiting for an opportunity to flee. We were gentle and patient, making sure he was fed and tended, but he'd rarely spoken.

After a few weeks, we received a letter from Liam's sergeant, filling us in a little about what had happened. Liam's ship had been torpedoed, we learned, when he'd been below deck. He'd been trapped in a compartment near the bow with two other sailors, completely surrounded by fire, but somehow he had managed, with the other two, to find an opening, and he'd shoved the other men through the flames to safety. But by then the ship had begun to sink, rotating on its way down, and a large pipe collapsed on top of Liam, exposing half his body to the flames as water rushed in on the other side. Realizing he hadn't made it out, the two men he'd saved rushed back with help, and they'd managed to free Liam in time. But the fire had ravaged the right half of him, from his face to his knees, and his survival had been touch and go at the hospital. The sergeant said in his letter to us that Liam had been saved by the hand of God.

Mum and I were now looking after him as well as caring for Dad. Sometimes when I came home, Dad and Liam were sitting together in silence in the shadowy living room, and I knew to leave them alone. In a way, Liam's suffering seemed to help Dad come out of his own shell. He was still weak, but he had to be strong for his son. But it was never enough, and Mum and I were exhausted.

"Read me what the notes say," Ian said, flicking the ash from his cigarette out the window. "Why are we out here?"

I opened the folder, but I already knew the contents by heart. "They're calling it the Battle of Bowmanville. Back in August, Hitler allegedly saw photos of four dead German POWs at Dieppe with their hands tied behind their backs. Binding prisoners is against the Geneva Convention, of course, so Hitler enforced his Commando Order. Since the Allies had broken the Convention at Dieppe, he ordered fifteen hundred British and Canadian POWs in Stalag VIIIB, one of the German camps, to be shackled." I suppressed a shudder. "For twelve hours a day for an entire year."

Ian stared straight ahead, at the highway, but I saw the muscles in his jaw flex. "Tit for tat. That's mature. Twelve hours a day? How are they eating? Sleeping? Uh, going to the men's room?"

I set the folder down. "These are just men, Ian. That's what I can't get past. These are men like my brothers. In war it's one side against another, but it all boils down to human beings. What I can't grasp is how men can treat other men like that." I paused. "I've also been reading about the Japanese internment camps in British Columbia. They're alarming too, but in a different way."

Ian raised an eyebrow. "I thought you were focusing on POW camps."

"I am. Those camps are somewhat similar, except they're full of regular citizens. Last year the BC government took more than twenty thousand Japanese men, women, and children from their homes. The men were sent to labour camps, where they were paid half of what regular labourers were paid. The women and children were housed in a livestock building, then moved to sprawling, filthy camps with no electricity or running water."

"They were concerned about national security," he suggested. "The enemy hiding among them."

I shook my head. "Before any of it started, the army itself insisted that Japanese Canadians were no threat to national security. Most of these people were born here. They've never even seen Japan. The orders came from prejudiced politicians. Why, the things I've read from them make them sound like Nazis discussing Jews. That's how much they hate the Japanese. Get this: the Japanese Canadians are basically paying for their own confinement. The government seized all their assets: they sold their fishing boats, their farms, their cars, their businesses, and their homes just to pay for locking these innocent people up. And nobody's talking about releasing them anytime soon."

"You have that look in your eye," Ian said. "Well, I can add to that a little. I read that the families of the British POWs, the ones who had been living in Hong Kong before the Japanese invasion, were all put in Stanley Barracks, near where D Company took their last stand. So they're basically in a camp as well. There's no food, and the buildings are practically demolished. Perhaps there are some parallels to draw from that in, say, a long-form piece? Mr. Hindmarsh would probably go for it."

I nodded, toying vaguely with the idea. The car raced past the sleeping fields, but my mind still peered through the barbed wire of the camps. Three years of war. When would it end?

Ian cleared his throat. "So, the shackling debacle?"

I returned to the notes in front of me. "Yes. Right. So this is all about Churchill demanding reciprocity. Since most of the Stalag VIIIB POWs are Canadian, the Bowmanville camp is under orders to get back at Hitler by shackling a hundred of their five hundred German prisoners. Of course, the German prisoners here want no part of that, so they're fighting back."

"How long's this been going on out here?"

I flipped back a page. "It started this morning."

"It'll probably be over by the time we get there."

"I doubt it. They've called in reinforcements."

After a while we reached the outskirts of town, and Ian nodded ahead. "There it is," he said. "It used to be a reform school for boys. Built back in '27."

He turned onto a tree-lined gravel road surrounded by farmers' fields. A white, two-storey building with a red-brown roof came into sight, and Ian slowed as we neared it. The guard, a man in uniform who looked to be in his midfifties, held up a hand, and we pulled over.

"This is it?" I asked as the guard approached. "No gates or fences?" Up ahead I could see long, plain rows of barracks surrounded by fields. "This hardly looks like a prison. Look! Cows!"

Ian stuck his head out the window. "Good morning," he said. "Ian Collins and Molly Ryan from the *Star*. And this is our photographer, Freddy Morris. We're here about the shackling incident."

"Corporal Griffen," the man said, shaking Ian's hand. "Yes, I'd been informed you were coming. I'll take you to the main building, but I have to ask you to be cautious." His eyes flitted to me. "We have five hundred POWs here, and hostilities are ongoing."

I frowned. "Is it safe?"

"Oh yes. Most of the prisoners have barricaded themselves inside the mess hall in the main building and we have them locked down inside. There are a few locked inside their own houses as well, but we have them covered."

He indicated where Ian should park, and once he had, the four of us set off at a brisk walk toward the main building.

"Can I answer any of your questions while we walk?" Griffen asked.

I asked about the fields and the cows, and he told me they had ten acres for farming. "Cows, chickens, pigs, whatever you want. The planting fields are out back. Why waste such glorious land?"

"Indeed!" Ian replied. "And you're saving the government money by feeding yourselves, to a certain extent."

"Exactly," Griffen replied.

I took in his white hair and moustache, surprised to see someone his age guarding the camp. I'd assumed guards would have to be fighting age. "How did you come to be stationed here?"

"We're all members of the Veterans Guard of Canada: veterans of the last war. Too old to fight, but fine for guard duty."

That explained his age. "There's not a lot of outside security, I've noticed."

"Why leave? Most of these fellas have it better here than they've ever had it before. Bacon and eggs for breakfast, fresh bread every day, full, hearty suppers . . ."

"Jeez. They eat better than us. Can the public come for supper?" Ian asked. "What do you think, Miss Ryan?"

That was my cue to say something witty to lighten up the conversation and keep the guard talking. I smiled. "Mr. Collins, if you ate here, there'd be nothing left for the rest of the men."

Griffen chuckled and continued the tour, pointing out the nine guard towers and the separate, well-maintained barracks for prisoners, as well as the ones for the Canadian guards. While Ian asked questions, I took notes, and Mo snapped photos of the camp.

Griffen pointed past the barracks. "Sports field over there, then they have the lake during the summer, and even a pool."

"Lake Ontario?" Ian asked. "That's pretty wide open. Don't they escape?"

"You might think it's crazy—I did at first—but the prisoners are required to give their word of honour that they'll come right back, or else they can't go."

"Their word of *honour*?" I exclaimed. "From *Germans*?"

Griffen shrugged. "Like I said, they have it good here. Plus, where would they go? We've never had even one try to break out. Right now, of course, we're having some problems with them, but it's under control. Usually they're out in the yard, playing soccer, baseball, whatever. The games are pretty competitive. Reminds me of my old days in service: navy versus army versus air force. In the evenings, some of them put on weekly plays. We even gave 'em musical instruments. Their band performs every Saturday night, both classical stuff and jazz. They're not bad. You might want to come back and hear them sometime."

"Seems you run a pretty comprehensive ship out here," Ian said.

"Oh, we've got even more than you see here. We have professors from the University of Toronto coming out here to teach the men," he said, looking proud. "I'll admit I doubted it at first, but the facility is in great shape, and so are all the men. It works real well."

My thoughts went to poor Arnie Schwartz with his messy black hair and wide smile, dying of an illness in a filthy Hong Kong camp. "We've been reading very different things about POW camps overseas," I said. "I didn't expect to see something like this."

"Well, that's good old Canadian hospitality for you." Griffen's smile faded. "Not all the camps in Canada are as nice as this one, but every one of them is better than what our men are suffering in over there."

Ian glanced at me, and I gave him a reassuring nod.

"Here we are," Griffen said as we arrived at the main building. "Now, I must warn you to stay back. The prisoners have armed themselves with sticks and iron bars and whatever else they can find. One of our own men is in hospital with a fractured skull from a flying jam jar. This morning was pretty rough, so we're taking a break now. Regrouping. We have the situation under control—about five hundred of our own soldiers are here too—but I don't want you getting too close, just in case. Especially you, Miss Ryan."

From outside, I could hear a ruckus inside the building, and adrenaline prickled through me. "It must be difficult to make them bend to your will, considering they've been given such royal treatment," I said.

"Yeah. Our men have guns, but the Germans see through that."

"What do you mean?"

"The guns aren't loaded. We don't want to turn this into an international event."

We stepped through the foyer, then stopped at a set of closed doors. Through the windows in the doors, I saw the prisoners pacing, talking to one another. Griffen asked us to remain there while he went to retrieve a few of the senior prisoners for us to interview. Before he left, Mo spoke up.

"Excuse me, sir," he said, startling me. He waggled one finger at the closed door. "Can I go in? I'd rather not shoot through the window. I promise to stay out of the way."

Corporal Griffen hesitated then gave a quick nod. "I'll have a guard posted to you."

Mo followed him through the doors, and within seconds I could see his trigger finger shooting away.

I scanned the room, taking in the angry faces, then paused, caught by a flash of red hair. I was staring at a German soldier, about the same age, same build as Richie. Same everything, save for his nationality. And the fact that he was alive. I blinked, remembering that awful fact, and I quickly looked away.

Griffen returned with one of the prisoners. "This is General-Major Georg Friemel," he said. "He's the German spokesman."

Friemel nodded coolly at us. Like Griffen, he was older, perhaps sixty years old, with just a few wisps of white hair covering his head. He stood before us, arms at his sides, waiting. Ian jumped right in, asking questions about the attitudes and health of the POWs, all of which Friemel answered in sharp, disciplined English.

I screwed up my courage. "And what's your general opinion on the matter at hand? Considering the shackling order has been put into place as a result of your führer's orders."

Friemel studied me. "We are in the service of the führer and obliged to follow his orders, not Churchill's," he said simply.

I knew what the Nazis were capable of, but with Friemel standing basically defenceless before me, I couldn't help but regard him and his men in the same light as our own POWs. They'd been following orders, nothing more. Though Friemel said nothing of the sort, I thought about how humiliating it must be for him and the rest of his soldiers, spending the duration of the war in a camp, unable to fight. I know how frustrated my brother Mark had been all along, waiting to join in the fighting.

But at the same time, seeing Friemel in that light brought back the reality of what was happening at other POW camps, and indignation swelled within me. How dare these men complain, when they were being asked to withstand a small inconvenience while basically living it up at the Ritz?

"How long do you think this standoff might go on?" I asked.

Friemel scowled at Griffen before he answered my question. "We will not be surrendering twice."

Interview concluded, Friemel was escorted back into the mess hall, and Ian, Mo, and I were asked to step out of the building. Griffen informed us that the guards had a new plan and suggested we watch through the outside window. As soon as we were out, the guards rushed in with high-pressure water hoses and soaked the POWs, pushing them to the back of the room. Through the glass, Mo tried to get photos of the soggy prisoners, slumped in defeat. I felt an unexpected pang of sympathy for their humiliation.

"What now?" Ian asked as Corporal Griffen accompanied us back to Ian's car. "Will they have to wear the shackles?"

"Oh, I think we'll probably have another day of disagreements, but in the end, they'll put them on. They don't have much choice. If our boys have to wear them, so do they." He handed Ian a card. "You can telephone tomorrow for an update, if you'd like."

The three of us climbed back into the car, lost in our own thoughts. Ian lit a cigarette, and when he saw me watching, he offered it to me. Still annoyed by what I'd seen, I nodded, surprising us both, then inhaled. I coughed, unfamiliar with the feel of the smoke in my lungs, but then I tried again. Something about the act of breathing in the smoke seemed to soothe my nerves.

"That was not at all what I imagined for a POW camp," I said, passing the cigarette back.

"Me neither." He glanced sideways at me. "What's going on in that busy head of yours? You're angry about something."

"I am. The Canadian POWs at Stalag VIIIB are suffering without food or any kind of comforts, plus they're surrounded by Nazis at all times—Nazis whose guns *are* loaded—and then Hitler up and decides that they'll be shackled for twelve hours a day. On the other hand, the German POWs we just saw have everything they need and more. Even if they are shackled, I doubt the guards will make it hard on them. It's all ridiculous and unfair. Hitler's too mean and we're too nice."

"Now, now, Miss Ryan. Truth and Accuracy. Fairness—"

"And Impartiality," I finished for him. "I know, I know. I'll stick to the code, don't worry. But don't forget the other one: humanity. I mean, think about our men over there. Can you imagine how demeaning it would be to have your hands tied behind your back all day, every day?"

"I imagine demeaning prisoners is only part of the plan. But I agree."

"Monsters," Mo muttered from the back seat.

"True," I said, turning to face him, "but now we're hosing them down with water and shackling them. I don't think anyone, in war or not, has the right to become monsters. When does humanity go out the window?"

Ian looked over at me. "You take the byline on this one," he said, surprising me. "And consider that longer form piece idea as well."

"You're sure?"

"You seem to have it all figured out. Just keep your journalistic distance."

Smiling, I held out my hand and took his cigarette again. "Yes, boss."

We arrived back in the city after five o'clock. I was tired but still energized by the experience, and I was anxious to get my first draft down on paper. Ian dropped Mo off, then he gave me a ride home.

"Thanks for the lift," I said.

"You know, we've been working together for a few years now," he said as he turned onto my street.

"But who's counting?" I teased.

"Best years of my career. Maybe of my life."

Heat rushed into my face. "Oh, you're being silly."

"I mean it."

His expression was soft, and I felt a rush of affection for him. "I've really enjoyed the past few months, too. I mean, after I came out of my daze. I needed time last Christmas, and you gave me all I needed. I really appreciate that. Even before then, when I wasn't being all that nice to you, you let me lean on you. And now, with Liam and everything, I mean."

I looked away, the weight of memories wrapping themselves around me. In two months it would be Christmas again. A year since Richie had been murdered. I doubted that would ever get any easier for me to accept.

He stopped the car in front of my house. I reached for the door handle, but he turned off the engine and faced me. "I was just glad I could be there," he said. "And I understood, you know, when you withdrew. You had so much going on. I just waited. I'm stubborn that way." He took my hand. "I'm very fond of you, Molly Ryan, as you well know." His thumb slid over my knuckles, raising goose bumps all over me. "And I was think-ing that maybe it's almost time for me to meet your parents."

The air between us hummed, and my eyes lowered to the soft line of his mouth. "Why?" I asked, unable to look away.

The corners lifted in a smile. "Because I'd have to ask your father's permission if I'm gonna ask you what I want to ask you."

nineteen

MOLLY

❦

lease, Mum!" I said, leading her to her favourite spot in the living room. "Honestly, you've been fussing around the kitchen like a chicken with its head cut off."

"But do you think he'll like the casserole? You know, the one with the noodles. Oh, it's so difficult to make anything special with all the rationing."

I placed her knitting in her lap. "Ian will eat anything, Mum. He'll love it."

"You're the best cook I know," Dad assured her.

I turned to Dad. He had shaved and dressed in his nicest suit, and seemed to be standing a little taller. "You're looking handsome," I said.

"I thought the occasion required me to clean up a bit," he replied, giving me his lopsided smile. "You don't often bring men home for supper."

After so many years, Dad was finally doing better. It had started when Liam came home, ruined in so many ways. Mum had been tired all the time, caring for them both, then one day Dad had gotten out of his chair, put on his hat, and walked around the block. Every day, he went a little bit farther, relying on his cane less and less. And recently Liam had joined him, wrapping his poor face in a scarf before leaving the house. They'd given me hope.

Outside, the fat, eager flakes of snow were piling up on the street. Of all the nights for me to invite Ian over, now we were being buried in the first snowfall of the year. Ian had said he was going to drive over regardless of the weather. I knew he wanted to make a good impression, but I was nervous about the slippery roads. Still, I had learned a long time before that there was no changing Ian's mind when it was made up.

"Do you think Liam will join us?" I asked.

"He thought it would be best if he didn't," Mum said. "It's a special night for you, Molly. He didn't want to take away from your big moment."

My heart sank. "He could never. I'll go talk with him."

"No, dear. Let him come around when he's ready." She brightened. "Your father and I are very excited about tonight. We want you to enjoy yourself."

I could practically hear wedding bells in her voice. Beside her, Dad shifted. "Molly," he said, his voice soft. "I know we haven't always done the right thing, but we love you. You're our only daughter, and we just want you to be happy."

Christmas 1941 had put the pain of my parents' betrayal behind me. I still grieved what might have been between Max and me if I'd received his letter, but that was years ago. As I'd told Hannah, I'd moved on.

"I know, Dad. You've always wanted that. And I am."

I turned to the window, my heart pattering with nerves. A couple of weeks ago, after Ian had made his intentions clear, I had lain in bed a long time, thinking about the decision before me. For so long, I had felt sad and alone. Then Ian had come into my life, a bright sun spreading energy and excitement. Once more, I had someone to talk to about the news, politics, and my ambitions. He had taken me under his wing and never once looked down his nose at me. After Max, I'd never expected to open my heart to anyone ever again, but Ian had found a way in. He was funny, smart, and unquestionably handsome, and he doted on me. What more could I want? I was twenty-seven years old. It was time. Hannah was right. If I wasn't careful, I would waste my life waiting.

At last, Ian arrived, his black coat sparkling with melting snow. When I opened the door, he filled the whole entrance, and his broad smile brought a new level of warmth to the room. I took his hat and coat while he stomped snow off his boots, and when he leaned down to give me a kiss on the cheek, Mum and Dad stood back, glowing like children seeing Santa Claus.

"So glad you're here," I murmured.

"Me too," he said.

"Did you really drive?" I asked, hanging his coat on the hook.

"I did." He grimaced. "The way it's coming down, I'll admit that might have been a poor choice."

I watched with appreciation as he greeted Mum, complimenting her on the kitchen's wonderful aroma and the general "beauty" of our tired old house. Then he turned to Dad, who had straightened to his full height. I smiled inside, recognizing the sergeant in him, still so proud.

Ian wasn't daunted. "Sergeant Ryan," he said, offering his hand. "It's an honour to finally meet you."

After a few minutes, Mum went to our brand-new white refrigerator to get her favourite cabbage and pineapple gelatin salad, then she ushered us all to the table, saying dinner was ready. Ian, Dad, and I took our seats, then Mum dished out the casserole. Ian was a perfect gentleman, saying, *This is delicious* and *Thank you so much for having me*, until those niceties were out of the way. Then Mum poured a little wine, and the conversation wandered into more uncharted territory.

"Why don't you tell us about yourself, Ian," Dad said.

Ian patted his mouth with his napkin then set it down, always happy to talk. "What is there to tell? You'll be glad to know, Mr. Ryan, that I'm of good Protestant Irish stock. My grandparents came over from Dublin in 1868, and they settled in Bowmanville, where I was born. Molly and I actually went there to research a story the other day."

I sat back, watching him in his element.

"Molly's told me about her *seanmháthair* and a few of her wonderful stories," he continued. "I recognized some of them from my own grandmother, God rest her soul."

"What about your brothers and sisters?" Mum asked.

"I'm an only child, I'm afraid."

She gave him a sympathetic look.

"That's all right," he said, flashing that contagious grin. "I make friends easily."

"He's a charmer, all right," I agreed, touching his toes with mine under the table.

Dad lifted a censorious eyebrow. "Is that right?"

"I believe it," Mum said, obviously warmed up to Ian already.

"And your job," Dad said. "You seem content there, are you? Writing for a living? Why is it you never enlisted, I'm wondering."

Ian's smile faded. "I would have if the doctor had allowed it," he said, sounding disappointed. I felt for him. He'd told me before that he was ashamed about being turned away by the military doctor. "I have a heart murmur. It's never once given me cause to worry, and I tried to tell the doctor that it wouldn't impede my abilities to fight, but he was adamant. So I'm doing my bit as well as I can, I suppose, by writing about the war. I started at the *Star* fresh out of school, and I was promoted to assistant editor recently, right around the time Molly became a senior reporter."

For the first time, I wondered if he'd had anything to do with my promotion.

"And you enjoy writing?" Mum asked. "Molly always loved to write."

Ian looked fondly at me across the table. "She's a natural, my girl.

From the first day our editor asked me to show her around, she impressed me."

"You were a good teacher," I told him.

"We've taught each other, I think," he replied gently, and his voice felt like a caress.

Mum leaned in. "How do you like the casserole?"

"Mrs. Ryan, I believe this is the best noodle casserole I've ever had."

By the end of supper, Ian was the golden boy in my parents' eyes, and he gave me a big wink after Dad turned to the living room and invited him to join him.

"Brandy?"

"That sounds just right," Ian said, squeezing my hand on his way out.

"He's perfect, Molly," Mum said softly, after he'd left.

"I knew you'd like him," I said, picking up the drying towel.

She looked up from the sudsy dishwater. "And you seem happy."

I held her gaze. "I am."

We cleaned the dishes in quiet, then Mum wiped her face.

"What's wrong, Mum?"

"I'm just being silly," she said. "Thinking about things. Like how fast you all grew up. Oh, the noise in this house. You remember. Now it's so quiet."

That was the hardest part for me about being home. For so many years I'd come home to the chaos of my family, my brothers all going in different directions, my parents trying to herd us to the table. Now all of it was gone. Richie would never walk through that door again, though Barbara brought his little daughters over when she could. Liam was still afraid to step outside most of the time, despite the thick, grey scarf he insisted on wearing year round. Mark and Jimmy were still gone, fighting somewhere far away.

"Jimmy and Mark will be home soon, Mum."

"Of course they will. But still." She flashed a weak smile. "You remember all those ball games we went to? Cheering on your brothers until we lost our voices? Life's thrown us a few curveballs these past few years, hasn't it?"

I set the dry plate aside. "Game's not over. We can still win."

"I know. And you and Ian are giving us a chance to have joy in our lives again." She put her hand on my arm. "Maybe someday you'll have a daughter, and she'll come see her grandmother, and I'll tell her stories so she can write them all down."

My heart ached, remembering *Seanmháthair*. "Do you think she would have liked Ian, Mum?"

"She would have loved him."

"How do you know?" Then I asked the real question. "How will I know?"

Her face softened with memory. "Your grandmother was a wise, wise woman. She told me something once, a long time ago. It was the day I was to marry your father, and I was filled with doubt as every young bride is. I asked her just what you asked me, and she told me, the thing about love is that you can never know until you know."

"What does that mean?"

"Tell me, Molly, when you look into Ian's eyes, what do you see? Do you see a friend? A lover? Someone who will always stand behind you?"

From the corner of my eye I spotted Ian poking his head into the kitchen. "Excuse me, ladies, but do you need help in here? Or if you're done, can you come sit with us? I think I'm boring your dad."

Mum smiled. "Oh, I doubt that, but yes. We're done in here." Ian turned back to the living room, and her eyes sparkled at me. "Come on, Molly. Let's go enjoy ourselves."

Dad poured each of us a glass of brandy, filling his and Ian's back up as he did so, then he raised his in a toast.

"I'm glad to know you, Ian. Thank you for making Molly happy."

Ian grinned, then wrapped one arm around my waist. "It has been my pleasure."

"Got an extra glass? It sounds like a celebration down here."

I spun around at the sound of Liam's voice. He stood at the bottom of the stairs, small and quiet, his scars shining with the candlelight in the room. In the next instant, Mum had placed a brandy glass in his hand.

"I'm so glad you came down," I told him. "I wanted you to meet—"

Ian held out his left hand, and I caught my breath, loving him so much in that moment. He'd remembered that Liam's right hand was useless and had offered him respect without hesitation. I saw a flicker of appreciation cross Liam's face as he took Ian's hand in his.

"Ian Collins," Ian said. "It's a privilege to meet you."

"And you," Liam replied, then he turned slightly, so only I could see, and he gave me a wink.

After an hour or so of warm, spirited conversation about politics and the war, always keeping Liam's sensitivities in mind, Ian thanked my parents profusely for the dinner, and I went to collect his coat and hat.

At the door, he paused, his eyes on mine. "Would you care to walk with me?"

"You'll need galoshes," Mum said out of habit. She and Dad were watching me like hawks.

I slipped them on, and Ian helped me into my coat.

The temperature outside was pleasant, but I shivered in spite of myself as we stepped down the walk toward the street, the snow sinking gently beneath our boots.

"I thought that went well," Ian said, taking my arm.

"It went very well. They loved you."

He stopped, studied my face, his own full of affection. "And what about you?"

"I love you too," I told him, and I meant it.

"You know what I'm gonna ask," he said.

"You aren't very good at secrets," I replied, then I lifted my chin a little. "But I won't give you an answer until you ask me properly."

"That's my girl," he said, then he knelt before me, right there on the snowy sidewalk, the streetlight shining down on him.

I laughed. "Not in the snow, you silly man!"

"Why not?" He grinned. Then he held out a gold ring, looking up at me through sky blue eyes while snowflakes caught on his lashes. "Molly Ryan, you're the most incredible girl I've ever met. You're smart and beautiful, and despite all your brains, you still put up with me. My favourite sound in the world is your laugh, and I promise to do everything I can to keep hearing it. So tell me, Molly, will you do me the honour of marrying me?"

I hesitated for only a heartbeat, and I didn't think he noticed. It was time. I held out my hand so he could slip the ring onto my finger. "Yes, Ian. I will marry you."

With a look of pure joy on his face, he rose, gathered me up in his arms, then kissed me with a bold, confident strength I'd never felt before. His passion swept through me, and my heart raced, keeping up to his.

"Woohoo!" he yelled into the night, our arms still around each other. "She said yes!"

He squeezed me tight against him, and as I looked over his shoulder at my house, I caught the shadows of my parents watching me. I raised my hand to wave, and as I did, the gold of my new ring shone in the pale light of the snow, and I blinked at the unfamiliar sight of it.

"I'm gonna make you happy," he whispered into my ear. "I promise."

The thing about love, Mum's voice reminded me, *is that you can never know until you know.*

"I know," I said, telling both him and myself. "I know."

July 1944

Dear Molly,

I thought you might like to know that this will be my final letter to you from jolly old England. That's right. I'm on my way home soon. After Normandy, when that pesky German gunner decided I no longer needed my leg, the Army decided they didn't need me. What a surprise! I guess there's not much market for a one-legged soldier these days. It's just as well, I suppose, because you have a shiny gold band on your finger now, and I haven't given this man my official stamp of approval yet. Hardly fair of you to go and do that without my say so, Big Sister.

Helen and I would like to welcome you both for a congratulatory dinner once I'm home and settled. I'm learning to get around with the crutches, and I've been told I'm up for a new leg when I get home, so you can come and tease me while I stagger around, even clumsier than usual.

Jokes aside, I was very happy to hear of your engagement, and I know we shall love this man as much as you do—almost! I cannot wait to get home and see you.

All my best, your loving little brother,
Mark

PART FOUR

— 1945 —

twenty

MOLLY

ᑌᑌᐤ

glanced up at the clock, my eyes burning from staring at paperwork all day long. Already 8:35 p.m. I'd wanted to leave hours ago, but Mr. Hindmarsh had asked all of us to stay late because he'd heard that Prime Minister Mackenzie King was going to make an announcement. No one had balked, because we all had a pretty good idea what this announcement was going to be about. Or at least we hoped we did. The news had broken about Hitler's suicide a week ago, and now it was like watching the very last leaf on a tree, waiting for it to drop.

I leaned over my desk, scanning the recent statistics about homelessness in the city, then scribbled more notes into my notebook. The number of men living on the streets had eased since the Depression had ended almost a decade ago, but I worried. With the number of veterans returning from Europe in various conditions, that issue could easily balloon again. The government had recently proposed plans to help reintegrate these men into the everyday world, so I'd calculated some of the social programme costs, hoping to come up with a substantial article that might forecast what would happen when our surviving men returned at the end of the war, whenever that might be.

I ran my finger down the column I needed and was just writing down the number I'd been searching for when Mr. Hindmarsh stepped out of his office in his usual plodding manner, his arms folded. The rest of us could read him like a battalion reads a general, so we all dropped what we were doing.

"Please turn up the radio," he said in his deliberate voice. "In about thirty seconds, Prime Minister Mackenzie King would like to speak to you all."

The blink of silence was followed by a ruckus of chairs being pushed back as everyone flocked to the big radio at the side of the room. This had to be it: the announcement we'd all been waiting for. Seconds later, the prime minister's voice crackled out of the speaker, his words rising and falling like a minister's sermon.

> "In the name of our country, I ask the people of Canada at this hour to join with me in expressing our gratitude as a nation for the deliverance from the evil forces of Nazi Germany. We unite in humble and reverent thanksgiving to God, for his mercy thus vouchsafed to the peoples of our own and other lands. Let us rejoice in the victory for which we have waited so long, and which has been won at so great a price."

The war was over. The newsroom burst into applause, and I sank onto the desk, relief flooding my chest and tears burning my vision. The nightmare was over. Our men would finally be coming home.

Ian swept me off the desk and kissed me in front of the entire room, just like in the movies. Everyone cheered louder, and I laughed against his mouth. "Let me go, you brute."

"Come with me," he said, grabbing my hand and leading me to the window.

The street below was filling with people, cheering, banging pots, making noise with whatever they could find.

Mr. Hindmarsh came to stand beside us, watching the crowds, a rare smile on his lips. After a while he turned away. "All right, all right," he said in his trademark monotone. "Back to business. I'll need pieces right away on the treaty, the ships coming back, what's happening with the wounded—"

Al Jones, one of our salesmen, suddenly jumped on his chair. "I just got a call from the mayor's office," he announced, waving a paper like a flag. "They've taken out a full-page ad to announce tomorrow's public holiday!"

As the room erupted, Mr. Hindmarsh leaned closer to Ian. "Mark my words," he said. "He'll ask church groups and synagogues and other community organizations to run their own parties. The less on his plate the better. He thinks that by closing liquor stores for the day and banning places from serving alcohol he's going to keep control."

Ian snorted. "Sure. Let's all celebrate the end of six years of war with a nice hot cup of tea."

UNCONDITIONAL SURRENDER was to be the headline on the front page, Mr. Hindmarsh said. *Surrendered last night at 8:41 Toronto time* would be printed beneath that, just above a summary of the official signing of the surrender in a schoolhouse in Reims, France. On the bottom right corner of the front page was a column beneath another headline:

40,000,000 CASUALTIES
AS EUROPE WAR ENDED

I knew too many of them.

Ian, his hair mussed and a pencil tucked behind his ear, paused by my desk a while later and set a coffee in front of me. "Looks like you could use this."

"You're a lifesaver," I told him, wrapping my fingers around the cup.

"I have to look after my fiancée," he said, winking.

"I'm surprised you have the time to even pour coffee," I teased. "What does Mr. Hindmarsh have you working on?"

"I'm waiting on a call from the prime minister's office. Get his statement. What are you going to write?" he asked. "Something that elicits tears, I imagine."

"I wouldn't have to do anything if I wanted to do that, just underline the forty-million-casualties headline."

He winced. "You're not writing more about the Japanese, I hope."

Lately I'd been educating myself more and more about events happening in the Far East. Germany always led the news, but I wanted to tell the world about what was happening because of Japan. Despite today's momentous announcement, we were still at war.

"Not this time," I told him. "I'm gonna write about Liam, Mark, and the other returning veterans."

His lips tightened slightly. "Yeah, okay. But the rest of the world will be celebrating, you know. You don't always have to play the guilt card and bring everyone down."

I bristled. "It's not guilt, Ian. It's reality."

He shrugged, then walked across the room to his own desk. Watching him go, I was more sure than ever that I'd picked the right topic. Ian might be in denial, not wanting to talk about it, but thousands of men were already returning here after unimaginable experiences. We needed to understand that.

I thought of Mr. Rabinowitz and his painful memories of the Great War, how they still lingered in his pale eyes decades later. So many veterans like him had wandered helplessly through life when they'd returned, never the same as before. Now another generation of survivors was coming home, and I was trying to learn everything I could about how to help them. They'd fought for us, and I planned to fight for them.

I thought of Liam. Of the permanent black line he had developed under his one good eye. Of the foot that never stopped tapping.

I thought of Mark. Of his empty trouser leg.

I thought of Jimmy, still out there somewhere. We hadn't heard from him in weeks, and I tried not to think about why.

Both Mark and Jimmy had been in Normandy—Mark joked that Jimmy had buzzed right over his head and never stopped to say hello. Mark had lost his leg on the beach, and just thinking about that made me dizzy with sorrow for him. But Mark had always been the most practical of us all, and he was determined not to let a little thing like a missing leg get to him. He was a master on his crutches by the time he was released from his convalescence at the Toronto General Hospital, and he'd had no trouble making himself at home in our kitchen when he and Helen had come over for dinner that first time.

I remembered the moment he'd walked into the house, with Helen behind him, practically glowing with happiness. I stood behind my parents, waiting for my turn to greet my brother, and when his eyes touched on me, I thought I might burst. First, though, he went to Dad. I knew Dad was unsure of how to approach his son; we'd had such a difficult time of it with Liam, and we were afraid to step past any boundaries we hadn't figured out yet. So Dad stepped stiffly toward him, holding out his hand.

But Mark wasn't put off. He reached for Dad's hand then gestured to his cane. "Is that a new cane? I like it. Maybe I can get one like it when I'm done with these crutches."

Ice broken, Mum moved to hug him, and when she pulled, back her cheeks were wet. She couldn't look away from the space where Mark's leg used to be.

"I'm all right, Mum," Mark said. I could see how hard he was trying to keep things light, worried for our feelings. He amazed me. "It's gonna save us some money, you know. I can use one pair of socks for twice as long."

"Oh, you," she cried, letting herself smile.

Then Mark turned to me, arms outstretched. "My big sister getting married. I thought I'd never live to see the day."

I rushed to hold him while Mum and Dad ushered Helen in. "I had to wait until you were home," I blubbered.

"I'm happy for you," he whispered in my ear.

I studied his face, needing to know. "Are you?"

"Helen and I are taking it all in stride," he said, a sad little twinkle in his eye. "Hey, where's my baby brother?"

"I'm here," Liam said, appearing in the doorway.

I saw the initial shock flash across Mark's face, but he covered it swiftly, using his crutches to take a step forward. "We're a pair, aren't we? Come here. It's still easier for you to come to me than for me to come to you," he said.

They sat beside each other at dinner, Liam hanging on Mark's words. He hadn't seen any other returning soldiers since he'd been back. He'd refused to have anything to do with the war at all, but by the time dinner was served, Liam had perked up more than I'd seen in a while.

"Have you heard from Jimmy?" I asked over dinner. "He doesn't write home as much as he used to."

"No." Mark shook his head. "But that doesn't mean anything. A lot of guys just aren't ready to talk about it yet. They may never be." He placed a hand on Liam's back. "But that's okay. What's done is done. What matters is what we do now."

Now I sat at my desk in the newsroom, thinking about how so many more would be coming home soon. Tomorrow, people would fill the streets, ticker tape would float from the rooftops, and strangers would embrace, their voices lifted in joy for a change. But when they raised their glasses, how many would think of those who would never come home? Or those who did, but lived with the scars and wounds of the battlefield, visible or not?

While the rest of the newsroom hurried about, working on their own VE assignments, I pulled out my notes, rolled a fresh sheet of paper into the typewriter, and began to type. I lost track of time while I wrote, and I was surprised to hear Ian's voice behind me.

"'*There is no programme the government could offer that might ease the pain of these returning heroes,*'" he read. "'*But the question of financial compensation, at least, must remain paramount in discussions.*'" He nodded. "I like it. Now let's go."

"Where?"

"It's time to celebrate," he said.

"Oh, I don't know. I'm not really great company."

"Doesn't matter. I am."

I looked up at him, puffed up with excitement. And why shouldn't he be? The war was over. He was right.

"Well, if you are, then that does it," I told him. "I'm ready. Where are we going?"

"Everyone's going to the press club. That's the only place we might possibly get a seat tonight. We'll get some food, have some drinks. Trust me. It's exactly what you need," he said, reaching for my handbag. "I won't take no for an answer. I've already told everyone you're my date."

I smiled in spite of myself. "Well, who else would be?"

"No one. You're the only girl for me."

I picked up my article. "Okay, let me just drop this off."

Ian held out my coat and scarf while I dropped the pages in Mr. Hindmarsh's tray, knowing he'd be pleased I'd kept it under five hundred words. I hoped he wouldn't edit too much out.

The temperature outside was barely above freezing, surprisingly cold for May, and it felt like rain might be coming. I hoped not. That would spoil tomorrow's citywide party. Ian grinned, squeezing my hand in his, and we wound our way between revellers on the street. We could hear the noise from the tavern from halfway down the block, and when we got to the door we had to squeeze through the crowds. Ian was almost a head taller than most of the people there, so he went first, holding my hand tight so he could clear a path. Halfway through, he checked on me over his shoulder.

"I'm fine!" I yelled over the noise, following him past a group of ladies standing on a table, singing the national anthem with great gusto.

"Gin and tonic?"

"Yes please!"

"Gin and tonic, and a scotch!" Ian bellowed, I assumed at the bartender.

There was no way to reach the bar through the throngs of people, so when we were about six people away, he passed the cash forward, and the people ahead of us passed the drinks back, toasting us along the way.

Ian's cheeks flushed with excitement as he handed me my glass. "To the end of the war!" he called, lifting his glass, and half the bar replied, "To the end of the war!"

The room was electric with happiness and alcohol. I left my concerns briefly behind, letting the energy infect me. Ian introduced me to practically everyone in the place, and he was right. I had a terrific time. I met new people and listened to the kinds of stories one could only hear in a roomful of reporters, and I drank far too much gin. When it was time for the evening to end, Ian went to retrieve my coat and hat.

"That was so much fun," I said, sliding into the front seat of his dark blue Chevy. My head swam with alcohol and warm, happy remnants of the evening. "Thanks for making me go."

"I told you so."

"Nobody likes anyone who says that, you know."

"You're wrong," he said, pulling into traffic. "Everybody likes me."

I chuckled and closed my eyes, letting the motion of the car lull me to sleep. Moments later, Ian gently jostled my arm. "Molly, wake up. We're here."

I blinked open my eyes and my street came into view, everyone's porch lights left on in celebration. After he parked beside my house, he went around to open my door.

"Thanks for the ride, mister," I said groggily, curling into him. He tugged me close, his lips on my neck, and a delicious thrill raced through me. "Why, you!"

"Molly?"

Startled by a new voice, I pulled away and peered at the dark shape sitting at the side of our front step, avoiding the light overhead. I took another step toward the house, unsure.

"Hey, Molly."

My heart stopped. "Jimmy?"

With the same slow, casual ease I'd known all my life, Jimmy got to his feet and set his hands on his hips. "Is this any way to welcome your b-b-big brother home?"

I felt as if an ocean wave crested on top of me. "Oh my God, Jimmy," I cried, rushing toward him. His arms closed tight around me, and I heard his heart thumping against my ear. "You're home. You're home. You're really home," I sobbed.

"Yeah," he said, his voice rough. "Here I am."

I didn't want to let him go, but Jimmy's hold eased, and I realized he was looking behind me, at Ian. I stepped back, and Ian offered his hand.

"Jimmy," he said. "It's an honour to meet you. Your sister never stops talking about you."

He eyed Ian's hand for a moment before taking it. "You must be Molly's fiancé."

I jumped in. "Jimmy, this is Ian Collins, assistant editor at the *Star*. And yes, he and I are engaged."

Jimmy didn't say anything, just studied Ian while I studied him. His face was a lot thinner than it had been when he'd left, and his uniform coat fell loosely over his frame. His blue wedge cap tilted off the side of his head, giving him a jaunty look that didn't match the weariness in his eyes. He noticed me looking and took it off, crushing it between his hands.

"God, it's good to see you," I said, hugging him again.

"It's good to b-b-be seen by you. There were times . . ." He left off, and I could tell he was embarrassed by his new stammer. I didn't care about that, though the reason behind it worried me. I couldn't stop staring at him, grinning like an idiot. It was strange to see his familiar face so changed by time and experience, but I could almost see the old him in the depths of his eyes, the tough little scrapper he'd once been.

"Let's go in," I blustered. "We can have a drink, and you can tell me when you got home. You've seen Mum and Dad already, I presume?"

He shifted uncomfortably. "Listen, I can't stay here."

I saw his pack at his feet. "I don't understand. Did Mum and Dad—"

"I saw them. And Liam. I just can't b-be here. Dad, he . . ." He shook his head.

I could imagine the scene: Jimmy blustering in with the usual chip on his shoulder, expecting Dad to knock it off. What Jimmy didn't realize was that we'd all changed over the past few years, including Dad. He would have been overwhelmed with relief at the sight of his son back home, but that's not how Jimmy would have seen it. I wished I'd been there to intervene.

"No, Jimmy. He wouldn't—"

"Drop it, Molly. I just stopped here to say hi to you, then I'll find a place."

Ian cleared his throat. "You can stay with me."

Jimmy eyed Ian, clearly suspicious. "Yeah? Just a night or two is all I need."

"However long you need," Ian said, filling me with warmth. What a good man.

After a moment, Jimmy picked up his pack and slung it over his shoulder. "Well, I appreciate it."

"It's the least I can do," Ian said. "You're a hero. We all owe you our thanks."

Jimmy's expression hardened. "I'm no hero. Don't call me that."

I touched my brother's arm, calming him.

His face squeezed briefly then returned to normal. "Sorry. I just . . . I'm no hero."

"Okay. Whatever you say," Ian replied. "You wanna go wait in the car? I'll be right there."

We watched him throw his pack in the back seat, then he opened the passenger door and slid inside to wait.

"Thank you," I whispered. "I'm sorry. He doesn't know—"

"He'll be okay. Just needs some time. I'll watch him." Then he took my hand, and he turned my ring gently between his thumb and finger. "So, before all this happened, I was thinking about something. Today's VE Day. And now that Jimmy's here, your brothers are home."

I knew what he was going to say, but I wished he wouldn't. My thoughts were on Jimmy. I was dying to run inside and find out from my parents what had happened. But he was waiting, expectation in his eyes.

"Yes, they are," I replied.

"So that means we can finally get married."

I smiled. I couldn't argue when he was looking at me that way. "Let's set a date."

twenty-one
MOLLY

꘎

By the time I got to work early the next morning, people were already crowding in the streets. I squeezed through them and into the building, then I headed to my desk, where Ian greeted me with a hot cup of coffee.

"How's Jimmy?" I asked.

He shrugged. "He took a glass of whisky into the spare bedroom and disappeared. He was gone this morning. Overall, a pretty easy house-guest, I'd say."

I tugged his collar so he'd come down for a kiss. "Thank you for doing that."

"Anything to make you happy, Molly. You know that."

"I'm so glad he's back, safe and sound."

He grimaced, knowing there was more to the story. "How did it go with your parents?"

"It was what I thought." After he and Jimmy had left, I'd knocked on my parents' closed door. They were quiet, and Mum's eyes were red from crying. "He cut Dad down as soon as he stepped inside. Dad never knew what hit him. He's devastated. Mum's a wreck."

He nodded. "That's rough. Sorry you have to be in the middle of all that. But," he said with a wink, "I have something that will put a smile on your face." He pulled today's *Star* from behind his back, folded open to my article.

"Page six!" I exclaimed. "That's my best yet!"

"You have a way with words that most writers would kill for, you know that? The guys never stop telling me how my future bride's going to keep me on my toes."

"Well, if the writing doesn't pan out, you do make a great coffee," I teased.

He laughed, a hearty sound that filled the room. "Say," he said, whispering conspiratorially, "how does August fourth sound? Is that enough time to plan?"

My phone rang, and Ian waited as I picked it up. It was a secretary at City Hall I'd been trying to reach a few days before, so my brain shifted to business mode, and I covered the mouthpiece with one hand.

"Can we talk later?" I whispered to Ian. "I have to take this."

His brow furrowed slightly. "Sure."

The morning passed in a blur, then at noon, Ian brought me my coat and we headed to the cenotaph with most of the newsroom, waiting for a formal announcement by the mayor. As we neared the monument, Ian and I wound between the merrymakers, soaking in the pulsing excitement of the city. I had thought we'd left the office in plenty of time, but I was wrong, so we couldn't get a spot at the front. I popped up on my toes to see what was happening, and when I put a hand on his arm to balance, he chuckled.

"You can't see?" Ian asked, and I suddenly thought of that day long ago, leaning against Sir John A. Macdonald's cold statue with Max. *Oh, Max,* I thought. Forty million casualties, and we'd still never heard a word about him. He had deserved so much better than that.

I took a deep breath, pasting my smile back in place, and pushed the memories back where they belonged. "No, no. I can see well enough. This is such a happy day," I said, pasting my smile back in place. "It feels like everything's going to change now."

On one hand, I was right. Things did change around the city. The streets filled once again with young men and cheerful couples, but also with beaten-down veterans and crutches. I saw some of the boys from baseball so long ago, like Snooky Rubenstein and Matteo Rossi, looking twenty years older than they had five years ago. When I said hello, they didn't appear to recognize me. Then I learned that Phil Burke had been killed fighting in Germany. Despite everything that had happened between us, I sat down and had a good cry. No one had deserved what this war had done.

On the other hand, I was wrong. Some things didn't change. The war between the United States and Japan raged on, and I found myself busier than ever, covering the conflict in the Pacific. At home, Liam still stayed in the dark most of the time, though he continued walking with Dad in the mornings, and he'd sit in the yard with Mark if he stopped by. So I suppose that was a bit of a change for the better, at least.

Jimmy was difficult to predict and always seemed to be on the move, though he never told anyone where he went during the day. Sometimes Ian came home to a houseguest, and sometimes he was alone. When I saw Jimmy, he was usually quite dirty but didn't seem to notice, and he only reluctantly agreed to my offer to do his laundry. Jimmy had always been independent, but this was extreme behaviour even for him. It hurt to see him so broken, but I was so glad to have him back I didn't tell him that.

One night he showed up unexpectedly at our house for dinner. Mum, Dad, Liam, and I all scrambled, making him a seat at the table and trying to ease through conversations, but Jimmy didn't say a word the whole time. I could feel anger rising off him in waves, but none of us had any idea where it was coming from. When it was time to clear the table, I stood and reached for his plate, and he shot out of his chair as if I'd struck him. The four of us stared in confusion as he grabbed his coat and left, slamming the door behind him.

"I didn't do anything this time," Dad said pitifully.

"No, you didn't," I agreed. "It wasn't any of us."

Mum had put her head in her hands, lost. Jimmy was back from the war, but we still grieved his loss in a way. I went to her side and hugged her, noticing the sharpness of her shoulder blades against my hands. Between taking care of Dad and Liam, helping Barbara and the girls, worrying about Jimmy, and still mourning the loss of Richie, she was weakening by the day.

"It'll be all right, Mum. We'll all be all right." But I hardly believed my own words.

Ian tried to be supportive, but after three months of letting Jimmy crash at his place, even he got frustrated.

"I don't know where he goes or what he does, but he always comes back reeking of booze and worse," he said. "He needs to get help, Molly. I can't look after him—I'm at work during the day."

"Just a little while longer. Please, Ian. He's the only big brother I have left," I pleaded.

"Okay, okay," he said, taking me in his arms. "But we can't keep doing this forever. We have to move on with our lives. We haven't even picked a wedding date yet."

We'd worked right through the August 4 date we'd agreed upon earlier, and I knew he was impatient, but it hardly seemed like a priority to me. My hands closed into fists behind his back, and I pulled out of his reach. "I can't think about our wedding right now. Mum's run off her feet, and Mr. Hindmarsh has me on so many assignments. You tell me, Ian. I kind of think writing about the end of a world war should trump booking the church, don't you?"

"Do you even want to get married?" he asked quietly.

"Of course I do," I said, immediately sorry. "I just have too much on my plate right now."

"All right," he said, holding up his hands in surrender. "I'm just impatient to be your husband. Can you blame me?"

I hopped up on my toes and kissed him lightly. "I'm sorry," I said. "I will get to it. I promise."

But the following week, Ian stormed into the office and pulled me aside, clearly upset. "Your brother's got serious problems. Last night I went out to the kitchen to get a glass of water, and he pinned me against the wall. I don't think he recognized me. I don't think he even knew where he was at first. To be honest, he scared me. Jimmy's wiry, but he's strong as an ox."

"He's scared too," I replied, aching for Jimmy. "Let me talk to him."

But Jimmy wanted none of my sympathy. "Look after Liam if you need to fix someb-b-body," he said. "I'm fine. All I need is a place to sleep at night, and if Ian doesn't want me there, I'll find somewhere else."

The next morning, Ian told me Jimmy had grabbed his pack that night and left.

From that day on, whenever I walked downtown and saw the sad, shadowy figures of veterans wandering or sleeping on the streets, I looked for my brother. I wondered if I would ever see him again. Jimmy had always done what he wanted. This time he'd wanted to disappear.

Not long after, Hannah rang me. "Come see me after work?" she asked. "You haven't been over in a while."

My first reaction was to tell her I had no time, but as I opened my mouth to say the words, I realized how much I needed to see her. She'd always been my strength.

"I'll be there."

Over a glass of wine, she told me she'd seen Jimmy and she was concerned.

"Where's he living, Molly? Because he doesn't look right. When I saw him, he was sleeping on the curb. He looked awful. Filthy. And he didn't know who I was."

I sagged. I'd spent all that time on VE Day writing my big, important ode to veterans, thinking I knew it all, and I couldn't even help my brother. "He's living where he can, I guess. He can't stand me or anyone else. He won't take help, and he won't listen to reason. My heart is broken for him, Hannah. I don't know what to do."

Hannah was quiet. "We knew this war would change them," she said. "Jimmy's so far down a hole he can't see the light. I guess we just have to wait for him to come out, and we all know how stubborn he can be. I promise if I see him, I'll make sure he's at least eating, okay?"

I thanked her, feeling a little relief now that she'd taken some of my burden on her shoulders.

"How are you?" she asked kindly, handing me a tissue. "How's Ian?"

"He's happy now that we've finally set a date for the wedding."

She sat up. "Oh, good! When?"

"Actually, Ian picked it." I twisted my mouth to the side. Ian and I had gone back and forth on the date. August was now just around the corner, so I'd suggested a winter wedding, thinking it would give me more time to plan, then Ian had mentioned a possible date. *We need to make happy memories to replace the sad ones*, he'd said. I had reluctantly agreed.

Hannah looked at me sideways. "What date did he choose?"

"Christmas Day."

twenty-two
MOLLY

❧

The doorman at the King Edward Hotel gave a little bow as Ian and I approached, then he swung the door open to welcome us in, scattering a few dried autumn leaves. We stepped into the elevator, then headed up to the seventeenth floor, where the doors opened to the glittering Crystal Ballroom and the lazy sound of a jazz trio. My stomach tumbled with nerves. Ian put his arm around my waist and squeezed, sensing that.

"You have nothing to worry about," he said. "You're the most prepared journalist in the room."

I had been looking forward to this reception for the past week, ever since Mr. Hindmarsh had received the invitation. Tonight we'd meet and speak with a few recently arrived prisoners of war from the Japanese prison camps. From all my research, I knew this was going to be tough. The stories being leaked were of starving, sick men dealing with horrific conditions, and from personal experience with my brothers, I knew it might not be easy to get full statements. But the interviews weren't what had me so nervous. My apprehension stemmed from the fact that Richie had been with these men out there. They had been his friends. Even if they could tell their stories, would I be able to listen without breaking down?

I noticed right away how different this event was from other receptions we'd attended recently. After VE Day, the returning men had been loud, boisterous, keen to open up over the free drinks in their hands. Some had flirted with me at first, and I'd let them, knowing I had to put them at ease if I was going to get them to talk. Ian was good at getting details in a man-to-man way, but I was better at getting beneath the surface, where emotions lurked.

Tonight the mood was quiet, but I had expected that. When Ian and I had gone to celebrate VJ Day on August 15, those crowds had been smaller than back in May. Since the majority of the fighting men and POWs had been in Europe, a lot of the city was already back to work by now, having left the war behind. It almost felt to me as if the tens of thousands returning from the Far East were an afterthought. If Japan ever came up in conversation, it was usually in reference to the atomic bombs that had been dropped over Nagasaki and Hiroshima in August, not about our men left behind.

I understood that, though. The bombs had shocked the world. The end of the war had come at a terrible price, and I was having a great deal of trouble reconciling that solution with the tens of thousands of innocent people killed. Now, as I stood in the same room as men who had been tortured for four years by the Japanese army, I wondered how they felt about it.

At the coat check counter, Ian took my coat and let out a low whistle of appreciation. "You look incredible, Molly."

I'd bought myself a new emerald-green dress for the occasion, with boxy shoulders, a trim, belted waist, and a dainty white collar at my neck. Ian always looked well put together, and tonight he was wearing his navy suit with a pale blue tie. I knew we had dressed right for the event, but I felt self-conscious among these men with their baggy uniforms and sallow faces. I also noted that, while there were a few other reporters and government officials in the room, all in all, there were very few women.

"We stick out like sore thumbs among all these uniforms, don't we?" I murmured.

"Mutts circling pedigree canines," Ian said, scanning the room. "There are a lot of horrendous stories of beatings and killings coming out of these camps. This is going to be interesting."

I touched his arm. "Don't say 'interesting,' Ian. That's cruel."

"You know what I mean."

"I wonder if they'll even be able to speak to us about what happened. My brothers barely can."

I'd been so proud of Liam lately. The light in his eyes had finally come back on a couple of weeks ago when Barbara had stopped by with Evelyn and Joan. Mum told me he'd come downstairs for tea, and the girls had run to him, wanting to play toy horses with him. At first, when they asked about the strange markings on his face and neck, he'd turned his answer into a gentle lesson about very bad people and staying away from fire. They'd nodded, wide-eyed, then they'd simply moved on to the game. Disarmed by their unaffected attentions, Liam had sat with them for hours while Mum and Barbara watched in astonishment. Mum told me that after they left, he'd started carving small toys for them, and the work was consuming him in a whole new, productive way.

Mark and Helen were expecting their first baby in the next two months, and they were on top of the world with the news. Mark always seemed fine, but despite his cheery outlook, he had never told me the truth about what had happened to him on the beaches of Normandy. I'd asked, but he just gave me a tight smile and looked away.

Then there was Jimmy. He hadn't returned to Ian's house in weeks, and neither Hannah nor I had seen him. I feared the worst, and as I had with the Red Cross and the government in '42, I returned to calling hospitals and shelters, pleading for someone to tell me they'd seen my brother. No one had.

The men we'd come to interview tonight had only just been liberated after almost four years of harsh imprisonment. I knew the military wanted to celebrate their return in front of the press, but I questioned the wisdom of dragging them into the public eye so soon.

"I guess we'll see," Ian said. "The army probably had to choose some willing to talk, poor fellows." He lit a cigarette. "First things first. Drinks. Gin and tonic?"

"Please."

As he walked away, I studied the room, trying to determine who I should interview. Men lingered in ones or twos, cigarettes and drinks silently burning through them. I thought I knew a fair amount about POW camps, but I also knew the press hadn't been told all of it. What exactly had these men survived? What would I learn tonight? I looked for someone standing on his own, someone with a certain energy in his eye, hoping to avoid anyone who might be too shy to answer questions. I pulled my notebook out of my purse and checked my notes one more time, making sure I had all my questions lined up.

Ian nudged me gently then handed me my drink. I took a sip, and we scanned the room together.

"Have you decided on anyone yet?" He raised his scotch to his lips.

I tilted my head toward a lone, dark-haired man with a thin moustache, a tumbler of whisky in his hand. "Maybe the officer over there."

"He looks relatively alert, though all of them look like they could sleep for a month, don't they?" The scotch in his glass sloshed a little as he gestured to the other side of the room. "There's a group of younger men over that way. They'll have something to say, I imagine." He frowned at his watch. "I'll meet you back here in, what, twenty minutes?"

"I might be late," I said.

He started toward the young soldiers. "Don't be."

I took another sip then meandered toward the officer. The corner of his mouth twitched when he spotted me coming, as if he was considering whether or not to bolt, so I gave him a warm smile.

"Good evening," I said brightly. "I'm Molly Ryan from the *Toronto Daily Star*."

Up close, the gaunt lines of his face were even more obvious, his toughened skin loose over the bones, but I'd been wrong with my first impression of his age. He'd looked much older from a distance. Up close, I could tell he was only about ten years older than I was, maybe less.

"Nice to meet you," he said. His voice was quiet and slow, and I leaned in a little closer to hear him. "Sergeant Robert Cox. I'd offer to buy you a drink, but—"

I held up my glass. "Thank you anyway. Really, I should be buying you a drink, to thank you for your service."

He nodded but didn't say anything in response.

I hesitated. "Sergeant Cox, I'm sure you'd rather be anywhere but here, but I hope you'll speak with me a moment about your experience as a prisoner of war. So many Canadians don't yet know what happened over there. Would you mind if I asked you a few questions?"

"That's why they brought me here." His smile twitched again. "But you might not like the answers."

"I hope you can tell me what you remember and not worry about my reactions. I'm tougher than I look. My brothers fought. I know a little about the war."

"So they survived?"

"All but one," I said, setting my glass on a nearby table before pulling out my notebook and pen. I was here to interview the men. I didn't want to talk about me. "You were in captivity for three years and eight months, am I correct?"

He took a big gulp of his whisky. "Yes. I was captured on Christmas Day in '41."

My mouth went dry. The same day Richie died at St. Stephen's. I'd known his answer beforehand, but it still hit me to hear it out loud. "Where were you captured?"

"Stanley Village."

My mind went back in time, recalling Hannah's bloodshot eyes on that terrible day, when she'd told me David had died there. This was too much for me, I realized suddenly. I shouldn't be the one here, asking questions.

But I was. This was my job. If I gave in to the voice inside my head telling me to run, I would be a coward. I owed Richie and David more than that.

I cleared my throat, determined to go on. "Do you remember anything about that battle?"

He looked away. "I do."

He shut down so quickly it was like a door slamming. I moved on, hoping Ian would get those details from one of the younger soldiers.

"Where were you taken?"

"North Point Camp near Victoria, Hong Kong. It had been a refugee camp to begin with. A few months later we were moved to Sham Shui Po in Kowloon. That place was originally built as a British army barracks, and it's where we'd stayed when we first arrived in Hong Kong in November '41." He smiled to himself. "Funny to think of how nice it was back then. Big, comfortable, fairly modern. When we returned to it as POWs, there was little left of it besides badly cracked walls."

He looked tempted to stop speaking again, so I asked him to describe the camp for me. I had found that men opened up more when they talked about physical attributes.

"Sham Shui Po had two main barracks with fourteen huts in each. Not nearly enough room for all of us prisoners. I don't think they'd ever imagined capturing so many men. The place was surrounded by ten-foot, electrified, barbed wire fences connected by guard towers. During the initial invasion, the place had been bombed, then the local Chinese had ransacked it and removed all the windows and wood. We ended up using metal roofing material as shutters to try and keep out the rain."

I scribbled away on my notepad, not wanting to miss a single detail. "What about the food?"

He winced. "All we were fed was watery, mouldy rice. Two meals a day of it, occasionally flavoured by rat droppings and maggots. It went right through us, if you'll pardon my saying. The whole camp was a walking boneyard. If I ever see another grain of rice in my life, it'll be too much."

As he spoke, I couldn't help but remember the POW camp Ian and I had visited in Bowmanville, with its daily fresh bread and healthy vegetables, of the lake where they swam without guards.

"Sometimes the Chinese people hiding nearby would try to pass food through the fence to us," he said, his eyes losing focus. "That wasn't allowed. The Japanese made sure they never tried it twice."

I wanted to know everything, but the sea of pain in his eyes was too deep for me to cross.

"And where did you sleep?" I asked.

"We had cots of a sort, but usually we chose the cement floor instead. Between the bed bugs, the fleas, and the lice, we figured we were better off sleeping on the ground. But then we had to worry about the red ants and tarantulas, the scorpions, the termites, and the rats." He seemed briefly lost in his memories. "Those rats tasted just like chicken, and they were big as cats."

I swallowed the bile that had shot up my throat, and he caught himself.

"We didn't have those too often, though. Rats are greasy, and all that grease was hard on a body if it hadn't eaten anything but rice in months. Speaking of which, don't ask me about the latrines. Trust me on that. When we got there, there weren't any. And we didn't have any tools to dig them."

I wished that what he described were shocking to me, but by that point, I'd read so many reports on the conditions of the camps, I was able to steel myself for the most part. But there was one piece of research I needed him to verify. I'd come across a list of regulations for prisoners, and the black ink on the page had detailed exactly which crimes would result in an immediate execution by the Japanese. I wasn't sure if the regulations had been exaggerated for intimidation purposes, or if they were true.

I flipped over a page in my notepad. "I've read that the Japanese were strict disciplinarians. Is that right?"

He huffed. "That's a charitable way to put it."

I looked up, allowing him to fill the silence. Before he spoke again, he took a long swallow of his scotch.

"Personally, I wouldn't call them disciplinarians. I'd call them sadistic monsters. We weren't allowed to talk without permission. We couldn't take a step without an order to do so. Even using more than two blankets was forbidden."

Those were a few of the crimes I'd read on the list. "And what happened if you did?"

He frowned slightly. "You sure you want to hear about that, Miss Ryan?"

"As you said, Sergeant Cox, that's what we're here for. To tell Canadians the truth of what happened over there."

His voice lowered. "Okay. I'll tell you about my friend, Albert. One day he picked up a used cigarette butt—we never could get full cigarettes—and one of the Kempeitai—that's what the guards were called—stormed over and whipped it out of his mouth. Well, my friend was pretty determined. He picked up that butt again then stared down the Jap while he lit it, like he was daring him. Albert was gutsy, but incredibly stupid." He took a breath, stared into his drink. "He was damn near beaten to death after that, then he was staked out in the yard for a week. We weren't allowed anywhere near him, and nobody fed him. He got gangrene in his hands and feet from the beatings. They put him in the hospital building after that—of course they wouldn't ever give us medicine, so I don't know why they bothered—and he died two days later."

My stomach rolled, thinking of Arnie. "Unspecified illness" was how his death had been listed. "What would have happened if anyone had gone to help Albert?"

"Nobody was that stupid." He took a big pull of his drink. "Once you see a man's head chopped off, you learn to obey orders."

My pen stilled in my hand, and I forced myself to ask, "Did that happen often?"

He nodded. "One time, after one of the guys tried to escape, they chopped his head off then put us into groups of ten. They told us that if one escaped, they would kill the other nine."

So it was true. I had read on that page that any offense was punishable by death, but Sergeant Cox's pragmatic expression and his plain, straightforward words made it real.

I realized I was staring. "How long were you at Sham Shui Po? Were you sent anywhere else?"

"You're asking about the Japanese POW camps now," he said, seeming pleased that I knew the facts enough to ask. "I was at Sham Shui Po for about a year. Then they stuffed about five hundred of us at a time into the bowels of small boats they called hell ships. We were like sardines in there. No food or water or sanitation of any kind. We were shipped up to Japan. They needed workers, I guess, because their men were all at war. It was hard to believe at first, but those camps were a hell of a lot worse than what we'd just survived."

"Those were labour camps, correct?"

He tapped my paper with his boney finger, and I noticed his brittle, cracked nails, with ridges around the nail beds from malnutrition. "*Slave* labour. Make sure that's in your article, if you don't mind. I believe most of the men had to work in the mines, but I worked at NKK, a giant shipyard near Tokyo. For years, we built and maintained Japan's war fleet." He smiled faintly and finished his drink. "During that time, we sabotaged everything we could get our hands on. At one point, Staff Sergeant Clarke and Private Cameron set fire to the pattern shop, where all the blueprints were stored, destroying the most vital war effort of the Japanese. I was so proud of those men. Nobody had a clue, and nobody gave them up for it, either."

I tried to imagine the courage that must have taken, knowing their captors wouldn't have hesitated to kill them upon discovery.

"Any more questions?" he asked.

"Yes, Sergeant. I have just a few more, if you don't mind."

He'd told me the facts. Now I needed to know what it all meant to him on a personal level. Even after all my research, I still couldn't grasp the whole of it.

"How did you survive this? I mean, the horrors just kept happening. The punishments, the starvation, the disease, the slave labour . . . How did you not just give up?"

He straightened his bent frame, and for the first time, he looked me straight in the eye. "We are Canadians, Miss Ryan," he said, matter-of-fact. "We were disciplined and determined. A united front. Not one of our men would ever even think of disgracing their uniform or letting their brothers down. In fact, I would say that the worse things got, the more determined we became. I swore that my men and I would see freedom once more, once the Allies were victorious."

It set me back, this steadfast belief in himself and the others in his unit. I understood duty, but this went so far beyond that. It went to the physical and psychological destruction of human beings by the enemy, and yet somehow, despite all the best efforts by the Japanese to destroy his body, they had failed to crush his spirit.

"Sergeant Cox, can you tell me how you feel, right now, about what happened to you?"

"Feel?"

I didn't like the sound of the question either, but I needed to get insight into the thoughts of these poor men.

"Yes. In your mind." I touched my chest. "And in here. Can you describe it?"

He didn't speak for a moment. "Well, I'm very proud to have served with this brigade, both in fighting and in the camps. Every man there should be proud."

I nodded, waiting for more.

"To be honest, I don't think I feel much at all anymore. When you see what I've seen, and when you have to walk past the headless bodies of your friends every day, you kind of put up a wall against feelings, I guess. I'm sorry I can't tell you anything more than that."

I almost put my hand on his arm to offer comfort, but he was ill at ease now. The empty glass in his hand shook noticeably. I couldn't blame him. He'd told me much more than I'd expected.

"Thank you so much, Sergeant. I really appreciate you sparing this time and your thoughts."

He offered a weary smile. "Did you get what you needed?"

"Oh yes. And can I say that I think it's very courageous of you to tell me all these things. My brothers can't speak of it."

He frowned. "I'm sorry one of them won't be coming home. Might I ask where he served?"

"In Hong Kong, as a matter of fact. He died at St. Stephen's."

"St. Stephen's?" He blinked. "Beg your pardon, but did you say your name was Miss Ryan?"

"Yes, Molly Ryan."

"Richie," he said softly, raising goose bumps all over my body. His eyes were taking me in: the red hair, the freckles, and I saw his sadness. "I'm very sorry. I was Richie's sergeant. He was a good man and a good friend. He served bravely."

I pressed my lips together, determined not to break down. But it was so hard. "Thank you, Sergeant. And again, thank you for your service."

"It was my honour." He lifted his glass. "And now I think I deserve another drink."

Mine was still full. I had forgotten all about it. "You certainly do."

He headed toward the bar, and my gaze wandered, heavier now with thoughts of Richie. Of all the men in Hong Kong, what were the chances I would have met my brother's sergeant? I took a deep breath, focusing my thoughts on the job at hand. Sergeant Cox had given me a lot of information and insight, but I needed more than one source if it was going to be a comprehensive piece. I scanned the room for someone who seemed more animated, who might—

My vision closed in around a group of three men, standing by the exit. The tallest of them had his back to me, but I knew the set of those shoulders, that deliberate, thoughtful nod. Heat roared into my body, and I started to shake.

It couldn't be, could it?

I began to move, every fibre of my being straining toward the dark, uniformed figure in the doorway. Step by step, I squeezed through the crowd, thinking twenty feet had never seemed so far before. Then all at once I stood behind him, close enough to touch. Frozen, I listened to the sound of his voice, and though it was more subdued than I'd ever heard it before, it was as familiar to me as my own.

One of the others had asked him a question, and he'd shrugged. "Nah, I didn't have much time before this . . ."

Then he trailed off, straightening slightly, as if he sensed me standing behind him. When he turned, I could only stare, filling my eyes and heart with the sight of him.

"Max," I breathed.

His jaw dropped. "Molly?"

Before I could think, I threw my arms around his neck, embracing the solid proof of him, breathing in his scent, feeling relief take hold of my entire body as his coat absorbed my tears. The bones of his shoulders were hard against my hands, no longer young and muscled, too weak to catch me or lift me as they once had, but still there. *Still alive.*

He didn't move at first, then I felt him relax slightly, and his arms wrapped around me. After a moment, I drew back, needing to look at him. To really see him.

"You're alive," I whispered, noting with sadness how the light in his deep brown eyes had faded. His skin was dull, his jawbone pronounced within his angular face, and strands of grey flickered within his dark hair. All those years and more were etched into his face. While we had carried on with our lives, he had been locked up in a cage. He'd been mourned and never forgotten, but he'd been left behind by everyone he loved.

"Molly," he said again, and I swayed at the sound. Confusion and pain flickered across his face, and I felt it everywhere inside me. "What are you doing here?"

It was so hard to breathe. To think. "I'm . . . I'm working. I'm—"

"Ah! There you are." From somewhere behind me, Ian appeared and held out a hand. "Ian Collins, the *Star*."

Max shook his hand, but his dark eyes were still on me.

Ian turned, taking in my tears, and his face filled with concern. "Hey, are you okay?" he asked, handing me his handkerchief. "You look like you've seen a ghost."

I took a deep, shaky breath. "Ian," I said, trying unsuccessfully to smile, "this is Max Dreyfus. Hannah's brother. I haven't seen him in—"

"About twelve years," Max finished for me.

twenty-three
MAX

⁘

Max hardly noticed the newcomer to the conversation. He couldn't take his eyes off Molly. Her hair was mussed from the ferocity of her hug, and her face was blotchy from crying, but she was still the most beautiful woman he'd ever seen.

"Hannah's brother? *That* Max? Whoa," the other man was saying. What was his name? Ian? Max turned reluctantly toward him. "Welcome back from the dead, sir. We sure had it wrong, didn't we, Molly? What a coincidence, for you two to run into each other here, of all places."

"I had no idea," she whispered. "We all thought . . . What about your parents? Do they know you're here?"

He nodded, taking in the freckles that dotted her nose, still not quite believing that she was standing in front of him. He tried to concentrate on her question. "I got back today. I cleaned up at their house, then my captain dragged me here."

"Today!" Ian exclaimed. "You must be exhausted."

He lifted one shoulder, let it drop. "I've been exhausted for years. What's one more night?"

"I'm surprised your parents let you go." Her hypnotic green eyes held him like a lifeline. All those years of trying to forget, and he still felt exactly the same way about her. "They must be so happy. Does Hannah know?"

"She wasn't there, but Mama will call her. They'll all be there tonight after this, I expect." The thought sent a skitter of anxiety through him. He might be here to speak with the press, but he wasn't prepared to answer his family's questions.

She reached out her hand, as if to check that he was really there, then thought better of it. Her fingers brushed his arm, and his skin danced with nerves.

"God, I'm happy you're home."

"She was a mess for months," Ian said. "The folks at the Red Cross and the war office know her well. She was determined to find you and all the others. She didn't give up for a long time."

He remembered that, how she never gave up when she had something on her mind. He remembered everything about her.

"Yeah. We found out on the way back here that I didn't make the Red Cross list," Max said. "Frankly, it probably wouldn't have made a difference on my end. Hardly anyone got letters in the camps, but I guess it would have been a big help to you."

"We thought you'd been killed. But nobody would tell us anything. It didn't make sense," Molly said. "After we heard about Richie, I knew you had to be there somewhere."

Max dropped his chin, eyes to the floor. "I'm sorry about Richie, Moll." She had no idea how sorry. He wasn't sure he'd ever be able to tell her the full story.

Ian had been watching intently, and now he turned to Molly. "Say, I have an idea. Stop me if I'm wrong, but we came here to interview POWs, and it looks to me like you two would like to talk. Maybe we could cover both."

She frowned at him. "What are you suggesting?"

"An in-depth interview." He focused on Max. "You and Molly can talk, and I can take notes. We could meet at a café, buy you lunch. What do you think? It would be more comfortable than standing here with all these people."

"Oh, no, Ian. I don't think that's fair to ask of Max." She hesitated then turned to him, and despite all the years between them, he recognized the spark of interest in her expression. She liked the idea. "Unless you want to?"

"We wouldn't even have to name you in the article if you'd rather stay anonymous," Ian said.

"Maybe we could talk about Richie?" Molly added, and he heard fear in her voice.

He found himself nodding. "I'm up for it if you are," he said, but he wasn't sure that was true.

"How's tomorrow?" Ian asked. "We can meet at the Senator at noon. Do you remember that spot, at Yonge and Dundas? It's a nice place. We can keep to ourselves in there. Will that work?"

"Sure. I—" He caught a movement behind Ian. "Um, I'm sorry, but my sergeant's waving us out. They have a car for us, and I guess it's leaving."

"Duty calls," Molly said, trying to smile. "At least this time I know I'll see you again. We have all the time in the world now."

"We sure do," he said, wishing he could hug her again.

Ian stuck out his hand. It was a strong grip, which Max appreciated. "It's so good to meet you at last, Max. Really." He nudged Molly and winked. "Guess this means we'll have one more invitation to send out for the wedding."

Max's stomach plunged, and his gaze slipped to the plain gold band on her finger. When he looked up, Molly's face was flushed a dark pink.

That's when he felt it begin again, the hardening of his heart, the construction of a wall that no emotions could penetrate. Over the past four years that wall had saved Max's sanity so many times. He'd come home with no expectations, and tonight, he'd leave this place with even fewer.

———

Every light in the house was lit for Max's return, and as he stepped out of the hired car, he wished they hadn't done that. Of course they'd want to see him, to talk. But right now, it felt like too much. He wanted to sit in the dark, alone.

The door flew open as he limped up the walk, and Hannah ran out to him, her arms held out.

She collided with him, sank into his chest, and he lowered his face to her hair. "Hannah," he said, feeling her whole body bump with sobs. She was a widow now, he remembered, thinking of David for the first time in a while, his body unmoving on the trampled grass. Guilt rushed through him. "I'm sorry. I'm so sorry, Hannah. I couldn't save him. I couldn't bring him home."

She leaned back, pale with understanding. "Oh, Max! I know you tried. I know you did. You couldn't do everything." She put her hands on his cheeks, holding his eyes with hers. "But you came home. Oh, God. I still can't believe it. Thank you. Thank you for coming home."

He held her again, and through his coat he felt her fingers digging into his back. Holding on tight. Over her shoulder he saw his parents, their faces wet with tears. But his own was dry. How long since he'd cried? He couldn't remember.

"It's all right," he said to Hannah, then over her shoulder to his parents. "It's all right now." They needed him to be strong. If only he could convince himself.

Hannah finally released him, and the family ushered him into the living room, their voices ringing with happiness and laughter. Hannah's children hugged his knees, so his progress was slow, and he had to stop himself from peeling them off him. He wanted to be here. He wanted to be with them. But their grips felt like bindings, and one of them was squeezing too tightly around his bum leg. He was relieved when he was able to sit and they left him alone.

The others settled into their chairs, happily commenting about what a wonderful day this was, watching him as if he were some sort of curiosity. Their eyes overflowed with love, and Max felt a tremor of panic. He'd seen their eyes before, at night, in the dark, with the rats scuttling nearby and the stink of men in his nostrils. He'd felt this love before, but only when he'd been beaten so badly he'd needed to cling to his memories for his own sanity. Was any of this real?

It had to be a trick. How could he possibly be here? Then his mother appeared before him, smiling with adoration, a plate of latkes held out like an offering. He'd seen her do this before, seen her stirring pots in the kitchen and bringing food to him. He'd seen it all in his mind as he picked at the rotten grains of rice, moving with maggots.

But those were just dreams, he remembered. Wildly imagined fantasies of one day leaving the camp and finding himself again. They filled his mind to punish him because he didn't deserve that, not when all his friends were dead.

"Don't touch me!" he cried, jerking away from the hallucination.

"But, *bubbala*—"

"No!" He sprang out of his chair, knocking his mother's hands, and the plate crashed to the floor in a mess of broken china and latkes.

With a squeak of alarm, Dinah raced behind Hannah's chair, but no one else moved a muscle, and no one said a word. In the silence, he studied their stricken faces, slowly realizing it was not a dream after all. Then it dawned on him that what he was seeing in their eyes was fear. They were afraid. Of him. He'd done that.

"I— I'm sorry," he whispered. "I'm sorry."

Hannah slowly moved toward him, keeping her movements small. "It will get easier," she said softly. "I promise."

"I just need sleep," he said weakly, taking a step away from her.

His mother's hands were bunched into fists in front of her mouth, and he could tell she was holding herself back. He was asking too much of her. If only he could let the anger go, hold her like she needed to be held. But he was afraid.

"Tomorrow is a new day for all of us," Hannah said softly. "I know you don't understand this yet, but you are our miracle, Max. You're home. We will help you."

For the first time, a knot jammed in his throat. He nodded quickly, burying his emotions again, then fled the room. Upstairs, nothing had changed in his bedroom. He marveled at the forgotten scene, thinking this made it seem like he'd only been away for a few hours, not five years. They hadn't packed up his things. They hadn't given up on him, even if he had.

Out of habit he moved slowly, afraid to make a noise, while he took off his coat and boots. He sat on the edge of his bed, feeling the softness of the mattress beneath him, letting his body remember the idea of comfort. Then he lowered himself to the floor, more at home with its hardness against his body. He was so tired. Weary to the marrow of his bones.

The knot in his throat loosened, and though it ached from holding back his tears for so long, at least he could breathe. He inhaled slowly, filling his lungs and hoping for peace, but anguish gripped him at the top. Grief came out in a groan, pushing from his gut, and the agony of the past five years rolled down his face. The images that had haunted him for years returned, stabbing him deeper and deeper: David's motionless body lying just out of reach. Richie's red, pleading eyes begging him not to leave. Arnie, wasted to nothing by the end, weighing no more than a child in his arms. He'd left them all behind, but their dead eyes still watched. He took a deep shuddering breath, needing to find control again, but it was much too far away.

Finally, he drifted off to sleep, and he felt the scratch of the barrack's cement floor on his cheek. He heard the men down the row counting in Japanese in their sleep. He saw the arcing sword as it sliced through men's necks, ending their misery. So many times, Max had envied those men.

But he'd had to come back. For David, for Arnie, and for Richie.

twenty-four
MOLLY

I slid across the vinyl bench at the corner booth at the Senator, then sat on my hands to still them. I was practically buzzing with nerves. I needed to stay calm, but I couldn't fathom how. *Max.* Max was *alive.* He was back, and he was going to sit with me again. Twelve years of missing him. Of wishing and hoping . . . and soon he would be here.

But the very thought of Ian, Max, and me at the same table had my stomach rolling with anxiety. Beside me, Ian was oblivious. He was reading the menu, humming to himself as if this were just another day. He had no idea. *It's just Max*, I told myself. But was it?

He arrived at noon, and when I saw him walk through the front door of the restaurant, I scrambled to my feet, short of breath. Ian caught my cue and stood to face him. Max was wearing a black overcoat and flat cap, and as he came toward us, I noticed with a pang of sympathy that he was limping. What had happened to him over there? Was it something permanent?

"Welcome!" Ian said, stepping back.

Max took off his coat and hat and hung them on the hook with Ian's. Before he took his seat, he scanned the room like he wasn't entirely sure where he was, almost like he was afraid. Then his eyes landed on me and his shoulders seemed to relax a bit.

"What?" he asked.

I realized I was staring. "I'm sorry, Max. It's just that I really never expected to see you ever again. It's . . ." I searched for words.

"Hannah called me the family's miracle," he said, his mouth twisted awkwardly.

"Well, she's right," I said. "You *are* a miracle."

He smiled lightly then looked away.

"Hungry?" Ian asked, directing Max to the bench. "I'm starved."

I glanced at Max, painfully aware of Ian's gaffe. "Yep, you look it," he said wryly.

"What?" Ian blinked, then he realized what he'd said. "I'm sorry. I didn't think."

"It's okay," Max said, accepting the menu I passed him.

The waitress had brought three cups of coffee, and Ian raised his in a toast. "Cheers to Max's homecoming. To all the men finally coming home to their families."

"I'll drink to that," Max said, settling in. "So, you two work together, and you're engaged. Is that difficult?"

My face burned, but Ian didn't seem to notice.

"Not at all," Ian said, flipping open his notebook. "We're great partners."

I eyed the two of them, wondering if I was imagining the slight tension across the table. I hoped I was. Today was about so many important things. I didn't know how long we'd be able to talk before it became too much for Max, but I was hoping to propose an in-depth series of articles to Mr. Hindmarsh. I'd mentioned the idea to Ian, and he loved it.

I set my coffee down. "I'm so glad you're okay with doing this." I hated that my voice sounded higher than usual. Max would know I was nervous.

Max spread his hands. "Whatever you need, Moll."

Was he trying to put me at ease? Was it a challenge? Was he angry?

"Okay." I cleared my throat. "Well, I've done a lot of research into POW camps—"

"You have?"

"She was like a dog on a bone," Ian said proudly, patting my hand.

"But why?"

"Because I didn't think anyone was paying enough attention to them. I mean, we heard all about Germany, and the atrocities they were committing, but it seemed like Japan wasn't on anyone's mind."

Max nodded. "That's what we kind of figured."

"What was?"

"That we'd been forgotten."

Heat rushed into my cheeks. "Not by everyone."

"Good to know." He took a sip of his coffee. "So. Researching Japanese POW camps. Sounds like some fun reading."

His tone was bitter, sarcastic, so unlike the Max I knew. Was it from his experience? Or was it because of Ian and me?

"I wouldn't call it fun, Max," I said, asserting myself. "But I would call it important. I know a fair amount, but the outside world was mostly kept in the dark. That fed the rumours, but there was no proof. So I'm hoping you can talk about it. Help people—like me—understand what went on over there."

He looked down for a moment, then back up at me. All I saw was fatigue in those brown eyes. Fatigue and defeat.

"Okay, I'll do my best. What do you already know?"

"I spoke with Sergeant Cox at the reception just before I saw you. He filled in a lot of details for me."

"Cox was my sergeant. He and I were together at North Point Camp, then Sham Shui Po."

"Yeah, I know. He told me that he was Richie's sergeant." I watched him, wondering if he'd let me hook him. I wanted so badly to know about my brother.

But Max skipped right over that, and I set my hopes aside for now. "I was glad to see him at the reception," he said. "I hadn't seen him in years."

"You didn't go with him to the NKK shipbuilding factory in Tokyo, then?"

He shook his head. "No. I got put on a hell ship along with a few hundred others and landed at Niigata Camp."

My heart stilled at the name. Niigata, on the northwest coast of Japan, directly north of Tokyo. He'd been sent to the mines.

"Can you tell me about that camp?"

He took a deep breath through his nose. "It was cold. In Hong Kong, we were constantly sticky with sweat. But Niigata was cold." His fingers curled around his coffee cup. "The minute we got off the boat, they bound our wrists with barbed wire."

My gut clenched at the thought, and I looked at his hands. They'd been such strong, capable hands. Hands built for baseball and medicine. Hands that, once upon a time, had held mine. Now I saw vague lines cut around the wrists, scars put there by hate. I thought of the German prisoners at Bowmanville, then their Canadian counterparts at Stalag VIIIB, shackled because of a random order. I remembered how the men had fought so heatedly at Bowmanville, determined to maintain their freedom. Max had never had the opportunity to fight back.

"We were often bound," he continued, his voice flat. "Sometimes with barbed wire, sometimes chains. We worked in the mines twelve hours a day, so we weren't bound then, of course. We couldn't have worked for them if we had been. Every day for over two years we were up around five in the morning for *tenko*, the daily roll call, where we all lined up and called out our number, one at a time. In Japanese."

"But how did you know any Japanese?" I asked.

Max gave a little huff of derision. "We didn't. But we learned real quick. If you stumbled on your number, you were dragged up and beaten in front of everyone. A couple of the guards looked the other way when they could, but that was rare. I got the impression most of them lived in terror of the senior officers. If they were caught being lenient, their pun-ishment might be even worse than ours." He took another sip of coffee. "I can tell you one thing for certain. The Japanese were great at doling out punishments, warranted or not. They hit us with anything they had on hand, and they hit us without mercy. A lot of my friends died from those beatings."

I studied him, discomfited by the lack of emotion in his voice. Then I remembered Sergeant Cox trying to explain to me about how he couldn't feel emotions anymore. Could Max?

Max patted his pocket and retrieved a pack of cigarettes. "Do you mind?"

"Go ahead," I said.

Ian leaned forward. "I imagine this must be difficult to talk about, but what you're doing is giving a voice to those who won't be coming home. They deserve to be remembered."

Max inhaled, let the smoke roll over his lips. "I know."

Sergeant Cox had also talked about the lack of medical treatment at the camps. That aspect would touch Max, I was certain.

"It must have been hard for you, being a doctor, to watch all the suf-fering."

Finally, I saw his jaw flex. "I've never felt so helpless," he said, his voice a low grumble. He drew on his cigarette again, and his voice returned to normal. "So many men died of disease. Dysentery, diphtheria, cholera, beriberi, pneumonia, gangrene, tropical ulcers, pellagra, skin infections. Without nutrients, some of the men went blind. Some lost all sensation to parts of their bodies. A lot of them screamed all night because of 'electric feet.'"

I raised an eyebrow.

"It's an illness that comes from starvation," he explained. "Relentless, agonizing pain in the feet, like needles being jabbed into them day and night. And the Japanese had an interesting way of taking care of the sick: they got even smaller rations. One less prisoner to feed. As a result, there were so many dead we had to load bodies into a wheelbarrow to take them to the crematorium."

I hesitated, trying not to imagine what he'd just described. "What about you?" I asked, needing to know. "Did you get sick?"

"Everybody got sick."

"What happened?"

He tapped his cigarette on the edge of the ashtray and stared blankly at the ashes. "The first thing to hit the camp was dysentery," he said. "That spreads like wildfire. It drained the men in every way possible. We already weren't eating, but then our guts got rid of whatever we did have. It was disgusting. And often lethal." His nostrils flared in anger. "So many of these diseases were treatable, even preventable. There was a diphtheria outbreak at Sham Shui Po, and men were dropping like flies." His hand went around his throat, as if he were being strangled. "Their necks swelled up, and their airways were cut off. They developed lesions all over their bodies, which then got infected. Some died of kidney failure."

This time, when he took a drag on his cigarette, his hand was noticeably shaking. "The only reason I survived was I'd had a vaccine for it back in school. But Arnie—" His brow drew in tight. "Arnie hadn't gotten the vaccine. He'd been off school, sick that day, and never got one. When he came down with diphtheria at the camp, I tried." He closed his eyes. "I tried. But he'd already suffered so much. His body couldn't fight it."

He stubbed out his cigarette and tapped another from the pack, but he didn't light it. "All Arnie needed was the serum, and the Japanese doctor had it all along. Oh yeah. The Japs had medicines for practically everything, but they wouldn't give the POWs any of it."

He swallowed. "So one day I went to the hospital and told the doctor I was a doctor as well. I begged him for medicine." He looked directly at me. "Oh, and by 'hospital,' I should clarify. It was four walls with no windows, doors, fittings, lights, taps, baths, or furniture. No beds, no chairs, no blankets, no disinfectants, and no bed pans. It was just a filthy, broken place where they put the sickest of us." He paused, returning to his thoughts. "But I knew that bastard had the medicine. None of their men were sick. I also knew the chance of my getting it from him was slim, but Arnie was really suffering. So at first I was subservient like they expected, bowing and scraping and all that, speaking as much Japanese as I could work out, but he wasn't interested in listening to what I was trying to say.

"It was the most frustrating thing I've ever experienced. I ended up yelling at him, which shows you how out of my mind I was. The whole time I was yelling, I knew what was coming. I mean, I'd basically slit my own throat just by raising my voice. I didn't even bother fighting back when they threw me out of the hospital, then a bunch of them took turns beating me. I couldn't stand up when they were done. I was afraid my jaw was broken at first, and at least a couple of ribs. After that, they—" His voice cracked. "They dragged me across the yard and shoved me into the shack for a week."

I swallowed the lump in my throat. "What's . . . what's the shack?"

"Exactly what it sounds like. A tiny, broken-down, floorless shed with nothing in it. Nothing but darkness and dirt, with half portions slid under the door when they remembered me. The rain was constant. And it was so cold." He shuddered and looked away. "I changed in there. I was no more than an animal. No. I was less than an animal. When I got out, Arnie was gone."

I caught my breath, imagining how that must have felt. Ian reached for my hand, but I slid it out of reach. It wasn't I who needed comfort.

"Is that when you hurt your leg?" Ian asked, breaking the silence.

"No," he said quickly, striking a match and finally lighting the cigarette.

I could tell he didn't want to talk about his injury, so I changed direction. I hoped we would discuss it eventually, but I'd never go where he didn't want me to go.

"Did the Red Cross packages help?" I asked. "I helped pack them, full of food and clothes and books, even sports equipment. Did they help at all?"

"I never got one," Max replied. "I think some of the guys got a couple over the years, but the Japanese mostly sold them on the black market. Someone said there was a whole warehouse full of them somewhere. The Red Cross wasn't allowed into any of the camps, from what I understood, except for one time at Niigata." He smiled. "They wanted the Red Cross to go back and report on what a nice, happy place our camp was. They sent us to the field to play soccer, for crying out loud, and they even gave us little bits of meat in our rice. But after the meal, one of the men tried to pass a note to the Red Cross people, telling them the truth, and a guard caught him. They waited until the visitors were gone, then they cut off his head."

My stomach rolled, and I had to look away. Ian was staring at his notepad, but his pen was still. I forced myself to turn back.

"What did you do?" I whispered, sick for him. "How did you survive?"

He met my eyes, and the most terrible longing twisted in my chest.

"I thought of you," he said simply. Then he went on. "I thought of home. Of Mama and Papa and Hannah and the kids. I thought of all of you over here, gathered around the fireplace, knowing you'd be thinking of us, or at least hoping you were. I thought of our summers together, of the fun we used to have, of baseball."

I wanted to tell Max that thinking of him had pulled me through the worst of times as well, but the truth was, I'd given up on him. The shame I felt was crippling.

Ian shifted on the bench beside me. I wondered if he could sense the torment ripping through me. "I knew this was going to be a hell of a story, but wow. Thank you so much for opening up to us this way. It can't be easy."

Max tapped his cigarette in the tray and finished what must have been cold coffee. We hadn't even ordered food, I realized, but I had no appetite now.

"I'd like to hear about the battle at Stanley Village. Can you tell us about that Christmas Day?" Ian asked.

Max looked down at his hands. He didn't say anything, but to me it seemed like he was asking himself permission. Then he nodded at Ian, but I could see the anguish in his eyes. I couldn't do this to him.

"You know what? I think that's enough for today," I said. "That's a lot for all of us. We don't have to do it all at once, and I'm sure Max would like to spend some time with his family. Maybe we could meet again tomorrow or Thursday?"

Ian bristled beside me, but gratitude shone in Max's eyes.

Two days later we met again at the Senator. But this time, we ordered our meals first. Max dug into his soup, swallowing four spoonfuls before Ian and I had even started.

"Hungry?" I asked kindly.

He looked sheepish. "Sometimes I forget nobody's gonna take it away, I guess."

"When's the last time you had a real meal?" Ian asked, his notepad and pen magically appearing.

"The Americans fed us after they rescued us. On the ship. That was swell."

"We've seen photographs of the men after they were liberated," Ian said. "I gotta say, you look all right. Not exactly robust, but not skeletal."

I thought about the photographs I'd seen. Men just like Max, with their boney arms hanging like twigs, stripped of muscle, slender and fragile as a child's. Of the ribs, the clavicles, the hip bones.

"I've gained back at least forty pounds in the past six or so weeks. About a week after the emperor surrendered, the Americans started dropping food over our camp. That was a sight to see: huge oil drums floating down on parachutes, filled with peaches, sausages, cigarettes, chocolate, you name it. Every time we opened one it was a surprise. We ate like millionaires for a while. The doctor says I'm almost one hundred forty pounds now."

The waitress came by to take Max's empty bowl, and he took the opportunity to order another one.

"And some bread please," I asked, then turned to Max with a small smile. "You've still got a ways to go if you're thinking of swinging a bat next summer."

Max gestured to his leg. "I'll never run bases again."

"Oh, I'm sorry, Max. I shouldn't have—"

"I'm six foot two," Max explained to Ian as he lit a cigarette. "In the old days I'd be somewhere around one hundred ninety. I'm lucky, though. Some of the men with me were well under a hundred pounds by the time the Americans got a boat in to get us. Some of them couldn't hang on. One of the fellows, a tough Italian named Stan Jilani, was real sick. His whole body was riddled with infection. He and I both knew he wasn't going to make it, but he stuck it out as long as he could. I brought him some chocolate and put a square in his mouth. He told me it never tasted sweeter. He was dead by morning, but I was glad I'd given him that at least. After years of hell, he got to taste a little freedom before he went."

My mind fell back a decade to when my family had all eyed the last slice of bread on the table, and how my dresses kept getting looser. I knew how hunger felt, but we had always been able to scrape something together when we needed it. I tried to imagine what it must have been like for those men, knowing their bodies were dying, waiting for food they believed would never come. And then, after all those years of waiting, to know help was in sight, but not close enough.

"Did you know about the bombs?" I asked. "When they dropped Little Boy and Fat Man on Hiroshima and Nagasaki?"

"The Americans told us on the ship going back. We had no idea."

"Right. That makes sense," Ian said. "So how did you learn about the surrender?"

Max tapped the ash off his cigarette. "That was a strange day," he began. "They ordered us out of the mine, and they made us sit in a circle on the ground. They'd attached speakers to the trees, and everyone got real quiet when a Japanese man started talking. We couldn't catch a word of what he was saying, but the Japs, well, they looked like someone just threw ice water over them. I actually saw a couple of them cry. But one fellow there—one of the nicer guards—came over and nudged me on the arm."

Max leaned back so the waitress could place the soup and bread before him. He took a couple of bites before speaking again.

"I still remember the look of wonder on that guard's face. The sheer relief." A broad smile stretched across Max's face, the first genuine one I'd seen. "He said to me, 'War is finished. Canada go home.' We all stared at him, and he kept saying. 'You go home.' It wasn't until the guards all left that we finally believed him."

"Then what happened?"

"Well, then we were on our own at the camp. We had nowhere else to go. We painted the roofs with the letters *PW* and hoped the Americans would find us, which they did, within a week. It took them about a month to get ships to a nearby port to pick us up, but by then, the food parcels had changed everything for us."

"Because they meant freedom," I said, searching his face.

He took in what I'd said, then he nodded slowly. "Yeah. They meant we were going home. After four years of surviving, we were finally getting the chance to live again."

Beside me, Ian cleared his throat, ready to ask another question, but I dropped a hand onto his leg to stop him. I knew how much he wanted Max to talk about Christmas Day, and how much I needed to know about Richie, but this wasn't about us. We couldn't push him. Max had told us about things that, no matter how clearly he painted the picture, we couldn't imagine. Like my brothers, he was scarred inside and out. But at least he was meeting my eyes now. He was trusting me again. I would go as slowly as he needed me to go.

He finished his second bowl, and the bread was long gone.

"How about we call it a day? We can come back tomorrow—you looked like you enjoyed the soup."

He smiled, slow but with a hint of confidence. "Yeah. It's pretty good. Tomorrow is fine with me."

———

I met Max almost every day, sometimes alone, sometimes with Ian. It was always at the Senator out of habit, and the waitresses started leaving a booth open for us. Until he changed his order, they automatically brought Max two bowls of soup every time. I wondered if they were doing it because they knew he was a veteran. That he'd offered his life for theirs. I hoped so.

Max had good days and bad ones. On the good ones, he talked on and on. On the bad ones he basically stared into his hands. The ashtray was almost always alarmingly full. The first time I tried to nudge him out of a daze, he looked at me like he didn't recognize me at all, then he'd simply left the restaurant. It reminded me of Jimmy's terse exit from our family dinner, though Max hadn't seemed angry, just confused. I learned not to press him when he was in one of his moods. But over time, he became more and more willing to talk, and the bad days were fewer in between.

At the end of one of our lunches, when it was just the two of us there, Max asked about my brothers. He sagged a little bit, hearing about Liam and Mark.

"It's Jimmy I'm really worried about though," I said, filling him in on all that had happened.

"Jimmy's a fighter," he said. "He'll pull through."

"How are you adjusting to being back? In your head, I mean."

After his first night at home, Hannah had called me, letting me know about his strange behaviour. She'd assured me he would recover, and I loved her for believing it. But no one knew what would happen with any of our brothers.

"I'm trying." He stubbed out his ever-present cigarette. "When I was in Newfoundland, then for a little while in Hong Kong, Hannah would write to me all the time, telling me stories about her kids. Used to break my heart, knowing I was missing so much of their childhood. Then, after we were in the camp, the letters stopped, and I started to accept that I might never see them again. I promised myself that if I ever did make it back, I'd be better than what I was. I'd be a better brother and uncle, and I'd be a better son." He nodded. "I'm trying. I'm trying to live."

But our conversations about family never went further than that. He still hadn't brought up Richie, and I was hesitant to ask. I didn't want to ruin the fragile bond we'd established.

One day, when he was telling Ian and me about working in the mines, I noticed him rubbing his wrists.

"What are you thinking right now?" I asked.

He lifted his hands, turning them so he could see his palms, then the backs. "I was thinking how strange it is not to have shackles on my wrists anymore. How unfamiliar I am with the concept of freedom. Freedom was something I took for granted all my life. I promise you, I never will again. No more barbed wire or ropes or chains. No more biting down on every single thing I want to say, knowing I was risking my life by saying it." He paused. "No more wishing that someone would either rescue me or kill me."

I'd never get used to this, I realized. The pain they'd inflicted on him, the way they'd reduced him in so many ways. "You never should have had to go through any of that. None of you should. Someone needs to make it up to you somehow."

"Not possible," Max said.

Ian nodded. "There'll be a compensation package, I imagine."

Max smiled. "There you go, Moll. Your next research project."

It was an innocent suggestion, but I felt Ian stiffen beside me. The past few weeks had been full of many intensely personal moments for Max. He'd told us almost everything about his experience in Hong Kong and Japan, but once in a while a comment or memory would slip out that made it clear we'd always been close. Nothing romantic was ever hinted at, just a very deep, lifelong friendship. Sometimes I wondered how much Ian noticed, and what he was thinking, but he never said anything.

The end of the year was drawing near. With everything else going on, December had snuck up on us, and our wedding would be here before we knew it. Ian had booked the church for Christmas Day, my mother had helped me sew my dress, and Hannah had agreed to be my maid of honour. Everything was ready to go.

Our interviews with Max were drawing to a close, which had to happen eventually, but I'd chosen to ignore that. I could have talked with him forever. One day, when Ian couldn't come, I decided to do something special for Max, as a thank-you. I called ahead and asked the Senator to serve him a dessert I had made myself. When the waitress brought it to the table, she set the plate in front of Max, and he stared in amazement.

"Is that *rugelach*?" he asked. "That's not on the menu."

The waitress smiled, in on the surprise. "Your girlfriend made them. She said you loved them as kids."

My face burned, but Max didn't correct the waitress. Instead, he reached for one. "You remembered."

"I remember everything, Max," I replied.

Our eyes met, and neither of us looked away. It was impossible not to know what he was thinking about, because I was thinking about that summer, too. On impulse, I reached across the table to take his hand, but my gold ring shone in the light, and he pulled away.

twenty-five
MAX

Max knocked on the door of Ian's house, then shifted in the cold. It seemed his leg hurt more in the winter, and his limp was acting up. While he waited, he reached into his pocket, checking for the letter he'd tucked in there before coming. Tonight was the night. He'd waited long enough.

A week after Molly had made him *rugelach*, she had called him and asked if he could come for dinner at Ian's house instead of lunch at the Senator. From the tone of her voice, he couldn't tell if it was her idea or Ian's, but he supposed it didn't matter. Sometimes Max wondered about Ian, and what he thought about all the time he and Molly had been spending alone together, but Ian had never complained. Lately, though, Max had caught something in Ian's expression that clearly said he wasn't comfortable with the whole situation anymore.

Molly was thrilled with everything they'd been doing. She said her editor was very happy with how the series was coming along, and that she'd be adding research from other sources so it would be a well-rounded piece. She positively glowed when she talked about it. Despite the memories the interviews dug up, Max would've continued doing them for as long as she wanted, just to see her happy. But it was one week before Christmas. Their time was running out.

He knocked again, and the door swung open. "Max," Ian said, smiling broadly and stepping aside so Max could enter. "You made it. Thanks for coming out this way for a change."

He took Max's coat and hat then ushered him through to the dining room where the smells of home hit him. Molly was there, her long hair drawn partly back by a light blue bow that matched her dress. She was beautiful. But then, she was Molly. She'd always been beautiful.

He stepped closer, checking the steaming bowls already on the table. "Is that goulash?"

She grinned. "I thought you might like something warm to counter the bitter cold outside. And you can have as many seconds as you like."

Ian pulled out the chair at the head of the table and gestured toward them. "Let's eat before it gets cold!"

Molly nodded at Max, suggesting he take the spot to Ian's left, then she claimed the chair across from Max. Her eyes were on him as he eased himself down, always careful not to bump his leg. She smiled, watching his reaction as he took his first taste.

"This is delicious, Moll," Max said, and it was. "Tastes like home."

Her face lit with the compliment. "I did learn this recipe in your mother's kitchen," she reminded him.

"Mama would be proud of you. I'll tell her."

"Yes, really good, sweetheart," Ian said, then he looked over at Max. "So about tonight," he said. "Since we're getting close to Christmas and all, I'm wondering if we could talk about Stanley Village. I think it's the final piece of the puzzle."

She shot him a look. "We talked about this. It doesn't have to be the final piece."

Ian reached for her hand. "One week left, Molly. It's time to put this article to bed."

Her gaze flickered to his own. The subject of their wedding had hardly been mentioned until recently, at least not during the interviews, and it felt a bit like a slap, being reminded of it that way. A couple of days ago he'd been sitting on Hannah's stairs while Dinah ran up and down them, fascinated by the "Slinky" Max had bought for her, and he'd brought up the subject of the wedding with his sister. He'd tried to keep his personal feelings out of the conversation, but she always saw right through him.

"He does dote on her, Max," she'd said, leaning against the bannister at the base of the stairs. "And Molly seems happy."

"She does," he allowed.

"Listen, Max. I warned you once before to be careful around her, and I'm going to warn you again, but not for the reason you think." She shook her head sadly. "You both have been through way too much. I'm not sure either of you could survive having your heart broken again."

She was right, of course. Even if Molly changed her mind about Ian and stepped over that line with Max, they could never be together. But it was so hard to think of her married to another man. To imagine Molly and Ian standing before a minister together, then to imagine them after the wedding. Whenever he allowed his mind to wander in that direction, it hurt.

Molly was holding up a spoonful of goulash and watching him. "He's right, you know. Stanley Village is the one thing we haven't talked about. Are you ready to talk about it?"

No, he wasn't. If he had a choice, Max would never again return to that battlefield or to any other thought from that day. Christmas 1941 had been the worst day of his life, until the camps. But if Molly wanted to go there, and of course she did, he would tell her everything she needed to know. Even if it broke her heart.

"Sure, Moll."

"Okay then," Ian said, producing his notepad and pen.

Molly scowled. "Ian, slow down. What's the rush?"

"It's okay, Molly," Max said.

Ian flipped through his pages. "Before we actually get to Stanley Village, I wanted to ask you about some concerning reports coming out about the Battle of Hong Kong. It sounds like the Canadians were woefully underprepared and lacking in proper weapons. Was that your experience?"

Instantly, Max found himself crouched in the dark jungle, the cold of that night at Lye Mun hardened in his bones. Panic clogged his veins once more. The Japanese were coming. They were almost there.

All Max had to do was close his eyes, and he could see his friends beside him, huddled in the trench. He saw Richie's confident nod. He felt Arnie tucking the grenade into Max's frozen fingers because he didn't know how to use it. Then he heard it again: the shrieking battle cry as the Japanese exploded from the water. In his mind, Max ducked beneath the orange flares of gunfire, cutting through smoke already raised by artillery explosions. *Retreat! Retreat!* And he fled with David and Arnie, Richie somewhere nearby, racing for the trees, for the rendezvous, then David screaming, "What do I do?" after the bullet sheared through Max's leg. Then David had gone, and Max looked down, down, down, diving toward the bloodshot blue eyes of Richie, mutilated, paralyzed, helpless.

He opened his eyes. Molly was watching him, waiting. How was he ever going to admit to her what he'd done?

He turned to Ian. "We were never trained for battle. We never should have been there. What are you hearing?"

Ian rattled off the basics: almost two thousand Canadians vastly outnumbered by over fifty thousand hardened, veteran Japanese forces with far superior firepower and training.

Max listened, confused. Ian's expression and tone were respectful, but what he was describing sounded so black-and-white to Max. Where was the cloying, coppery stink of blood? Where were the screams of men cut short as their throats were slit? Where was the terror of that relentless, starving, exhausting two weeks of hell in the mountains?

Ian hesitated. "There's a story going around that the Canadian troops broke and ran during the battle."

Max stared, aghast. "That's a damn lie." He hated that his voice shook, but his body vibrated with anger at the assumption. "Nobody ran. Nobody broke. We were outnumbered fifty to one, and we gave as good as we got. I can tell you without any reservation that I was proud to be a Canadian in Hong Kong. Nobody could have been more courageous than our men. Who the hell is saying that?"

Ian didn't answer, but his pen was busy.

"That's why your story is so important, Max," Molly said gently. "People need to know the truth."

Ian looked up from his notepad. "Let's move on. Christmas Day, Stanley Village."

Max took a deep breath. Molly was right. If someone was claiming his men were cowards, this was his chance to set the record straight, even if revisiting it killed him.

"On Christmas Day, we went in knowing we were going to die," he started, reluctantly letting his mind drift back. "There were only one hundred and twenty of us left in D Company, and they'd told us there were only a few Japanese in the village. Fifteen, someone had said. But they'd lied. There were hundreds of them, and they had all the ammo in the world. We rushed in, making all the noise we could, and somehow we got past the initial guard. David, Arnie, and I just kept running. We couldn't believe it. We felt invincible, euphoric, as though we might actually make it." His smile faded. "But we should never have been so confident. When the Japanese pulled themselves together, it was more than just seeing them assemble, it was like feeling a force of nature swelling against us. The world blew up around us, shaking the ground so hard that men were knocked over. I saw some blown in half. I saw them cut apart by shrapnel and bayonets. I saw so many things that day." He rubbed his forehead hard, pushing the memories out. "We never had a chance. We were forced to retreat, but they kept firing at us. We ran as fast as we could go."

David's face swam in front of his eyes, and he paused, needing to breathe. "David was running right in front of me. He turned to help me, because my leg was bad, and I couldn't keep up. He was reaching for me, and—"

He dropped his head into both hands, feeling it all again. The help-lessness. The agony in his leg. The knowledge that this, this was *it*.

"We can stop," he heard Molly say from far away.

"He's fine," Ian said tightly. "Probably do him good to get it out."

Max bristled at the challenge. He fished for his cigarettes then lit one, inhaling deeply as he squinted across at Ian. He visualized the smoke trav-elling through his trachea, flooding his lungs, then filling and burning every bronchiole. What did he care? David, Arnie, and Richie were gone. Molly wore Ian Collins's ring.

"I can go on," he assured them calmly, exhaling. His voice had dropped. The armour was back, hard and impenetrable. "If you want me to stop, you'll have to tell me, because I haven't talked about this with anyone over the past four years. I might get carried away."

"Ian, let's stop," Molly said with concern.

"No," Max snapped, louder than he'd intended, then he lowered his voice. "People need to know what happened, right? People need to un-derstand we fought with all we had."

He looked at them both, noting the pain in Molly's eyes, then he braced himself and ripped through the barrier.

"They shot David in the face. He fell, and . . . I picked him up and tried to carry him off the field." Even now, he could see David's face, his open, unseeing eyes. "That's when they shot me. I dropped, and David's body rolled away." He held out his hands, but if he reached out for the rest of his life, he'd never get close enough. "I couldn't just leave him. I couldn't. So I started crawling toward him. The next thing I knew, a Jap had his gun on my head, and I raised my hands. Because in that moment, I knew I was about to die."

Molly's fist was pressed against her mouth. Ian was transfixed, his pen hovering over his paper.

"What happened? Why didn't he kill you?" she whispered.

"Turns out the Brits had already surrendered. In fact, they'd surrendered before David had been killed. Stanley Village was all done in vain." He inhaled, letting the smoke leak through his lips and cloud around him, wishing he could disappear within it. "One hundred and twenty men went out. Twenty-six were killed. Seventy-five wounded. Trust me. I've had years to do the math. That's an eighty-four per cent failure rate."

Molly sat unmoving, then without a word, she got up and went to the kitchen. He knew she was getting coffee, but it sounded like she was making extra noise to cover her sobs. When she returned, her cheeks were bright, but her eyes were clear. She set the coffee before them, then resumed her seat.

"I have more numbers for you, Max." Her expression was set, and both men sat back to listen. "From what I've learned, the original C Force was made up of 1,985 men. Of those, two hundred and ninety-six were killed or unaccounted for between December tenth and Christmas Day. The rest were taken as POWs. I've had time to do the math on that, too. That is a hundred per cent failure rate," she said. "And of those POWs, about five hundred had been wounded in battle. Then over two hundred and fifty died at the camps." She lifted her chin, which quivered with anger. "When you said you never should have been sent there, you were absolutely right, Max."

Max let the figures soak in. He had only known the ones from D Company, because Arnie had eventually filled him in. He'd said Cox was waiting for him as he ran off that field to safety, and tears were rolling down their sergeant's face as he witnessed the devastation.

Ian gave a low whistle. "Those are sobering numbers," he said. "So that's when you and the others officially became prisoners of war."

Max nodded once. "They tied us up and marched us to North Point Camp. I could barely walk. I'd been hit at the very beginning of the battle, when the Japanese had first invaded the island, and I'd doctored myself as best I could, but the second bullet at Stanley did me in. As we started to walk, my leg collapsed, and I went down. Arnie dropped to help me, and he was in a panic. The Japanese were yelling something at us, and Arnie kept screaming that I'd better get up or I was gonna get a bayonet in my gut. I looked around, and that's exactly what they were doing." He was back on that road, with the bodies of his friends falling, then screaming, then lying still. He could still smell the death, a thick tang in the air that burned. "Anyone falling by the side was getting stabbed then left behind. So I got up. I don't remember doing it, but I did."

"What happened with your leg?" she asked.

He looked up, startled. For a moment he'd forgotten where he was. He looked down at his leg, lost briefly in the wonder that it was wrapped safely in a trouser leg. They'd marched into Hong Kong that November, clean and starched in their regulation army shorts, but those had fallen apart over the years. By the time they'd finally been freed, they'd worn little more than bits of cloth. With all the heat and filth in Hong Kong, he'd never understood why infection hadn't latched onto his leg and pulled him under.

"I told myself it was just a cut, but as you can tell by my less-than-nimble gait, I was wrong about that. I'm pretty sure the first bullet broke part of the bone off, and it's still floating around in there. The second one went right through."

"Is it all right now?"

"I still have it," he said, putting out his cigarette.

Molly looked away, and he remembered her brother Mark. "I'm sorry, Moll. I didn't mean anything by that."

"It's fine." She paused, giving him a moment. Or was it she who needed that? "But I have to ask you about something else," she said, her green eyes glittering with determination. "St. Stephen's."

He'd always known she would ask. How could she not? He'd written to her; she'd known he and Richie were in Hong Kong together. If anyone knew about what had happened to her brother, it would be him. And he did.

"I know about the massacre." She tilted her head to the side, toward Ian. "Ian did the research for me, so I know what the Japanese did that day. And I know Richie was there, because they told us he died there. But I don't know why he was in that hospital. Do you?"

When the survivors of the massacre had joined the rest of them at North Point Camp, the stories had leaked out a bit at a time, as if they were testing to see if it was safe to speak. Then, like a wound ripped open again, details had poured out of the men's weeping mouths: the murders, the atrocities, the unthinkable evil that had rained down on that quiet, defenceless hospital on Christmas Day.

Max hadn't wanted to hear the stories. He didn't want to believe any of them. Especially after he combed the survivors' faces and found Richie's wasn't among them. The guilt he'd felt for years after that day, the knowledge that he had personally put Richie in the face of danger, had never dissipated. Back in that terrible jungle, with the enemy all around, Richie had begged Max never to leave him, and yet he had.

"I sent Richie to St. Stephen's Hospital," he said, bracing for her reaction.

She paled, and Ian's hand covered hers. "What? You?"

"He got caught in the initial invasion onto the island a week before. The same time I was shot. He was a mess." He was back in the tunnel now, Richie's blood black on his hands. His heart was beating so hard he could barely hold his hands still. "I . . . I had to amputate his arm in the field, and patch up his leg and face."

Tears streamed from her eyes as her brother's long past death suddenly came alive in her mind. He hated himself in that moment, putting her through it.

"I did all I could," he said, needing her to understand. To forgive, even. "Then I sent him to St. Stephen's. I didn't have a choice. And at the time I believed it was the safest place for him to be. Why wouldn't I? It was a goddamn hospital, and he was wounded real bad."

She shook her head quickly, swallowing back sobs. "No, no. I understand. I do. You were saving his life. You had no choice."

Max took a breath for courage. "I have something for you," he said quietly. "It's from Richie."

She stared at his hand as he pulled the old envelope from his shirt pocket, then laid it on the table in front of her. The paper was dark and sweat-stained, grimy from hiding it inside his clothes for all those years. He'd held on to it for so long, he'd come to think of it as his good luck charm. He'd never opened it. He still didn't know what it said. But in a way, knowing it was there, and knowing it was his responsibility to bring Richie's letter across the sea, had kept him alive. And it had brought him back to Molly. Now he had to let it go.

"He gave it to me the last time I saw him. It's for your family."

She touched the seal gingerly, as if it might break. Then she picked it up, and from the look of astonishment on her face, it was as if Max had given her the world.

"I think he knew something was going to happen to him, because he already had this written," he said, remembering Richie's desperate expression. "I know it's important."

Her fingers traced the lettering on the envelope. Richie's handwriting, smeared almost illegible by the years. "Thank you, Max. I can't imagine how hard it was for you to keep it all this time. This means so much to me."

"You gonna open it?" Ian asked, his eyes wide.

"No," she said, pressing the envelope to her chest. "I'll wait for my parents. Maybe it will give them peace at last."

Ian sipped his coffee, regarding Max. "You've been to hell and back. That was an incredible story. I feel honoured that you told us."

"I want people to know," he said. "I don't want our men to be forgotten."

"We'll make sure of that." Ian shook his head, marveling. "After everything you went through, it must be such a relief to be home. To know it's finally over."

"You think it's over?" The words lashed out. "If you think that, then you haven't been listening. This will never be over. Richie and David and Arnie and hundreds more will never come home. I may never have to push another wheelbarrow of corpses, but I sure as hell will never get that stink out of my nose."

Ian blinked. "Of course," he said. "I didn't mean to belittle anything you just said. I apologize if I offended."

Max closed his eyes, embarrassed. "No. No. I'm sorry. My temper is pretty fast these days. But I meant what I said. For some of us, the war will never be over." He drained his coffee, then pushed his chair back from the table, done with all the stories. "That's it. You have your final piece. Think you can sell a bunch of papers with all this?"

Ian tapped his notebook with his pen. "Everyone has heard traumatic stories, but those are usually about women or children. To hear of strong, young Canadian men devastated to this extent? Yes, we will. Thank you."

Molly cut in. "We aren't naming him, remember? It's an anonymous source."

"I know. Too bad, though. We could make you famous, Max."

"No need," Max said, suddenly in a hurry. Before they could stop him, he was headed for the door. "I gotta go. Thanks very much for dinner, Moll. I'll tell Mama how great her recipe tasted."

He was grabbing his coat and hat as Ian reached for his own. "Hang on a minute," he said. "I'll get the car keys and drive you both back."

Max held up a hand. "Thanks, but I'd rather walk. Clear my head a bit."

"Would it be all right if I walked with you?" Her voice was small. Fragile. How could he say no?

Ian was watching her, a slight crease in his brow.

"I guess," Max said. "If it's all right with Ian."

Ian gave a short laugh. "Hey, Molly's not mine yet. She can do what she chooses."

Molly tucked the letter into her pocket, and he waited for her to pull on her coat and hat, then wind a scarf around her neck. He held the door for her, and they stepped out into the quiet, crisp night. Max breathed in the air, feeling lighter than he had in a long, long time.

"I'm sorry I snapped back there," he said as they walked.

"It's okay. I'm sorry we pushed you so hard. And for so long. Thank you for doing that, Max. I think you'll be really happy with it when it's done."

He didn't answer. He wasn't sure he wanted to read it. He'd already lived it.

They walked in silence for half a block, and he thought how strange it was, to feel awkward, walking beside her on this sidewalk where they'd grown up. Once, she had chattered in his ear the whole time. Now, he didn't know how to speak to her.

After a little way, she tugged at his sleeve, and he stopped beside her. "There's something I need to tell you," she said, facing him.

What was that look in her eye? She'd kept something from him. Something important. He didn't like that feeling.

"I wrote back to you," she said. "I mean, the second time. After you wrote to me from Hong Kong. Of course, you never got my letter, but I thought you should know." He saw her hesitate, then she met his gaze again. "But what it said was that I'd found out my parents burned your original letter from 1933. I never even saw it."

He stared, his chest tight with confusion. "They *burned* it?" His mind raced back to the conversation he'd had in Sham Shui Po with Richie, when Richie had accused him of leaving her behind without a word. He'd said Molly was devastated. Max had assumed the letter had been lost along the way, shuffled among the millions of letters constantly traveling around the world, and he'd reluctantly chalked it up to bad luck. Learning that her parents had deliberately destroyed their friendship that way explained so much.

"Things were so tense back then," she was saying, her pale eyes sparkling in the streetlight. "They thought they were doing the right thing, keeping us apart. They've apologized since then, and I know they're sorry. But it's hard for me to forgive."

"Why?" he asked, his breath catching. "Why would they have burned it?"

"Because I would've written back." She searched his eyes. "Surely you must know that."

All those years he'd spent longing for her, wondering why she had never responded. The dreams he'd dared to have, of being with her despite the rest of the world forbidding it, of living his life with her and loving her every single day. Now here she stood, telling him he could have had it all. That she'd always wanted him the same way.

But it was too late.

Max started to walk on, adrenaline pumping through his veins. He could discuss the worst the war had to offer, but he couldn't have this conversation with Molly. Not yet. Maybe not ever. He was too broken.

"It's for the best," he said bitterly as she caught up, then he softened, seeing her smile was gone. "You've moved on. Ian seems like a great guy."

"But Max. What I'm trying to say is—"

He walked faster, needing to escape the pain. "What, Moll? What do you want from me?"

She grabbed his sleeve this time and jerked him back to face her. Her cheeks were blazing with emotion. "I can't lose you again," she said. "I can't."

He knew the ache in her heart, because he felt it so deeply. He knew her regret, because he would always, always feel that. He never should have left her. He should have stayed and talked it all out with her. But he'd gone away. He'd left her behind. He'd left it all behind.

"You'll never lose me," he said, hating himself for what he was about to say. "I'll always be around. But we both know that you and I could never be together anyway. We shouldn't have started something we were never meant to finish."

"I couldn't have stayed away," she said quietly. "Could you?"

No, he wanted to say. *You're all I ever wanted.* He opened his mouth to answer, then stopped, distracted by the sounds of conflict. A fight had broken out on the street, and he made out four men, he thought. Three on one.

Max took a step toward the four, needing to see.

"Max? What are you doing?"

Then the one who was at the receiving end turned slightly, trying to avoid a punch, and the streetlight caught his face.

Max started to run. It was Jimmy.

twenty-six
MOLLY

✤

Even with his limp, Max outran me. He barged in on the brawl, unafraid, and when one of the men wouldn't release Jimmy, Max slugged him in the face. Jimmy staggered back, and I caught him while Max chased off the instigators.

Jimmy slumped against me, and I gagged. He reeked of garbage and booze and vomit, and his face was a mess from the beating. "What's happened to you?" I cried, unable to stop myself. "What have you done?"

He blinked up at me as if his eyes had been glued shut, and he had to break through the seal. "Hey, Molly. Nice to see you."

I grabbed both his shoulders. "C'mon, Jimmy. Can you stand?"

"Is he okay?" Max asked, returning to us.

Jimmy's eyes widened at the sight of Max, and he stumbled backwards, landing on his backside. "No, no, no, no," he pleaded, hands up.

I looked between them, mystified. "Jimmy, it's just Max."

Max took it all in stride. He crouched beside Jimmy, and his hands went to my brother's smashed face, checking his injuries. Jimmy watched him with a kind of horrified fascination.

"Are you real?" he asked, poking Max's chest. "Is it you?"

"Sure is," Max said, then he turned to me. "We need to move him. He's gonna need stitches, and I don't want to do it out here."

We each took one of Jimmy's arms and half dragged, half carried him home, both of us holding our breath. Occasionally he'd look at Max and smile the best he could, and one time, I heard him say, "Maybe there is a God after all. Jeez, it's good to see you, Max."

"He may not say that in a minute," Max told me. "Your mom still have all her sewing supplies?"

We barged through the front door, and I rushed ahead to clear the kitchen table.

"Put him here," I said, patting the top, then Max laid Jimmy out flat while I ran to get Mum's sewing box.

My parents thumped noisily down the stairs. "What's going on?" Dad demanded, then they walked into the dining room and stopped short.

"Max!" Mum exclaimed, astonished. She collected herself as best she could. "We'd heard you were home."

Dad stayed back, but I saw the remorse play out on his face. "We thought you were dead, son. Welcome home."

"Thank you, sir," Max said, and I thought I might cry, hearing the civility between them. It had been years since he'd stood in my parents' house. Maybe the past really could be the past.

"I'm sorry to wake you," he said, "but Jimmy—"

"Jimmy?" Mum rushed to my brother's side then covered her mouth and nose, alarmed. "What's happened? Is he all right?"

"He will be," Max said. "Could I bother you for some clean cloths and hot water? And a razor?"

"A razor?"

"He's not going to like this. His lip is split. I have to take off that impressive beard of his."

While Max worked, I went upstairs and filled the bathtub for Jimmy. Now that I had found my brother again, I wasn't going to let him go. He would stay here, where I could take care of him. I'd take some time off work, maybe. Mr. Hindmarsh would understand, I was sure. Especially after he read Max's story.

"Drink this," Mum was saying to Jimmy when I returned. He was sitting up, his face stitched and bandaged, and wiped mostly clean. The beard was gone, and Jimmy looked so much younger. More vulnerable. I smelled strong coffee in the air.

Jimmy mumbled something, and Dad put his face in his son's. "Please, Jimmy."

I didn't think I'd ever heard him say those two words together in my life.

Liam appeared on the steps. "Max!" he cried. "Jesus Christ, it's really you. We all thought—"

"Yeah," Max said, grinning. "I'm hearing that a lot. I think my new name will be Lazarus."

Jimmy dropped his legs over the side of the table and was threatening to try and stand, but Max and Liam stepped in, putting his arms over their shoulders.

"Let's go," I said, and against Jimmy's protests, I led them up to the bathroom. When they came out without Jimmy, I eyed them nervously. "Think he's all right in there on his own?"

Max nodded. "He'll be okay."

I slumped back against the wall, my hands at my sides, feeling drained by so many emotions. I moved my hand slightly and felt a crinkle of paper in my pocket. Richie's letter. I headed down the stairs, calling everyone to the living room.

"I know it's late, but we need to talk about something." Looking confused, they sat, then I held up the yellowed envelope, stained by years of sweat and secrecy. "It's a letter from Richie. It's for all of us. Whatever it is, I know he would have wanted you to hear it. Please stay."

A hush fell over the room.

Mum stared at me, uncomprehending. "From Richie?"

"How?" Dad asked, suddenly pale.

"Max brought it back with him," I said quietly, and everyone turned to where Max stood in the corner. "He kept it safe for all those years, and he never even opened it. It's addressed to all of us, but I want him to hear it too."

I held the envelope out to Dad, but he shook his head. "You open it, Molly."

With the utmost care, I opened the envelope then gently unfolded the paper. The ink was faint, but it was undeniably my brother's messy writing. I skimmed my fingertips over his words, braced for the unknown, then began to read aloud.

To my dear family,

If you're reading this letter, that means I'm dead. But I guess you already know that.

I hate to say it, but after you read this, you might be glad that I'm gone, and to my eternal shame, I know I deserve that.

You see, I did something. I made a mistake. I mean, I've made a lot of mistakes, but one in particular has haunted me. At one time I thought I could take this secret to my grave, that no one would ever know. But I've had lots of time to think recently, and I understand now that I can't lie to you any longer.

I had obviously hoped to see you again and explain in person, but fate had other plans.

I threw the brick that changed everyone's lives. It was me. It wasn't Mr. Dreyfus, and it wasn't a stranger. I did this to you, Dad. I did this to all of you.

I know you remember what I was like that summer, hanging out with Phil's gang. But things changed for me on the night of the riot. I looked down over the field, where we were just supposed to play baseball, and I saw a war. Thousands of men cracking heads.

Over what? Protestants versus Jews. But why? Why were we going after each other for something that was so personal? Whose business was it whether they went to a church or a synagogue? Everything had gone way too far. And when I saw Dad beating Max, caught up in the craziness of the fighting, something in me changed. I couldn't get there fast enough, not from where I was standing, so I threw the first thing I could get my hands on. I never meant to hurt you, Dad. I just wanted the fighting to stop.

Every day since, I've thought about what I should've done. Now, the only thing I can do is tell the truth. I wanted an end to the fighting, but I was afraid to admit my part in all this. My silence only made things worse. And I have lived with that guilt ever since.

So now you know. They say confession is good for the soul, but mine feels terrible right now. You didn't raise your boy to be a liar, and I'm ashamed of myself for not telling you sooner. I'm sorry I'm not there in person to apologize. I love you all so much. I hope you can find it in your hearts to forgive me someday.

All my love,
Richie

I stared at the letter, unable to move. My face burned. All this time, it had been Richie. Long ago, I had accepted the consequences of that night, of the damage that brick had caused, but now it all came back, and anger boiled inside me. Richie's need to save Max had caused all that pain to both our families, but it was his cowardice that had ripped us apart.

I looked at Dad, who was bent over, his head in his hand. He was a different man from the proud sergeant he had once been, broken in body and spirit by Richie's fear. Beside him, Liam held Mum, and she was quietly weeping. Where, I wondered, was their anger?

Dad eventually lifted his head, and his eyes moved to Max, who was staring silently at the wall. "That's a hard lesson. Richie's deed was done out of love for his friend. I'd like to say that in that same position, any one of us might have done the same, but I'm not sure that's true." He allowed a faint smile. "I guess we should have known it was him. Richie was the only one with an arm that good. The real harm was done out of shame." He looked at Mum. "I just wish he could have come to us. Trusted us with the truth."

She nodded weakly. "Our poor boy. Poor, poor boy."

Dad's words slipped around me like an embrace, his forgiveness overshadowing any anger I had felt at first. I looked down at the letter again and felt a glimmer of hope.

Max was frowning slightly, still absorbing Richie's message. Was he thinking of their childhood? Was he remembering more recent times the two of them had spent together?

From the corner of my eye, I saw Mum gather herself, then look up at Max with so much love in her expression. She'd always loved him. I knew the division between our families had been hard on her. Seeing her now, my heart swelled.

"Dear, dear Max." She looked from me to him, and I knew she was thinking of the letter they'd burned. "I'm so sorry for the pain we've caused you."

With effort, Dad got to his feet and went to Max, holding out a hand. "A lot of wrongs were done, Max. I'm asking you to forgive me."

Max hesitated, but just for a moment, then he took his hand. "There's nothing to forgive, Mr. Ryan."

"Will you tell your mother?" Mum asked, wiping her eyes. "I want to come see her. We have years to catch up on."

"I'll tell her first thing tomorrow."

I walked him to the door, then I handed him Richie's letter. "Read this to your family. There should never be any secrets between us."

After he was gone, Mum, Dad, Liam, and I came together, wrapping our arms tightly around each other. I knew we were all thinking of Richie, wishing more than anything in the world that he was there with us, knowing he was forgiven.

"What am I missing?" came a hoarse voice from the doorway, and I laughed through my tears, seeing Jimmy, bruised and battered, but clean. Wearing nothing but a towel.

"Come here, fool," Dad said fondly, holding out his arms.

And there was nothing more that any of us needed to say.

twenty-seven
MAX

❦

Bright and early the next morning, Max stepped out of his house and onto a fresh layer of sparkling snow. His hands were full with a plate of *sufganiyot* his mother had sent along for Mrs. Ryan, a first step in rekindling their friendship. His parents had been waiting up for him when he'd come home last night, worried something had happened to him, so he'd sat them down and shown them Richie's letter. He watched their expressions melt as they read, then his father reached for his mother's hand.

"Good," his father had said, looking more at ease than Max had seen in a while. "Richie did the right thing."

Max knocked on the Ryans' door, and as Molly opened it, he heard Jimmy's voice. She was laughing at something he'd said, and Max figured that was a good sign.

"How's our patient?" he asked.

Stitching Jimmy up had brought Max back to the days when he'd felt satisfaction from the career he'd worked toward his whole life. After so many years of feeling useless at the camp, he'd enjoyed using his skills to finally do some good. Now Max wondered if he could help heal more than just Jimmy's physical hurts. He'd seen the ghosts in Jimmy's eyes, so similar to his own. All the time Max had spent speaking with Molly, telling his stories, had helped ease the guilt he'd felt at coming home when so many had not. Maybe, he thought, he could help do the same for her brother.

She tilted her head toward Jimmy, who sat at the table with a cup of coffee and a cigarette. "He's been up for an hour now, telling me about flying without landing gear."

Max looked at Molly, surprised. "He's talking about combat already?"

She nodded, waving him in. "Come on in and sit. Everyone else is still asleep. It was a long night."

"Hey, Max," Jimmy said, raising his coffee cup in greeting.

"I bring treats," Max announced, setting down the plate of jam-filled pastries, then grabbing a seat at the table.

Jimmy wolfed one down as Molly placed a coffee in front of Max.

"Your stitches are holding," he said, studying Jimmy's face. "That's good."

A lock of Jimmy's unruly black hair had fallen over one eye, but he didn't seem to notice. Jimmy hadn't been in a POW camp, and he'd been back for months, and yet he was almost as thin as Max was. Max moved the plate toward him.

"Here, have another one. You look like you could use it."

"Says the skeleton," Jimmy replied in kind.

Molly took a seat and looked at Jimmy. "Tell Max what you just told me. About your plane."

"I was out on exercises one day," he said, "and my landing gear broke off. B-b-bang!" he yelled, grinning. "I'll admit, it was a bit of a b-bouncy landing, but I stuck it. Impressed the b-boys, too. What a time."

"I can imagine that," Max said, noting Jimmy's stammer. He hadn't heard it when Jimmy's system had been clouded with alcohol.

"I loved flying, you know. Just me and my squadron and the plane and the clouds. Such a feeling of freedom up there." Jimmy frowned at the steaming coffee then took a long gulp, seemingly oblivious to the heat. " 'Course it had its moments. Those Germans sure could fly. When they snuck up on you, you had to b-b-be ready."

"Can you tell us about Normandy?" Molly asked gently.

Max recalled the patient look on her face from their own conversations, and felt an odd twinge of jealousy. It felt strange, not being the object of her attention for once.

Jimmy was frowning, considering her question. "Our job was to patrol Juno Beach on D-Day," Jimmy said after a moment. "I've never seen military might like that day. On b-b-both sides. Flying over that, well, yeah. It was really something. What a show."

The three sat like statues around the table, steam rising from their cups, and the past flickered behind Jimmy's eyes. This was the moment when he could choose to let his story out and share his pain, or he could decide to keep it to himself. It was all up to him.

"We were providing cover for the ships," he said slowly, his eyes on his coffee. "And going head to head with enemy fighters. They'd painted our planes in b-black and white stripes so nobody could mistake us for Krauts. We looked like goddamn zebras, for Christ's sake. We'd flown on a patrol the night before, in the south of England, just a skip away from the Channel. In the morning when we got there, we could see the invasion was underway." He looked up at their faces. "I was flying behind my b-b-buddy Jocko. We were each other's wingmen all along. Great guy. He was a nickel miner from Sudbury."

Jimmy stopped, and all the colour drained from his face. There it was, Max realized, his heart twisting with sympathy. Jimmy's ghost.

"It's okay, Jimmy," he said. "You can tell us."

"There were more planes in the air that day than I'd ever seen." His voice was soft, coming from somewhere high above, hunting planes through the clouds. "Lots of b-b-bombers, but my eye was always on the fighters. I had to come down low when I passed over the b-b-beach. I'll tell you, I'd never seen anything like that in my life. I was close enough to see things." His hand went to his head, his fingers sinking into his hair so it stuck out like a hedgehog. "Men were sloshing through red, bloody water, wading through the b-b-bodies of their friends. I saw a leg here, a torso there." Anger flashed in his eyes, and he looked directly at his sister. "Nob-body ever prepares you for things like that."

No, they didn't, Max thought, his own mind crowding with the guns, the blades, the blood, and the hopelessness. The unimaginable cruelty he'd experienced at the hands of fellow men.

"I'd had my eye on a group of our soldiers trying to get off the b-b-beach, but they kept getting picked off one by one. They were almost to the ridge. So close. Then I saw the Germans aiming. They couldn't miss." He stretched out his arms to the side, like wings, then tilted them slightly. "So I swerved off course to warn them. It was stupid of me. I knew b-b-better than to think I could change anything. I kept yelling, yelling at those guys, as if I could stop them." His hands bunched into fists. "They couldn't hear me. How could I think they would? I was irresponsible and reckless, and I was off course."

"What happened?" Max asked.

Jimmy looked directly at Max. "I flew through the flames of Jocko's plane after he b-blew up. I saw his face as he went down." He made a V with his fingers then held them toward his eyes. "He was looking right at me, asking why I was off course. He still is. He's always looking at me, wanting to know." Then he gritted his teeth. "I see him when I'm sleeping. His mouth is always moving. He's asking me, *Where did you go? Why weren't you where you were supposed to b-b-be?*"

"It's not your fault," Molly whispered.

Jimmy slammed his fist on the table, and Max forced himself to stay still. He knew the anger, knew how hard it was to control it.

"How do you know that, Molly?" Jimmy demanded. "How do you know he wouldn't still b-b-be flying around up there with me, if I'd just stayed where I was meant to? If I'd looked out for him instead of getting distracted. If I'd—"

Max cut in. "Molly's right. Your being off course couldn't have blown Jocko's plane up. He flew into something. Somebody fired on him. There's nothing you could have done."

"How can you say that?" Jimmy cried, his face twisted with anguish. "I let him down!"

God, Max knew that agony. Seeing David's face a moment before he was shot; holding Arnie in his arms as he dwindled; the men in the hospital who had cried out, dying for want of medicine that was only a few feet away but always out of reach.

"It was the worst day of my life," Jimmy said, slumping with defeat. "I hated the world for putting me there, b-but I hate it more for b-b-bringing me home."

"Don't say that, Jimmy," Molly said, her eyes brimming.

But Jimmy was telling the truth, sharing with them what possessed his mind and heart. The torment, the guilt that was swirling inside Jimmy, was real for Max as well. Hannah had called him a miracle, but how could he be a miracle when so many of his friends hadn't made it back?

He touched Molly's hand. "Give me a minute?"

She studied his face, then nodded. "I should be heading to work," she said. "Jimmy, I'm sorry."

After she'd gone, Max took a breath and turned to Jimmy. "I understand."

He told him about the ghosts he saw every time he closed his eyes, and the disembodied voices of his friends—even of Richie—that screamed through his nights. It was getting easier to talk out loud about them, and the more he did, the quieter his nights became. Lately, there were moments when he could think back and smile, remembering the good times instead.

"They sent us to places nobody should ever have gone," he said, his voice wavering with the memory of Richie's bloodshot, pleading eyes. "We watched our friends die while we lived. But we survived. For whatever reason, we were spared and we came home. Now we have another battle to face." He tapped his temple, then touched his chest. "In here, and in here."

He'd never forget his family's faces the night he'd come home, how he'd frightened the people he needed the most. Recognizing that he was responsible for their unease had motivated him to work harder, and Molly had helped with that as well. The people here had grieved for years, thinking he was dead, so now he needed to show them he knew how to live.

"Our head and our hearts might still be back there, but our lives are here now. We have to pay attention to the people around us, or else we'll lose ourselves entirely."

"I feel like I already have, Max. I can't shake this. Jocko is like, he's like . . ." He lifted his hand. "He's like my hand. Always there. Part of me."

Max searched Jimmy's face for the scrappy kid he used to know, wondering how to reach him. His favourite memories of Jimmy were at the ball games, then talking and laughing about them after. So Max returned to the ballfield to find him.

"It's the bottom of the ninth, Jimmy. Bases are loaded, but the other team's brought in a new pitcher. You know he's got the goods to beat you. What's your move, Jimmy? You gonna pass the bat to someone else?"

Jimmy stared at him, and it took a full beat before he could respond. "No?" His voice was weak as a child's.

"Don't ask me, Jimmy. It's not up to me. It's up to you. Maybe you're too scared. You can walk away and lose, then hope to play another day. Or you can fight back right now. Hit that home run." He could see Jimmy's need to understand. He was almost there. "I'm sorry Jocko died. I know what that feels like. And I'm sorry you were there at all, just like I'm sorry I was there. I'll never stop being sorry that Richie, David, and Arnie never came back. But you and me, we're here now. We need to live our lives. People here depend on us. Respect Jocko's memory by being the guy he knew."

A tear slipped down Jimmy's cheek and dropped onto the table. "I can try."

Max nudged the plate of *sufganiyot*. "You can start by having another one of these. You need to put on some pounds if you're going to go up to bat."

The corner of Jimmy's mouth lifted slightly, then his smile grew, reaching toward his eyes. They crinkled at the corners, in a way Max remembered so well. "You know, Max, I could say the same about you."

Max patted his ribs. "Should've seen me before."

"No," Jimmy said. "Not about that. He reached across the table and tapped his nail against Molly's cold cup of coffee. "I think you'd better step up to the plate soon, Dreyfus. You're letting the pitcher win."

twenty-eight
MOLLY

I set my fingers on the keys of my typewriter and waited for the words to come. They always came. They were my thoughts. My feelings. Myself. But nothing came to me. Not even a whisper.

I'd thought I could write this POW story. That I could be objective. Listening to the men's stories and writing them all down was so important for them, for me, for everyone. But I hadn't counted on what they'd do to me. Their memories had seeped into my subconscious. When I closed my eyes, I saw their nightmares. I had awoken this morning, sweating and shivering.

"Molly," Ian said, coming up to my desk. "You're looking . . ." He hesitated and took a seat on the corner of my desk. "Actually, you're looking a little rough. You okay?"

I shook my head. "I didn't sleep last night. After I left your house, my night got a little wild."

His eyes widened when I told him how Max and I had come upon

Jimmy, being beaten up on the street, then how Max had sewn him back together.

"I left Max with him this morning. They were still talking when I left for work. Jimmy's a mess, as you know, but I think if anyone can help him, it'll be Max. Jimmy always looked up to him as a kid."

"You guys were all pretty close back then, huh? Why'd you drift apart?"

"Oh, it happened a long time ago. After the riot. Remember that night?"

He did. I'd told him long before about the brick that had led to my father's stroke, but I hadn't told him that Mum had blamed Max's father all this time. There hadn't been a reason to tell him, until now.

Ian leaned back, taking in this new information.

"That's what Richie's letter was about. We read it together last night."

"Wow," Ian said. "I missed a busy night. But I'm glad for you. It must feel good to know the truth after so long. I imagine Max's family is relieved too." He frowned. "So, Richie threw the brick to stop your dad from beating up Max. I get that. But I don't think you ever said why your dad was going after Max in the first place. He was a cop. Had Max done something? A fight like that sounds like something personal."

Heat shot up my neck. "Oh, it was nothing."

He sat up a little taller. "Well, now you've got me curious. From the shade of your face, I'd say it was more than nothing."

"It was a long time ago. It doesn't matter anymore." I looked over at the stack of papers on my desk, searching for an exit. "I'm sorry. I really should get back to this article. It's taking forever."

He was watching me, the oddest expression on his face. "Did something happen between you and Max? Is that why your Dad went after him?"

My skin burned.

Ian took my silence as confirmation, and his eyebrows lifted. I couldn't read his mind, but he definitely wasn't smiling. "I see," he said, almost to himself. "That explains some things."

"We were young," I said quickly. "It never would have worked, and we've both moved on." I tilted my head, beseeching him to let it go. "I'm with you now. And we're getting married."

Ian rose, looking unsure. I could see wheels turning behind those blue eyes, and my stomach churned with shame.

"What?" I asked.

"I guess I just wondered why you didn't tell me before," he said.

My skin prickled with guilt. "I had no reason to."

"Huh. Yeah, I guess." He took a step away, and my heart twisted at the hurt look in his eyes.

"Ian, it's nothing. I promise. It's all in the past."

"Sure. Yeah. Don't worry about it."

He was moving away from my desk, his face unreadable, but I could tell. No matter how I urged him to forget about it, the truth about my past was only wedging deeper into his mind.

I watched him walk away, and when I put my fingers back on the keys, they were trembling. What had I just done? I should have left it unsaid. But I'd *told* him it was history. Shouldn't he accept that? It's not like he'd ever told me about any of his past girlfriends.

I took a deep breath, turning to my work. I couldn't think about Ian. Not now. I took out my notes, and slowly the words came to me, though the story was so much more difficult to write than I'd ever imagined it would be. Hours later, I pulled the final page from my typewriter and sat back, drained but proud.

Wanting to share, I looked over to Ian's desk, but it was empty. I scanned the room and spotted his profile, standing in Mr. Hindmarsh's office with the door closed. When he came out, he seemed distracted. He went straight to his desk, and I followed him there.

"What's up?" I asked.

From the look on his face, I'd startled him. "What?" Then his expression softened, realizing why I was asking. "Oh, nothing. Just chatting with Hindmarsh about stuff. What's up with you?"

"I did it," I said, holding out the pages.

"Aha!" He managed a smile. "Good for you. I can't wait to read it."

His lacklustre response threw me off. "I was hoping you would, you know, put your finishing touches on it, or do whatever you think before I give it to Mr. Hindmarsh. It's by both of us, after all."

"Of course."

"Are you angry at me, Ian?"

His handsome face was pained. Had I caused that?

"You thought he was dead all that time," he said. "What if he hadn't been?"

"What?"

"For the longest time, it felt to me like something was between us. Was it him?"

I flushed. "It doesn't matter, Ian."

"Sure, it does. Since he's been back, you're different."

"That's not fair. Lots has changed. He's here, and my brothers are home. I have a lot on my mind."

For the first time, I couldn't recognize the look in his pale blue eyes. Then his attention was drawn past me, to the door. "Someone's here to see you."

It felt wrong, leaving the conversation unfinished, but he was still looking toward the door. I turned reluctantly, then rushed over, surprised, but so happy to see Hannah. It had been way too long since I'd stopped by her house. "Hi! What are you doing here?"

"Have lunch with me?" she asked.

Max would have shared Richie's letter with her, I realized. "Of course. One second." I ran to my desk and grabbed my coat and handbag then tucked my arm through hers. "There's a cafeteria in the basement, or the deli around the corner."

"Deli sounds good," she said, squeezing my arm against her side.

We got a spot at a cozy booth and settled in, anxious to talk about what had happened, and yet a nervous silence stretched between us. It wasn't until after we placed our orders that Hannah spoke.

"Richie's letter," she said.

"I'm so sorry, Hannah. Richie never should have done what he did."

"It's okay," she said. "It actually is. What a shock it was to read, though. I wasn't sure how I felt at first. Angry in the beginning, for sure."

"Me too."

"Then I spoke with Max, and he told me the two of them had reconciled over there. The more Max talked, the more I realized that Richie had been trying to do the right thing that night, but it went too far. He made a mistake and was just too afraid to tell us after. I only wish we'd known."

"I'm sorry," I said again. "I know his silence hurt your family. It hurt all of us."

"You have nothing to apologize for," she replied, covering my hand with hers. "You and I made our peace a long time ago. Richie's letter didn't change that for me." Her face brightened with a smile. "Oh, and I thought you should know that your parents and mine all met up this morning and had a good, long overdue talk over *sufganiyot*."

"I'm so glad to hear that."

"Yeah. Family's so important," she said, her smile dimming.

I knew where her mind had gone. "Have you talked to Max? About David?" I asked softly.

She looked at her hands. "Yes, he eventually told me what had happened. As awful as it was, it was something I needed to hear. I know now. I don't have to keep making things up in my mind."

I nodded, understanding exactly what she meant. How long had I wondered about Richie?

"I know Max is struggling with being back, but I think the interviews with you have helped him. Mama says he comes home tired, but the weight on his shoulders seems a little lighter. He's been so good with the kids recently. Especially Dinah. She worships him. I'm glad she finally has her uncle back."

I imagined him there, sharing his laughter with the children, and I envied them that time. But that's where he was supposed to be. Max was back. He was part of their family, as he'd always wanted to be. But he'd never be part of mine again.

"So, the story's over," Hannah said. "When will it run?"

"It's actually going to be a four-part series, and it starts next Monday."

"That's wonderful, Molly," she said.

Our meals arrived, and we sat quietly for a moment, picking at them. I was aware that Hannah was studying me like she always had, like she could hear my thoughts. It had been a while since I'd felt that sensation, and I clamped down hard on any secrets I might be harbouring.

After a moment, she set her fork down. "Molly, as your maid of honour, I need to know: Are you sure you want to marry Ian?"

I choked. "What?"

"If you are going to marry Ian, you have to be sure, without a shadow of a doubt. No regrets, no lingering thoughts."

I stared at her, stunned. "I don't understand. Why are you asking me this?"

"Max is back," she said slowly. "And any idiot can see that after all this time, nothing has changed between the two of you. My brother loves you. He always has. I want him to be happy. And I want you to be happy."

My whole body tingled with nerves. *The thing about love is that you can never know until you know*, Mum had told me. Back then, I'd thought I'd known. Back then, before the world had changed.

"Of course I want to marry him," I said quickly, dismissing the thought. "And you'll be the best maid of honour anyone could ask for."

But her words hummed in my head all the way back to the office. I was still deep in thought when I got to my desk.

"Miss Ryan."

I glanced up. "Yes, Mr. Hindmarsh?"

"May I speak with you a moment?"

I rushed into his office, still in my coat, fresh nerves skittering down my spine. Mr. Hindmarsh always made me nervous, no matter what. He didn't mean to, that's just how he was. He indicated my chair, then he handed me a file. I opened it and saw the story I'd finished that morning was on top. My stomach rolled with apprehension. Where were his usual red editorial markings? Was it that bad?

"I think this is your best work, Miss Ryan," he said, and relief blazed into my cheeks. "Some of my editors should consider taking lessons from you."

"Oh, I—"

I was about to correct him, tell him that Ian and I had written this together, but then my eyes fell on the byline, noting that Ian had taken his name off. That was strange. I'd ask him about that as soon as I was finished here. Confused, I shuffled to the next article in the folder, my original story from VE Day, talking about the returning veterans. Behind it, I spotted others. Near the bottom of the pile, I saw Mr. Rabinowitz's story. The last page was my original letter to the editor, from 1933.

"You have quite an impressive collection there, Miss Ryan. You've come a long way from writing church bazaar notices, haven't you?"

My smile flickered. Where was this going?

"Yes. Well, if you have a few minutes, I wanted to speak with you about an assistant editor position that's just come up here at the paper."

My jaw dropped in disbelief. It was a good thing I was already sitting, because I felt dizzy with surprise. Twenty minutes later, when I left his office and headed back to my desk, I was walking on air.

Ian had left a note on my typewriter, where I couldn't miss it, asking me to come to his house for dinner. Unexpected nerves wriggled through me. Between his reaction this morning and my lunch with Hannah— and then my recent promotion—we had a lot to discuss. I just wasn't sure what I was going to say.

He was at the stove when I arrived at his house. He'd lit a candle on the dining room table, and the soft light felt romantic. Two empty wineglasses waited by our places, and I wondered if we were celebrating my promotion. He'd been in Mr. Hindmarsh's office earlier, I recalled, and a thought hit me. Did he know about it already? Had he recommended me for the position?

"This looks so nice," I said, my voice slightly higher than usual.

"It's just spaghetti," Ian said, plating two dishes. "It's the only thing I can make."

I helped him carry the plates to the table, then he went back for wine while I sat. When he returned, it struck me that he looked older in the candlelight. He looked tired.

The uneasiness from this morning still hovered over us like a cloud. When he sat across from me, he avoided my eyes. He poured the wine, and I squirmed in my seat, not sure how to react. We'd always been able to talk about anything.

"Mr. Hindmarsh called me into his office today," I said, breaking the ice as Ian poured the wine. "He actually offered me an assistant editor job. I didn't even know there was a position open."

"I hope you took it," he said, lifting his glass.

"I did."

His smile was warm, but sad. I didn't understand.

"I'm happy for you, Molly. You deserve this. Your piece on Max was brilliant. I knew everything you were going to put in there, but you still brought me to tears and taught me new things. Your talent, your insight, your dedication. It was yours and yours alone."

"Thank you," I said, blushing. "But why'd you take your name off the byline?"

"Because it was your article. We both know that."

"We did it together, Ian. Some of those questions were too hard for me to ask. Not sure I could have done it without you."

"Yes, you could have," he said, taking a sip. "It was all you and Max."

I hesitated, hearing that note of sadness in his voice. "Did you say something to Mr. Hindmarsh about the job?"

"No," he said. "It wasn't my idea. Mr. Hindmarsh wanted you right from the start." He put his napkin on his lap, then he took a deep breath. "What he didn't tell you—and I asked him not to—is that it's my position."

"Your position?" I echoed.

"I've been offered a job in Boston."

My hand stilled on my glass. "Wh-What? What's going on?"

His bright blue eyes shone. "It took me a little while, but then I couldn't miss it."

"You've been looking for a job? And you didn't tell me?"

He shook his head. "No, Molly. It wasn't that. It's . . . I saw how you looked at Max, and how he looked at you. How could I not?"

My heart sank, hurting for both of us.

"I won't say that it didn't hurt. I'd never actually felt my heart break before. But I watched you both, and I listened. And as much as I didn't want to, I came to understand. Max isn't just your old friend. You've loved him your whole life."

I bit my lower lip. I couldn't deny a word of it.

"You and I," he said gently, "we are the best of friends. Do you agree?"

"Absolutely," I whispered.

"If we got married, I know we would be happy. Content." He reached across the table and put his hand on mine. It was warm, familiar, and soft with love. "But you, Molly, you're not an average girl. You're something special. I knew that the minute you walked into the newsroom. And I think you deserve more than 'content.'" He took another breath. "So I'm setting you free."

I couldn't breathe.

He squeezed my hand. "It's your choice. Come to Boston with me, or stay here."

If I'd ever truly loved him, it was in that moment. I saw the pain shining in his eyes, and I longed to soothe it. But he was waiting for my answer, and he'd sense if I was being honest. And that's when I knew. *You can never know until you know.* Despite the affection Ian and I felt for each other, he wasn't the one for me.

Gently, I withdrew my hand, and he closed his eyes, accepting my decision.

"I don't even know if Max would want me, after all this," I said after a silent moment.

"Molly, if there's one thing I know, it's how a man looks when he's in love." He managed a small smile, then his eyes fell to my hand. "But you'll never know if you go in with my ring on your finger."

"Oh, Ian!" He always knew how to make me laugh. Even through tears. "Our mothers are going to be so disappointed," I said, placing the ring in his palm. I curled his fingers over it, then looked at my own hand. My finger looked so plain now. But it also looked right.

"They'll be okay," he said.

We looked at each other a long time, accepting what had just happened.

"I will miss you, Ian Collins."

"And I will miss you." He softly kissed the back of my knuckles. "Molly Ryan, I need you to promise me one thing."

"Anything."

"Be happy. Do what makes you happy."

twenty-nine
MAX

❧

Max hopped off the streetcar and made his way toward home, a lift to his step despite his limp. He'd been down to the Toronto General Hospital, where he'd met with the chief physician about a job. The chief had been impressed with his résumé and his references, and since the hospital was overflowing with patients and low on doctors, Max was feeling positive about his chances. It would be good to get back to work and leave the past five years behind.

He wasn't the only one feeling better about the future. Since sharing Richie's letter, things had warmed between the Ryans and the Dreyfuses. Both Molly's mother and his had been over at each other's houses, baking and sewing together, and one day when Max came downstairs, he'd walked in on a roomful of women and children. Richie's wife, Barbara, had brought her two, Mark's wife, Helen, had her new baby, and Hannah had her three. The grandmothers beamed over the whole brood. He was vaguely surprised to see Liam sitting in the corner of the room, smiling his odd little smile, but he knew the simplicity of the children calmed him. The poor man would never be able to walk down the street again without being stared at, but he was finally realizing he wasn't the only one. They'd all come back with injuries, visible and invisible, and they found the most solace in sharing their stories. Just yesterday, Max and Jimmy had joined the Legion, where they met and remembered and played pool over beers. Liam was considering going with them next time.

At the end of the block, Max perked up a little, spotting Molly standing outside his house. She was wrapped in her black coat with a faded green scarf tied around her neck, and her nose was bright red from the chill. He could see her smile from five houses away.

"Hello, Miss Ryan," he said, feeling a familiar pang of loss, remembering that name would change in just a few days.

"Hi," she said, her eyes twinkling in the sunlight. "Where've you been?"

"I just applied for a job," he told her. "What are you doing out here in the cold?"

"Waiting for you. I have something to show you," she said, then she took off her mitts and handed him a folded newspaper.

He opened it up and gaped. There, on the front page, was her story. His story.

WE NEVER SURRENDERED

*The Story of Canadian Soldiers in Hong Kong,
and Their Brave Survival in
Japanese POW Camps*

"It's just one column here," she said quickly, bubbling with excitement. "But it continues on page six. Everyone's going to read it, Max. They won't know your name, but they're all going to know you were heroes in Hong Kong." She paused. "Even if you don't believe it."

He felt his eyes prick with tears as he read the first paragraph. "Molly," he breathed. "You don't know what this means to me."

"I couldn't have done it without you," she said. "You were the one to encourage me to be a journalist in the very beginning. All these years later you trusted me to tell your story. Thank you. For trusting me."

"I'm so, so proud of you." His eye went to the byline. "Where's Ian's name?"

"Ian's actually left the *Star*," she said lightly. "He's taking a job at a paper in Boston."

He stepped back, his heart plunging. Boston? He searched her face. "You're moving?"

"Um, no. I'm staying here." She tugged at the scarf around her neck, and he stared at her hand. Her ring was gone. "Ian and I aren't getting married."

His throat jammed with relief. He hadn't dared to imagine that possibility.

She closed the gap between them, just as she had all those years before, and anticipation swooped through his chest.

"Max, you must know how I feel about you. How I've always felt about you."

Thoughts flew through his head like bullets. For so long, this was all he had ever wanted, but the obstacles hadn't changed.

"Molly, I can't give you what he can. I can't give you a ring."

She took a breath, and he heard it catch. "I don't need a ring to be with you, Max. After all we've been through to find each other again, I'm not going to let that come between us."

He felt it in his heart first. A cautious sense of hope, like the first rays of a sunrise breaking free of the horizon. The sound of the American planes spotting them for the first time.

"God, Molly. I thought that we—" Then he stopped, unsure all over again. "I'm not the same man I was. I'm not sure you'd know me anymore."

"I know who you are, Max. You know I do. And I know you're suffering, but we'll get through it together." She hesitated, and fear crossed her face. "If you still want me, I mean."

He looked her straight in those startling green eyes. "If I still want you? How can you even say that? Of course I still want you, Molly. It's always been you."

She took another step closer, and he reached for her, drawing her into his arms and feeling instantly whole. He lowered his face to her silky hair.

"You're trembling," he murmured. "Are you afraid?"

She shook her head against his chest then drew back to look at him through shining eyes. "I'm never afraid when I'm with you, Max."

Her arms wrapped around his neck, bringing them even closer, and he felt as if the entire world had just opened up for him. His life wouldn't ever be carefree again, he didn't think; he worked through self-doubt and grief and guilt every day. But he was no longer worried about the battles ahead. With Molly at his side, they would fight those together.

"Max," she said softly.

He smiled, their lips inches apart. "What?"

"I've been waiting over twelve years for you to kiss me again."

It felt like a dream, bringing his lips to hers, then feeling her kiss him with such a sweet desperation. He could hardly catch a breath, but he didn't care. Because it wasn't a dream. Her love filled his heart, his mind, and his body, as real as the sunshine beaming down on them, here in the middle of their street. He was home now, and he was safe. And there would be no more good-byes.

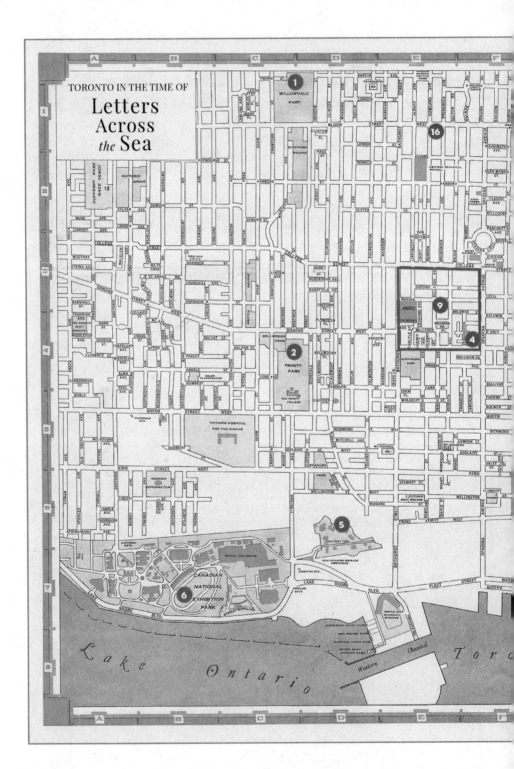

TORONTO IN THE TIME OF
Letters
Across
the Sea

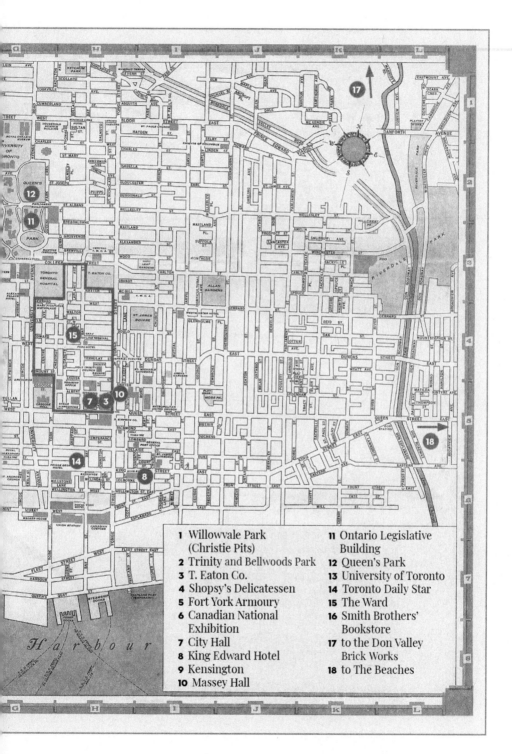

1 Willowvale Park (Christie Pits)
2 Trinity and Bellwoods Park
3 T. Eaton Co.
4 Shopsy's Delicatessen
5 Fort York Armoury
6 Canadian National Exhibition
7 City Hall
8 King Edward Hotel
9 Kensington
10 Massey Hall
11 Ontario Legislative Building
12 Queen's Park
13 University of Toronto
14 Toronto Daily Star
15 The Ward
16 Smith Brothers' Bookstore
17 to the Don Valley Brick Works
18 to The Beaches

KOWLOON

Belcher Point

VICTORIA

Bowri

MOUNT DAVIS

VICTORIA PEAK

MOUNT
PARISH

MOUNT
GOUGH

Wan Chai
Gap

Pok Fu Lam

MOUNT
CAMERON

H   O   N

Aberdeen
Reservoir

BENNET'S
HILL

Lit
Hong

WEST BRIGADE
TWO COYS 1ST MIDDLESEX
ELEMENTS 5/7 RAJPUT
2/14 PUNJAB
2ND ROYAL SCOTS
WINNIPEG GRENADIERS
HONG KONG VOLUNTEER
DEFENCE CORPS
PLUS VARIOUS
DETACHMENTS

Aberdeen

2ND BN
229TH
JAPANESE
INF REGT

BRICK
HILL

HONG KONG
18-25 DECEMBER 1941

0   1   2   3
MILES ├─────────────────────────────────────┤ MILES

Ground over 50 metres ____   Approximate British Front
Ground over 150 metres ____   Line at Times Indicated ____
Ground over 300 metres ____   Japanese Lines
of Advance ____
ONLY PRINCIPAL ROADS SHOWN

MAP 1

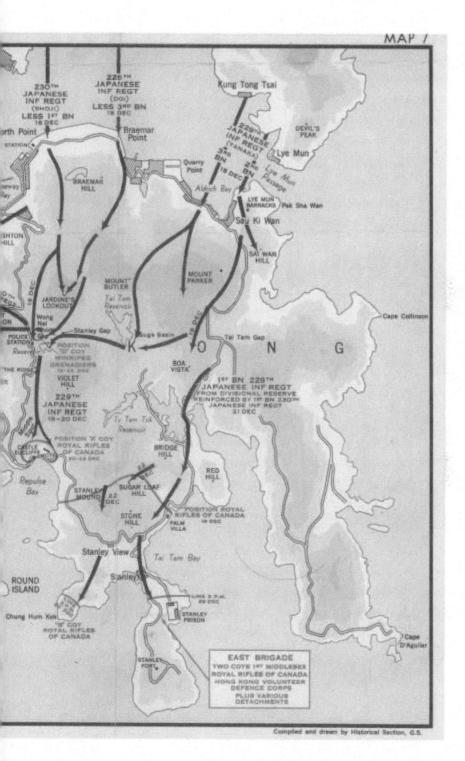

A Note to Readers

What I love most about writing historical fiction is the ability to take something ordinary, like a black-and-white photo, and make it into something extraordinary. To bring that wrinkled old piece of paper, or whatever it is, to life. For example, there is a plaque at Christie Pits in Toronto—also known as Willowvale Park—that commemorates the riot. Just a plain, metal plaque that people walk past on a regular basis. I like to think about what's behind that plaque. About why it was put there. I love to bring that story to life, so it sticks in people's minds long after they've walked away.

I am constantly on the hunt for little-known stories in Canadian history. When I heard about the Christie Pits Riot, the largest ethnic riot in Canadian history, I thought about all the societal reasons that had caused the event. Considering today's volatile climate, I also thought it would be interesting to learn about past riots and protests in our cities. After all, we are not the first to witness unrest in our streets. What did they look like before? Why were they happening? What, if anything, did they achieve?

In 1933, Toronto was a regular Canadian city, filled with regular Canadians, and yet beneath its veneer as "Toronto the Good," the city simmered with an ugly, hateful tension. Just like today, the press played a large role in creating divisions. As Molly, Max, and Arnie sat in the sun on that beautiful July day, they spoke about the different ways in which the *Toronto Daily Star*, the *Evening Telegram*, and *Der Yidisher Zhurnal* covered the news coming out of Germany. Everything they said was true. Not only did the *Telegram* deny the stories about the mistreatment of Jews, they frequently ran anti-Semitic editorials in their paper throughout the 1930s. The *Telegram* even accused the Jewish community of having incited the Christie Pits Riot, despite the fact that it was the unfurling of the swastika-emblazoned blanket that set off the fight. Their front page headline the following day read "Jewish Toughs Begin Trouble Says Witness." When the *Star* eventually began to report properly on what was happening in Germany and around Toronto, the *Telegram* began to refer to them as "the Big Brother of the Little Reds."

In January 1933, Adolf Hitler became the chancellor of Germany, and by March, the Enabling Act basically gave him free rein as a dictator. But his strength was in propaganda, and once he and his Nazi thugs shut down all competing radio, newspaper, and news reels, he had the airwaves all to himself. He denied any wrongdoings, stoked the nationalist fire, and didn't bother with the five principals of ethical journalism that Ian reminded Molly about: Truth, Accuracy, Fairness, Impartiality, and perhaps most importantly, Humanity. As some international press rode that wave of Nazi rhetoric, anti-Semitism rose around the world—including in Canada.

While different points of view are a sign of individuality and free thinking, trouble occurs when we are told what to believe, and we don't question why. As Molly pointed out, the *Telegram* went beyond bias to censorship, and these stories were partially responsible for the emergence of the hateful Swastika Clubs. From what I could learn, there were approximately four thousand badge-carrying members of the Toronto clubs that occupied areas around Toronto, like the boardwalk near the Balmy Beach Canoe Club and Willowvale Park, or Christie Pits. Interestingly, there was also a Swastika Club at Roches Point and Balfour Beach in Lake Simcoe, and one in Kitchener, Ontario.

At the same time as this was happening, thousands were out of work because of the Great Depression, and they struggled to feed their families. Labour unions demanded non-existent jobs for their workers, and women sought better wages and working conditions. But they were largely unsuccessful, as Molly tells Max when he invites her to the July 11, 1933, rally. In February 1931, five hundred members of the International Ladies' Garment Workers' Union (ILGWU) walked out on a general strike, seeking a 15 per cent pay raise, recognition of their union, and impartial mediation in Toronto. But the populace regarded their demands as greedy and shouted them down. After two and a half months, public pressure forced the ILGWU to abandon the cause.

During the Depression, mass unemployment led to protests of all kinds. Here is an iconic photo of The Single Men's Unemployed Association parading to Bathurst Street United Church in Toronto in the 1930s.
Toronto Star / Library and Archives Canada / C-029397.

As a writer of historical fiction, I'm always looking for a personal thread that will bring the history to life. With everything going on at that time, Toronto was like a bed of dry straw, ready to burst into flame. I decided to light a match by creating a love story between two characters from opposite sides.

It wasn't too difficult for me to imagine all this, since I grew up in Toronto in the 1970s and 1980s. While it was a different time, I do know those roasting-hot summer days and nights before air-conditioning was a given in every house. I have ridden along the same streetcar tracks as Molly and Max. My family and I spent countless days downtown, mostly enjoying Chinatown (I am a dim sum fanatic), but I know the fashion district of Spadina as well. Once upon a time, I had a gorgeous leather jacket and the softest gloves I've ever owned made in one of those old buildings. In elementary school, I remember being taken to Kensington Market with my class, and the father of one of my best friends owned a Mexican restaurant in Cabbagetown. And of course, I've also been to Christie Pits.

In Toronto, there are wonderful little pockets of culture, like Chinatown and Little Italy. Growing up, I knew certain areas were mostly Jewish, and others were primarily Catholic or Protestant. To me, the city's "patchwork quilt" of people, as Max described his neighbourhood, was part of Toronto's charm.

Until I learned of the Christie Pits Riot, I never could have conceived of the anger that erupted that hot August night in 1933. At the beginning of the ball game between Harbord Playground and St. Peter's, approximately two thousand spectators were in attendance, and those were eventually joined by thousands more who drifted over after the Native Sons and the Vermonts game. St. Peter's won the game against Harbord Playground around seven o'clock. That's when a group of youths standing on the slope of the hill south of the ball diamond spread out a large white blanket bearing a black swastika, and the field erupted in a furious game of capture the flag. Once word got out, reinforcements raced in from around the city, building to a massive crowd of ten thousand. Both sides came prepared with sawed-off metal pipes, pool cues, baseball bats, and bricks.

It was no secret that something big was going to happen that night, but the police didn't show up for the first forty-five minutes. Then again, it might not have made that much of a difference if they had come earlier. According to Cyril Levitt and William Shaffir's *The Riot at Christie Pits*, by 9:30 p.m., "the police on horseback and motorcycle and on foot had formed a complete circle around the park, [and yet] the trucks of reinforcements still managed to break through." Young Jewish boys rode their bicycles through the streets, hollering, "*Gevalt, me shlugt yidn!*" (Help, they're beating Jews!) inspiring truckloads of Jewish men—and Italians, since the two communities were close—to head to the park. The fighting went on until after midnight, splintering into smaller gangs, and spreading through the streets. In the end, there were ten noted injuries, most of which were head injuries, plus a possible fractured rib. Two arrests were made: one for carrying a knife (the offender claimed he was carrying it because he was a fishing guide and needed it for scaling fish), and the other for being caught standing over a prostrate man with a wood-and-metal club raised over his head. He was locked up for two months for that.

I wondered about the far-reaching effects of the riot. Globally, it was a signal of what was to come, with World War II on the horizon. But in Toronto, what did the riot mean for Molly and Max?

Molly understood that incorrect or incomplete journalism could change everything, and how easily trust could be broken between the press and the people. The riot was her first real opportunity to look at an event and see all sides to the story, then capture it in words.

As a female reporter determined to tell the truth, Molly had her work cut out for her, and she had quite a role model in real-life journalist Rhea Clyman. Rhea led a remarkable life. Born in Poland in 1904, she moved to Toronto with her parents when she was two. At five, she lost part of her leg in a streetcar accident. The following year her father died, and so at age eleven, she went to work in a factory to support the rest of her family. But Rhea had big dreams. She moved to New York, then London, working for various newspapers. As a single woman with a disability, a Jewish-Canadian, and a feminist, Rhea was a rarity in an industry primarily run by men. At twenty-four years old, she traveled to the Soviet Union as a foreign correspondent. Before they expelled her—to international headlines—she became one of the first North American journalists to report on the Holodomor, a man-made famine (*Holod* = hunger, *mor* = extermination) in which at least five million people perished from 1932 to 1933. As the Nazi party rose to power, Rhea moved to Germany and attended rallies so she could write about them. Remember, she was *Jewish*! Like Molly, I am in awe of Rhea's courage.

When I learned about the Battle of Bowmanville, I knew Molly had to report on it. The connection between Stalag VIIIB, a German prisoner of war camp in Poland, and the Bowmanville prisoner of war camp is real. According to reports, Hitler saw a photograph of a small group of German prisoners at Dieppe with their hands bound, which was against the Geneva Convention. The Germans demanded an apology from Britain, and when they didn't get one, they tied the wrists of hundreds of British and Canadian POWs at Stalag VIIIB with the red string from Red Cross parcels. The prisoners were bound for twelve hours a day and were only untied at night. They suffered ulcerated sores on their wrists, had trouble eating and visiting the latrine. After Molly, Ian, and Mo left the three-day riot at Bowmanville, the hundred German POWs were indeed forced to wear the shackles, but Canadian public opinion was strongly against it. The guards weren't fans either, and they reportedly dropped keys around the camp so the prisoners could take them off between roll calls.

Over my years of research, I have grieved over moments of inhumanity, but I have also celebrated acts of human kindness. In dark times, those are the stories we must remember. One such story took place at Stalag VIIIB, where some of the Allied POWs captured by the Nazis were Jewish soldiers. Not surprisingly, the Nazi guards treated them more harshly than their fellow prisoners. What the Nazis didn't expect was for the prisoners to stand in solidarity. When the guards planned to withhold the much-needed Canadian Red Cross parcels from Jewish prisoners, the rest of the prisoners declared that if their Jewish fellows couldn't have the parcels, well then, they wouldn't take them either. They were all in it together. During those terrible times, it was friendship that kept the men strong.

As for Max, when war broke out, I knew he would be eager to fight the Nazis as so many young men were, and I took special inspiration from Torontonian Ben Dunkelman. In Cyril Levitt and William Shaffir's book, they included the following quote from Ben: "As a Canadian, it's my duty to volunteer. As a Jew, I have a special score to settle with the Nazis." I had Max paraphrase this when he told his family that he was enlisting.

I had originally planned to send Max to Dieppe. There, he would have been captured by the Germans and taken to Stalag VIIIB. There are many stories about Stalag VIIIB and other German POW camps that deserve to be told. But then I stumbled across a piece of Canadian history that I had never heard of before, one that has largely been forgotten: the Battle of Hong Kong.

There's a reason this battle is not often discussed. I've read military accounts and articles as well as journals and interviews of veterans who survived, and they all tell the same shameful story: the Battle of Hong Kong should never have happened. In fact, it was the only battle in WWII that was 100 per cent a failure. As Molly said, 1,985 men went in and 296 were killed in battle. The remaining 1,689 were sentenced to three years and eight months in brutal POW camps where their Japanese captors had no interest in following the Geneva Convention. Private Robert "Flash" Clayton of the Royal Rifles fought in the Battle of Hong Kong. In the documentary *Savage Christmas: Hong Kong 1941*, he said, "The government of Canada knowingly put 2,000 men as lambs to the slaughter in order to meet some political expediency."

Why were they there? As of 1941, the Canadian Army was the only branch of the Canadian military that had not yet seen combat. At that point, Japan had shown no aggression toward the West, but Britain wanted to make a show of force in their colony of Hong Kong to discourage any potential attack. British soldiers were busy fighting Germans, so the Brits asked Canada for reinforcements. Prime Minister Mackenzie King's government reluctantly sent two battalions for—what they expected to be—garrison duty.

The Canadians sent to Hong Kong were members of the Royal Rifles from Quebec and New Brunswick and the Winnipeg Grenadiers. Together, they made up C Force. Before they sailed to Hong Kong in November 1941, C Force was officially labelled "unfit for battle" due to undertraining and inadequate weapons. They were told that was all right; they had nothing to worry about. After all, they said, there were only about five thousand weak, poorly trained Japanese soldiers, against which the Brits who were already stationed there could easily defend. In fact, there were ten times that many, and they were hardened Japanese veterans loyal to the unflinching Bushido code of conduct, known as "the way of the warrior."

The Japanese attack on Pearl Harbor on December 7, 1941, was a signal to the rest of the world that Japan was in the war. Just ten hours later, they turned their attention to Manila, then Hong Kong, of which they took control within five days. They demanded the British surrender, but despite there being no hope of relief from outside the colony, Hong Kong's military commander refused, choosing instead to depend upon the remaining, inexperienced soldiers to defend Hong Kong. That included C Force.

The December 11 ferry ride across the Lye Mun Passage was only three kilometres long, but it must have been a terrifying journey for the Royal Rifles and the 7th Rajput Regiment, one of two Indian infantry battalions also assigned to Hong Kong. When the Japanese attacked one week later, sending four boatloads of seasoned fighters through the dark night, the defending forces had no chance. Arnie and Max said they didn't know how to throw a grenade, which echoed what many of the survivors later recorded. Despite their serious shortage of weapons, the undertrained Canadians fought back as hard as they could, but the Japanese inflicted heavy casualties right away, and they kept on pushing. After an impossible week of fighting in the brutal, unfamiliar mountains of Hong Kong Island, the Canadians finally withdrew to Stanley Fort, on the Stanley Peninsula. On Christmas Day, they fought it out at Stanley Village, where those who didn't die were taken as prisoners.

While that was happening, two hundred Japanese soldiers carried out the atrocities at St. Stephen's College hospital. I had Ian hold back some of the most gruesome details, but the horrifying truth is that the Japanese army killed sixty or so wounded men in their beds, dismembering many of them as they lay motionless, anesthetized in preparation for surgery, and then they gang-raped and murdered most of the nurses. Incredibly, there were survivors, and when I read their personal reports, I wept.

When it came time to write about the valiant soldiers in the ranks of C Force, I couldn't leave out Gander the dog. In order to bring him into the story, I took a little creative license and transferred Max, David, Arnie, and Richie from the Royal Regiment in Toronto to the Royal Rifles and posted them to Gander, Newfoundland, in 1940. In reality, the Royal Rifles picked up men later, when they made their way west to Vancouver in 1941. At the time, Gander air base was the largest airport in the world, and when the Royal Rifles were stationed there, they were given a purebred Newfoundland dog, whom they named after the base. Before departing for Vancouver, they promoted Gander to the rank of sergeant so they wouldn't have to leave him behind.

The Royal Rifles with their mascot, Gander, aboard HMCS Prince Robert *en route to Hong Kong on November 15, 1941.* Canada. Dept. of National Defence / Library and Archives Canada / PA-166999.

Sergeant Gander, with his fondness for cold showers, beer, and a good scratch, would prove to be a hero. Almost invisible in the dark of night, he charged at enemy soldiers who usually fled rather than face him. Later, when the men were taken as POWs, the Japanese interrogated some of them about the "Black Beast," thinking the Allies were training vicious animals. Eventually, Sergeant Gander made the ultimate sacrifice, rushing in to retrieve a grenade, then carrying it away, saving the lives of seven Canadian soldiers.

When Ian and Molly interviewed Max, Ian mentioned that C Force had been accused of fleeing like cowards, and I felt Max's indignation at that. I read personal accounts and listened to interviews in which survivors argued vehemently to the contrary. For eighteen days, the Canadians had been continuously bombarded by the Japanese's heavy arsenal of artillery on land and in the skies. It is a testament to the Canadians' bravery that they never surrendered, despite their own lack of reinforcements, food, water, rest, battle training, and adequate weapons.

In the Japanese Bushido code, it was considered better to endure death rather than live with the shame of surrender. So when the British surrendered to Japan on Christmas Day 1941, the Japanese automatically considered the Allied POWs to be worthless, contemptible cowards, and they were treated accordingly. There were occasional reports of some Japanese guards who treated the prisoners better, engaged in friendly conversation, even befriended them, but they did so at risk of their own lives—and those of their families.

The Geneva Convention is made up of four conventions. The first protects wounded and infirm prisoners of war as well as captured medical personnel. Without discrimination, it grants rights to proper medical treatment, and it prohibits torture, assault, and execution. Japan did sign the Geneva Convention; however, they never ratified it. While some countries showed an occasional lack of regard for the rules (as evidenced by the reason for the Battle of Bowmanville), the Japanese paid no attention to them at all. They committed horrible atrocities in the POW camps.

The descriptions shared with Molly by Sergeant Cox and Max about what the prisoners ate in the camps come directly from journals and interviews with POW survivors. A soldier or average male doing manual labour requires 3,500 calories per day. At North Point Camp on Hong Kong Island, each prisoner was reluctantly given 600–1,200 calories, which consisted almost entirely of rice and chrysanthemum tops. If men were sick, they were given half portions. In the German POW camps, Allied prisoners relied on the Red Cross parcels to help them survive their incarceration, but the Japanese rarely allowed any of the parcels to reach the prisoners. They were usually stolen by the guards, and often sold on the black market.

During my research, I came across a typed-up list of infractions the Japanese captors considered worthy of immediate execution. Sergeant Cox listed some of them off for Molly. Among the offences were: talking without permission and raising loud voices, walking and moving without order, and using more than two blankets. All were punishable by death.

The camps in Hong Kong were horrible, but those who were shipped to Japan on board hell ships fared even worse. Max was one of more than 1,100 Canadians who were stuffed into the boats like sardines and given barely any food or water. When they arrived at the camps, they were covered in waste and vomit. Max was imprisoned at Niigata, where prisoners worked in a mine ten to twelve hours a day, swinging a sledgehammer by a white-hot furnace, pushing hoppers filled with coal up steep railway inclines, or other similar tasks.

Besides the physical beatings and punishments, and the lack of nourishment, medicine, and sanitation, the Japanese were also extremely lax in reporting to the Red Cross exactly who they had in their camps. For months, even years, Canadian families like the Ryans and the Dreyfuses had no idea if their fathers, brothers, and sons were dead or taken prisoner.

Emperor Hirohito's original plan had been to execute all POWs if the Japanese were forced to surrender. Some reports claim the mines the men were digging were actually large burial caves for the prisoners. But because the atomic bombs were so quickly and unexpectedly dropped, the war ended too abruptly to carry out that plan. That's not to say they didn't manage to kill the prisoners in a more drawn-out manner.

Canadian and British prisoners of war being liberated from Sham Shui Po in Hong Kong in August 1945. Despite the smiling faces, you can see how thin some of the men are—and this was after a month of receiving food drops. The men who would be liberated from the Japanese camps were in even worse shape. PO Jack Hawes / Canada. Dept. of National Defence / Library and Archives Canada / PA-145983.

Two hundred and sixty-four POWs died in those camps. Here's a statistic that Molly didn't know, but we do now. During WWII, 4 per cent of Allied POWs held in German and Italian camps died in captivity. In the Japanese camps, that number was *at least* 27 per cent. Some reports I read suggest it was up to 38 per cent. Between May 1946 and November

1948, the International Military Tribunal for the Far East (IMTFE) took place in Tokyo. Eleven justices from Canada, the United States, Australia, China, France, Great Britain, India, the Netherlands, New Zealand, the Philippines, and the Soviet Union tried twenty-eight Japanese military and civilian leaders for war crimes, crimes against peace, and crimes against humanity in what is known as the Tokyo Trial. All twenty-eight were found guilty. Two died of natural causes during the trial. One had a mental breakdown during the trial, was sent to a psychiatric ward, then was released in 1948. Seven were found guilty of inciting or participating in mass-scale atrocities and sentenced to death by hanging, including the former prime minister of Japan Hideki Tojo. Sixteen were given life imprisonment, and two, lesser terms. Three of those sixteen died between 1949 and 1950, and the rest were paroled between 1954 and 1956. They committed crimes against millions of people, and they served fewer than eight years in prison.

The list of those *not* indicted is disturbing. For example, Emperor Hirohito was never tried; General MacArthur decided to leave him on the throne in an attempt to help the Japanese people accept their defeat and occupation. There were other notable exceptions, such as the heads of the Japanese military police, or Kempeitai—the Japanese equivalent of the Nazi Gestapo. Those responsible for rounding up tens of thousands of young, non-Japanese women to serve as "comfort women" were never pursued, nor were those who forced non-Japanese men into military service. Secret immunity was granted to a group of officers and scientific researchers in Manchuria who conducted lethal experiments on thousands of prisoners and civilians, on the grounds that they share their research results with the Americans. A number of the guards at Niigata, where Max spent most of his imprisonment, were tried and found guilty of mistreating or causing the deaths of prisoners; however, no one was ever charged for what happened on board the infamous hell ships.

On the other hand, not everyone turned a politically blind eye. The victimized Asian countries sought justice beyond the Tokyo Trial. They tried an estimated five thousand Japanese, executed as many as nine hundred for war crimes—including acts of cannibalism on Allied POWs and civilians—and sentenced more than half to life imprisonment. Reports vary, some saying the cannibalism was done purely out of hunger, but others claim the flesh of Allied prisoners was given to Japanese troops by their commanders to give them a sense of victory.

Of the 1,985 Canadians sent to Hong Kong, 1,425 eventually came home. Initially, Canadians were outraged at the treatment of their men, but their attention was quickly drawn elsewhere. After all, far more men had been killed, wounded, and taken as prisoner in Europe. The world was also in shock over the revelation of the atrocities carried out in Nazi concentration camps as well as the human toll of Hiroshima and Nagasaki on Japanese civilians.

After I completed writing this book, I made the most astounding discovery: the great-uncle of a close friend of mine, Lance Corporal Philip Doddridge of the Royal Rifles, is one of the five Canadian Hong Kong veterans still alive today. It broke my heart to hear him say in an interview, "I think we're largely forgotten, if not ignored." The terribly sad fact is that Molly's POW series was fictional; there were no substantial articles written about Doddridge or the other Hong Kong POWs until decades later.

Every returning Canadian prisoner suffered chronic health problems. Eighty-seven of the men came home blind. Two hundred died before the age of fifty. After nearly four years of being denied calories and essential vitamins, the survivors suffered from avitaminosis, which caused wet beriberi (shortness of breath, rapid heartbeat, swollen limbs, possible heart failure) and the unremitting stabbing and burning agony of electric feet. Two years after they returned home, more than 70 per cent of Canadian POWs still had intestinal parasites, whipworms, hookworms, and threadworms. Very few doctors of the time had experience dealing with tropical parasites, and since the POWs had gained back most of their weight by their return, thanks to the American care packages, the doctors didn't think to worry about starvation.

All this was made much more difficult by the fact that the men were so traumatized by what they'd survived, they often chose not to tell any-one about their experiences, so their doctors saw little need to follow up. As a result, many veterans didn't have medical records to prove that the increasing health problems they experienced over the years stemmed from their incarceration and maltreatment.

For decades following their return, the dwindling number of veterans battled the Canadian government to demand compensation and an apol-ogy from the Japanese, but they heard only crickets. In fact, the Cana-dian government legally absolved Japan of any financial responsibility in 1952. Over fifty years later, the Japanese prime minister expressed "deep remorse" and stated "heartfelt apologies" to the people who suffered in World War II, but he did not specify the Allied POWs. Finally in 2011, Japan's Parliamentary Vice Minister for Foreign Affairs issued an apology to the POWs.

When it became obvious that the veterans were passing away so quickly there would no longer be anyone left to tell their story, a group of their sons and daughters established the Hong Kong Veterans Commemorative As-sociation, a registered charity, in 1995. They lobbied for better pensions, benefits, and compensation. Because of their efforts, in December 1998, the Canadian government granted compensation of $24,000 to each sur-viving Hong Kong POW or POW's widow. The association also pushed for greater recognition for the veterans and education about their experi-ences, and in 2009, more than sixty years after the men returned home, they erected a memorial wall in Ottawa. Sadly, by then, most were dead.

As for Sergeant Gander, in 2001 he was posthumously awarded the Dickin Medal for Gallantry by the People's Dispensary for Sick Animals (essentially the Victoria Cross for animals) and the twenty surviving members of his regiment attended the ceremony. His medal is now on display at the Canadian War Museum in Ottawa, and his name is listed on the memorial wall along with the other slain Canadians.

Letters Across the Sea began as a novel about the Christie Pits Riot. In the years following that event, many of the same men who had come to blows in Toronto fell against a common enemy and were buried side by side, Jews and Gentiles together. On Remembrance Day each year, we honour those who gave their lives so that we might live ours. The men who not only fought at the Battle of Hong Kong, but also endured forty-four months as prisoners of war at the hands of the Japanese, came home and were largely forgotten. Their story is not taught, and it is barely told except by their children and grandchildren. Learning about these men has added another dimension to that day of remembrance for me, and I hope it has for you as well.

Letters Across the Sea

Genevieve Graham

A Reading Group Guide

Topics & Questions for Discussion

1. The novel begins during the Great Depression. How has the economic downturn affected Molly, Hannah, and others in their neighbourhood?

2. Max describes Kensington as a patchwork of different communities. Using the Ryan and Dreyfus families as examples, discuss how Canada is a country of immigrants. What did they leave behind? And what problems do they still face?

3. Molly says that the Orangemen nicknamed the city "Toronto the Good," but in the opening of the novel, we see a place teeming with unemployment, protests, and civil unrest. What people and behaviours are considered "good"? What happens to those who are thought of as second-class citizens or outsiders?

4. Did you know about the rise of anti-Semitism in Toronto before reading this book? Were you surprised to learn about the Swastika Clubs and signs banning Jews from businesses and beaches? What does the novel suggest might be some of the causes of this racial prejudice? Consider the characters of Mr. Ryan, Richie, and Phil.

5. Molly wants to become a journalist, but she drops out of school and puts her dream on hold to help her family make ends meet. Discuss the expectations of women during this time period. What opportunities are available to them? How do Molly's and Hannah's paths differ? How are they the same?

6. During the scene at the beach, Molly, Max, and Arnie talk about

the *Star* and the *Telegram*, and the difference between bias and censorship. In light of our current media landscape, what did you make of this discussion? Do you think we can ever know the truth?

7. Even though Molly and Max grew up together as friends, there is still a line between them that they are forbidden from crossing. What does this suggest about the bonds of family? As second-generation Canadians, do Molly and Max view community and tradition in a different light? If so, how?

8. On page 96, Mr. Ryan tells Molly that "there will come a time when it's us versus them" and that she'll "not be able to walk away from that." How is this borne out in the novel? When is it not?

9. During the riot, Mr. Ryan goes after Max, thinking that he's protecting his daughter. What does this say about the power of love, both parental and romantic? And given what we later learn about Richie, what does this scene say about the power of friendship?

10. How does the riot at Christie Pits forever change the Ryan and Dreyfus families? How does this event shape your own understanding of race relations in Canada?

11. When Molly goes to work at the *Star*, she is one of the few women in the newsroom. How is she treated by her colleagues? Despite trailblazers like Rhea Clyman, what stereotypes still exist?

12. When Max enlists in the army, he tells his family that "as a Canadian, it's my duty to volunteer . . . As a Jew, I have a personal score to settle." Discuss Max's obligation as a Jewish Canadian. How have the events of 1933 impacted his decision so many years later?

13. In Hong Kong, Max expresses frustration about not yet seeing action. Why does Max feel so restless as opposed to someone like Richie? Does it have to do with who they are fighting for and what they left behind?

14. What are the central friendships in the novel and how are they tested? What seems to unite friends again? And what new friendships are forged?

15. Did you know about the fate of Canadian troops in the Pacific Theatre during World War II before reading about the Battle of Hong Kong? Do you agree that they shouldn't have been sent there to begin with? How were they unprepared for the conflict they faced?

16. When Max becomes a prisoner of war, his voice drops out of the narrative. Did you think he had died in Stanley Village along with David?

17. For a long time, Molly puts her career before romance. Why does she decide to give Ian a chance? How did you feel about their blossoming relationship?

18. After the Battle of Hong Kong, Molly throws herself into research- ing German and Japanese POW camps and she even visits the camp in Bowmanville. What are some of the differences between the prisons? Molly says, "I don't think anyone, in war or not, has the right to become monsters." What do you make of her statement?

19. Discuss the theme of storytelling in the novel. Consider Molly's and Max's grandparents, Mr. Rabinowitz, and the many veterans from both world wars. What is accomplished when the charac- ters share their stories with one another? What happens when they don't?

20. Consider the portrayal of PTSD in the characters of Max, Jimmy, Liam, and Mark. In what ways do they struggle to adapt to life after witnessing the horrors of war? What scars do they have? And what helps them heal?

21. When Molly interviews Max about his experience as a prisoner of war, he describes the moment they saw the American planes flying overhead and says, "after four years of surviving, we were finally getting the chance to live again." What's the difference be- tween surviving and living?

22. Max returns from war guilty that he survived when so many others did not. What makes him tell his story to Molly and Ian? What did you make of his decision to remain anonymous?

23. What role do letters play in the novel?

24. Discuss the importance of forgiveness. What other characters redeem themselves by the end of the novel? How do the losses of war soften their hearts?

25. Were you surprised by Richie's revelation? What reasons does he give for his actions the day of the riot, and after?

26. In many ways, the novel is an epic love story. What do you think drew Molly and Max together in the first place? And what continues to bind them to one another after so many years?

27. Consider the title of the novel. What does *Letters Across the Sea* symbolize?

1. Walk the streets of Toronto with Giles Hodge as he takes viewers through the night of the Christie Pits Riot in "History Happens Here: The Riot at Christie Pits." https://www.facinghistory.org /resource-library/video/history-happens-here-riot-christie-pits

2. Hear from firsthand survivors of the Battle of Hong Kong by watching *The Fence*, a documentary written and directed by Viveka Melki. In this film, she interviews two POW survivors as well as a young girl who was trapped in Hong Kong during the Japanese occupation. http://thefencedoc.ca/
   Or check out Brian McKenna's 1991 film, *Savage Christmas: Hong Kong 1941*, on the National Film Board website for a critique of Canada's involvement in the Pacific Theatre. https:// www.nfb.ca/film/savage_christmas_hong_kong_1941/.

3. In chapter 18, Molly mentions the internment camps where more than 90 per cent of Japanese Canadians living in British Columbia were detained and dispossessed under the War Measures Act. Joy Kogawa was one such girl. Read her award-winning novel, *Obasan*, to find out more about this dark chapter in Canadian history.

Acknowledgments

First of all, this book never would have become what it is without the brilliant, dedicated, and creative work of my incredible editor, Sarah St. Pierre. I can't say that enough. This was the most difficult book I've ever written, and she was instrumental in helping me find the story within all the pages and pages of research. We were partners through it all.

Thank you to the generous Jewish readers Nicole, Cori, and Merle for sharing their time and cultural expertise, and to suspense author extraordinaire and fellow Simon & Schuster Canada author, Samantha Bailey, for helping me out with my ongoing Jewish queries! The author community is truly a wonderful place to live, where everyone helps each other.

There's a lot you can learn online via websites, but nothing beats personal connections. The moment I posted on the official Facebook page of the Hong Kong Veterans Commemorative Association of Canada, I wondered why I hadn't headed there long before. Just like with the British Home Children descendants I talked to for *The Forgotten Home Child*, I discovered people who are passionate about learning and teaching the history of the Battle of Hong Kong and the subsequent prisoner of war camps where the brave men of Canada's C Force spent so many horrible years. The members of that page, most of whom are the children and grandchildren of the soldiers, are determined not to let the sacrifices of the Canadians in Hong Kong be ignored or forgotten. When I asked for personal stories, I received messages and emails right away, full of information about and letters from their dads and granddads. They're still coming in, but I would like in particular to thank Lincoln Keays, and salute his father, Rifleman Richard Keays, as well as Judy James, Wendy Jarvin, and Mona Thornton, who helped me see into their fathers' lives. Wendy and her friend Wilma were keen to point out that, just like with the British Home Children and Canada's residential school system, those who returned from the POW camps had deep scars that affected future generations. Intergenerational trauma is a very real, very underestimated issue, and I'm glad that it is finally being recognized, at least for some.

Thank you to Em Gamelin and Sarah Glassford from the Canadian Red Cross Archives for helping me with research on the precious Canadian Red Cross POW parcels—very few of which ever made it to the actual POWs, since they were mostly taken and often sold by the Japanese guards.

I already mentioned my editor Sarah (her name bears repeating!), but I also need to thank the talented and enthusiastic team behind me at Simon & Schuster Canada. President Kevin Hanson has a wonderful group of experts, including publicist Mackenzie Croft, marketing associate Allie Boelsterli, cover designer Elizabeth Whitehead, director of sales Shara Alexa, sales rep Sherry Lee, and the manager of library and special sales Lorraine Kelly, all of whom babysit me beautifully and make sure to get the stories out where they belong.

And without the expertise and guidance of my esteemed literary agent, Jacques de Spoelberch, I most likely wouldn't have met any of them, so thank you again for everything you do for me, Jacques!

Thank you ALWAYS to all the amazing readers out there, so many of whom have (incredibly!) added my books to their "auto-buy" lists. What an honour for me! I will never stop being grateful for all your support, your messages, your letters, your book clubs—boy, oh boy, am I ever "zooming" to book clubs these days!—and for recommending my books to your friends and family. I love what I do. I love learning about our country and sharing my findings with you through characters I love as well. What a wonderful way to live!

Last but never least, thank you to my wonderful husband of almost thirty years, Dwayne. He was incredibly understanding, considering this book tried my patience more than any other. He's the hardest-working man I know, and yet when he comes home and sees the strain in my expression, he still somehow finds the energy to make dinner for us—after he brings me my end-of-day glass of wine. He has resigned himself to watching and rewatching World War II and 1940s movies whenever I feel the need. Actually, I think he rather likes that. We have a perfect partnership, and he is already helping me figure out my next book.

Also by
GENEVIEVE GRAHAM

National Bestsellers

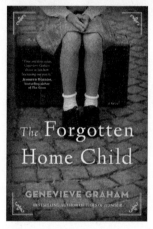

"Time and time again, Genevieve Graham
shows us just how fascinating our past is."

JENNIFER ROBSON,
internationally bestselling author of *The Gown* and *Our Darkest Night*

SIMON &
SCHUSTER